Praise for *City of Dreams*

"The action keeps your heart racing. . . . Martin can spin yarn after yarn that keeps you guessing, holding your breath, stunned. . . . A fun, fascinating tome with [an] almost epic sweep."

—*The Providence Journal*

"Two years ago, Bill Martin told me about this story, and I immediately wished I'd thought of it. The plot is novel, smart, and ingenious. Exactly what every thriller writer searches for. A great 'oooh factor' and an even better 'so what.' Don't miss this one."

—Steve Berry, *New York Times* bestselling author of *The Paris Vendetta*

"Martin has a winning formula . . . and it shines through!"

—*Booklist*

"Is William Martin the author's real name? I'd swear Dan Brown and David McCullough coauthored this nonstop page-turner. *City of Dreams* is the showstopper to end all showstoppers."

—Douglas Preston, *New York Times* bestselling author of *Impact*

"This is a solid story, well told, fast paced, and interesting."

—*Historical Novel Review*

"Before Robert Langdon in *The Da Vinci Code*, there was Peter Fallon. Before *National Treasure*, there was William Martin. In Martin's Fallon thrillers, history comes to life. Not since James Michener has an author swept so smoothly through the big events of America's past. . . . You'll rush through New York history and run for your life in modern Manhattan. You won't be able to stop reading, and you'll think about it long after you're done."

—David Morrell, *New York Times* bestselling author of *The Shimmer*

"Plenty of action and intrigue . . . This is definitely a unique twist on the 'search for buried treasure'-style adventure, handled well and made more thrilling by the rapid pace of the plot (in both eras)."

—*Mysterious Reviews*

"William Martin's books are an addiction. A fine mix of historical fiction and modern quest novel, with plenty of action and bad guys, they are pure fun, storytelling at its finest."

—Stephen Coonts, *New York Times* bestselling author of *The Assassin*

"William Martin is one of the few contemporary writers who can resuscitate history by means of crackling good storytelling."

—*The Barnstable Patriot*

"A delight. Martin again pulls me into a novel while simultaneously teaching me history. I live in the 'City of Dreams,' next to places he describes . . . I had no clue about many of the fascinating things that happened right in my neighborhood."

—John Stossel, *New York Times* bestselling author of *Give Me a Break* and host of *Stossel* on Fox Business Channel

BOOKS BY WILLIAM MARTIN

The Lost Constitution
Harvard Yard
Citizen Washington
Annapolis
Cape Cod
The Rising of the Moon
Nerve Endings
Back Bay
City of Dreams

CITY OF DREAMS

WILLIAM MARTIN

A TOM DOHERTY ASSOCIATES BOOK
New York

CITY OF DREAMS

A Forge Book
Published by Tom Doherty Associates, LLC
175 Fifth Avenue
New York, NY 10010

www.tor-forge.com

Forge® is a registered trademark of Tom Doherty Associates, LLC.

ISBN 978-0-7653-6162-2

First Edition: May 2010
First Mass Market Edition: April 2011

Printed in the United States of America

0 9 8 7 6 5 4 3 2 1

For the Ancestors of my Children.
They came from Mayo and County Cavan,
From Lithuania and Bavaria, too.
Some came to Boston and some stayed in New York,
But they all saw America first as the City of Dreams.

ACKNOWLEDGMENTS

Some rainy Saturday afternoon when you're cleaning out your attic or flipping through a bin in your favorite secondhand bookstore, you may uncover a pile of flimsy, crudely printed notes from the American Revolution. They may appear to be nothing at all, but be careful with them, because they may be New Emission Bonds.

Of course, you won't be able to call Peter Fallon for an opinion, because he's a fictional character. But I was lucky because whenever Peter Fallon needed an opinion, I could call Ned Downing.

Ned is one of the nation's leading scripophilists and scholars of eighteenth-century American capital markets. He first told me about the bonds, more properly called New Emission Money, over a decade ago.

And what a story. A struggling Congress attempts to finance the Revolution by printing money and issuing promissory notes backed mostly by air. Alexander Hamilton takes the financial reins of the new government and tries to make good on all the promises, and those that remain unfulfilled, including interest payments on the New Emission Money, he calls debts "of honor." Two centuries later, modern collectors and historical institutions attempt to redeem the New Emission Money, which may still be accruing interest.

And then what happened?

I told Ned that some day I would write a novel about the New Emission Money. Now I have put Peter Fallon and Evangeline Carrington on the case in New York. But I could not have written this book without the generous advice, insight, and historical perspective that Ned Downing has offered at every phase of the process. As I say of a character in the book, he introduced me "to a new way of seeing American history." He answered all my questions during the research and writing, and he read the manuscript, too.

I have, of course, taken a novelist's liberties in fashioning my historical fiction out of the story of these flimsy pieces of paper and their passage through New York history. But the broad contours and most of the specifics are true, thanks to Ned.

There are many others who deserve my thanks, too. They have offered research help, insights, advice, reminiscences, eyewitness accounts, and friendship.

So, my thanks to Mark Bartlett and the staff of the New York Society Library, Alice Beale, Thomas Cook, Peter Drummey and the staff of the Massachusetts Historical Society (which owns a collection of New Emission Money), Patty Garcia, John Harrison, John Herzog, who founded the Museum of American Finance and graciously gave me a personal tour, William Kuntz, Katherine Kunz, Stephen Martell, Linda Nakdimen, Joseph Riley, Patricia Resnick, Andy Rosenwach of the Rosenwach Tank Company, John Spooner, Susan Terner, Pamela Thomas, Martin Weinkle, and my research assistants, Corwynn Crane and Lauren Dye.

Also a more general thanks to the Sons of the Revolution in the State of New York, who own and operate the Fraunces Tavern Museum; to the staffs of the Federal Hall National Memorial, the Lower East Side Tenement Museum, the Morgan Library and Museum, the Museum of the City of New York, and the New-York Historical Society; to the priests and parishioners of Trinity Church and St. Paul's Chapel, in Lower Manhattan, and the Sacred Heart of Jesus Church on Fifty-first Street.

Thanks for their continued support to Bob Gleason, my editor at Forge; and to Tom Doherty, my publisher; and to Robert Gottlieb of the Trident Media Group, my agent for a quarter century.

Thanks to my kids, Bill, Dan, and Elizabeth. They're spread around the country, but they still offer their opinions and can now offer professional judgments, too, on subjects as diverse as IPOs, dramatic structure, and human psychology.

And thanks as always to Chris. She makes the hard work much easier.

WILLIAM MARTIN
December 2009

CITY
OF
DREAMS

ONE

Monday Afternoon

Peter Fallon read the caller ID, pushed the Talk button, and said, "I am *not* moving to New York City."

"That isn't why I'm calling," said Evangeline Carrington.

"But that's where every conversation ends up."

"Listen, Peter, I'm in a bookstore."

"What are you doing in a bookstore?"

"Buying you a wedding present."

"I have enough books."

Peter was sitting in his office. *Books everywhere.* And in the outer office, more books. But not just *any* books: a Shakespeare Second Folio from 1632, a first edition of Adam Smith's *Wealth of Nations*, a signed first of *Tales of the South Pacific,* the rarest Michener, three million dollars worth of books, all bought, sold, and brokered from the third floor of a Boston bowfront, above an art gallery that was above a restaurant.

"If you think I'm getting you golf clubs," she said, "forget it."

"I'd love a new Callaway driver," he said. "We

can play on the honeymoon. Nice golf courses in France."

"Forget France," said Evangeline. "I want you to come to New York."

"See? I told you. This is where every conversation ends up. I don't want to live in New York. And there's a wedding in ten days. In Boston. There are details."

"Name a detail that I haven't already taken care of."

"I have to put the dance tunes on my iPod. I have to shuck the oysters—"

"Peter, get serious."

He sat up straight, as if she were in the room. "Okay. I'm all ears."

"I'm in Delancey's Rarities on Fourth Avenue, in the back. I'm going through a bin of engravings, because I know how much you like them, and this bag lady comes in."

"A bag lady? In New York? There's news. Does she smell?"

"Of rum. I can smell it back here. But she doesn't sound drunk, or old, or especially derelict. That's what's got my attention."

"Eight million stories in the naked city, babe."

"She's saying how Delancey is an expert in old money, and so is she, so they should team up, because she knows where there's a lot of it, and if they work together—"

"Smart bag lady. She knows enough to go to Delancey. A major player in the scripophily market."

"Scripophily?"

"Collecting old money. Antique stock certificates, bonds . . . it's hot right now."

"Oh, hey, wait a minute . . ."

Peter could hear Evangeline breathing. He could almost hear her listening.

While he waited, he clicked the Internet and glanced at the stock market. The Dow was dropping—and fast—in the last half hour of trading.

Then Evangeline was back. "The bag lady says she has something that'll impress Delancey. But she'll only show it to him on her turf."

"She sounds batty. Don't let her hear you or see you, or she'll make herself *your* pain in the ass instead of his."

"She can't see me in the back. And she can't hear me because I'm whispering, and Delancey's playing his old-timey music."

Peter could hear the music, too. "That's Benny Goodman. The term is timeless, not old-timey."

"Okay. Timeless. Now they're talking about a room papered in old money. You know, Peter, I think we should see what this is about."

"*We?*" Peter laughed. "Aren't you always saying, 'Peter,' in that cold, calm voice you get when you're pissed off, 'Peter, I'm just a travel writer. Don't be dragging me into your treasure hunts.' "

"Peter," she said in that cold, calm voice, "ten days from now, what's mine is yours and what's yours is mine. Right?"

"Right."

"You were the one who turned down the prenup. Right?"

"Right"—Peter put his feet up on the desk—"because I'm after your money."

"So if this is something big, and it pays off, it's community property. Right?"

"Right."

"And it could make a helluva wedding present . . . wait a minute"—her voice rose an octave—"she's showing Delancey a picture. Peter, this could be . . . *something*."

"Right." Peter tried to control a laugh. "Something."

"I can see you smirking, Peter. Stop it. Oh, hey . . . she's leaving. The bag lady's leaving. Do you think I should go after her?"

"Yeah, sure. Why not?" Peter laughed.

"Peter, *screw you*." And she clicked off.

PETER SPUN IN his chair and looked out the window.

He realized that if this marriage was going to work, he had to learn the difference between smart-ass and plain-vanilla ass.

He thought about calling her back, but that would only make things worse. So he just pictured Delancey's store.

Peter's old mentor, Orson Lunt, once said, "Whenever you're in New York, go down to Book Row. Stop in at the Strand, of course, then go to Delancey's. It's dark, it's messy, but it's a treasure trove. Look around, go through the bins, get to know Delancey, ask him as many questions as you can, but answer as few as possible, because he's sharper than Gillette, and he doesn't miss a trick. . . ."

Orson was retired now, but Delancey was still going strong, the kind of guy who'd probably die in his store some day, get to heaven, and go looking for Bill Shakespeare, just to ask him where he'd buried his manuscripts. Then Delancey would figure out a way to come back to life, dig them up, and sell them to the highest bidder.

Of course, Delancey had done pretty well in this life, too. He played the poor bookseller in the dumpy shop, one of the last holdouts on Book Row, but he also owned the building, and every year or so, he sent Peter an e-mail that went like this:

Dear Pete—

Strike one: Peter hated to be called Pete.

I've been doing business with a New York stockbroker who also happens to be a major collector. Considering his interest in our field, I think you might be interested in his services. Business to business, so to speak. This is some chance. He does not take on many clients. And believe me, there's no one in Boston who can match this guy's heat.

Strike two: Peter had a Boston broker who delivered all the "heat" any investor could want, without New York's high overhead or taste for two-hundred-dollar lunches.

So give it some thought. Minimum investment, five mil.

Strike three: for Peter to come up with that much money, he'd have to sell his inventory, his condo, his car, and he'd still be scrambling.

Peter often wondered what Delancey got out of the relationship beyond a loyal customer, and he almost called Evangeline to warn her about a sales pitch. But he knew she was too smart to fall for one.

So he imagined her walking from the back of the store, past the long bookshelves, toward the afternoon light flooding the front . . .

. . . AND SHE WAS.

She stuffed her cell phone into her purse and hurried through the American history section and up to the big windows that looked out onto Fourth Avenue.

The bag lady had left and turned south toward the Bowery. She was pushing a shopping cart full of boxes, bottles, a plastic trash bag, and a scruffy little dog.

Evangeline couldn't see her face, just a dirty raincoat and a dirty Mets hat over a mess of dirty brown hair. Should she follow?

"Find anything?" Delancey said "find" with a New York accent that made it come out *foiwnd*. Though it was early May, he was wearing a gray wool vest sweater over a white shirt and skinny brown tie. And his comb-over reflected—literally—his talent in the lost male art of creating something out of nearly nothing but Vitalis.

Strictly old-school. That was what Peter said

about Oscar Delancey, and he meant it as a compliment.

"I didn't find any priceless engravings of Lincoln, if that's what you're asking." Evangeline craned her neck to watch the bag lady rattling away.

"Bowling Green, eleven o'clock tonight," said Delancey.

"What?"

"That's where I'm supposed to meet her."

"Who?"

"I heard"—*hoid*—"you on the phone. Did you say hi to Pete for me?"

"Of course I did, and don't call him Pete."

"Did you tell him about the crazy broad who just left?"

Busted. Evangeline stepped back from the window and gave her blond hair a little flip. She knew that he liked looking at her. To a man in his late sixties, a woman of her age was just a kid. That was why she had worn a skirt and a heel. She always made better deals if Delancey was in a good mood. She noticed his eyes flick down to her legs, so she turned her foot to give him some calf. But when his eyes stopped at her chest, she folded her arms and said, "Of *course* I told him. A bag lady walks into a bookstore and starts talking about a room papered in money? How in the hell could I miss that?"

"*I* was talking about a room papered in money. I was telling her that I hear stories like hers all the time, about old grandmothers findin' old bonds underneath old wallpaper in shitty old bathrooms on the Lower East Side, and if I go and look, I don't find anything but old cock-a-roaches." Delancey dropped into his chair and swung to his computer. "I'll bet Pete told you to leave her to me."

"He did, but if you're not interested in what that bag lady—"

"Honey, she's one of the reasons I put in a buzzer system." He pressed a button beneath his desk and the door lock gave an electric hum. "I've got one of the best inventories of rare books in Manhattan, and I never worry about the bad guys, but pain-in-the-ass old bums with b.o. drive me crazy, male or female."

"So why let her in?"

Delancey shrugged. "Eh . . . I'm a soft touch. What can I tell you?"

"She showed you a picture just now."

"An old house on the West Side. It was a fancy estate in Washington's day. An eyesore in Lincoln's. Torn down in Teddy Roosevelt's. She used to come in all the time with cockamamie stories like that. Now she says if I meet her tonight, I'll learn somethin' big. I'm not bitin'."

"Why not?"

Delancey gave a bigger shrug. "What do I look like? Stupid? I'm a businessman, for chrissakes. I'm not into cops-and-robbers stuff. Not like your boyfriend."

"So why does she bother you instead of some other dealer?"

"Eh . . . she must read the papers before she sleeps in them." He looked at her over his glasses, as if trying to decide how much to tell her, and said,

"I sold a couple of old bonds to an uptown buyer and it made the papers."

"Who?"

"Well, I wouldn't tell you except that—"

"Don't say you wouldn't tell me except that you like my legs."

Delancey chuckled. "I wouldn't tell you, except that his identity made the papers, too. My stockbroker. Austin Arsenault. You heard of him?"

She shook her head.

"I sold him two Revolutionary War bonds that he's now trying to get the Treasury to honor. Gone all the way to the Supreme Court. It's a big story in the scripophily biz."

"Does this make you the scripophily stud?"

"Yeah. But the pretty girls ain't flockin'. You know any pretty girls you could send my way?"

"Maybe." Evangeline sat on the edge of his desk and swung her leg. "I also know that a room papered in money might make a pretty nice wedding gift."

Delancey watched her leg for a moment.

She was playing him, and he knew it, and she knew that he knew it.

Then he said, "If you really want to meet this bag lady, have dinner with me tonight. Then we'll see if she shows up."

"And if she does?"

"I'll split the commission. But half of nothing is still nothing."

She stopped swinging her leg and offered her hand. "Deal."

He took the hand and grinned. His teeth were

stubby, mostly yellow near the roots, mostly white toward the ends, as if he only brushed halfway. "Bring a friend. And wear something that shows your . . . assets."

"Good that you said 'assets.' If you'd said 'tits,' I would have been mad."

"Well, you can show them, too, if you want to humor an old man."

"You're not old," she said. "Just horny."

PETER FALLON WAS asleep in front of the television when the phone woke him. He saw the green of Fenway. He heard the announcer's voice: "Red Sox three, Yankees two." He grabbed the remote and pressed Mute, then he picked up the phone. "It's ten thirty. This better be good."

"I'm having dinner with Delancey," said Evangeline. "I'm in Fraunces Tavern."

Peter could think of no more incongruous sight than the little building that sat at the corner of Pearl and Broad Streets, surrounded by the giants of Lower Manhattan. In Boston, you were always stumbling across redbrick reminders of the Revolution. But a third of New York had burned to the ground in 1776, and a lot more had gone up in the 1835 fire. And the rest had fallen to progress once the concrete march from the Battery to the Bronx had begun. In the whole fourteen-mile length of Manhattan, there were only four or five buildings where the sunlight still slanted through the windowpanes of the eighteenth century. Fraunces Tavern was one of them.

The New York Sons of Liberty met there before

the Revolution. British officers dined there after chasing off the Continental Army. George Washington said a teary good-bye to his officers there after the Revolution. And when the Federal government opened for business in New York, Alexander Hamilton moved his Treasury Department into one of the upper chambers. Now it was restaurant downstairs, museum upstairs.

"Eating pretty late," said Peter, "even for a New Yorker."

"Delancey and I are supposed to meet this bag lady at eleven o'clock, on the Bowling Green."

"You're still on that? Why couldn't you meet her in Battery Park at lunchtime?"

"I'm not calling about the logistics, Peter. I didn't plan this. The bag lady did."

"Good way to do business. Let crazy customers call the shots."

"Be quiet and listen. It's about Delancey. We were having a nice meal. The usual chitchat. He jokes with me about how disappointed he is that I didn't bring him a girlfriend. We order. He's telling me about the business—"

"I bet he told you it was terrible."

"He was telling me about these Revolutionary bonds he sold, and just as the food comes, he gets this funny look, like he's seen someone or . . . some*thing*. He pops up, says he has to go to the can, and leaves."

"For the night?"

"He never comes back."

"You mean he stiffed you?"

"He sent me a goddamn text message: 'Evangeline, something has come up. Go home. I'll fill you in tomorrow.' The son of a bitch."

Peter didn't like the sound of this. Delancey was cheap. He had never left a hot meal uneaten in any restaurant, fancy or greasy or anywhere in between. "I'd do what he's suggesting. Pay the check. Have the restaurant call you a cab. Go home."

"Like hell, Peter. I didn't come all the way downtown at this hour just to—"

"Let me try calling him, see what's going on."

"He's not answering. Like you say, he stiffed me."

Peter suddenly felt very helpless. She was two hundred and twenty miles away. She was pissed. And she'd probably had a glass of wine. He hoped she hadn't had two.

He said, "Remember what you told me last time? 'Peter, from now on, we don't go looking for trouble. Nothing dangerous.' "

"How dangerous can it be to meet some bag lady on the Bowling Green?"

"Plenty dangerous, if this is a setup."

"Peter, you're the one who's always saying to trust our instincts."

"I also tell you to trust the process, and the process is all about research, logic, and—" He knew he wasn't reaching her. He had to try something to keep her in the restaurant until she calmed down a bit. "Hey, is it busy there?"

"About half the tables are taken in this room, half in the other room, and it sounds pretty noisy in the taproom, too."

"Can you take a few pictures with your cell

phone? They might show me something. But be subtle about it. Send me the pics. I'll look at them and call you back."

A FEW MINUTES later, Peter had mail. He muted the TV again, clicked the attachment on his laptop screen, and opened the file.

Three pictures appeared.

They were more shadowy than sharp. Not surprising. No flash on a cell phone. And the restaurant went for eighteenth-century ambience, which meant low-key electric candle sconces on the walls and real candles flickering on the tables.

He could tell that she was sitting by a window in the Tallmadge Room, the one with the cherrywood paneling and the working fireplace.

There was a young couple directly behind her, a group of hard-drinking businessmen at the table next to her, two old couples by the fireplace.

And sitting at the table near the doorway to the Bissel Room was a lone diner, male. Peter tried to blow up the photograph to get a look at him. But there wasn't enough light to make it worthwhile, and what was unusual about people dining alone?

So he called her back. "I got nothing."

He could tell that she was outside. He heard cars, footsteps.

"Where are you going?" he asked.

"The Bowling Green."

"Evangeline, don't—"

"Peter, don't always be saying 'don't' to me. I've been in scarier places than the Bowling Green on a Monday night in May. And if we're getting married, you have to get used to me following my instincts once in a while. Trust *that* process. I'll call you later."

He could almost hear the *pop* of her phone as she flipped it shut.

There was nothing for him to do, so he turned back to the ball game.

IN MOST OF New York, the parade went on day and night. But Lower Manhattan was different after dark, especially since 9/11. It was more like Houston, a business district that emptied when the workday was done. And it had always reminded Evangeline of Boston, with streets that were narrow, twisty, unpredictable, the streets of the ancient city, streets with a pattern that would not have been unfamiliar to Alexander Hamilton or even Peter Stuyvesant.

The night was cool. She was glad that she had worn a camel's hair sportcoat over her silk blouse, along with Antik denims and comfortable cowboy boots. Her heels echoed behind her as she followed Broad Street to Stone Street to Whitehall.

She stopped in front of the entrance to Bowling Green subway station, a modern arch of glass and steel. For a moment, it enticed her down.

Maybe Peter was right. Maybe this was crazy. Just jump on the 4 or the 5, make the change at Fulton Street, and be back on the Upper West Side in no time.

But she was committed now. She had always been the one dragged kicking and screaming into Peter's hunts for lost tea sets or Shakespeare manuscripts or drafts of the United States Constitution. What better way to begin their marriage than to drag Peter into something? What better way to remind him that she was still going to be as independent as ever? And if it paid off, what better wedding present?

The area was quiet but not especially dark. Floodlights sculpted shadows onto the neoclassical façade of the old Alexander Hamilton Customs House. Quaint street lamps lit the tree-lined oval of grass where the Dutch had run a market, where the British had bowled the jack, where the Americans had torn down a statue of the king.

So Evangeline glanced at her watch—almost eleven—then she went through a gate in the wrought-iron fence surrounding the Bowling Green.

And suddenly, it *was* especially dark. The tall sycamores seemed to suck up the light. The sound of the fountain in the center of the oval—the alien sound of running water in the heart of the city—drowned out the hum of the few cars passing by.

Broadway ran down the west side, Whitehall down the east. Two cabs were idling at the corner of Whitehall and Beaver. The cabbies were standing outside having a chat. An NYPD cruiser glided slowly down Broadway. That made Evangeline feel better, because the sidewalk in front of One Broadway was covered by construction canopy: pipe staging and plywood to protect pedestrians from overhead work, also good for hiding muggers, thieves, and other phantasms of the New York night.

She stood a few moments more, thinking that something might happen quickly if it happened at all. She was glad that it was a small park. She knew that she could make it to the safety of the street in a few strides. So she went toward a bench on the north side of the fountain and sat . . .

. . . and listened to the running water . . .

. . . and looked at her watch . . .

. . . and scoped out the entrances, one at the south end, one at the north . . .

. . . and took out her cell phone and checked her messages . . .

. . . and jumped when she heard footsteps behind her.

But it was only a jogger. He did not even glance at her. He pounded past the fountain and went out by the south gate.

So she checked her messages again . . .

. . . and left the phone open on the bench, like a little night-light, or an alarm . . .

. . . and listened to the running water . . .

. . . and watched a middle-aged man and a girl in her twenties stroll into the park. They stopped in a shadow, kissed, kissed again, pawed each other, then noticed Evangeline and turned quickly for the subway.

She knew their story: the husband had told the trusting wife that he was working late. He had not told her what he was working *on*: a pretty secretary, perhaps, or a client with 36DDs.

Evangeline had been the trusting wife once, married to a dermatologist whose motto was "the softer the skin, the better." She called it her sandwich marriage, after her time with Peter Fallon the young man, before her time with Peter Fallon the grown-up.

Grown-up? Perhaps there was a better term . . .

She looked at her watch: 11:09. Six minutes and she was out of there, due diligence done, curiosity not satisfied but reputation for stubborn sense of purpose upheld.

She glanced again at her phone. No new messages in the last three minutes . . .

. . . and set the phone down . . .

. . . and gazed up at the façade of the Customs House . . .

She had read that once there was an old fort there. She imagined torchlight instead of floodlights. She imagined Alexander Hamilton and his artillery company out at the Battery. She imagined two- and three-story buildings instead of skyscrapers, and . . .

She heard something behind her.

Rattle-ka-thump-rattle-ka-thump-rattle-ka-thump-thump-thump.

She looked over her shoulder.

"No need to turn around."

Rattle-ka-thump-rattle-ka-thump-rattle-ka-thump-thump-thump.

The bag lady's shopping cart had a bad wheel. She pushed it right up to Evangeline's feet and scowled. "Where's Delancey?"

Evangeline smelled rum, but not much in the way of b.o. or bad breath or any of the other smells she expected from someone wearing a raincoat so greasy it reflected the light of those quaint street lamps.

She said, "Delancey thought it would be better if I came in his place."

The bag lady's dirty little fuzzball of a dog popped out of a pile of rags and stood with his paws on the edge of the cart and growled at Evangeline.

The bag lady began digging through the trash barrel next to the bench. "If I hadn't seen you in the store, I wouldn't be talkin' to you now. I came here to talk to Delancey. Why didn't he come?"

Evangeline decided to offer a bit of truth. "Something made him nervous."

The bag lady stopped rooting and looked up, "I make a lot of people nervous. Do I make you nervous?"

Evangeline looked around. "This whole thing makes me nervous."

"Well, I do business on my turf, or I don't do business at all."

Evangeline swallowed. Her mouth was dry. "I . . . I can understand that."

"You can understand? Well, isn't that fuckin' sweet of you." The bag lady pulled a Pepsi bottle out of the barrel, checked for a bar code, then threw it into the cart.

Evangeline said nothing. She saw no point in antagonizing this woman, who was not nearly as old as she appeared from a distance. The hands were dirty, the hair matted into dreadlocks, but the face didn't have the leathered appearance that a lot of homeless developed. Evangeline put her somewhere in her forties.

The bag lady pulled out a bottle of rum and took

a swallow. "We're all nervous these days." She offered Evangeline the bottle.

Evangeline wondered if it would be better to accept the offer and make this a meeting of the drinking sisterhood, or decline the bottle, the germs, and the honor, but leave the bag lady with a little more rum. She declined.

The bag lady laughed, revealing two neat spaces where her front teeth should have been. Somebody must have knocked them out, thought Evangeline, because the rest of her teeth looked pretty good.

The bag lady dropped the bottle into her pocket and said, "Who wouldn't be nervous these days? You got your government spending, your limp-dick recovery, your crash of 2008 caused by the subprime mess, which you can blame on slick lenders and stupid borrowers who don't know that if it sounds too good to be true it probably is—I call it thieves selling garbage to morons—oh, and don't forget the politicians on both sides of the aisle, that fat Massachusetts fuck Barney Frank, sayin', 'when it comes to affordable housing, I'm willin' to roll the dice'—yeah, his dice, our money—or that slithery Texas snake Phil Gramm—don't you think he looks like a snake?—comin' up with the bright idea to repeal Glass-Steagall, so that bankers become brokers and brokers become bankers and you can't tell who's a good guy and who's a bad guy and—shit, they're all bad guys—say, I'm not borin' you, am I?"

Evangeline shook her head.

"Good. I hate to be a bore at all those fancy uptown cocktail parties, so I practice my chitchat on the Bowling Green." She went back to the trash barrel and pulled out a newspaper. "*New York Post*. Did you know Alexander Hamilton founded this rag?"

"As a matter of fact, I was thinking about Hamilton while I was sitting here."

"Bullshit. You were thinkin' you have to tinkle you're so scared to be sittin' here in a park with a crazy hag like me at this time of night."

Evangeline said, "I'm not scared. Not with a watchdog to protect us."

She reached out to pat the dog, and he bared his teeth.

"Down, Georgie." The bag lady laughed. "You know why I like this place? It's where the Dutch had their first hog-and-cattle market, so this is where the money changers first met in New York. That makes it the birthplace of American trade, which makes it the birthplace of American money. And all our troubles are about money."

"My name is Evangeline." She offered her hand. "What's yours?"

The bag lady said, "Call me Frivolous Sal, a peculiar sort of a gal."

"Okay, Sal."

"So, are you Delancey's assistant or something?"

"More like a new partner."

"So, how much of the story do you know?"

Evangeline did not want to say "absolutely nothing," so she said, "As much of it as Delancey knows."

"I'll bet you don't know about this." Frivolous Sal pulled a small brass crown from her pocket. "Do you?"

"No."

Frivolous Sal looked around the Bowling Green. "You see all the posts holdin' up this fence? There were little crowns like this on all of them. Little crown finials. But the rebels tore 'em all off the night they tore down the king's statue in 1776."

Evangeline extended her hand. "May I hold it?"

Frivolous Sal gave her a squint, then asked the dog, "What do you think, Georgie? Do we let this lady hold a piece of history?"

The dog looked at Evangeline and sniffed.

Frivolous Sal said, "Georgie likes you. He thinks you're honest."

She dropped the crown into Evangeline's hand. It was heavy brass, polished and shimmering in the lamplight. A hole had been drilled though it and a leather lanyard passed through the hole, as if it were a talisman of a more noble past.

"Is this what Delancey was supposed to see?" asked Evangeline.

"This is just the preview." And something cracked through Frivolous Sal's voice, something hard, trained, professional. "But the real story is coming right . . . about . . . now. Coming in at the south entrance, coming this way, coming fast."

A man appeared from the shadows beyond the fountain. He wore a gray suit and rimmed glasses. He was tall and skinny. His stride was long but more frightened than confident. He carried a briefcase.

Evangeline tried to catch his features, but they were bland, square, conventional. She didn't think, in the moments she watched him flicking in and out of the pools of light cast by those quaint street lamps, that she could ever give a police sketch of him.

"Slow down there, cowboy," said Frivolous Sal. "You're supposed to be bringin' a message to Delancey."

"I don't see Delancey." The man never broke stride. "And I've been made."

"Made?"

"I told you this would happen. Even on the Bowling Green late at night." He was heading for the north entrance. "Two of them, under the canopy over by One Broadway."

Frivolous Sal looked over her shoulder. "Fuck." Then she looked to her right, as if she was expecting backup from somewhere on the other side of the Bowling Green.

The man with the briefcase began to run. And the dog did what dogs do. He jumped out of the carriage and ran after the running man.

Frivolous Sal cursed again and ran after the dog.

Evangeline looked back toward One Broadway: two men were appearing from under that plywood and pipe canopy, moving toward the south entrance of the park.

But she had seen enough. Whatever was happening, she didn't want any more of it. So she jumped up and ran.

The dog was barking near the north entrance. Now the bag lady forgot the dog and started after Evangeline. "Come back, you silly bitch. Stop, thief!"

Evangeline was running straight for a cab still

parked at the corner of Beaver Street. The fence rose between her and the cab, but Evangeline did two circuits around the Central Park Reservoir every other day. So she was in shape enough to grab a spoke and vault over, right into the middle of Whitehall Street.

At least there were no cars coming.

So she sprinted across the street and grabbed the handle of the cab door.

Frivolous Sal let out a scream and began to wave her hands to attract attention, but two or three cars went past. Just another crazy bag lady making a scene.

Evangeline jumped into the cab and said to the driver, "Seventy-ninth and Columbus. Fast." Then she looked out at the shadows on the Bowling Green. The man with the briefcase had disappeared . . . into a cab or a car or onto a bicycle, she couldn't tell. Another man was crossing Whitehall Street and vaulting the fence. And those two from under the canopy were still advancing.

Evangeline reached into her pocket for her cell phone. Instead, she felt something harder and heavier and far older. In all the excitement, she had forgotten to grab the phone but had kept the crown finial.

TWENTY MINUTES LATER, Peter Fallon's cell phone rang. *Evangeline.* He pressed the button. "What now?"

"I don't know. You tell me." It wasn't Evangeline. It was some guy.

"Who's this?"

"My name's Joey. I picked up this cell phone from the sidewalk on the Bowling Green. Your number's on it." He spoke with a Brooklyn accent.

"The sidewalk?" Peter's stomach turned. His focus split and split again. *Who is this? What's happened to her? Who do I know in New York who can help?* He decided the best thing was to play it cool. So he asked, "Did she drop it?"

"That would be why it was on the sidewalk, don't you think?"

"And she didn't notice?"

"If she did, she might've picked it up."

This guy was annoying, thought Peter, but don't mouth off . . . yet.

"She jumped into a cab," said Joey. "I'm sure she wants her cell phone back. What's her address?"

"You want her *address*? Listen, pal, I was born at night—"

"Yeah. Yeah, but not *last* night. Ha-ha. Very funny. A smart-ass. I should write it down to call you whenever I need a laugh. Now I got your girlfriend's cell phone, so—"

"We'll get it in the morning," said Peter.

"It's your phone, too? This your wife? Is she there?"

"No."

"No, she's not your wife, or no, she's not there."

"Both," said Peter. "Just tell us where to meet and when. We'll give you a hundred bucks for your time."

"A Benjamin? Nice. I'll take a hedonistic sage over a dead president any day. You like that? *He-*

donistic sage. Bet you thought I didn't have an education."

"I just want the cell phone back."

"Meet at the Bowling Green, tomorrow morning at nine thirty. I'll be wearin' a blue windbreaker and a Yankees hat."

"I'll have on a blue blazer and a blue button-down with an open collar."

"That'll make things easy. Only about a million guys in New York wearin' Yankees hats. Only about a million more wearin' blue blazers and button-downs."

"I'll have my girlfriend with me, too," said Peter. "You'll recognize her, right?"

"I never forget a face, especially a pretty one, even at night. I might forget their names in the mornin' but—"

"Are we done?"

"See ya tomorrow, Peter Fallon from the Boston area code."

Afterward, Peter called Evangeline's landline. She answered on the fifth ring. She had just gotten in. She told him what had happened and admitted she had panicked.

He said he'd be there in the morning. "We'll go to the Bowling Green together."

She took the crown finial from her pocket and turned it over in her fingers. She wondered what it was she had really seen that night, and how it had all begun.

TWO

July 1776

Gil Walker cared nothing for the rebellion until the night he broke a finial off the king's fence.

He believed that rebels and kings would do what they always did, and the less time he spent worrying about them, the better. The smart man looked out for himself and looked for help to no one but his friends.

Gil had three. They called themselves the Waterfront Boys. They had met before their voices changed. They had schooled together and worshiped from the back pews together and gotten into trouble together, too. So it was only natural that they would join the rebellion together.

They did it on a hot July night and did not regret it until the next morning.

They had gone to the Common, the triangle of grass where the Post Road forked off Broadway. They had gone because General Washington had mustered his troops to hear the new Declaration of Independence, and the Boys wanted to hear it, too. If New York was to be occupied by the Continental Army, or attacked by the British, or blockaded, or burned, or left to rot by three-quarters of the people who once lived there, Gil Walker at least wanted to know what the fight was all about.

And hundreds of New Yorkers thought the same way, because they ringed the Common and stood at the edges of the trampled grass and listened in the blood-red sunset, right along with all those ranks of ragged soldiers.

And Gil would never forget the resounding words, "When in the course of human events . . . ," followed by the resounding cheers, then the resounding riot.

After the reading, soldiers and townsfolk mingled and chanted and poured down gallons of rum, then they poured down Broadway toward the Bowling Green, where a gilded lead statue of King George III sat atop a gilded lead horse galloping to nowhere.

And like a river topping its banks, the mob swept everything before it, including the whores who worked the Holy Ground, the streets and the churchyard surrounding St. Paul's chapel. They all joined with giggles and shrieks and gales of caterwauling laughter, as if a little noisy patriotism might be just the thing to boost business.

When Gil Walker heard the high-pitched laugh of Loretta Rogers, his favorite at the Shiny Black Cat, he stopped in midstream.

But Big Jake Meigs grabbed Gil's arm. "None of that. No quiff sniffin' when there's *real* trouble to be makin'."

"You're right." Gil snatched a rum bottle from Big Jake and took a gulp. "I got no money, anyway."

"And as my mother used to say, you can't do nothin' in New York without money."

"So we should be tryin' to make some from all this," said Gil over the roar, "instead of just followin' the crowd."

"Ain't you heard?" Big Jake gave out with a big laugh. "After the rebellion we'll all be rich. That's what the Sons of Liberty keep sayin'. And this here crowd's doin' some fine rebellin', which means we're doin' somethin' to get rich this very minute."

"Is that what's called logic?"

"Well, it ain't common sense," said Big Jake. "Now come on."

Gil glanced back toward Loretta, but she had already disappeared into the crowd. So he took another gulp of rum and gave the bottle back to Big Jake.

Gil would think about Loretta later, because he thought about her plenty. And whenever he went to the Shiny Black Cat, he asked for her, because he saw something more in her than other men did.

He had glimpsed her in the early mornings, when she made her way to the fish market, when she *wasn't* wearing her face paint or the high-topped wig that smelled like a perfumed mouse or the corset that pushed up her titties like two cupcakes in a baker's window. The morning light made her seem sweet, almost virginal, the kind of girl that a young man would take home to his family, if he had a family.

But Gil Walker had never known his father, and his mother had died of consumption when he was fourteen. So, he had taken the Waterfront Boys as family: a gang of young men who made their way doing the work of the city . . . most of it legal, some of it not, most of it menial, some of it smart . . . and some of it smart enough to give Gil Walker dreams of bigger things.

But Big Jake Meigs, who strode beside him, dreamed mostly of rum, and he was slinging the bottle to his lips even then.

Rooster Tom Ramsey, red-faced and pugnacious, dreamed of fighting any man who was bigger than he was, and most men were. So he strutted ahead, flinging slowpokes out of his way while he looked for trouble in every direction.

And Augustus Bethel, expelled from King's College for striking the headmaster, dreamed of writing broadsides to inspire rebellion or books to inspire the world, and he always carried a sheaf of papers and a novel in the pouch over his shoulder. So his friends called him "the Bookworm."

But the Boys followed Gil's lead, because Gil was the tallest and the smartest, and his innocent smile made people trust him implicitly, even when the Boys were up to no good. Gil also dreamed the biggest dream of all: to make himself rich. So whenever the work of cargo slinging or grave digging slowed, he led his friends to some busy coffeehouse to wait outside until the brokers and merchants called for messengers.

You could learn a lot, he always said, just by carrying order slips around the waterfront.

But since the arrival of Washington's army, there had been little shipping and even less brokering. So a bit of noisy rioting seemed like a fine outlet on a summer night.

As the crowd surged toward the Bowling Green, their shouts hammered against the walls of old Fort George, and they forced their way through the gates of the wrought-iron fence that surrounded the oval green, and when they couldn't get through quickly enough, they started clambering up and over.

It was a good fence, thought Gil, strong enough to hold the weight of dozens of grown, angry men. But as he grabbed one of the little brass crown finials that topped the posts supporting the fence, it came off in his hand and he fell backward.

He hit the ground in the midst of all those stamping, scuffling, stumbling feet, and somebody stepped on him, and somebody else kicked him, and Big Jake Meigs shouted, "Stay there! You make a fine ladder." Then Big Jake took another swig of rum, dropped the bottle into Gil's lap, put a foot on Gil's shoulder, and leaped over the fence.

Then Gil heard someone laughing, and he saw the dirty hem of a red satin dress.

"A kiss for a tot there, Gilbie boy!"

It was Loretta. She was wearing her working dress and that wondrous corset, but she had joined the mob before she finished dolling herself, so she hadn't painted her face or put on her satin mules or that wig, so she looked like the virgin at first light and a lady of the night, too.

Gil had never seen a finer combination. From his knees, he smiled up at her. And she smiled down.

Then a rope made a long arc through the dusk-silvered sky above her head and snagged the king by the neck. This brought a thunderous roar from the crowd.

Gil shoved the little brass crown into his pocket and stood.

People were pushing all around them, but Gil and Loretta were shouldered against the fence and anchored in place. So she reached for the bottle in his hand.

Gil pulled it back. "Kiss first," he said, over the roar of the crowd.

"Come on now, Gilbie boy. I get me goods in hand 'fore I give out with the sweets, whether we're talkin' about coins or rum." She took the bottle and drank a gulp big enough to make a sailor go stupid. Then she raised herself onto her tiptoes and brought her mouth to his.

Inside the fence, Big Jake was shouting, "Tail on, boys! Tail on!" And people were stumbling over one another to get a piece of one of the ropes that now had the King of England and his horse lassoed half a dozen times.

Then someone shouted, "One!"

And someone else shouted, "Two!"

And a gang of people shouted, "Three!"

And everyone on the ropes began to sway like a wave rolling over the green. And then they all shouted, "Heave!" and came swaying back and shouted, "Ho!" And again, "Heave!" And again, "Ho!"

But Gil Walker was focused on Loretta's tongue. In all his visits to the Shiny Black Cat, she had never once given him an open-mouthed kiss.

"Heave! Ho! *Heave! Ho! HEAVE! HO!*"

The lead legs of the king's horse began to bend.

And Gil pivoted Loretta against the fence, so

that he could keep his lips on hers while the stiffening in his breeches found purchase against her thigh.

The king was falling, the roar was rising, and so was Gil.

Loretta whispered, "Now, Gilbie, no pokin' without payin'."

He pushed the rum bottle back to her lips. "Have another swallow."

And as the mob gave out with a roar that must have been heard all the way down at the Narrows, the king began to fall backward.

"Ah, hell"—Loretta took the bottle—"we should be celebratin' tonight." She swallowed down another gulp, then gave Gil a devilish grin and dumped a big splash over her breasts. "Have a lick, Gilbie. The king is dead. Long live Washington!"

"The hell with Washington." Gil Walker buried his face in the soft, sweet, rum-soaked flesh and pushed his hips against her.

"Feels good in a crowd, don't it?" She pressed her thigh to him. "All these people raisin' hell, and you're the only one with a stiffy. But if you pop off in your breeches, you'll be owin' Madam Fanny, just like we was in the Cat. You might be a big boy, but she's got Leaner McTeague, who's as strong as a draft horse—"

"He don't scare me."

"Maybe not, but he always collects when customers pop off uninvited like."

The crowd was roaring, chanting, ranting. Men were dangling on top of the pedestal and someone had produced a hammer and chisel and with a great clanging that echoed through the statue and out into the crowd, he began to decapitate King George.

And for a few moments, the crowd fell silent, as if this truly were regicide. *Clang. Clang. Clang.* Then the head came off and the crowd gave out again.

But Gil's mind was on one thing.

So Loretta gave him a knee to get his attention. "If you want *more,* Gilbie, you gotta *give* more."

"I got no money." He pressed his face against her breasts.

"But you got choices, Gilbie. You can have another lick of my nice rum titties, and we'll call it square. Or you can *hit* a lick for Gen'ral Washington and have yourself a whole hour with me on the end of your dick."

Gil raised his face from the glorious valley where her breasts met. "Washington?"

She took his chin and pointed it toward the edge of the crowd, where a burly man in an eye patch stood next to a drummer boy. The sticks were moving in the drummer boy's hands, but the crowd was so noisy that Gil couldn't hear the tattoo.

Loretta said, "That's Captain Bull Stuckey. A seafarin' man who don't have a ship no more."

"Like a lot of seafarin' men these days," said Gil.

"He's formin' a company of militia, all New York City lads. Sign on with him, and I'll give you a free one."

"Sign on?"

"Us gals is nicer to soldiers than we is to local dock rats." She slid her hand down his breeches. "So let me take you over there." She gave him a tug. "You can sign your name or make your mark—"

"I know how to write." He pushed himself against her hand. "*And* read."

"Ooh, an educated dockhand, then. They might just make you an officer. Or considerin' the size of this"—she gave it a stroke—"they might make you a *bat*man."

And before the night was over, all four Waterfront Boys had joined Stuckey's company of New York militia, while Loretta Rogers and her friends had made more money in commissions from Bull Stuckey than ever they had from servicing a dozen men.

As for the king . . . they paraded his gilded head around town on a pike, then they dragged the rest of him off to Connecticut and melted him down and turned him into forty thousand musket balls.

"Good riddance," said Gil Walker.

ii.

But nothing good happened to New York or the Waterfront Boys after that.

The British fleet, which had begun arriving in June, grew from a small grove of masts into a dense forest in a few weeks. And from that forest emerged the largest army ever sent forth by a British king. First, they built a city of white tents on the hills of Staten Island. Then they began to drill. And every afternoon their bayonets glinted in the sun, and every evening the music of their regimental bands floated across the harbor.

The Waterfront Boys listened from their post near the Grand Battery.

"We didn't sign up to fight *them,*" said Rooster Tom.

"I fear that we did," answered Gil.

Worse, they had signed up with a man used to meting out shipboard discipline. His recruits could sleep in their own homes. They were local militia, after all. But the man who did not appear within five minutes of the drummer's tattoo would be marked as a deserter and dosed with thirty-nine lashes.

So Gil and Big Jake continued to live under the eaves at the Queen's Head, where they did the heavy lifting for master Sam Fraunces. Rooster Tom lived with his old mother, who kept house for a Jew merchant named Haym Salomon. And Augustus the Bookworm lived by his wits and his charm, which had endeared him to every pretty housemaid in every manor house from Richmond Hill to Harlem Heights. But they all slept with an ear out for the sound of the drum.

"We didn't sign up to dance a jig whenever Stuckey gives us a beat," said Big Jake.

"I fear that we did," answered Gil.

And worst of all, the girls at the Shiny Black Cat were no better to militiamen than they were to anyone else.

"Those doxies lied to us when we signed up," said the Bookworm.

"I fear that they did," answered Gil.

Most of the time, when Gil showed up with a few shillings, Loretta was busy. So he would go off to spend his money at some house where the ladies looked decidedly less virginal in the morning light.

This, Big Jake explained as they walked down Broadway one August eve, was a good example of the old saying about living and learning. Business, he said, should always be business. "Answerin' a muster 'cause we think it might get us a bit of free finky-diddlin' ain't the way to join a rebellion."

"*Now* you tell us," said Rooster Tom.

"If I'd been sober," said Big Jake, "I woulda told you that joinin' any rebellion is fool's work. We should be tryin' to get rich off of all this, like Gil always says."

"I didn't do it for any free finky-diddlin', nor knob jobs, neither," said Gil.

"No. You did it because you're in lo-oo-ove." The Bookworm made a graceful little bow-and-step, like a courtier in a silk waistcoat.

Gil kicked him. "I did it because it seemed like the right thing to do at the time."

"It don't seem so right now," said Big Jake.

The Bookworm laughed. "At least Loretta's a pretty one."

"They're all pretty at night," said Rooster Tom, "and they all give you the itch in the mornin'." He stuck a hand into his breeches and grabbed. "And what are *you* lookin' at?" he said to an old man stepping out of a nearby tavern.

If the old man was startled to see Rooster pulling his pecker in the middle of the street, he didn't say. Rooster's quick-match temper was known in every ward, and men said that a challenge from him should be met with a pistol or a polite retreat. The old man chose the latter.

So the Waterfront Boys strode on, as if this were any New York night . . . before there was a Continental Army on the Common or a British fleet at the Narrows, a normal night when rich men entertained in their parlors and whores entertained on the Holy Ground and young men rambled from alley to avenue in search of whatever entertainment they could find.

A few days earlier, Washington had issued orders for civilians to evacuate the city. Most had already left, and those who remained were too old to travel, or too young, or too impoverished, or too fearful of losing whatever they owned, or too opportunistic to flee when the war had given them the chance to change life's odds.

And the Waterfront Boys were nothing if not opportunists.

Rooster Tom had shown his mates half a dozen vacant Tory houses where pewter candlesticks and Turkey carpets and pipes of good port had been left behind. The Bookworm knew about a few, too, because he knew the maids in most of them. And since it was in the natural order of things that *someone* would eventually take *anything* valuable in a vacant house, the Boys had taken that responsibility onto themselves.

What they took they carried to a pawnbroker who lived in the First Ward. What the pawnbroker gave them they spent on rum and girls.

And they had spent plenty already that night. Rum and girls. Girls and rum. Now they were looking for a different kind of fun . . . a gang of soldiers throwing dice, perhaps, or a few Massachusetts militiamen worthy of a fight, or maybe a Tory to ride on a rail.

Most nights, the streets teemed with soldiers and militiamen who were as undisciplined, drunk, and troublesome as the Waterfront Boys could be. But New York was quiet and tense, because Washington had moved half his army across the East River to Brooklyn. A fight was coming. So Broadway was mostly empty, and the Boys walked all the way to the Bowling Green without finding a bit of bother.

As he kicked along, Gil fingered the crown finial in his pocket. He had kept the piece of brass, as large as the palm of his hand, because whenever he was about to do something stupid for patriotism or lust or any other emotion, high or low, the finial reminded him that acting without thinking had its consequences.

The Bowling Green lay in darkness. But torches flickered in front of the fine house that Colonel Henry Knox now occupied at One Broadway. And Fort George glowered in the shadows beyond.

There were two soldiers in blue uniforms guarding Knox's door, two more guarding the gate in the picket fence, half a dozen more lounging by a row of horses tethered to the fence.

Rooster went sauntering up, and the guards snapped to attention.

"Easy, lads," said Rooster.

"Yeah." Big Jake came out of the shadows. "We're just lookin' for a game of dice."

"We don't throw dice," said the big sergeant at the gate. "So move on."

"Move on, is it? In our own town"—Rooster rose on the balls of his feet, then dropped back, then rose up again, then back—"you're tellin' me to *move on*?"

Gil grabbed Rooster by the tail of his leather waistcoat.

The Bookworm stepped in front of the soldiers. "We're sorry."

"We ain't." Rooster whacked at Gil's hand. "We can go anywhere we want in our own town."

Gil said to the soldiers, "He's just a bit—"

"A bit what?" An officer with a blue sash appeared under one of the torches.

"A bit"—Gil fumbled—"a bit . . ."

"What unit do you men belong to?" said the officer.

"None of your damn business," said Rooster Tom.

"What *unit*?" demanded the officer. "Or are you deserters?"

Gil knew, from their size and fine uniforms, that these weren't ordinary soldiers. They were the life guard for Washington himself. He said, "No deserters, here, sir."

The officer turned on Gil. "I think you're lying. I think you're all deserters . . . lying and desertion. Do you belong to one of the units the general moved to Brooklyn today? Lying, desertion, and cowardice. Good for fifty lashes. Take them." He swung his arm and two of the Continentals grabbed Big Jake, and two more grabbed Gil.

"I'm no deserter," cried Gil.

"Then what *unit*?" demanded the officer.

"Mine!" A slight young man emerged from the shadows. He wore a blue uniform with deerskin breeches and brass buttons that flashed in the torchlight. "Captain Hamilton, New York Provincial Artillery."

And before another word was said, the door of Henry Knox's house swung open, and out stepped the tallest man that any of them had ever seen. *George Washington.*

All the soldiers presented arms. The captain pulled out his sword and raised the hilt to his chin in salute.

Washington said a few more words to Henry Knox, the *widest* man that any of them had ever seen, then he pulled on his gauntlets and strode toward the street.

One of the guards brought over his horse. The others formed a wall between Washington and the Waterfront Boys.

Washington grabbed the bridle and swung a leg onto the horse. He didn't even look down until he was mounted, sitting flagpole straight, left hand holding the reins, right hand braced against his hip. "Did I hear word of deserters?"

"We're not deserters, sir," said Gil Walker.

"Then rejoin your unit, or face a flogging." Washington kicked his horse up Broadway, with his life guard mounting and galloping after him.

Alexander Hamilton watched them go, then pivoted on his heels and said to the Waterfront Boys, "Come along, men."

Once they were out of earshot of the guards, the

Bookworm said, "I want to thank you, Alexander . . . on behalf of all my friends."

"I won't see New York boys bullied," said Hamilton, "and I don't forget favors."

"Favors?" said Gil.

"Augustus here saved me from a beating or two at Kings College. Pity he couldn't save himself."

"A pity," said the Bookworm.

"So, then"—Hamilton was heading for the Grand Battery, the row of cannons at the tip of the island—"what unit *are* you from?"

"Stuckey's militia," answered Big Jake.

"That explains it," said Hamilton. "You're lucky."

"Lucky?" said Rooster Tom. "We'd be lucky if we wasn't in this militia at all."

At the Battery, half a dozen men were crouched under a torch. One of them was tossing dice against a wall. Another noticed Hamilton and cried, "Attenshun!"

The men leaped to their feet and stuck out their chests. Someone dropped a rum bottle that rattled on the cobblestones.

Hamilton picked it up and threw it into the water. Then he said, "At ease."

"How are we lucky, sir?" asked the Bookworm.

"The British are moving on Long Island," answered Hamilton. "It may be a feint, or they may be after Brooklyn Heights. Local units will be held here to protect the city. I expect the general thinks we'll fight harder for our own homes."

"That's for fuckin' sure," said Rooster Tom.

"Your friend is very rude, Augustus," said

Hamilton without looking at Rooster. "Rejoin your unit, all of you."

The Bookworm said, "Thank you, sir."

Gil peered out at the lights of the British fleet, like harmless fireflies flicking on and off in the distance. Then he said to Hamilton, "You saved us from a floggin', sir. It's not somethin' we'll soon forget."

THE BRITISH BEAT the Americans so convincingly off Brooklyn Heights that only a lunatic would think that fledgling independence would not die in its nest. Washington's escape from Brooklyn, accomplished under the cover of dark and dense fog, seemed an act of abject desperation.

And the Boys saw it all because Stuckey's company covered the New York ferry landing during the retreat. From midnight to dawn, the boats landed and left, landed and left, disgorging troops who had been beaten, bloodied, and had barely survived. The men came ashore dragging their muskets and sometimes their mates, and many simply drifted off in search of the nearest grogshop or the quietest whorehouse.

"Scary thing," said Big Jake.

"What?" said Gil.

"That we're the most disciplined unit in sight," said the Bookworm.

"I got a good mind to desert this damn army," said Rooster.

"You'll desert nothin'," said Gil, "not while we're watchin'."

"Aye," said Big Jake. "Do it when we're not lookin'. I'll go with you."

"We signed our names," said Gil. "If a man's to be anything in this world, if he's to get anything, signin' his name ought to stand for something."

"Still and all," said Big Jake, "it's a helluva way to get rich."

THE DEFEAT TURNED Washington's army into a mob, and for a time, no amount of flogging made a difference in their behavior. Some men deserted, simply picked up their bedrolls and shouldered their muskets and started walking. The rest got after the most serious drinking, whoring, and looting yet.

Gil told his mates that they could never quit their own city, but there could be nothing wrong in looking out for themselves. So when they were released from duty each day, they "visited" more vacant Tory houses and brought more goods to the pawnbroker, so they had more money to spend.

And with so many soldiers deserting, Loretta had more time to spend with Gil.

He told himself that he was not in love with her, that she was just another person trying to make her way in a hard world, and what they did was all business.

So he paid his shillings at the Shiny Black Cat. And she loosened her corset and raised her dress and let him poke her for as long as he could hold it.

Usually, she dropped her skirts when he was done and stepped out to the yard for a quick douche. But sometimes, she stayed and talked, and talk, he knew, was something she saved for her "specials." And he liked being a "special."

So one night, he brought her a present. In a deserted house, he had "found" two fine mahogany boxes with brass fittings—a matched set. They were empty. But he had discovered that if he slid a small piece of side molding, the bottoms of each box opened to reveal inner compartments where might be hidden jewels or money, though they were empty, too.

Still, when he gave her the boxes, she acted as if they were full of gold.

And she repaid him the best way she knew. She didn't simply raise her dress and petticoats. She took them all the way off. Then she paraded in front of him in nothing but the corset, red satin mules, and white stockings. She let him see her front and back, arse and cunny and sweet rum titties, too. Then she pushed him back on the bed and pulled down his breeches and rode him until he was spent. Then they talked.

"So," she said, "what's your plan for when the British attack the town?"

"Do what Stuckey tells me to do."

She got up and pulled on her petticoats, then her dress, but she left her breasts exposed so that he could look at them a bit longer. "I hear that you boys visit the houses of Tory toffs who went runnin' . . ."

"I need to make my money to pay you." He got up and pulled on his breeches.

"I know a Tory house where there's hard coin hidden." She tightened her corset. "Gold guinea coins."

"Gold guineas? Why didn't the owners take them?"

"Because they ain't left. The wife's sickly. So she don't much care that her husband has me come in to 'cure' him once a week."

A thumping started in the next room, accompanied by the deep groaning of a man and the theatrical urging of a woman.

"Where is this house?" asked Gil.

Loretta stepped closer to him. "I won't tell you, but I'll *show* you."

"Then what?"

"Why . . . we can run . . . together."

The thumping played more steadily against the wall.

Loretta glanced at the mirror vibrating above her little dresser and said, "We'd all like to get out of here, Gilbie. And gold'll do it. No matter who wins the next fight, gold'll get us through."

"I'm *in* the next fight, thanks to you."

"Don't be blamin' a girl for doin' what she has to do." Loretta pressed her breasts against him. "And remember, I believe in this fight as much as you do."

"How do you know what I believe?"

"You signed up, didn't you? You signed up 'cause the only way for the likes of us to have a chance—without robbin' houses or whorin'—is to get free. Freedom's the thing, Gilbie, whether you're a young yob waitin' by a coffeehouse for a merchant to give you an errand, or an orphan girl whose uncle sold her into . . . this."

Gil grabbed Loretta by the shoulders. "Why should I trust you?"

"Because I like you, Gilbie, and you like me."

Footfalls thumped down the hallway, followed by a knock and Fanny Doolin's phony-sweet voice. "Hurry up, Loretta, dearie. This here's a business, don't forget."

Loretta glanced at the door, then turned her eyes back to Gil. "And because you and me, we're two peas in a pod. We both grew up without a pa, we both seen our ma's die afore their time, and we both want to do better than we done."

Gil Walker saw honesty in her eyes, no matter how obscured by mascara, more honesty than he had seen in the eyes of all the brokers on the waterfront or all the preachers in their pulpits or all the Sons of Liberty that ever met at the Queen's Head.

She smiled. She had all her teeth, all white as milk teeth, not yellowed, not tobacco-browned, not wine-stained. And she had hope, too. "Just trust me," she said. "If you trust me, I'll trust you."

HAD THEY ATTACKED New York in those first days after Brooklyn, the British might have ended the rebellion right there. They could have lined the Post Road with gibbets from the Battery to Harlem Heights and hanged a rebel from every one.

But they waited almost three weeks, as if to give Washington the chance to regain a bit of discipline, as if it would not be sporting to beat so disorganized an enemy. Or perhaps they were amused to see Washington spreading his troops up and down Manhattan like a poor man spreading butter on stale bread. Once he had put troops in Harlem and at the Grand Battery and on all the beaches along the East River and in all the little dirt forts that he had built to control the city, the British began to move.

Stuckey's company spent a Friday night on duty in a new trench that cut across Bayard's farm, about a quarter mile north of the Common. Then Stuckey allowed them to go home to sleep. Gil expected it would be the last night that they would sleep in their own beds for a long time. So he dropped onto the feathers under Sam Fraunces's eaves and slept with the same sense of purpose that a miser banks his pennies.

But just after dawn, he and Big Jake were awakened by a pounding on the door.

Gil popped up first. "The tattoo! We missed the tattoo! It must be the attack!"

Jake rolled over. "Hunh?"

Gil leaped to his feet. "Get up. Get dressed. Or we'll get lashed."

"It ain't that," said Fraunces through the door. "There's a woman downstairs . . . says she's a friend of yours."

"A friend?" said Gil.

Big Jake popped up. "A woman?"

LORETTA WAS WAITING on the street. "Fraunces wouldn't let me come up."

Gil turned to Big Jake. "You can go back to bed."

Big Jake gave them a wink. "You want the room for a bit?"

"No," said Loretta. "That ain't what this is about."

So Big Jake shrugged and went shambling back up the stairs.

Gil looked at the sharp shadows slanting over Broad Street. "It ain't much more than six o'clock. I was on the line all night."

"If the big fight's comin', time to show you the house, the house with the gold guineas."

So Gil followed her through the deserted streets.

She wore common clothes and loosed her hair, and he almost told her that she looked beautiful in the morning. But he already knew her answer: Any woman would look beautiful in the morning, if she was leading a man to a stash of gold. So Gil said nothing.

They headed up Broad Street and turned onto Beaver, which was lined with gabled Dutch buildings that housed the merchants who traded the pelts that had given the street its name. But rebellion had put most of the trading houses out of business, so most of the stores were shuttered.

Then they turned onto New Street, the first street that the British made after they took the city from the Dutch. At the lower end lived artisans, craftsmen, and mechanics, who did business on the first floors and kept families on the second. But the neighborhood changed as they headed toward the Presbyterian Church that sat on Wall Street and stared down New Street like the all-seeing eye of God. The dwellings grew larger, taller, *newer*.

Halfway up the street they came to the intersection of Fluten Barrack, which cut from Broad Street over to Broadway.

Loretta stopped on the corner, near an old man who had built a fire on the street and was stirring a large pot of coffee over the flame.

"Mornin', folks," he said. "Care to buy some coffee?"

"Coffee?" said Gil. "Where did you get coffee?"

"Been savin' it. Last coffee in New York, but the redcoats'll be in our lap soon enough. So I'll drink it now, and what I can't drink I'll sell. No tree bark nor ground-up shoe leather. Just fine roasted beans."

Gil pulled three copper pennies from his pocket.

"That'll do." The old man snatched the coins, took a dipper from the side of the pot, and ladled out a measure of coffee.

Gil had a sip. It was hot and bitter and tasted better in the early morning than rum at midnight. He offered the dipper to Loretta, but she ignored it because her eyes were fixed on a house across the street.

"Old man," she said. "There's guards in front of that house."

"You mean John Blunt's? The Tory? Colonel Silliman of Connecticut moved in there the other day. Colonel *Gold* Silliman. Some name, eh?"

Gil stepped closer to Loretta and whispered, "That's his actual name. *Gold*. And that's as close as we're gettin' to the gold in that house, I think."

"Did I hear someone say *gold*?" Big Jake's voice came up behind them.

"Go back to bed," said Loretta dejectedly. "I'm doin' the same. Alone."

They watched her scurry off, then Big Jake said

to Gil, "I been at your side since we was boys. You hold out on me when some whore tells you about a stash of gold—"

"There's no gold, only a colonel named Gold." Gil started walking back to the Queen's Head.

"You better not be lyin', boy," cried Big Jake. "That there would be somethin' to break up a friendship."

"Coffee, mister?" said the old man to Big Jake.

"Coffee?" Big Jake turned. "Where in hell does a feller get coffee these days?"

iii.

The next morning, Gil Walker heard thunder though the sky was clear. A second later, he felt it rumble in his chest, then its echo rolled across the green farmlands and before he could turn toward the sound, he heard a second clap, even more powerful.

The British naval bombardment had begun.

The Waterfront Boys were back in their trench.

At the center of the line, on Bayard's Hill, rose a fort that looked to Gil Walker like a giant dungpile. Captain Hamilton had built it, and his provincial artillery had been moved there, so now half a dozen cannon poked out of the dirt like strands of straw grass poking out of the dung.

And from the smell that rose after that first cannon blast, Gil wondered if the whole trench might not fill with dung before the day was over. Someone had shit himself.

Gil jumped up onto the lip of the trench and looked to the north. A white cloud was rising from the East River, and the thunder was rising with it.

"What do you see?" Rooster scrambled out of the trench.

"Five British ships openin' up on the beach. Looks like Kip's Bay."

"Kip's Bay? That means we're cut off."

"You men!" Bull Stuckey came striding along the top of the trench. "Get in line."

"But, Captain," said Big Jake, "we thought the redcoats would land down at the Battery. Ain't that why we pulled back to here? To form a second line?"

"No tellin' where they'll land," answered Stuckey. "So we got Washington up in Harlem, and Henry Knox in the city, and good men up and down the island."

"But if they're landing north of us and south of Washington," said the Bookworm, "they'll cut us off like one of the heads of Cerberus."

"Save that fancy talk," said Stuckey. "Do as you're told or take a floggin'."

"Well, I ain't stayin' to get flogged nor trapped neither." Rooster reached down to pick up his musket, and Bull Stuckey kicked him square in the ass.

Rooster went headfirst into the trench, then he popped up with the musket clubbed. "No man lays a hand to me, and no man kicks me, neither."

Stuckey's answer was a kick to the jaw that knocked Rooster cold. Then Stuckey pulled out his pistol and looked up and down the trench line. "The next man who challenges me, I'll shoot him down like a dog, so help me God." Then he strode off.

And Big Jake looked at Gil. "Rooster was right. We should have deserted."

* * *

ALTHOUGH IT WAS the Sabbath, the Supreme Being did not seem offended by the British attack. Otherwise, thought Gil, he might have done something to stop it.

Soon Henry Knox himself was retreating from the city, bringing cannoneers but no cannon, and bringing the thousand men in Colonel Gold Silliman's brigade but no gold (as far as Gil could tell). Silliman's Connecticuts crowded into the trench with the New Yorkers, and Gil smelled more shit. He knew it was not any of his friends. He hoped it was not any of the New Yorkers.

All morning, the Waterfront Boys watched and listened and waited. They saw the glinting of shouldered muskets as other American units retreated across the folds in the green landscape. They saw flashes of red—British soldiers, expanding their beachhead from east to west across the island. They saw flocks of birds flushed from cover before the advancing troops. And still the men on Bayard's Hill waited.

Then, just before noon, a rider approached from the north. He wore the blue sash of a major and was flanked by two big dragoons.

"That's Aaron Burr," said the Bookworm. "A Princeton man."

"Princeton, eh?" Gil took a drink from his wooden canteen. "That means he should have more sense."

"It means he's an educated man," said the Bookworm.

Big Jake laughed. "We're *in* this fix thanks to educated men."

Burr reined up in front of the dungpile fort and shouted, "Who's in charge here?"

Colonel Silliman, who was striding back and forth atop the trench, stopped and said, "I am!"

Colonel Knox, who was striding back and forth atop the rampart, stopped and said, "I am."

Burr looked from rail-skinny Silliman to mountain-belly Knox, and said to Knox, "You should retreat, sir, or your whole regiment will be cut off."

"We've received no orders," said Knox.

"Stay here and be sacrificed, then," said Burr.

"We have no orders, and no option for escape," Knox shouted, "so we'll put our faith in Captain Hamilton's cannon and our strong position."

Hamilton's little cocked hat appeared on the rampart above his little red face.

"My compliments to the captain for his skill at piling dirt upon a hill," answered Burr. "But your fort has no bomb-proof and no water, and it's a damned hot day for September, sir."

"I'll say." Big Jake upended his empty canteen.

"It's my opinion," Burr went on, "that a detachment of British could take this . . . *fort* . . . with a single howitzer."

"We will defend it, Major!" shouted Knox. "Defend it to the death!"

"Death?" whispered Rooster, who had come to. "No one said nothin' about defendin' *anythin'* to the death."

Burr turned to Silliman. "You'll be cut off soon enough if the British keep moving west, but I grew up on this island. I know every trail from here to Harlem."

"I know every trail and every *girl,*" whispered the Bookworm.

"So why ain't you 'tween a pair of pretty legs," said Big Jake, " 'stead of in this fix?"

"Because I'm takin' a stand," said the Bookworm.

Rooster muttered, "Damn fool."

"He's no damn fool," said Gil Walker. "It's the right thing."

"Right thing . . . wrong thing"—Rooster kicked at the dirt—"I say we're all damn fools. Let's disappear while we still can. Get back to bein' New Yorkers, lookin' out for no one but ourselves."

"And your mother," said the Bookworm. "Don't forget her."

"Aye, and don't forget the gold," said Big Jake.

"Gold?" said Rooster.

"What gold?" said the Bookworm.

"Ask Gil," said Big Jake.

"There's no gold." Gil kept his eyes on Burr, who was now leading his horse along the trench, so that all the men could hear what he said next: "If you stay here, half of you will be killed or wounded, the other half hung like dogs."

Men all along the line looked at one another, murmured, fidgeted. Gil fidgeted with the finial in his pocket. The possibility of hanging made most men fidget. So did lying to your friends. But why was he lying? Did he not believe Loretta? Or did he believe that there was something more important than gold? In that bright sun, he was not sure. But the Bookworm was right. They were making a stand, and it was the right thing to do.

Silliman shouted at Burr, "You'll not address my men without permission, mister. Now, we've received no orders from General Putnam."

"But *I'm* General Putnam's aide, sir," said Burr.

"But he did not order anything," said Silliman.

"Therefore," boomed Henry Knox, "*I'm* ordering that we defend this place . . . to the death. Unless we receive orders to the contrary."

Aaron Burr seemed to lose all patience. He pulled his reins so hard that his horse nearly went over. Then he and the dragoons galloped about a quarter mile north to a barn in a field. They disappeared behind it for a few moments, then they came galloping back.

"What *is* he doin'?" Rooster asked his mates.

"Playactin'," said Gil. "Savin' us by playactin'."

"Helluva way to fight a war," said Big Jake.

Burr reined his horse again, looked up at the ramparts again, shouted again: "I now bring orders from General Putnam. You are to place yourselves under my command and allow me to conduct your brigade north with as much baggage as you can carry."

Skinny Silliman looked up at fat Knox. "That's good enough for me, Henry! I'm takin' my men out."

Knox gave a snort and turned to Hamilton: "Prepare to remove your fieldpieces."

THE POST ROAD, which ran up the east side of the island, was now in British hands. But the Bloomingdale Road, which began north of the Common, led up the west side, through farmers' fields and past rich men's manors, and it was still open. And west of it were smaller roads, trails, cart paths, and ancient deer runs where a man who knew his way could confound anyone who was chasing him.

Soon, a thousand Connecticut infantry, along with Stuckey's company of New York militia and Hamilton's provincial artillery were seeking to confound the most powerful army on earth.

Their column stretched over a mile. They turned west toward the woods, then north along the river. They went four abreast, as any good army did, but that was their only similarity to a *good* army. Gil knew that this was no more than a freshet of human panic running uphill for Harlem. And by some quirk of military fate, the Waterfront Boys were the last men in that last unit, the absolute rear guard.

"The redcoats must've stopped for tea," said Gil, "else they could have cut straight across the island and trapped us."

"Don't like movin' north," said the Bookworm.

"Quiet in the ranks!" Aaron Burr, who seemed to be everywhere on his lathered horse, galloped past them and up to a little rock outcropping. He pulled out his spyglass and peered into the woods, then slammed it shut and turned back.

"Captain!" he said. "If the enemy advance party strikes, turn your men and hold."

"I have scouts back there," said Stuckey. "They'll sound the alarm."

"'Turn your men,'" muttered the Bookworm. "That means us."

"That's means we'll have to fight," said Big Jake.

"Instead of that," said Rooster, "what say we drop out and go get this gold?"

"We signed our names," said Gil. "We give our word. I mean to see we keep it."

And they marched in and out of woodlots, up and over gentle hills, across orchards and cornfields, along pathways that kept them out of the enemy's sight for much of the afternoon. And when they were a bit more than halfway up the island, they swung back to the Bloomingdale Road.

The Dutch had called this area Bloemendael, and the name told a tale of purple asters and yellow sunflowers and orchards heavy with apples. In every September of his life, thought Gil, the upper reaches of Manhattan Island had appeared as garden paradise. But—

That was when they heard musket fire in the woods to the east. A moment later three Americans came crashing through the underbrush, shouting that light troops were coming fast.

Stuckey bellowed, "New Yorkers! Fall out."

Gil said to his friends, "That's us, lads."

Rooster gave a hoot and unshouldered his musket. If there was a fight, Rooster became a fighter, even when he didn't want to fight.

"Now we'll see how bookworms do it, eh, Augie?" said Big Jake.

Augustus the Bookworm answered by vomiting onto his shoes.

Aaron Burr galloped out of the same woods

and called to Stuckey, "What's your disposition, Captain?"

Stuckey glanced at the Bookworm. "We got a few pukers, and a hundred and fifty men ready to do their duty."

"Get them into that field yonder," said Burr. "Volley on my pistol shot, and my dragoons'll strike the redcoats in the flank."

A few bellowing commands sent Stuckey's company scrambling over a split-rail fence and trampling through hip-high asters.

Stuckey and two sergeants put themselves in front and directed the men into two ranks.

The Waterfront Boys took their positions on the far left of the first rank.

Gil looked at Jake. Jake looked at Rooster. Rooster looked at the Bookworm. And the Bookworm whispered, "I think I'm gonna puke again."

Then the brass buckles on the British crossbelts glinted through the trees.

"There they are," said Big Jake. "Shinin' like gold."

"Speakin' of gold," said Rooster, "you better not be holdin' out on us, Gilbie."

"Poise your firelocks!" shouted Stuckey.

And the New York muskets rattled into place.

"Cock your firelocks!" shouted Stuckey.

Gil grabbed the hammer and pulled it back.

Stuckey raised his saber. "Take aim."

For a moment, the British captain, now just forty yards away, seemed to reconsider an attack, then he called his men into line.

Gil thought he might puke, too.

Fifty or sixty redcoats were pulling tight into two ranks. Their sergeant was shouting and the men in the front were kneeling, so both ranks could fire at once.

"I read how they do this," the Bookworm was saying. "They put up as much lead as they can, then they come with the cold steel."

"You read too much," said Rooster. "One volley from *us* and they'll all be down."

Then Aaron Burr's pistol popped off in the woods.

"Fire!" shouted Stuckey.

Gil pulled his trigger and the musket kicked. Thunder erupted to the right and the left of him. Smoke billowed so thick that he could not see the British. But their musket balls came whizzing into the cloud.

Gil heard one scream past his ear. Another whipped over his head and another thumped into something on his left. He heard Rooster give out with a strange grunt, and as the musket smoke blew off, Rooster dropped down among the trampled flowers.

Stuckey was screaming for the front rank to pull back and the second rank to step forward, as if men who had drilled a few times on the Common could execute complicated field maneuvers in the face of the hardened regulars now lowering their bayonets and preparing to charge.

"Rooster!" cried the Bookworm.

Rooster was curling on the ground, clutching his chest, groaning, "Goddamn it, I'm shot through."

"Front rank, fall back!" shouted Stuckey. "Second rank, forward!"

Gil ignored the order and bent to help Rooster, so Stuckey smacked him with the flat of his saber. "I said front rank fall back! Second rank forward!"

But the second rank faltered. The Americans were about to do what they had become famous for in New York—break and run, this time before a unit half their size.

Then Burr and his dragoons swept out over an outcropping and galloped straight at the British.

And nothing so unnerved infantry in line, even British infantry, as the sight of cavalry attacking their flank, even if it was no more than three mounted men waving sabers. Whatever courage had inspired this small redcoat detachment to take on the rear of the American line vanished, and so did they, back into the woods.

"HE EITHER MARCHES or we leave him." Stuckey took off his hat and wiped sweat from his forehead.

"I can walk." Rooster knelt on all fours, then lifted himself to his knees.

Stuckey said, "Those redcoats'll have the main body on us right quick. We have to move, now."

"I said I can *walk*!" Rooster looked down at his bloody shirt. "Just don't take me for one of the redcoats and shoot me again."

"All right!" bellowed Stuckey. "Fall in!"

With the help of his friends, Rooster managed

to walk another half mile before he sank to his knees next to an orchard heavy with red apples.

Stuckey came stalking back. "He's gut shot. It's a wonder he made it this far."

Gil knelt beside his friend in the middle of the road. "We can't leave him."

Stuckey pulled his saber again.

And Gil stood. His face was covered in sweat, and a long streak of black powder ran up his right cheek. He leveled a gaze at Stuckey that said, Do not strike me again.

And Stuckey seemed to soften. He pointed the saber toward a big house about fifty yards back from the road. "That's the Woodward Manor. The squire's a patriot. He's even entertained General Washington. A wounded soldier'll be safe there."

"I know the maid," added the Bookworm.

"You know all the maids," said Rooster.

Gil thanked Stuckey and said, "We'll take him there, then rejoin you."

"No," said Stuckey. "Pukin' Mary here can take him. You two, step off now."

"But we're militia," said Big Jake. "There's militia desertin' all over this island."

"There'll be no desertin' from my unit." Stuckey puffed himself up. "I won't lose two men who stood enemy fire like you boys just done."

Rooster held his hands to the bloody wound and said, "Get goin', but Gilbie boy, don't be holdin out on us . . . that there would be somethin' to break up a friendship."

So Gil and Big Jake marched on toward Harlem Heights.

iv.

By ten o'clock that night, Gil Walker had come to a conclusion: no man ever got rich swinging a shovel. He got calluses and a sore back. He got dirty. He got tired. And no man ever got rich in an army, either. He got shot at, and chased, and yelled at, and sometimes he got killed, and sometimes his friends got killed.

And no army had ever spent more time digging than this one. The only thing they did more than dig was run. And such an army would never win freedom for anyone.

Gil's mother, who had scrubbed floors in the homes of rich Tories, who had seen as best she could to his learning and his faith in the Anglican church, had told him that he was made for bigger things, but here he was, in the miserable drizzle, at the end of the most miserable day these new United States had yet seen . . . digging a trench. And behind him, men were digging more trenches, and behind them, more men were digging.

And out there, beyond the greasy tallow light of the American torches, lay the British army.

Gil did not say what was on his mind, because Stuckey was too close. So he swung the shovel and tossed the dirt. Swung the shovel and thought his thoughts. Swung the shovel and stopped for a moment and fingered the brass finial in his pocket.

"Keep diggin'," muttered Big Jake, who dug right

next to him, "or that one-eyed dog fucker is liable to come down and hit you with the shovel."

"Dog fuckers . . . educated fools . . . officers who don't march for common sense but do for a bit of playactin' . . . these ain't the men to be desertin' your friends for, Jake."

"Nope. No honor in servin' fools. No gold, neither."

The shovels crunched. The dirt thumped. And the smell of turned earth reminded Gil of an open grave.

"It was a bad idea to start," said Big Jake. "It's a worse idea now. Best thing would be to slip away, find the others, then find that gold. Pretend like we was never in this army."

"Well, I do have to admit it"—Gil swung the shovel again—"sure is a helluva way to get rich."

"Quiet down there!" shouted Stuckey.

And Gil Walker made his decision. He put down the shovel, picked up his musket, gave Big Jake a jerk of the head, and dropped into the shadows of the hillside on the far right of the American line. He did not worry that he was now a deserter, a fugitive who might be hunted by two armies instead of just one. He was on his own again, answering only to the few friends he trusted.

GIL AND BIG Jake knew the woodlands and meadows of Manhattan Island as well as Aaron Burr did. These were places where they had hunted as boys, places that were like old friends, even in the dark. And nature was a friend, too, bringing a steady drizzle that dampened the sound of their movement and settled into the folds of the landscape so that they could disappear when they saw a British patrol or a pair of British officers clopping along, passing a bottle between them, drunk with port and the arrogance of victory.

Rich men owned most of what they crossed that night. The land north of the city had been divided into farming estates not long after the Dutch had bought Manhattan from trusting natives for a pile of beads. The names of some of the estates, like Hoagland's and Vandewalker's, still spoke of olden times. Others, McGowan's and Apthorpe's, told of the British who had come later.

When Gil and Big Jake spied a line of torches, tents, and tethered horses—the forward units of the great army—they reckoned that they were still a mile from the Woodward estate. So they dropped again toward the river and meant to swim if they ran into pickets on the beach.

But the hallmark of the British was professional contempt for the amateur rebels they faced. So they had not bothered to extend their line to the water, as if they could not imagine a flanking attack launched through the mudflats and along the Hudson.

So Gil and Big Jake skittered along the bank until they saw, perhaps a quarter mile ahead, torches burning at Woodward's Landing. The house would be up above. But even from this distance, they could see redcoats on the dock.

"Do you think they have Rooster?" asked Big Jake.

"If he's alive."

Then something much closer caught their attention, a rustling in the water to the right. The bank here dropped down from the trees onto a little plain of brush and mudflat dotted with deeper pools. And standing in one of the pools was a woman.

They had not noticed her at first because they had been moving with their eyes on those British torches. Now they were mesmerized.

She was washing herself. Her naked body seemed almost silver in the gray-black darkness of a cloudy night. She rubbed the bar of soap on her neck, then passed it over her breasts. Then she raised an arm to wash the tuft of hair beneath, a motion that caused her breasts to rise and Big Jake to gasp.

Gil whispered, "Close your mouth."

"But I know her. She was one of the Bookworm's girls. She—" Big Jake's words caught in his throat as she dipped, rinsed, then stepped out of the water altogether.

When she bent to pick up her towel, Gil and Big Jake dropped down from the tree line. Startled, she pulled the towel against herself.

"Don't be afraid, miss," said Gil.

"Damn you." She sounded more annoyed than afraid. "Can't you leave me be for a minute? You all been gawkin' at me ever since you got here . . . wait a minute . . . you ain't redcoats." And she took a step back, as if she suddenly *was* afraid.

Big Jake said, "We're Augie's friends."

"Augie? The Bookworm?" She looked from face to face. "Gil and—"

"That's right, Gil and Big Jake." Big Jake gave her a grin.

She ordered them to turn around, dropped her towel, and pulled on her shift.

Gil looked off toward the torchlight and said, "We come to get them, but—"

"Augie's gone, and Rooster"—she pulled on her shirt, then she picked up her skirt and shook the twigs off it—"Rooster's gone, too."

Gil turned. "Dead?"

She stepped into the skirt. "When we heard the redcoats comin', I told Augie to run. I stayed with Rooster till he passed. I come down here to wash the blood off. Couldn't do it up there, not now, not tonight. There's officers in the house and dragoons in the barn. And every one of them looks at me like they want to"—she glanced at Big Jake—"they look at me like you're lookin' at me now."

"I told you to close your mouth," said Gil to his friend.

The girl picked up a bloody shirt and skirt from the bushes.

"Rooster's blood?" asked Gil.

"Aye. They drug him out and left him for the meat wagon. They say there'll be plenty more bodies by tomorrow."

She boosted herself up from the bank, up into the trees above.

"You're going back?" asked Gil.

"I serve breakfast at dawn. The British are braggin' on how they'll bag a fine fox in the mornin'. And Squire Woodward, he's a lot more of a loyalist than he ever let on."

"I'm thinkin' most folks'll be loyalists by tomorrow night," said Gil.

"Miss—" Big Jake boosted himself up and stood next to her.

"My name's Nancy. Nancy Hooley."

Big Jake touched her hand. "I'd like to thank you for helping our friend."

She took the hand. "Augie told me about you boys, said you was like family."

"Where did he go?" asked Gil.

"Back to the city. Back to tell Rooster's mother."

Big Jake said, "We're goin' back to get—"

"Get back to normal," said Gil. He feared that Jake was so mesmerized by her beauty, he might tell her right there that they were going back to get a stash of gold in a Tory house.

She wished them luck and said, "I'll tell you what I told the Bookworm. In the city, act innocent. I hear the British sayin' they'll round up the arrogant Yanks and the ones who go about armed and the ones who pull long faces. But they can't arrest everyone. So don't attract attention, and you'll be all right."

THREE

Tuesday Morning

At eight thirty, Peter Fallon crossed the Henry Hudson Bridge at the northern tip of Manhattan.

The traffic had gone all-aggression-all-the-time at just about the spot that he started picking up 1010

WINS news radio. That would have been an hour back on the Merritt, when the Manhattan-bound businessmen started tailgating him at seventy-five, tripping the switch that turned him from the relaxed I-84 cruiser into Mr. Cut-the-other-guy-off-and-beat-him-to-the-tollbooth-too.

He could have taken Amtrak. The first Acela left South Station at 6:15, scheduled arrival at 9:40 in New York. And when it worked, it was the only way to go. But he'd missed too many early meetings because of signal problems, power failures, work crews, and trucks broken down on Connecticut grade crossings, so he wasn't trusting the train on a day when his nerves woke him up after two hours of sleep.

Instead, he was sliding toward the E-ZPass lane on the highlands where Washington and his Continental Army had dug their trenches in 1776.

Continental Army? Stop thinking about them and watch out for that bastard cabbie trying to sneak into your lane before you get to the toll.

He outmaneuvered the cabbie, then he felt bad about it.

Just another guy working for a living, who maybe had a fare who needed to get somewhere in a hurry . . . like a hospital. So Peter reset his driving switch and tuned the radio to the morning market report.

He hadn't come to New York for fun or history. He wouldn't have come at all but for that phone conversation. He wasn't letting Evangeline go downtown alone to meet some guy named Joey, who was wearing a Yankees hat. Sure, she'd been around the world on her own, but Peter didn't like the sound of the guy's voice. He didn't like the part about the Yankees hat, either.

From the tollbooth, the Henry Hudson dropped quickly down to the river for one of the finest approaches to any city in the world.

The first explorers thought the Hudson was the fabled Northwest Passage. In the Revolution, the Americans and British fought over it, because control of the river meant control of the continent. In the nineteenth century, a visionary named Dewitt Clinton cut a canal from Lake Erie to the Hudson, so the riches of the heartland could ship straight to the wharves of Manhattan, guaranteeing that New York—not Boston or Philadelphia—would become America's first city. And in the twentieth century, master builder Robert Moses had imagined a beautiful road and a beautiful park on the Hudson mudflats, and . . .

Enough with the history. Turn up the radio.

"Dow futures are lower on the heels of China's announcement that they will be sitting out Thursday's auction of U.S. Treasuries. Secretary Robert Lappen says there is no correlation between this announcement and the growing crisis over Taiwan, but . . ."

Peter turned at Seventy-ninth and headed straight for a parking garage. He had long ago learned that when driving into the city, the best thing to do was to get rid of the car as quickly as possible. And the farther from Midtown you parked, the cheaper.

* * *

EVANGELINE CARRINGTON SPENT half of her time in New England, but she considered herself a New Yorker. And why not, with a two-bedroom co-op on the corner of Columbus and Seventy-ninth, a prewar building, twelve stories, big rooms, and that favorite real estate phrase, good bones? She also had a view over the Museum of Natural History and across Central Park.

That was like having good bones and a pretty face, too.

Peter stopped at the desk in the foyer: a marble podium with brass trim, glass apron, and Art Deco flourishes.

"No need to sign, Mr. Fallon," said Jackie Ryan, the desk man. "With you two gettin' married and all . . . it'll be like you live here, even if you *are* from Boston."

"Thanks." Peter put his pen back into his pocket. "Is Miz Carrington in?"

"You mean the future *Mrs.* Fallon?"

"Jackie"—Peter looked over the tops of his sun-glasses—"you've been around her long enough to know that even if we were married by the Cardinal in St. Patrick's on Easter Sunday, she'd always be *Miz* Carrington."

Jackie chuckled. "Yeah, you got that right. And no, I haven't seen her go out."

Peter pressed the elevator button. "How's the left hook?"

"Haven't used it since I decked Marvin Hagler."

In his younger days, Jackie had been a club fighter and a club bouncer. When he couldn't take the punches anymore, he took a job at the night desk in an East Village flophouse, then he worked his way uptown. But his uniform jacket still looked like a display case for his thick fists and broken nose.

"You fought Hagler?" said Peter. "I'm impressed."

Jackie let out a loud "Pah" at a joke on the guy from Boston. "If I did, I wouldn't be sittin' here. I'd be rich or dead."

"Dead, most likely." Peter got onto the elevator. As the doors closed, he said, "Go Red Sox!" and heard another "Pah."

On the eighth floor he gave a little tap, the chain lock rattled, the door opened, and Evangeline peered out. "So you decided I'm not crazy after all?"

"Not crazy," he said. "Just misguided."

"Misguided to be marrying you."

Her eyes were puffy. Her hair was tousled. She was wearing a blue terry cloth bathrobe and silk pajamas. She looked just fine to Peter.

He followed her into the large living and dining area.

The morning sunlight poured through the front windows. The traffic hummed eight stories below. The coffeemaker burbled in the little kitchen.

"Are you all right?" he asked.

"Aside from being scared to death last night, I'm fine."

"But if you're scared, it means you might be onto something."

"So that's why you came down? Because I'm onto something? I thought you came down because you wanted to protect me."

"I came down because if you want us to live in New York, I should see if I can stand the commute."

"That's an argument for another day."

"Oh . . . and you *asked* me to come down."

"Coffee's almost done. Toast some English muffins while I shower." She reached into her bathrobe pocket and pulled out the crown finial. "And have a look at this. See if you can figure out what it is."

EVANGELINE SAID THAT the best way to get around Manhattan was on foot or the subway. So they rode downtown to Rector Street, and walked the rest of the way because it was a nice day.

A charging bronze bull greeted them at the Bowling Green. The bull had been sculpted by an Italian named Di Modica, who deposited him one night in 1989, right in front of the New York Stock Exchange. Di Modica said the bull was a gift to the American people, to celebrate their resilience after the crash of 1987. Not quite as majestic as Lady Liberty, thought Peter, but that statue from France had helped to define the city and the nation in 1888, and this one from Italy said plenty about America a century later.

Peter gave it a rub as he went by. He wasn't the first. The head and horns shone, as if a thousand hands polished them every day. The balls shone, too.

But Evangeline barely gave the bull a glance. "Time for someone to sculpt a big bear and put it right here, just to keep that stupid bull from breaking any more china."

"Is the bear a female?" he asked.

"You mean, do we need a female to keep the male from doing something else stupid or greedy to this country?"

"A different way of putting it, but . . . yeah."

"Another question for another day."

Right behind the bull was the Bowling Green, which looked far more innocent in the sunlight, a perfect little oval of grass, trees, and park benches surrounded by that fence. In the sunlight, it felt like one of the centers that held, rather than a lonely outpost of greenery in a big city.

Peter said, "This is the kind of place I love. A pinhole in the fabric of time—"

"Oh, God, not another pinhole, Peter. I just want my cell phone back."

He pretended to ignore her and kept talking. "—where you can feel the past, even see it. Once there was a statue of the king—"

"Do you see him?" said Evangeline.

"The king? No. They melted him down—"

"The *guy.* Do you see the guy? The guy who called himself Joey? The guy with my cell phone."

Peter looked around at the suits and secretaries and coffee drinkers. "I see a few guys in Yankees hats. But no one seems to be looking for a Bostonian in a blue blazer."

"Maybe you should have worn a Red Sox hat."

"I'm not *that* crazy."

"Just misguided . . . have you figured out that little brass crown?"

He took it from his pocket.

"While we wait for Joey . . ." She slipped it from his hand and led him over to one of the posts that supported the long, curving runs of fencing that surrounded the park. Then she told him to put his hand on top of the post. "What do you feel?"

"Aside from foolish?"

"On top of the post . . . what do you feel?"

"A little nob. It feels rough, as though something was hacked off . . ."

She gave him the finial and told him to feel the bottom.

He ran his thumb across it. "That's rough, too."

She looked around. "That little crown was torn off the top of one of these posts in 1776. So if this park is a pinhole, the posts are the pins. The bag lady said that the whole story begins with that finial."

"What story?"

"We . . . ah . . . never got to that."

Peter raised the finial, as if to see if it would fit on top of that post.

"I wouldn't do that if I were you." A man in a Yankees cap and blue windbreaker was standing on the path a few feet away.

Peter shoved the finial back into his pocket.

"Not that," said the man. "The grass. I wouldn't stand on the grass. The sign says keep off the grass."

Peter looked at Evangeline. "New Yorkers obeying signs . . . we must be in a parallel universe."

"And you must be the Boston guy. A smart-ass on the phone, a smart-ass in person. But I like smart-asses. I'm Joey." He was stocky but solid and a bit swarthy, and there was a kind of polish about him, a bit of street-styled professionalism, an air that you sometimes smelled around a beat cop who'd finally made detective or a wiseguy who'd finally made his bones. He offered his hand.

"Do you have my cell phone?" asked Evangeline.

"What? No small talk?" asked Joey. "You sure seemed interested in yappin' with that bag lady."

Evangeline said to Peter, "This must be one of the guys who was here last night."

"I wasn't here," said Joey. "Not when you were here, anyway. But humor me. How 'bout them Yanks?" He glanced at Peter. "That's my small talk, especially with a guy from Boston."

Peter offered his hand. "*Them* Yanks. They prove that even in baseball, money talks, Mr.—I didn't get your last name."

"Call me Joey B. Or Joey Berra."

"What are you?" asked Evangeline. "Yogi's son or something?"

Peter whispered to Evangeline, "That's not his real name."

"I *get* it, Peter."

Joey Berra made a gesture—follow me—and led them toward the coffee wagon at the southern edge of the park. He chattered the whole way about baseball and New York and the drive down from Boston in the early morning.

Peter kept up his end of the conversation. But Evangeline didn't say anything. She just watched and listened. She knew this Joey Berra wasn't some guy who had happened onto the Bowling Green the night before. He had been in on it, whatever *it* was.

Joey bought three coffees, passed them out, and jabbed his chin toward a bench.

Evangeline glanced at her watch. "I have an article to write."

Peter gave her a jerk of his head—come on. Let's see where all this leads.

So they all sat on the bench, with Peter in the middle.

Joey took a swallow of coffee. "Did you know, the fence around us right now is one of the oldest things in New York City?"

"Not enough respect for the past in this town," said Peter.

"Nah, too much goin' on in the present. Not like that little burg up north."

"Where half of New York sends its kids to be educated." Peter noticed a bulge beneath the windbreaker: Joey was carrying.

Evangeline noticed something else. Out at the north end of the park, out by the bull, a guy was taking pictures. He was wearing a windbreaker, too, but no hat. He might have been taking pictures of the bull—tourists did all the time—but Joey had picked a bench that had a clear view of the bull's backside, which meant that the guy with the camera had a clear view of them.

She nudged Peter and gestured toward the camera guy. By then, Peter had noticed two other guys, one black, one white, one on Broadway, one on Whitehall, one drinking coffee, one reading the *Daily News*. If this was a setup, Peter had walked right into it.

Some pinhole.

Evangeline leaned around Peter and said to Joey,

"Any chance I can get my cell phone back before lunch?"

Joey took another sip of coffee. "I told you that it would cost you."

Peter said, "You told *me.*"

"Oh, right. The boyfriend."

"Fiancé," said Evangeline.

Joey said to Peter, "There's still time. You have a very pretty lady"—he leaned around Peter and gave Evangeline a wink—"but she likes hangin' with smelly old broads in New York parks at night. Somethin' a little weird about that."

"I don't need this." Evangeline jumped up and pulled out a hundred dollar bill. "Here."

Joey looked at the bill and sipped his coffee. "You know, miss, your . . . fiancé . . . is kind of a sucker, offerin' a C-note for a celly you could buy for a song on Sixth Avenue. He does that, I think maybe I can get a little more, or maybe there's numbers on that phone that are—what?—sensitive."

Evangeline said to Peter, "Give me your phone."

He handed it to her.

She made a call. "I'd like to report a lost cell phone."

"Easy there, miss," said Joey.

She clicked off, but she did not give Peter back his phone.

"I'll tell you what," said Joey. "Instead of the C-note, I'll take that little brass crown you were flashin' around a minute ago."

"It's not ours," said Evangeline. "It belongs to that bag lady."

"Well, that's where you're wrong," said Joey Berra. "It belongs to the New-York Historical Society. It was stolen along with a box of other stuff about three months ago. They're offering a reward because, as far as anyone knows, it's the only brass crown that survived the riot in 1776."

"How big is the reward?" asked Peter.

"Ten grand. You're walking around right now with ten grand in your pocket."

"And you were willing to take it from us?" said Evangeline.

"You can't hate a guy for tryin'."

"And you brought backup, in case I resist?" asked Peter.

"What backup? That mongalooch with the camera? The soul brother with the coffee cup? The one lookin' at the pictures in the *Daily News*? They don't work for me."

"Who do they work for?" asked Peter.

"Don't you mean, 'For whom do they work?' You went to Harvard and I went to CCNY, but even I know that."

After a few minutes with him, Peter wasn't surprised at anything this Joey Berra knew. He didn't even bother to ask *how* Joey knew about Harvard. So Evangeline did.

Joey said, "If I'm tryin' to squeeze someone, I check out his Web site. Fallon Antiquaria. Very fancy. Rare books and all. Means you know what you're doin' when it comes to findin' stuff, right?"

"Hard work and dumb luck," said Peter.

"A good combination." Joey reached into his pocket and pulled out the cell phone. "Here you go, miss. But I'd be careful about receiving stolen property. I'm no cop, but having that crown in your possession could get you in trouble."

"Are these guys after it?"

"They could be." Joey scanned the park. "But I think they're after me."

"After *you*?" said Peter.

"Yeah. I had you meet me here to pull them into the open and get a look at them."

"Thanks a lot," said Peter. "And who do you work for?"

"I wouldn't worry about that," said Joey Berra.

"I would," said Evangeline. "I'm a worrier."

"Just say I work for the American people. But if these guys work for the people I think they do . . . it's them I'd be worried about. Now"—Joey's good nature disappeared—"I'm walkin' right out past the bull. Don't follow. Don't watch. I know what I'm doin'. You two head the other way, down into the subway. If one of these guys follows you, you'll have to lose him down there."

"What's going on here?" said Peter.

"I'm tryin' to figure that out myself." Joey pulled a business card from his pocket and handed it to Peter. "If you figure it out first, give me a call."

"Why should we do that?" asked Evangeline.

"Because I'm about to draw these guys away from you." Joey stood. "I might be savin' your life right now. I might save it later." Then he headed for the bull. "Get goin'."

"Who was the guy last night?" Evangeline called after him. "The guy with the briefcase?"

Joey Berra didn't answer. He just said, "Go out through the south gate."

Peter took Evangeline by the elbow, and together they stood.

"See," she said, "I told you this was something. I wasn't making all this up."

"I never said you were. Don't take out your MetroCard till we're on the escalator. And don't run unless I tell you to."

"Why not?"

"Predators react to movement. If one of these guys is after us, he'll run if we do."

"You've been watching too much Animal Planet."

"Just walk." He led her down into the subway while she fumbled to pull out her yellow MetroCard.

As they crossed the upper platform, they heard the rumble of a train arriving below. People all around them picked up their pace, scurried for the fare machines, hurried for the turnstiles, dodged the panhandlers, avoided each other.

"Okay," Peter said, "move faster. Once you swipe the card, run."

"What about the predator business?"

"We're in the herd now, honey. Gazelles bounding all over the place. The sound of the train makes them all nervous. The jackal won't know which way to look."

They swiped the card twice and began to run. Down the stairs, down to the platform, and onto a crowded uptown number 4, just arrived from Brooklyn.

Stand clear of the closing doors, please.

And Mr. *Daily News* got on at the other end of the car, forcing himself into the crowd of straphangers and newspaper readers.

"Damn," said Peter.

"From gazelles to sardines," said Evangeline. "So, how far are we going?"

"As far as it takes."

Next stop, Wall Street.

"Peter, this train goes all the way to the Bronx. I am *not* going to the Bronx."

"We could go to the zoo. Keep with the theme."

"Screw the zoo." She looked down the car, past all the other commuters. *Daily News* was tall, skinny, pockmarked, and he kept his head buried behind the newspaper.

"Notice anything about him?" she asked.

"Like Joey said, he's only looking at the pictures."

"The tattoo on his neck. Did any of the other guys at the Bowling Green have tattoos? Maybe they're part of—"

"Baby, sometimes a tattoo is just a tattoo."

"You've never heard of secret societies?"

"Only in novels and the movies made from them."

In and out of Wall Street Station they went. A few people got off: men in suits, women in suits with running shoes. Then a few people got on. Mr. *Daily News* moved a bit but stayed in position.

Stand clear of the closing doors, please.

The train lurched. Legs buckled and locked. Hands grabbed for railings. But heads stayed down, focused on papers and books. These commuters were professionals.

Next stop, City Hall.

Evangeline was still peering toward the other end of the car. Finally she whispered, "So you're not interested in the tattoo?"

"I'm interested in how we lose this guy. We can wait for him to get bored somewhere between here and the Bronx, or we can run."

"I'm not dressed for running," she said, "so let's use our wits instead."

The train slowed again, and as soon as the doors opened, Evangeline stepped off.

Peter had no choice but to step right off with her.

And *Daily News* folded his paper under his arm and stepped off, too.

Twenty or thirty other people piled off behind them. *Stand clear of the closing doors, please.* The doors *thunked* shut and the train began to roll again.

But Evangeline grabbed Peter's elbow and gave him the eye. Then she stopped. And he stopped. And the commuters poured up the stairs as quickly as the train was sucked back into the tunnel. Evangeline pivoted Peter against a concrete pillar and gave him one of those kisses that wouldn't quit. But she didn't close her eyes. Neither did Peter. Finally she pulled back.

"Is he still there?" asked Peter.

"Still there, still looking at the pictures."

"So, we can stand here and make out, or we can run. We'll hop a cab as soon as we get upstairs. Or we can fight him, which is never my choice."

"Let's stay with the plan and use our wits."

"I didn't know we had a plan," he said.

"I didn't know you had any wits," she answered.

She pulled a New York subway map from her pocketbook and handed it to him. "Pretend you're studying it. Pretend you're confused by how big the Big Apple is."

"But—"

"Just act like a Bostonian."

"Okay." He looked at the map, furrowed his brow, turned the map upside down, scratched his head.

"Another Brando," she said. Then she walked right up to Mr. *Daily News*.

The guy's eyes widened. He raised the newspaper and buried his face in it.

Evangeline put on her best tourist smile. And she had a good one, considering that she had spent the last five or six years writing travel articles. "Excuse me, sir. Will this train take me to Forty-second Street?"

"Yeah. Get off at Grand Central."

"Thank you." She turned and went back to Peter. "Honey, the gentlemen says this is the right line after all."

"Oh, good, honey." Then he gave a wave. "Thanks."

And now they heard the rumble of the train, felt the push of air, then the sudden roaring rise of sound and the screaming of brakes.

They headed for the rear doors of the third car, and as they expected, *Daily News* headed for the front doors.

Peter said, "The old step-on, step-off trick?"

"With a twist. I've confused him by talking to him."

"Not the first time you've done that."

"I've made him wonder if we're really riding to Forty-second. And all we need to make this work is a bit of hesitation. So"—she took him by the elbow—"step on."

Stand clear of the closing doors, please.

"Now," she said.

She jumped off. He squeezed through right after. If he'd had a tail, the door would have closed on it.

But someone blocked Mr. *Daily News,* and he couldn't get off. In an instant, the train was gone.

"See," she said. "I've learned a few things hanging around you."

"Did you get a look at the tattoo?"

"Yeah." She pushed through the turnstile and started up the stairs.

"What did it say?"

"It was a heart with an arrow through it and the words, 'Boris loves Mary.' So at least we know that his name is Boris."

"Or Mary," said Peter.

"Did you look at Joey Berra's business card?"

He pulled it from his pocket and held it out so that they could both read the simplest business card a man could carry: the name, Joseph P. Berranova, and a telephone number.

"That clears up a lot," she said.

THEY CAME OUT on City Hall Park.

This had been the Common in the eighteenth century, the drilling ground for Washington's troops and the place where they heard the Declaration of Independence. In the nineteenth century, the streets around it, Broadway on the west and Park Row on the east, had been the site of newspaper offices and entertainment, including the famous museum of P. T. Barnum, who proclaimed the philosophy that some of the newspapers practiced, too, the one about a sucker born every minute.

All of that was gone now, replaced by office buildings, businesses, booming traffic. But a fountain sent a jet of water sparkling into the May morning sun. Tourists took pictures and read the timeline of Manhattan history on the plaza around the fountain. Trees and shrubs gave some cover to the barriers and other security measures that protected City Hall from whatever the terrorists might try next in New York.

Peter pulled out his cell phone and started to walk.

"Now what?" said Evangeline.

"I'm calling James Fitzpatrick."

"At the Massachusetts Historical Society?"

"I don't have many friends at the New York society. But I think we need to get the story on this ten thousand dollar finial. James will know, or he'll find out for us."

"Ask him about old Revolutionary War bonds, too."

"Let's go step by step," he said. "Finial first."

"So where are we stepping now?"

"Over there." He pointed to the little church.

Though it was at the southwest edge of the park, near the spot where Broadway and Park Row met, it was true north to Peter Fallon. It sat surrounded by concrete and limestone and glass, just like everything else in New York, but it was unlike anything else in America.

It was St. Paul's Chapel, and it symbolized the resilience of the city, of its people, of the nation itself. That's what Peter told Evangeline as they crossed Broadway and stopped at the corner of Vesey Street.

"This," said Peter, "is one of the only eighteenth-century structures left in Manhattan." Peter pointed down the street that bordered on the northern edge of the chapel property. "Vesey Street and Church Street were lined with whorehouses once."

"Whorehouses? Around the church?"

"The bishop owned the land and made money from the rents. And the whores even worked in the graveyard behind the chapel. They called it the Holy Ground. If you were going to the Holy Ground, you might be going to get yourself right with Jesus or—"

"Get your ashes hauled?"

"Think of the souls spinning around this neighborhood. Some spiritual and—"

"Some carnal?"

"Maybe that's why it's survived. It says so much about us. God favored it when the Great Fire burned up the West Side in 1776, and he sure favored it again on 9/11."

"She," said Evangeline.

"What?"

"*She* sure favored it."

He laughed and looked up at the little church, separated from the world by a fence, surrounded by oak and sycamore trees that cast cool shadows onto the street and the graveyard. But there was a powerful light at the rear of the property, a light that the trees could not shield, an unnatural light that seemed to emanate from the earth itself, from the massive, thirteen-acre hole that stretched from Church Street all the way to West Street.

That was where the World Trade Center had been.

When the towers collapsed, said Peter, they sent down a horrifying cascade of debris that destroyed buildings all around them. Then had come the cloud that surged along the streets and spread out onto the rivers and across the harbor. Nothing, Peter had thought as he watched that day on television, had ever looked more like the end of the world. Nothing could have survived beneath that.

But when the cloud had settled onto Lower Manhattan, when it had buried the little cemetery and City Hall Park and every surface for blocks in a blizzard of concrete, steel, glass, paper, aluminum, gypsum, plastic, electronics, avionics, human remains, hopes, and happiness, all of it pulverized to dust, the little chapel still stood.

She tugged his elbow. "Let's go in. Say a prayer. Thank God for outwitting Mr. *Daily News*."

"And thank God for this building. Then we'll go up to Book Row and talk to Delancey."

As they walked into the old church, Peter's iPhone buzzed. He pulled it out: a text message:

> Mr. Fallon: Friends speak well of you. Can I interest you in saving America? Avid Austin Arsenault.

FOUR

September 1776

By dawn, Gil and Jake had hidden their muskets and shot pouches under a rock on Greenwich Road. Then they had come down Broadway and stopped at the corner of Vesey Street, right in front of St. Paul's Chapel.

They wanted to visit the Shiny Black Cat, but the street was overflowing with British sailors queued up in front of the Cat and Quaker Fan's and all the other whorehouses that ran down to the Hudson.

While the rebels had been retreating the previous day, the military governor had landed with a detachment of Royal Marines. Tories who had been housebound for months—or confined aboard British ships—had come out to cheer them, and now, even the whorehouses were flying the Union Jack.

"Nothin' makes a man so randy as conquerin' a city," said Big Jake into Gil's ear, "but we need to talk to Loretta. If there's gold to be got, we're gettin' it. Won't be much good livin' in this city otherwise."

"Might not be much good anyway, but easier with gold."

The sight of two Yanks peering down Vesey Street attracted a redcoat corporal who was standing in front of the chapel. "Oy, you there. What are you after?"

Gil touched the brim of his hat. "We was hopin' to get a bit of the old in and out, but you lot have been away from the ladies a lot longer than us, so we'll just be on our way."

"You look a touch suspicious to me." The corporal came off the sidewalk and unshouldered his musket. He was tall and rangy, red-faced and pock-marked. He and the others leaning against the chapel fence wore the leatherneck collars of the Royal Marines. "You ain't spies, are you?"

"Spies?" Big Jake laughed. "Us?"

The redcoat leveled his musket at his hip. "Spies."

"They're not spies." Reverend Inglis, the rector of Trinity and St. Paul's, stepped out of the chapel.

Gil had not seen him in some time. He had left the city shortly after the Declaration of Independence. But here he was back, a tall, slender, spectral presence, all in black but for the white wig and priest's collar.

"They're handymen about the town," the rector went on, "and they've done a goodly share of grave digging for this parish. So rest easy, Corporal Morison."

That much was true.

Gil and Big Jake both doffed their hats and thanked "his Reverence."

"They're good Loyalists, then?" said the corporal.

"They're loyal members of our church." Inglis arched his eye at Gil. He could arch his eye as well as anyone in New York.

Corporal Morison put up his musket and gave

them a jerk of the head. "Be on your way, then, but I'll be watchin' your faces."

"You won't see nothin' on 'em but smiles," said Big Jake.

The two Waterfront Boys pulled their hats low and put their eyes on the ground. There were plenty in town who knew that they had been part of Stuckey's company, and plenty waiting to trouble any rebel who had troubled them. The wheel of vengeance and victory was turning. When Gil and Jake saw two men painting the letters *GR* on a house, they simply walked on. *GR* stood for *George Rex*, which meant that the house, which had belonged to some departed Son of Liberty, now belonged to the king.

IT WAS NEAR seven thirty when they sneaked down an alley from Broad Street into a little backyard. Chickens were pecking about. The door to the privy was closed. The door to the kitchen was open.

Gil peered in. A pot of cornmeal mush was bubbling on the grate, and it set Gil's empty stomach to growling. He swallowed and whispered, "Hello?"

In answer, the privy door slammed open and a man holding a brace of pistols stepped out. "Hands up."

"We're friends." Gil shot his hands into the air.

"Friends of Rooster Ramsey," said Big Jake.

"We've come to see his mother," said Gil.

Haym Salomon lowered the guns, and the boys lowered their hands.

Gil had only seen the Jew once or twice before. His face was symmetrical, his cheekbones high, his nose a bit stronger than most. Only the accent, which sounded German, marked him as an outsider.

"The one called the Bookworm, he brought bad news last night." Salomon looked from face to face. "But Rooster's mother, she did not cry. She said she always expected him to die hard. She never expected he would die fighting for his country."

"Fighting for his country?" Gil glanced at Big Jake.

"We may all die fighting for our country." Salomon set the pistols down. "The British are arresting some of us and watching the rest."

"Why don't you leave?" asked Gil.

"I should. I'm a Son of Liberty, but"—Salomon shrugged—"I have a business here . . . and a girl."

Gil nodded. *Business and women.* Those were things a man could understand more easily than windy ideas like liberty. "Where did Augustus go?"

"Back."

"Back?" said Gil and Big Jake together.

"Back to find his friends on Harlem Heights. He meant you . . . yes?"

Gil said, "We come lookin' for *him*."

"And we ain't goin' back," said Big Jake.

"But it may be dangerous for two deserters," said Salomon. "I will hide you if you want."

"We won't be hidin'," said Big Jake. "This is our town."

"We work for Sam Fraunces," said Gil, "so we have reason to be out and about."

"And if the British stop us," added Big Jake, "we'll say that we're doin' his biddin', deliverin' wine to the whorehouses."

"Right," said Gil, "so British officers'll have somethin' to tickle their palates while the girls tickle their pricks."

"Pricks?" Salomon nodded. "Pricks are something they can understand."

Big Jake gave him an elbow. "Something every man can understand, eh?"

Salomon offered a thin smile and said that Rooster's mother had taken to her room with a bottle of whiskey. They could have a bowl of mush and wait for her to come out, or they could come back later.

Gil doubted that there was much they could say to her. And if the Jew was being watched, best not to be seen with him. They could eat later.

Salomon said it spoke well of them that they would endanger themselves to comfort an old woman. He wished them luck as they hurried off. Then he kicked the chickens out of the way and went back into the privy.

After a short walk, Gil and Big Jake ducked into another alley and peered across Broad Street at the Queen's Head, Sam Fraunces's tavern, where half a dozen Royal Marines were taking their ease in the early morning sunshine.

Fraunces ran the best tavern in New York—the best food, the best wines, all served in a four-story brick building that contained the most comfortable attic that contained the most comfortable bed that Gil ever slept in—and after digging and fighting and retreating and digging and deserting and returning, after covering twenty-four miles up the island and back in twenty-four hours, his eyes were starting to spin . . . and his legs . . . were . . . feeling . . . just . . . a . . . bit . . . wobbly. . . .

"Let's move," Big Jake whispered. "We're stickin' out here like stiff dicks."

"If anybody can help us, it's Fraunces."

"But the redcoats must know he was one of the Sons of Liberty, too, and he let the rebels hold meetings, and—"

British bayonets poked against their backs. British questions came quickly and less warmly than the bayonets: "Who are you?" "Where do you live?" "What are you doing?"

The answers were in part truth and in part the kind of invention that two smart street men could conjure even when their wits were clotting for lack of sleep. "We work for Sam Fraunces. We live in his attic. And we were bringing wine"—then came the part about palates and pricks and the pleasure of British officers—"and British soldiers, too."

The redcoats liked that last part. So they took the boys into the tavern, to see Major General Robertson, the new military authority.

At the sight of these two dirty Americans, Robertson pulled a handkerchief from his sleeve and held it to his nose. He didn't look like a fighting man, thought Gil, and his handkerchief smelled of rose water. But he was probably another British career soldier, the kind who could run a city or lead a regiment.

Robertson sent for one of Fraunces's slaves, to vouch for their story, because Fraunces had fled.

But the British weren't going to hang Fraunces, said Robertson, since he was the best innkeeper in America. They were going to bring him back and put him to work, and his family would be safe, so long as he continued to "serve the gustatory needs of His Majesty's officers as attentively as he has always served New York's."

A slave named Joshua vouched for everything that Gil and Big Jake had said. He told Robertson that they were the trusted musclemen of the tavern, and if the British wanted to keep up good service until they brought Fraunces back, these men should be part of it.

So Gil and Big Jake slept again in those attic beds, and by the next morning, they were hauling ale barrels off British ships, splitting stove wood, slaughtering chickens, and listening to the chatter of His Majesty's officers, most of whom were amused by the rebels' amateur leadership and by the redoubts they had raised around the city, piles of dirt that had proven worse than useless for defense. Washington might hold the high ground, they said, but soon enough they would get behind him, and soon after that, they would get him on the gallows.

Gil Walker agreed.

He told Big Jake that they had made the right decision, no matter where Augustus the Bookworm had gone. Now they had to keep their heads down, obey orders, and grab their chance to get the gold.

BUT TO DO that they needed Loretta. They needed to know exactly where to look and when. And they needed to act quickly before more British officers returned from Harlem and an old Tory like John Blunt threw open his doors to lodge them.

So Gil waited each morning along the route that Loretta took to the fish market. And finally, on Friday, four days after the British landed, he saw her.

She was walking down Broad Street with a basket under her arm. She wore a loose dress and shawl, and she moved with a kind of bowlegged stiffness, as though she had been kicked, or badly used in another way.

He stepped out of an alley behind her and said her name.

She stopped, turned, held the basket against her chest as if for protection. "Gil? Gil Walker? I thought you was on the line."

"I've come back."

"You deserted?"

He brought a finger to his lips. "If anyone asks, we been here the whole time, just good loyal lads servin' in the absence of Master Fraunces."

She brought a hand to his chest. "I'm glad you're back."

He grabbed her by the arm and pulled her into the alley. "I've missed you."

Usually when he said something like that, she laughed in his face. This time, she looked down, as if to hide a tear. "I can't be offerin' any free gifts. Fanny give me the mornin' off. Workin' double shifts for a week ain't too good for the"—she glanced at her midsection—"for the scuttle, if you know what I mean."

"How would you like to tell Fanny to go diddle herself?"

"Diddle herself? But she bought my indenture from my uncle. Five years."

"We'll buy you back. We'll buy your corset, too, and throw it away."

"Buy me back? With what?"

"John Blunt's gold."

That made her laugh. "We missed our chance. There's British soldiers all about now, watchin' over the loyal Tories and watchin' all the good loyal lads like you, too."

"Just tell us where the gold is. We'll watch the Tory's house tonight, make a plan, and move tomorrow."

The bits of mascara around her eyes tightened into a suspicious web. "And then?"

"We'll get out of here. There's boats slippin' away every night. We'll get over to Jersey, buy horses, and be gone."

"How do I know I can trust you?"

He kissed her, but she did not respond. She barely inclined her head.

So he pulled back and said, "Because what you once told me is true."

"What was that?"

"You and me are different. We were born low, but we have dreams. We're two peas in a pod." He kissed her again and this time, she opened her mouth against his and leaned into him, as if to tell him that he had said the right thing.

Then she slipped her arm into his and said, "Walk

with me." And as the sun rose, she told him everything she knew about John Blunt's house and his gold.

ii.

By nightfall, the wind was rising out of the southeast.

It was a warm wind riding the edge of some distant autumn storm, and it sent ragged clouds running like spirits across the New York sky. A younger Gil Walker would have wandered away from the waterfront and gone beyond the town to some slope like Bayard's Hill, all the better to feel the wind booming over the harbor and thundering up the Hudson and losing itself somewhere beyond the Jersey highlands. His mind would empty, and he would feel the force of nature, the breath of God himself, reminding him that he was part of something bigger.

But not tonight.

"Tonight," Gil told Big Jake, "this wind will mask the sounds."

"Sounds? What sounds? I thought we was just watchin' tonight."

Gil reached into his pocket and pulled out an iron cat's paw and a hammer. "We *do* it tonight. Less chance for Loretta to act nervous in front of old Fanny Doolin."

"Good." Big Jake took a bottle of rum out of his pocket and swigged. "Just as easy to cut her out as cut her in."

Gil stopped beneath a street lamp. The wind made

the flame in the lamp flicker and almost blew Gil's hat from his head. "I didn't say nothin' about cuttin' her out."

"You ain't thinkin' about cuttin' *me* out, are you?" asked Big Jake. "You and her, runnin' a cathouse in Jersey . . . there's a pretty picture."

"You're my oldest friend and you say somethin' like that?"

"You wouldn't tell us about the gold when there was four of us. Now we're just two, thanks to Loretta and her cunt friends lurin' us into the militia. And I'm gettin' my share. If the Bookworm lives, he gets his share, too."

"You been sippin' too much rum," said Gil.

Big Jake brought the rum bottle to his lips and took another long drink. Then he said, "Let's get the gold. We'll worry about the rest later."

And they hurried through the deserted streets, Broad Street to Beaver to New, which connected Beaver Street to Wall. The street lamps cast high flickering shadows. The Presbyterian Church stared down from Wall Street. And there, at the intersection of New Street and Fluten Barrack, was the house of John Blunt.

And *there* was John Blunt, a bloated old man in white stockings and disheveled wig, lurching down the street behind two big Airedales. The dogs were running about, stopping, snuffling, lifting their legs. And Blunt was singing between swallows from a silver flask. It sounded like "God Save the King."

Another Tory, thought Gil, whose world had been righted.

One of the dogs made a few circles around a spot in the street and squatted.

John Blunt said to the other one, "What about you, Prince? Have a dump for your old master. Don't want you whimperin' to go out in the middle of the night or shittin' on the rugs, now, do we?"

But Prince was ignoring Blunt. He was looking toward two shadows in a doorway.

"What do you see, boy?" Blunt peered in the same direction.

Gil grabbed Big Jake and pulled him back out of the light.

The dog glanced back at his master but held his ground.

Gil wrapped his hand around the cat's paw and waited.

But dogs were distractable creatures, especially good ratters when they saw rats, and as the other dog finished his business, he must have seen one, because he jumped up, kicked his legs at his leavings, and went racing back up the street.

Blunt called to Prince, "Come on, boy! Your brother just found quarry."

Prince looked again toward the shadows, then he turned and followed his master.

Gil waited a few moments, until he heard John Blunt cry, "A nest of 'em! Go get 'em, boys! A dirty nest of rebel rats!"

Above the wind came the sound of hunting dogs flushing prey. Somewhere in the next block a window opened, a man shouted, "Quiet out there!"

Then the contents of a chamber pot splashed into the street.

Gil whispered to Big Jake. "Let's go."

"But the wife?"

"Her light's just gone out." Gil pointed up at the second story. "Likely she's took to bed with a hair across her arse at a drinkin' husband who loves his dogs more than he loves her. Come on."

The door was no problem. As with almost every front door in New York, the rebels had stripped it of brass fixtures—knockers, handles, knobs—so the key assembly would not work. A bolt or chain would be the way to lock it.

So Gil used a Tory's wealth against him. Only the rich could afford sidelights—little panes of glass on either side of the front door—that allowed a person to look out and the sunlight to flood in. With the end of the cat's paw fitted neatly and a few gentle taps of the hammer, Gil broke away the glazing, lifted out the thick pane, reached inside, and threw the bolt.

As soon as he did, the wind caught the door and blew it out of his hand. He leapt to grab it before it banged against the stopper and woke the wife.

Then he and Big Jake stepped into the foyer. Gil closed the door and raised his hand—wait, listen. Nothing except the distant barking of the Airedales. Gil slid the bolt back into place. "Blunt and his dogs must come in by the back," he whispered.

An oil lamp flickered on a side table. Gil took it and led the way.

The dining room was to the left. The polished top of a mahogany table reflected the light of a street lamp. On either side of the fireplace were raised pine panels. Loretta had said that the gold was behind one of the panels on the left of the fireplace in the dining room.

Gil handed the lantern to Big Jake, then he tapped on each panel, but they all sounded hollow. He ran his fingers along the ridges, but he could feel no hinges or metal edges, nothing to indicate a compartment behind. He tried it all again with no more luck. Then he stepped back and looked at his friend.

"That trollop better not be lyin' to us," whispered Big Jake.

A powerful gust of wind caused one of the shutters to rattle. Gil and Big Jake both looked toward the window. They waited and watched, and Gil mentioned that everything seemed a little brighter for some reason, maybe a little redder.

"Just your eyes playin' tricks around this lamp," said Big Jake.

Gil turned back to the wall. A thick molding ran along the top, where the paneling reached the ceiling. Gil told Jake to hold the lamp higher. And there it was . . . a small lever hidden in the layered molding. Gil reached up and pulled and, miraculously, one of the lower panels swung open.

"Aha." Big Jake lowered the lamp and peered in and said, "Shit."

"What?"

"A strongbox, with a lock, mortared into the brick."

Gil took out a key ring containing awls of different sizes, perfect for lockpicking. He slid one into the lock on the strongbox . . .

And they heard someone running up the street, then a cry of "Fire! Fire!"

"Fire?" Big Jake's eyes widened.

"That's why the light looked different." Gil kept his eyes on the strongbox.

There was barking in the street now.

"Shit," said Big Jake again. "Blunt and his dogs."

And while Gil probed the lock, this came from the street:

"Fire? Where?" "Call off your dogs." "Baron! Prince! Come!" "It started in Fightin' Cocks." "But that's down on the waterfront." "Look in the sky, mister. Firebrands blowin' everywhere. And the rebels took all the church bells so there's no way to sound the alarm. Buildin's catchin' fire all over!" "My God! Samantha! Samantha! Fire! Fire!"

The dining-room ceiling thudded as feet hit the floor in the room above.

"Shit!" said Big Jake.

"Stop shittin' and hold the lamp." Gil slid a second probe into the lock.

Big Jake brought the lamp over Gil's shoulder. "Hurry up."

There were footfalls on the staircase now.

And Blunt was pounding on the door and shouting for his wife.

And his dogs were barking.

And someone else in the street was screaming, "Fire!"

And the lock popped.

The strongbox held two trays, each containing a hundred gold guineas, beautiful glittering coins stamped with the chinless profile of the king himself.

Gil pulled two canvas bags from his pockets, grabbed a tray, and dumped it into a bag.

"Hurry up," said Big Jake.

"We'll get out the back," said Gil. "But let's get what we come for."

In the hallway, Mrs. Blunt was screaming as she pulled back the bolt, "John! There's men in the house."

"Shit." Big Jake turned toward the foyer.

The door swung open and the dogs burst in.

Big Jake dropped the lamp, grabbed a mahogany dining chair, and slammed it down on a dog. At the same moment, the lamp was shattering, and the whale oil was rolling toward the long drapes gathered on the floor, and the flame in the lamp was following the oil . . .

Gil filled the second bag just as the second dog flew into the room.

This one got hold of Big Jake's leg.

There was an angry growl, followed by Jake's yowl, then the explosion of a pistol in close quarters. It seemed that old John Blunt went armed.

And the oil reached the drape, followed by the flame, and the fabric ignited.

Now Blunt was coming at them with a raised saber. "Get out of my house!"

Gil put a shoulder into the old man's chest and sent him flying across the room, right through one of the windows, and into the street.

"John!" screamed Mrs. Blunt. "My dear God! John! John!"

The dog still had Big Jake by the leg. But Big Jake had his knife out and was driving it into the dog's side.

And the drape erupted into red flames.

"My God!" screamed the old woman. "Fire! Help!" She rushed for the door.

But Gil and Big Jake leapt past her, got out the door first, and slammed it behind them. Then they turned toward Beaver Street.

But that way lay the fire, just a few blocks to the south.

People were stumbling from their houses to look up at the pulsing red beast inhaling buildings and exhaling sparks and smoke. Some stopped and stood and watched in awe. Others turned and rushed into their homes to grab what they could before they ran.

And Mrs. Blunt burst from her house: "Stop! Thieves! Firebrands! Stop!"

Gil hefted the bags on his shoulder and glanced back. The old lady's flowing white hair and wind-blown white nightgown made her look like an angry spirit that might fly after him in an instant.

And rushing up from Beaver were half a dozen British sailors, shouting "Fire! Fire! Turn out! Fire! We need men! Fire! Fire!"

The old lady was screaming and pointing at Gil and Big Jake. "They started it! They started the fire! They started the fire in my very house!"

"Rebels!" cried one sailor. "Firebrands!" cried another. "Let's get 'em!" And the sailors came after the Waterfront Boys.

"Come on," said Gil. "The other way."

But as Big Jake turned, Gil saw the blood on his friend's chest.

Blunt's pistol had found a target.

So Gil grabbed Big Jake by the arm and started to pull him along.

The old lady tried to get in their way, and as they passed, she screamed at them, "I curse that money. I curse you both. So drop it right now."

That Gil would not do, curse be damned.

But he could not get Big Jake to keep up, because now there was blood coming out of Jake's nostrils, and his legs were wobbling. Then he just stopped in the street, looked down at the blood on his shirt, and said, "A helluva way to get rich. Go on without me."

"No. You're comin' with me!"

But the sailors were almost on them, and the old lady was still screaming.

"Go!" said Big Jake. "But do somethin' good with that gold." Then he turned and threw himself into the sailors.

Three of them went down in a heap under him, while a fourth came at Gil, who swung a bag of gold and sent the sailor sprawling. But there were more coming and old Mrs. Blunt was screaming still, screaming that Gil and his friend had started the fire, had started all the fires.

So Gil turned and sprinted across Fluten Barrack toward Broad Street. His last sight of Big Jake was one that, in all the horrors ahead, would remain the most horrible.

They were dragging his friend toward the Blunt

house and throwing him through the shattered window, into the fire that he himself had started.

At least Gil did not hear the screams.

At Broad Street, Gil glanced over his shoulder. He was putting distance between himself and the vengeful furies chasing him. But instead of turning straight down Broad Street, he ran another half a block, ducked down a dark alley, then scuttled through dooryards and jumped fences and never made a false turn, because he had taken these paths a hundred times before.

He thought about dropping the gold into the privy behind some deserted house and coming back for it later, but instead he was heading toward his only home: the attic room in the Queen's Head . . .

He made his way through the shadows until he reached Duke Street, and as he turned again toward Broad Street, he was struck by a wave of heat so powerful that he thought his eyebrows might singe.

Two terrified horses were galloping toward him. A man in a nightshirt was chasing the horses. At the intersection, a man was on fire. People were slapping at him with hats and coats to put out the flames. The horses thundered past, while two old women scurried along with satchels under their arms. One shouted at Gil, "Run, sir. Run. The rebels are burning the city! There's incendiaries everywhere."

And so it seemed. Everything on the west side of Broad Street was burning. And the beast was roaring higher into the sky. And Gil knew that the Queen's Head fronted on Broad Street, so he feared that it, too, would be consumed if it hadn't been already.

So what to do with the gold? He had to protect it. He had paid far too much to get it. And Loretta . . . he had to protect her, too. The gold was her dream, too.

So he turned and ran with the wind, ran with the flaming blizzard of firebrands and sparks blowing northwest across the sky, ran through streets now lit by a hideous red-orange glow, turned and ran for Loretta.

He raced back to Wall Street, one of the few streets that cut a straight line from the East River to Broadway. A century earlier a wall had stood here to keep out the Indians. Now there were businesses, coffeehouses, the domed and pillared City Hall casting a proud gaze down Broad Street, and the Presbyterian Church.

And at each corner, the crowd and the confusion grew, as more people poured up from the waterfront. There were blank-eyed merchants clutching their ledgers, stumbling drunks clutching their bottles, terrified wives clutching their terrified children, who clutched their doll babies and toys. And frightened rats were skittering everywhere, causing a riot of stamping and scuffling and screaming.

Gil kept on toward Broadway and the mighty steeple of Trinity Church, the tallest thing in New York. As he passed New Street, he could not resist a look toward the Blunt house. It was a giant pyre pouring flames a hundred feet into the air, and the southwest wind was pushing the firebrands toward Broadway. And the firebrands were landing like seeds and blossoming like flowers all over Trinity's cedar shake roof.

When Gil ran out of Wall Street and onto Broadway, what he saw made his senses curdle.

The fire was roaring now on both sides of the Bowling Green. And the thunderous boom whenever a building collapsed sounded more frightening than the British bombardment of a week before. And the moaning scream that rose from people in the street sounded more frightened than the moans of the soldiers beneath the bombardment. And the smell of smoke and melting metals and burning flesh clogged his throat and made him want to vomit.

So he ran north, away from the flames, just one of hundreds of people fleeing up Broadway toward the Common.

He did not stop until he had reached the corner of Vesey Street. Then he looked back as flames leaped out of the Trinity belfry. For a few moments, the fire danced on the top of the spire, making it seem like a giant candle. Then flames burst from the roof itself and engulfed the most enduring symbol of God's favor and royal power in the city of New York.

"Oh, good Lord, help us!" cried a man in front of St. Paul's Chapel.

"The Lord helps those who help themselves!" shouted Rector Inglis, who was rushing up from Trinity, now a lost cause. "Find buckets. Find men to haul 'em! We'll wet down the roof with water from the well and from the river. We'll save the chapel at least."

A man came running with a ladder, another with buckets.

And Gil heard Inglis calling to him. "You there! Gil Walker! Will you help us?"

Gil shifted the bags on his shoulder and tried to answer.

But the rector kept on: "Whatever's in those bags, Gil, it can't be more important than what's in God's house! So set them down and fetch a bucket."

Gil wanted to help. *But the gold . . . the dream.* He turned down Vesey Street.

"Many thanks!" cried the rector. "The Lord will reward you!"

Gil did not say what he was thinking: since the Lord helped those who helped themselves, that's what he was doing. Instead, he shouted over his shoulder that he would be back. He was not certain that the rector heard him.

He ran with the chapel on his left and the ramshackle whorehouses of the Holy Ground on his right. And people were pouring out of most of them to gaze up at the storm of sparks flying across the sky, and they became a stream of humanity flowing toward Broadway, while Gil swam in the other direction.

A big British soldier came lurching toward him with a girl on each arm.

Gil recognized him as Corporal Morison, the one who had stopped him a few mornings earlier.

"Oy!" called Morison. "You there!"

But Gil kept going. He heard Morison tell the girls that he would be right back, that he needed to teach an ignorant Yank a lesson. Then Morison called for Gil to stop.

Gil knew he couldn't lead this redcoat to the Shiny Black Cat, because that would lead him to

Loretta. So he ducked into the graveyard behind the chapel.

Here the shadows were deep, and the rain of sparks falling from the sky sizzled harmlessly onto the old headstones and the canopy of leaves.

On some nights, the whores did business against the headstones and atop the crypts. Gil and Loretta had used a few cool stones themselves on hot July nights. But as New York faced a cataclysm, even the whores had stopped doing business.

"Oy!" Morison called. "I told you to stop."

Gil kept going until he led the big soldier deep into the shadows.

"I'll say it again. Stop, or I'll skewer your kidneys and cook 'em in a pie."

And now Gil heard the unshouldering of a musket, so he did as he was told.

"That's better. No rector to save you now, Yank, so I'll ask you a question, and you'll answer, like a good subject of His Majesty. What's in the bags?"

"Lead." Gil turned and with all his strength, swung upward.

A bag caught Corporal Morison on the chin. He fell back, and his hat flew off, and he struck his head on the edge of one of the crypts. Then he lay motionless.

Gil did not bother to see if he was living or dead. Unconscious was enough.

It was the crypt that caught Gil's attention. The large stone container, topped with a heavy lid . . . a perfect strongbox, if he could get into it, because he realized that he couldn't be seen in the whorehouse with two bags of gold.

Several other crypts were scattered among the headstones. He picked a small one—easier to move. And it was made of sandstone, lighter than granite, easier still.

He dropped to his knees and crouched so that from the street, his shadow was all but invisible. The cat's paw gave him just the leverage he needed to lift the slab. His head was too full of smoke to catch the puff of decay that rose. He peered inside at the top of a coffin. He reached down and felt another coffin beneath it, a second layer.

He slid the bags into the space between the lower coffin and the crypt wall. Then he dragged the top back and set it into place with a loud thunk. Then he read the family name, "Lawrence," and the names beneath it, a husband, a wife, a daughter, the dates of their time upon the earth, and the family motto: "The Lord seeth all and loveth all."

And he laughed, because this had been the crypt on top of which he had once fucked lovely Loretta Rogers. *Now to find her.*

WHEN GIL STEPPED into Fanny Doolin's parlor, he smelled rose water. She scattered it about to keep down the smells that wafted through a house dedicated to the joining of bodies—any bodies, young or old, washed or filthy. A chandelier burned cheap oil that sent smoke curling up to the ceiling. A girl in a corset and mules sat on the sofa. A blind Negro played a flute in the corner.

Fanny was counting money at a desk directly in front of the staircase. "Why, good evenin', Mr. Walker."

"Where's Loretta?"

"Done for the night." Fanny wore so much mascara that when she batted her eyes, they flashed like the slave's. "You'll have to come back in the mornin'."

Gil leaned on the desk, a motion that caused Fanny Doolin to snatch at the coins between them. But Gil kept his eyes on that mascara mask. "I need to see Loretta. *Now.*"

Fanny gave him a phony smile and said, very loudly, "A man here for Loretta!"

Gil knew what she was doing. She was calling for help.

Leaner McTeague stepped into the parlor. They called him Leaner because he liked to lean in doorways and fill them with his bulk. In taverns, he did it just to start fights. Here, he did it to control the movement of customers and girls. And he was big enough that it usually worked.

Fanny said to Gil, "My girls need their rest." Then she put out her hand. "Unless you pay double."

Gil said, "I'm not here for fuckin', and I got no money."

"Well, dearie, this here's a business. And time is money. We sell time with pretty girls. You can do with it what you want. Ain't that right, Leaner?"

Leaner grunted.

Gil brought his face so close to Fanny's that he could smell the grease in her makeup. "If that fire gets here, you won't *have* a business. So instead of callin' in the Leaner to scare me, you should put him up on the roof with a bucket of water."

The blind Negro stopped playing the flute. "I do smell smoke, Miz Fanny."

The old whore licked her yellow teeth and shifted her eyes to Leaner. "Maybe you better see what's happenin' outside."

Leaner went for the door. The music started again. And Gil went up the stairs.

"That'll cost you, Gil Walker," cried Fanny. "Or Leaner'll beat it out of you."

On the second floor, a man was stepping out of a room. He did not make eye contact with Gil. In a whorehouse, some customers would look a man in the eye and some looked at the carpet. Some were flush and free, some were married and skulking.

Gil pushed open Loretta's door: a bed, a chest, a woman sitting in front of a mirror, combing her hair. She stood and pulled her shift around herself. "Gil!"

He picked up the carpetbag from the corner and threw it onto the bed. "Pack your things. I have the gold. I've hid it. We're leaving."

"But, Gil—"

"No time to waste."

"But . . . Fanny and the Leaner."

Gil pulled the linen sheet from the bed, picked out the corner that looked the cleanest, and tore a piece with his teeth. "Wipe your face."

She took the linen, hesitated a moment, as if she knew the step she was taking, then she did it. The rouge and white powder left streaks, and tears washed down through her mascara. But she smiled.

"That's better," he said. "Now hurry."

She finished wiping, gave a quick glance in the mirror, then shoved her things into the bag. Dresses, shoes, shifts, the matched mahogany boxes he had given her. Then she picked up the corset.

He snatched it from her and told her she wouldn't need it.

"I was hopin' you'd say that."

"And put on comfortable shoes. We got some runnin' to do." He glanced out the window at the reddening sky. Then he took her winter cape from the back of the door. "Wear this. It'll keep the sparks off."

"But, Gil"—she grabbed his arm—"can we really get away?"

"You have my word." He reached into his pocket and pulled out the crown finial. "I don't have anything fancy to give you just now. But take this. The night I got it, things stared changin' for me. It's my promise that they'll change for you, too."

FANNY AND THE Leaner were waiting at the bottom of the stairs.

"Why ain't you up on the roof?" Gil said to Leaner.

"Fire may never get here," said Leaner. "I looked."

Gil tried to push past him. "Out of the way."

"I want my pay," said Fanny, "and she's goin' nowheres."

"Ain't you heard?" said Loretta. "It's a free country. You was there when they read the Declaration."

"The country might be free for streetwalkin' whores," said Fanny, "and it might be free for reg'lar folks—"

"Say, Miz Fanny," said the slave, "is it free for blind niggers, too?"

"Shut up and play." Fanny kept her eyes on Loretta. "I made a contract on you, dearie. Hot food and a roof over your head, so long as you do your work in bed."

Gil slipped his hand around the cat's paw in his pocket. "There'll *be* no roof, soon enough, so there'll be no contract neither."

Leaner moved toward them, and Gil snapped the cat's paw into Leaner's jaw, dropping him where he stood.

Fanny screamed, "Murder!"

Gil and Loretta raced out the door and into the rain of firebrands and sparks. The beast had eaten its way to within a few blocks of Saint Paul's Chapel. The sound of it was like a great hurricane wind.

Gil said, "This whole neighborhood's goin'. Let's get the gold and get to a boat."

They hurried across the street and went through a gate into the churchyard.

"Did you bury it?" asked Loretta.

A man ran past them from somewhere with a ladder over his shoulder.

"We need help! Help!" The rector stood at the foot of a ladder leaning against the back of the chapel. Nearby two men were working well pumps, while others were trying to organize a line to pass buckets all the way from the river. And the buckets were rising up the ladder, and water was playing onto the roof, and sparks were sizzling angrily.

"We need more men," cried the rector, "on the other side of the roof!"

"The church, Gil," said Loretta. "Can we help? The rector been good to you. He been good to us."

"That he has."

A firebrand landed on the roof. Someone shouted to stomp it out, and the rector called again for help.

And Gil Walker did something he had been doing more often. He stuck his neck out. He told Loretta to stay close to the church because it was made of good New York stone. Then he told the rector, "I promised to come back, Reverend."

"Well, bless you, Gil Walker. Take the pump."

Gil grabbed the handle and went to work, while Loretta jumped up on the ladder and slung buckets.

Gil pumped and pumped, bucket after bucket, and knew that he was doing something good in all this terror, saving something worth saving. So when his right arm began to stiffen he changed to the left and pumped some more.

Then he heard a shout: "There's one, right at the pump! Arrest him!"

Gil realized then that he should have killed Corporal Morison, because here he came, sobered by fire and filled with anger, leading a group of marines through the streets.

The rector shouted that they could not arrest a man who was saving God's house, but Corporal Morison said, "There's soldiers comin' right now to help you, Father, but this here is one of the incendiaries. We're arrestin' him."

And as they dragged him away, Loretta shouted, "Gil! Gil! Where should I go?"

Gil might have shouted the name of the Queen's Head, but he feared that the tavern was gone . . . or of Haym Salomon, but he feared that if the British were rounding people up, the Jew was sure to be one of them. So he said, "The Woodward house. See a maid named Nancy. Tell her you're a friend of the Bookworm. She'll help you."

She held up the finial. "And what about this?"

"The Lord seeth all and loveth all!" he answered.

iii.

The fire burned west to the river, north to the campus of King's College.

By morning, a swathe of smoldering black rubble reached from the Whitehall slip, up Broad Street, across Broadway at the Bowling Green, and eight blocks north. A third of the city lay in ruins. Even mighty Trinity Church was no more than a chimney and a pile of charcoal.

Hundreds of new-made homeless had fled to the grassy safety of the Common, where some collected now in clusters, and some wandered in search of loved ones, and others simply sat and stared at the ground or at the smoke still blowing like fog across the face of the sun.

But St. Paul's remained, its roof glistening with the baptism of water that men had been pouring all night to fight a baptism of fire. Dr. Inglis had opened the chapel doors and set up tables to serve hot tea that even rebel sympathizers did not reject.

On the northern edge of the Common, two stone buildings also stood. The Provost Jail and Bridewell Prison rendered unto Caesar (and the king) as St.

Paul's rendered unto God (and the king). The Bridewell faced Broadway. It was long and low, built in that style of balance and symmetry named for the king's own father. The Provost, on the Post Road, resembled a college building with dormers, cupola, and foursquare four-story solidity.

But symmetry and solidity served only discipline (and the king). In both jails, the usual debtors and criminals had been joined by rebels captured on the battlefield and by some two hundred suspected incendiaries rounded up during the fire.

Gil Walker stood in the Provost's Chain Room, one of two long cells on the second floor. He could not sit down because scores of men crowded in around him. Some he knew, most he had never seen before, but all smelled of soot and sweat, of fear and the faint odor of urine.

The British had been in power for barely a week, but the reputation of the provost marshal, a burly thug named Cunningham, had spread like an infection. Before the war, the Sons of Liberty had made him kneel on the Common and decry the king. Then they had ridden him out of town on a rail. Now he was taking his revenge, torturing some prisoners and hanging others, all without due process or the permission of General Robertson.

Cunningham . . . Robertson . . . what did it matter? If the last week had made anything plain to Gil Walker, it was this: he was no longer the master of his own destiny. When he faced his fate—a musket ball or a ball of flame—it would be no use to avoid it. Like all the souls crammed into that cell, he was part of something so large that it would roll on under its own weight and grind them all to dust in its own good time. So the best course was simply to do what was right and let fate make its decisions.

Nevertheless, when the doors of the Chain Room swung open and the guards shoved prisoners in or pulled them out, Gil put as many men in front of him as he could, because those who were pulled out seldom came back.

Around noon, he felt his eyes droop. He wanted to sleep, but there was nowhere to lie down, and when he closed his eyes, he saw the horrors of the night before: . . . *the old woman cursing . . . Loretta crying out as he was dragged away . . . the erupting spire of Trinity Church . . . Big Jake with blood bubbling at his nostrils, saying . . . what?*

Someone moved, and Gil was able to slip into a space along the wall. He leaned a shoulder against the cool stone, closed his eyes, and heard a thirst-rasped voice:

"Perhaps you wish now that you rejoined the Bookworm at Harlem, eh?"

Gil looked into the face of Haym Salomon. "They arrested you, too?"

"In some places they would arrest me because I am a Jew. Here, they arrest me because I am a patriot. They took me as a spy last night. They brought me before General Robertson this morning."

"Robertson, not Cunningham?"

Salomon shrugged. "I was lucky in that, anyway."

There came a sound of clanking chains, a heavy key turning in a heavy lock, the cell door swinging open. Four tall Hessians in blue uniforms and mitred brass helmets forced their way into the cell, bayonets first, and began to growl in that aggressive guttural language. They were calling a name: Hiller. John Hiller.

Gil noticed a skinny little man, whose clothes marked him as a schoolmaster, cowering in the corner.

The Hessians swung their bayonets around and again growled the name.

Those who knew John Hiller moved aside, as if they preferred that his fate should visit him rather than them.

The little man looked up at the Hessians and said, "I have done nothing."

The Hessians gestured with their bayonets and spoke more German.

Then Haym Salomon spoke . . . *in German.*

The Hessians turned to the sound of their own language and answered.

Salomon smiled and said, "*Danke schöen, herr soldats.*" Then he looked to the corner where John Hiller was trembling in a puddle of his own piss. "You can go. Your Tory master says that his children need their tutor and that you are no incendiary. He has vouched for you to the provost marshall."

The little man stopped trembling but finished pissing. He thanked Salomon and added, "I am no incendiary."

"None of us are!" shouted a burly blacksmith who pushed through the cell and shouted it again, right into the face of one of the Hessians.

The guard looked at him for a moment, as if he were a dumb beast, then skulled him with the butt of his musket. Then two Hessians led the tutor to freedom while two more dragged the blacksmith out by the feet.

THAT NIGHT, GIL and Salomon sat together and took their first prison food, a cloudy broth that tasted like chicken fat and trampled grass.

"They use the Hessians as guards because there are so many of us," said Salomon, "and the Hessians are so brutal."

"Ferocious fighters, too, or so I've heard," said Gil.

"Mercenaries, mostly . . . peasants, vassals to the prince of Hesse-Cassel. He sells their services to other monarchs, like the British king. Their discipline is harsh. Their pay is a pittance. Their profit comes from plunder. But I will speak to them in their own language. It may bring us better treatment."

"Until they hang us."

"Or release us," said Salomon.

"Release us? You Jews are dreamers."

"We *Americans* are dreamers. Otherwise we would not have rebelled."

"My friends said we were fools to rebel. Now, two of them are dead . . . or three."

"Then honor them," said Salomon with sudden anger. "Do not despair. Despair is a sin against God and the gift of life he has given you."

Gil sipped at the soup and looked around at the stone walls. "Most of the men in this cell are in despair."

"Despair? You think you are in despair? Let me tell you about despair." Salomon drained his soup.

"About a boy who had to leave his family when he was sixteen."

"You?"

"The Poles decided to tax Jews for being Jews. My parents could not pay for me. So I left home . . . in despair. But I left determined. I worked in many countries, Spain, Germany, France. I learned their languages. I learned the business of currencies and how to exchange one for another and take a little profit along the way. I brought this knowledge to America, and New York welcomed me. So don't despair."

"Were you ever in jail before?"

Salomon shook his head.

"It's easier not to despair," said Gil, "if you're in France and not jail."

Salomon shrugged, as if to say that he had no answer to that.

So Gil finished his soup and put his head back. This time, the images went away and he slept. And when he awoke in the morning, he remembered Big Jake's last words: "Do somethin' good with that gold."

OVER THE NEXT few days, Gil watched Salomon make friends with the Hessians, talk to them in their own language, and earn better rations for the men in the Chain Room.

Then, on the fourth morning, two Hessians came in, came straight for Salomon, and dragged him out.

And that, thought Gil, was the last he would see of his friend. Respectful speaking meant nothing in the Provost Jail, especially for a Jew charged with spying. And once Cunningham was done with the spies, he would turn to the incendiaries.

The British believed that Americans had started the fire to deny them winter quarters. The Americans believed that the British had started it themselves. A few believed that it had begun by accident in a tavern. But people all over New York wondered why so many fires had erupted so quickly, not only on Beaver Street, but on Broadway and Broad Street, and in John Blunt's house on New Street, too. At least the Queen's Head had survived.

This was what men discussed in the Chain Room, because their loved ones had been allowed to speak to them through the grate in the front door, usually for a price.

Gil hoped that none of them had been on New Street the night of the fire, or they might kill him right there, for all the trouble he had brought on them.

And he wondered why Loretta had not come to the grate to speak to him. Had she fled? Or had Fanny Doolin found her and forced her back to her indenture?

Those questions soon faded, however, because two Hessians came in, came straight for Gil, and dragged him out, too.

In the hallway below were two chambers. A turn to the right led into the office of Cunningham—judge, jury, and executioner. A turn to the left led into the Long Room, where guards awaited Cunningham's bidding.

The Hessians pushed Gil into the Long Room.

And the first face he saw was beefsteak red,

edged in a white wig: Cunningham himself. The burly provost was stalking toward him, looking him up and down as if he were vermin, and stalking out.

So, thought Gil, there would not even be an interrogation, only a condemnation.

He peered toward the end of the room, expecting to see the hangman holding his noose or a pair of Hessians holding truncheons. Instead, he saw Haym Salomon, a Hessian officer, and a Tory named Mr. Tongue, a small and precise man who wore no wig and dressed in the brown coat and waistcoat of a working merchant.

Tongue was reading from a report. He looked up and said to Gil, "A Corporal Morison testifies that he saw you running through the street the night of the fire. He says you assaulted him with a bag. This Jew says that you were working for him."

Gil looked at Salomon, whose impassive expression told him that the question was no trick. So Gil said, "I work for many men. I work at the Queen's Head, too."

"Yes," said Tongue. "They vouch for you."

"Ze bag?" said the German.

Salomon said to Gil, "General Heister wants to know what was in the bag. But as I told him, you were carrying bottles of wine."

"Yes," said Gil, picking up on a story that he had told Salomon earlier. "I was bringing wine to the Holy Ground, so British officers would have something to . . . to tickle their palates while the girls tickle their . . . their pricks. . . . Beg pardon, sirs."

"Pricks?" said the German general.

Salomon translated, and the general laughed.

That, thought Gil, was a good sign. No nooses, no truncheons, and a laughing officer in Hessian blue.

It seemed that General Heister had heard about the Jew who could speak their language and understood exchange rates. He had concluded that such a man would be a helpful one to work with Tongue as a purveyor of goods for the Hessians in New York.

So Salomon had been given his parole. And he had asked for an assistant, a bright young man also held in the Chain Room, one who knew where to find the fattest guinea hens, the freshest fish, and the nuttiest ale in New York, all thanks to his days in the employ of Sam Fraunces.

Since General Heister held more power than the provost marshall, it was done. The Jew would be freed, as would Gil Walker, if he agreed to work for the Jew.

iv.

The next day, Gil sat in Salomon's kitchen while Mother Ramsey ladled a stew of codfish, bacon, and peas and told them that it had been Rooster's favorite meal.

Gil told her that he would do what he could to honor her son's memory by doing all that he could to help Haym Salomon.

"Well, good for you, Gilbie," said the gray little woman, "good for you." And her voice trailed off as she did.

Salomon tasted the stew and said how delicious it was after the awful prison soup.

"I don't know how to thank you, sir." Gil dipped his spoon.

"You know the roads and pathways from here to our lines at Harlem?"

Gil nodded and tried the stew.

"Then we will find a way for you to thank me, but you will violate your parole—"

"Violate my parole?"

"In a good cause. And while you wait, I will teach you about money. About gold and specie and credit, too. It is what you have wanted all along, is it not?"

"I want to learn to be a broker some day. I want to do something good with my"—he caught himself before he said gold—"my future. I want to make money from money."

Salomon nodded. "Making money from money is an honorable thing, especially here, especially now. Credit will save America."

"Save it?"

"The American army must have food and weapons and powder and shoes. But our government has no money. We will have to borrow money from European governments that would like to see the British Lion bloodied . . . like the French."

Gil picked a fish bone out of his mouth. "No one ever give me credit."

"*I* just gave you credit," said the Jew. "I gave you fish stew and you promised to pay me by rendering me a service in the future."

Gil studied the fish flakes and bacon bits on his spoon. "I'd best enjoy this, then."

"America will not survive unless our credit is good, unless we can borrow and build our future on our borrowings, then pay back what we owe."

"But isn't credit debt?"

"It is. But it is good if used properly. Credit is a lender's faith in his fellow man and a debtor's faith in the future. Finish your stew."

THAT AFTERNOON, GIL stood on the Bowling Green and scanned the devastation. Already, the dispossessed and homeless were moving back to the burnt-over ground. They used the remnants of chimneys for fireplaces. They pitched tents and raised canopies of sailcloth. They called it Canvas Town.

Gil walked north through the ruins. He went past people still sitting and staring, others who were already rebuilding. He passed men who asked for work and others who scowled at him because he wore clean clothes and did not look hungry.

He walked up Church Street, and as he came by the back fence of St. Paul's graveyard, he heard the familiar sound of a flute playing something sad and slow. And there was the blind slave, sitting in front of a tent, a block south of where the Shiny Black Cat had burned to ashes.

Leaner McTeague was standing outside with his arms folded.

After a few moments, the tent flap opened. A British soldier stepped out, straightened his waistcoat, and hurried along Vesey Street.

Fanny stepped out of the tent and called after him, "Thanks, dearie. Don't be a stranger." She gave a big wave, but as soon as he was out of sight, her grin collapsed. She weighed a few coins in her hands and shook her head.

She gave the coins to Leaner and sent him off on some errand.

Then she headed toward the corner of Vesey and Church, where someone had put up a makeshift privy behind the pile of rubble that once had been her brothel. She drew a bucket of water from the pump, then she stepped into the privy.

And Gil made his move. He approached the old slave. "Afternoon, Ezekiel."

Ezekiel stopped playing. "Mr. Walker? We thought you was dead."

"Is Loretta here?"

"No, suh."

"She never came back?"

"No, suh. Once the house burn, all the gals took off. It's down to me and Leaner and Miz Fanny, tryin' our best to drum up business. Y'interested? Miz Fanny be back from her female ablutions in a minute."

"Female ablutions?"

"That what she call it when she go off to clean her scuttle after a customer."

"No, thanks." Gil pressed a shilling into the slave's hands. "Do an old friend a favor, Ezekiel, and don't tell Miz Fanny I was here."

Gil left by Partition Street, south of the graveyard. As he walked along the fence, he peered in at the crypt with the sandstone top. It did not look as if it had been disturbed. But with so many people sick in New York, and so many now exposed to the elements, he knew he had to get the gold out before another member of the Lawrence family died.

The gold was his future. And it might mean something for the future of America, because as Salomon had said, a man who held gold could give credit, and credit would make America. And if he could use the gold to help America—and help himself, too—he would not have betrayed the memory of his friends. He would make something good out of his own bad deed.

So that night, he put General Heister's safe-conduct in his pocket, took the cat's paw, and slinked through the darkened streets.

It was raining, which was good. Those who had roofs over their heads would be enjoying them. Those who didn't would be wishing they did. And the rain would dampen the sounds of a man at work in a small graveyard.

Again, Gil crouched low and kept out of the few shafts of light.

Again, he read the motto: "The Lord seeth all and loveth all."

Again he pulled the cat's paw from his pocket and pried, then pushed.

Again he reached down into the darkness where the bodies of the Lawrence family moldered toward the resurrection. And he felt . . . wood . . . and stone . . . and nothing else.

The gold was gone.

For a moment, Gil Walker thought about climbing into the crypt himself. Then he heard a British patrol on Vesey Street, and he sneaked off in the other direction.

ALL NIGHT, THE questions tormented him: Did she take the gold and flee? Or had she gone to Woodward Manor? Had she even gotten the clue about the Lord seeing all and loving all? Or, the worst possibility, had someone else found the gold? Had Corporal Morison been awake and watching when Gil slipped the bags into the crypt?

Gil could not venture six miles to the Woodward estate. That would violate his parole, and if he was caught, he and Salomon might both end up back in the Provost.

So he wrote to Nancy Hooley, then went to the Fly Market and found a farmer who had come in with a cart of squashes and paid him to deliver the note. It said he would wait in the market on Tuesdays and Thursdays for an answer.

Then Gil began to ask in the taverns if a big British corporal named Morison had passed any gold guinea coins. The answer everywhere was no.

That, at least, was good news.

GIL THREW HIMSELF into the business of procuring the best of everything for the Hessians. And he learned all that he could about bills of exchange and the movement of money. And he went with Salomon every other day to the Provost, to deliver their procurements and fulfill one of the terms of their parole.

And every Tuesday and Thursday, he went to the Fly, one of half a dozen market sheds that survived the fire, but the farmer who had taken his letter never returned.

However, hundreds of others appeared every day, now that the British were in power. The markets once again began to work. From the dairy farms of Brooklyn came milk, cheese, eggs. From the orchards of Bloomingdale came apples and pears. Chickens peered stupidly from their wooden cages. Big salt-cured hams could set a man's mouth to watering on sight. Herbs hung drying. Tins and barrels and jars of preserved foods—pickles, jellies, honey—awaited pantry shelves. And sacks of barley, oats, and cornmeal promised that those who could pay would not go hungry . . . for now.

But how long such plenty would last Gil could not tell. The farmers in the countryside were a productive lot. Many times before the rebellion, he had heard it said that no European yeoman lived better than an American farmer. With thirty thousand British soldiers in New York, however, and more refugees arriving all the time, there would soon be shortages.

Still it was better here, thought Gil, than outside the city. Farmers were businessmen. They would sell where they would get the best price. So they would much prefer to take hard coin from British purveyors than paper money and promissory notes from American rebels.

Then, on the first Thursday of October, Gil saw the crown finial.

Nancy Hooley was wearing it around her neck. She was standing near a wagonload of cider apples. Yellow jackets swarmed in the sunlight above the apples, and the aroma of cider vinegar filled the air.

He went up to her. "You're wearing—"

"Loretta said you'd see it from a fair distance."

"Loretta? Is she here?"

"She come to my door about two weeks ago. Scared silly. I didn't know what I'd do with her. But one of our scullery gals, she'd run off with the rebel army, so Loretta stepped right in. Works hard. The squire likes her."

"Why didn't she come to tell me?"

"She says she's afraid to be seen in the city. She's afraid of somebody called Miss Fanny." Nancy reached into her cape. "But she sent this."

The note was written in a raw, untutored hand.

Dear Gil,
The Lord seeth all and loveth all. I remembered. I am safe and so is our future. Come soon.

Gil Walker realized that his stomach had been clenched like a fist for two weeks, because at that moment, it released its grip. He laughed. He was so happy that if the blind slave had been there, Gil would have ordered up a tune and danced a little jig.

He sent back a message:

Work hard and be patient. I will see you soon.

He would see her just two nights later.

It was a cool October evening with the promise of the first frost in the air.

He had returned to Salomon's after delivering a

load of haddock to the Hessian officers in the barracks behind the Provost. He stopped the wagon in the alley beside the house and heard Salomon's voice: "Don't unhitch."

They went round to the front of Salomon's shop, where he offered an inventory of sundries, dry goods, and other English imports for sale. In the corner stood two barrels of flour, which they loaded onto the cart. Then they headed back to the Provost. They arrived at seven o'clock, full dark in October, and pulled up to the loading dock.

Salomon explained to the guards that they were delivering flour and picking up empty barrels.

Under the torchlight, the Hessian soldiers took the barrels inside. Then Gil heard the rumble of the two other barrels rolling along the stone floor.

He looked at Salomon, who had told him nothing, though there was plenty strange about this. Salomon didn't usually deliver goods and never after dark. And while one of those barrels rumbled as though it were empty, the other sounded full . . . of something.

Gil said, "Is there—"

Salomon just shook his head, wiped a bead of perspiration from his upper lip, and smiled at the officer who had come out to observe.

The two barrels rolled across the dock and onto the cart.

Salomon reached into his coat pocket and pulled out a bottle of wine, which he handed to the officer. "*Auf wiedersehen, mein herr.*"

"*Reisling. Danke,*" said the officer. "*Auf wiedersehen.*"

Salomon was silent as the cart rumbled down Nassau Street.

On this side of Broadway, life seemed to be returning to normal. Lamps flickered in windows. People hurried along, finished for the day with their business. The smells of suppertime floated in the air. But Gil could also smell the tension radiating off Salomon like sweat.

In the alley beside the house, Gil jumped down and went to light a lantern.

"No," said Salomon. "No light." Then he stepped into the back of the cart and rolled one of the barrels over to Gil. "Careful," he said. Once it was down, they rolled it across the yard, into the kitchen, and Salomon asked for the cat's paw. As Gil and Mother Ramsey watched, the Jew pried off the lid.

Mother Ramsey spoke first. "Holy Christ Almighty."

"Holy Christ," said Gil, then he looked at Salomon, "Moses, too."

Salomon said to Gil, "I was not certain it would go this well. I did not want you to know what we were doing until it was done."

A stench rose from the barrel, then a man rose from the stench. He was skinny, bearded, pallid, except for his eyes, which were both bruised black.

"Lieutenant McQueeney?" said Salomon.

The man looked from face to face, as shocked by his fate as Gil was by the sight of him. "Yes," he said. "Lieutenant Robert McQueeney, Second Massachusetts Infantry."

Salomon clapped him on the shoulder. "You

must've thought you were bound for drowning, once they put you into that barrel."

"I've been tortured," said the lieutenant. "I thought I was condemned."

While Mother Ramsey ladled out pea soup, Salomon explained: in his visits to the Provost, he had gotten to know several of the younger Hessians. He had given them small favors, sweetmeats, bottles of wine, cakes. He had told them of the wonders of America and promised that if the Americans won, any man would have the opportunity to rise as high as a European prince, even a man who had deserted an enemy army.

As Salomon talked, the Massachusetts lieutenant ate. He ate like a man who had been starved for weeks. He ate like a man who had never expected to eat again. Pea soup. Bread. More soup. Bread. A swallow of ale. Then another ladle of pea soup.

Salomon watched like a parent watching a child well fed. "I proceeded carefully with the Hessians, but now my caution bears its first fruit."

"If they all eat like this one," said Mother Ramsey, "it better bear more than fruit."

Salomon chuckled. "If I can encourage Hessians to desert, I hurt the enemy. If I can encourage them to free American prisoners, I help the cause."

By now, Gil Walker had lost his appetite. He took a sip of his ale, studied the bedraggled soldier, and asked Salomon, "Has my debt come due?"

"Consider Lieutenant McQueeney your first installment," answered Salomon.

An hour later, McQueeney had shaved, bathed, and dressed in clean clothes.

Gil had wrapped a scarf around his face, but this would not look suspicious to British patrols, because it was a chilly night. The two pistols he carried beneath his coat were another matter. He prayed that he would not have to use them.

Gil's job was to get McQueeney to a promontory of rock about eight miles up the Hudson shore, about two miles beyond the Woodward dock. A farmer named Dibble would be waiting in a rowboat to take him the four miles around the British lines.

There were British checkpoints on the Post Road and the Bloomingdale Road, at the line of abandoned American earthworks on Bayard's Hill. And to the west, there was a checkpoint on the Greenwich Road. Slipping through the area between these was easy enough, and Gil soon had led the lieutenant into the tangle of cart paths and trails that he knew so well.

And for once, fearing the worst proved an empty exercise. Gil and McQueeney avoided every British patrol, a few feral dogs, and a skunk the size of a well-fed raccoon.

At midnight, they reached the promontory. A bell rang aboard the British man-of-war anchored in the river. The reflection of her stern lights danced in the dark water.

To summon Farmer Dibble, Gil was supposed to hoot like an owl. But he admitted that he was not sure of how to give a good hoot.

The lieutenant obliged with a perfect *hoot-hoot-hoo-hoo-hoo-hooot.*

A few moments later came an answering hoot.

McQueeney said to Gil, "You try."

So Gil gave a *hoot-hoot-hoo-hoo-hoo-hooot.*

Then they heard the oarlocks clanking, followed by an angry voice. "You're only s'posed to hoot once, goddamn ye. When I hoot back, just shut up and let me find you. Otherwise, the redcoats might."

Gil recognized Farmer Dibble from the market. He was a round man with a round face who looked as if he might roll the rowboat over if he moved right or left.

"Come aboard, whichever of you is comin'," he said. "And keep down."

McQueeney shook Gil's hand. "Thanks to you, sir, and to Haym Salomon, too."

"Godspeed," said Gil.

"Enough of that," said Dibble. "Time to go. And tell the Jew that this here's dangerous work. I'll do it as long as I can, but there may come a night when I ain't here. Then it'll be on you, whatever your name is, to get your man to the American lines."

An hour later, Gil put a hand over the mouth of the sleeping Loretta Rogers.

Her eyes popped open. She screamed against the hand.

He whispered. "It's me. It's Gilbie."

She stopped struggling and threw her arms around his neck. Gil felt her warmth and wanted to crawl into the bed with her. Instead, he gestured to the door.

Shortly, they were on a path that led away from the little outbuilding where Squire Woodward's scullery girls slept. Loretta was wrapped in a blanket. And Gil's arm around her warmed him as much as it did her.

"It's dangerous for you to come here, Gil. There's British officers here."

"Every night?"

"Often enough. And sometimes, there's dragoons or a night patrol in the barn, and sometimes they come sniffin' around, lookin' for bit of it from any girl they can find."

They reached the spot where Gil and Big Jake had first seen Nancy Hooley. The river glittered in the starlight, more like a path than a barrier to the opposite shore.

"Is tonight the night?" she asked.

"Where's the gold?" he asked.

"Hid good. Not far from here. When I figured out what you meant by the Lord seein' and lovin', I snuck back to the churchyard and done what I thought you wanted. And the whole time, I could hear Ezekiel tootlin' right across the street. I kept waitin' for the Leaner to find me and drag me back. But I'm never goin' back."

"You don't have to," said Gil. "Just keep the gold safe till we can do somethin' good with it."

"Helpin' ourselves to get out of here is somethin' good."

"We'll help ourselves, but . . ." He hesitated. He had been thinking hard on some things, and they bubbled up now. "We have to do somethin' to help the cause."

"The cause?"

He stood there, shivering . . . from the cold and

from the sense that he was stepping ever deeper into the trouble he had tried to leave to others on Harlem Heights. "We have to make up for how we got that gold. It's the only way to get the freedom we want."

Loretta wrapped her arm around him. "Then we will. As soon as we cross the river."

"That could be a spell. I give my parole. If I run off, it could go bad for Salomon, and he saved my life."

She shivered. "So . . . we can't run tonight?"

"We missed our chance for runnin' on the night of the fire. When the rector—"

" 'Twas the right thing to do." She took his face in her hands. "And remember this, Gil Walker. No matter what folks say about two street rats like us, we're good people. And good people does what's right. So keep doin' what you're doin', and I'll wait." The steam from her breath sparkled in the starlight.

GIL TOLD LORETTA to work as dutifully as always. And every night, she should go down to the bathing spot on the river and look for the signal.

If she found a rock in the knothole on a certain oak, she would know that he had passed with another escaped prisoner. She would then go back to the bunkhouse and lie awake until she heard his owl hoot. Then she would get up and go out to the privy, so that any of the girls awakened by her movement would think nothing more of it. Then she would sneak down to the riverbank.

If there were British dragoons in the barn, she

and Gil would talk briefly. He would tell her the news of the city. She would tell him the gossip among the officers. If there were no redcoats about, she would lay her blanket on the riverbank. He would lay his coat over both of them, and they would make love.

Then they would talk of the future.

"When does it start?" she asked him one warm night some two weeks after his first visit. "This future of ours?"

"Salomon says they trust us now, so they may release us from our parole, so we can come and go as we please. Then he'll send me on a scavenge into the countryside, and if I don't come back, he'll blame highwaymen. I can disappear, if I want."

"Do you? Do you *want*?"

"I can't quit yet, not with Salomon riskin' everything to help prisoners escape, and the prisoners so all-fired ready to get into the fight again."

His voice trailed off, and he rested his face against her breast.

She stroked his hair. "Like I said once before, we got choices in this life, Gilbie. We made ours. Gold don't wear out. The longer we keep it, the more valuable it gets."

V.

Two weeks later, Gil Walker led another escapee across the orchards north of the city. With each journey, he had learned a bit more about how to time the British patrols, how to wait till the right moment to rush over open ground in the moonlight, and how to keep his latest charge moving northward until they arrived at the rocky promontory on the river.

This one was a Rhode Islander named Eph Dolliver, tall and wiry and without much to say. He had been so weak that he had spent three nights in Salomon's cellar while Mother Ramsey fed him. Then he said that he was ready to get back to fightin'. He even asked Gil for one of the pistols. And along the path west of the Bloomingdale Road, he picked up a heavy branch. He said it would make a good club.

When they passed Woodward's dock, Gil put the rock in the knothole.

From what he could see, there were no soldiers around the manor house that night. The British army had moved north to get behind Washington. But Washington had escaped again. So the two armies were now stumbling about Westchester County. The only American troops on the island were the twenty-eight hundred who garrisoned Fort Washington, an earthwork on a bluff overlooking the Hudson.

That was where Farmer Dibble would be taking Dolliver.

Once Gil got to the promontory, he gave an owl hoot.

Out on the British man-of-war, the midnight bell rang.

Gil waited. He could hear music—a squeezebox—coming from the ship. After a few minutes, he hooted again.

Then he heard the splash of oars. But when Dibble did not hoot back or start complaining, Gil put his hand on his pistol and pulled back the hammer.

At the sound, Eph Dolliver cocked the pistol Gil had given him.

There was a sliver of moon, so Gil could see the rowboat coming in, but the man in the thwart was not round enough to be Dibble.

Then Gil heard movement on the rock above him and a familiar voice somewhere behind him. "I been watchin' you for a while, Yank. Now I got you dead to rights."

Corporal Morison.

At the same moment, a second man rose from the rowboat and a musket cocked on the rock above. Four against two, a nice ambush.

But Eph Dolliver had the right instinct. He went for the one above, the one silhouetted by the moonlight.

The prime in his pistol gave a little pop, then blew a ball upward, then the soldier was falling and his musket was clattering down with him.

In an instant, a string of muzzle flashes caught bursts of motion in the dark.

A soldier was rising to fire from the boat.

Gil was spinning and firing toward the flash of Morison's pistol.

Dolliver was raising his club as a soldier charged from the boat with his bayonet.

Gil was on his knees, grabbing for the musket dropped from above.

The soldier at the oars was firing a pistol.

Dolliver was parrying the bayonet of the charging soldier.

Gil was firing the musket at the soldier in the boat.

Dolliver was slamming his club off the head of the charging soldier.

And then the flashing stopped. The gunfire echoed out across the river.

Gil crouched in the darkness, and looked at the shadows and shapes around him.

Dolliver was standing with the club cocked.

The four British soldiers were all down and motionless.

Then Dolliver slammed the club viciously onto the head of the one who had come at him with the bayonet. The head crunched like a melon.

"Stop it." Gil's knees began to wobble, but he willed himself to rise.

"He won't stick anyone else with that thing," said Dolliver.

"Did he stick you?"

"No. But I took a ball in my leg meat."

Then Morison groaned.

Gil went over and poked him with the bayonet.

A dark stain had begun to spread across Morison's midsection.

Gil knelt next to him.

"I been watchin' you, Yank," said Morison, "watchin' since a publican told me you'd been askin' about me and some gold guinea coins. Gold guineas? says I. What's . . . what's this, then? I done some askin' and some thinkin' and—" He groaned and curled up around the pain in his belly.

"Kill him," said Dolliver, "or he'll turn in the Jew."

Morison managed to smile. "I stopped at Woodward's, 'fore I come here."

"You what?" Gil crouched closer. "How did you—"

Morison tapped his forehead. "I may be slow, but I remembered what you said to your whore the night of the fire. . . . Now I got you."

"What did you do at Woodward's?" asked Gil.

Morison groaned and his eyes fluttered.

Dolliver smashed his club down onto Morison's forehead.

Gil jumped back, more shocked by that than by the ambush. "Are you insane?"

"Time to go."

"Then go," said Gil.

"We're both goin'," answered Dolliver. "I'm bleedin' like Jesus. My shoe's fillin' with blood. And I don't know one damn bit about that dark water out there. You're rowin' me to Fort Washington."

But Gil had to get back to back to Woodward's to find out what this redcoat corporal had done: Exposed Loretta? Found the gold?

Dolliver fished some coins from Morison's pockets and took another small pistol from his belt.

"No gold guineas, are there?" asked Gil.

"Nope. Just another redcoat carryin' shillings. Now let's go."

Gil said, "My job is to take you this far."

The Rhode Islander raised Morison's pistol. "Your

job is whatever I say it is. Now we can go easy, Gil Walker, or we can go hard, but we're goin'."

AN HOUR LATER, Gil could see torchlights outlining the ramparts some two hundred feet above the river. The foliage had dropped, so the earthen fort hulked in the moonlight like a wounded beast.

The bank here was nothing but a steep hill approached by a narrow path of switchbacks. And somewhere in the dark, sentries were protecting it.

Gil shipped oars and tried to decide what to do.

The current grabbed the boat and began to push it downstream, and he had worked too hard to get here, so he decided to give out with an owl hoot.

A voice came from the bank. "Virginia!"

Gil knew that was the password for the night. He was supposed to know the countersign. If he didn't, the guards were free to open fire. Gil hoped that the pickets might have been expecting Dibble's rowboat, so he said, "Dibble is dead! I—"

The response was a blast of musket fire from the bank.

He saw the flash, then he saw nothing.

GIL WALKER AWOKE to piercing pain and blackness.

He tried to open his eyes, cried out, and fell back into a stupor.

Later he awoke again and saw moving lights, torchlights, but only on one side. The pain was not as bad. He hardly felt it at all.

He groaned and brought a hand to the bandage covering his eyes, but another hand took his wrist.

Then he heard a familiar voice: "Gil, Gilbie boy."

The Bookworm?

"Just lie still. You're in the fort. They've given you laudanum. They say it makes you feel—"

"Like floating," mumbled Gil.

And he floated. Time passed. Daylight burned through the fabric and the burning pain burned again into the left side of his face. He groaned.

He heard the Bookworm: "Can't you do something for him?"

Another voice: "We've given him all the laudanum we can. We're runnin' out."

And a third voice: "Serves him right for desertin'."

Then the bandage was off and he was looking into the eye of Captain Bull Stuckey. "As soon as you can shoulder a musket, you'll be in the line."

Gil brought his hand to the left side of his face. "My . . . my eye."

"I'll give you one of my patches," said Stuckey, then he was gone.

But Augustus the Bookworm stayed close.

"What happened?" asked Gil.

"Musket ball caught you on the corner of the cheek. Played hell with your eye. It's . . . it's ugly, Gilbie boy, but another half an inch and it would've blown your head off. Killed that Rhode Islander as it was."

And soon, it was night again. The dark of November had come, so each day promised nothing but a quicker trip back to blackness.

At least the dark lessened Gil's pain.

So did his friend. The Bookworm saw that Gil

got soup when there was any, and fresh water when it was fetched up from the river. And each night, he helped Gil to bathe the ruined left side of his face in cool, wet cloths.

WITHIN A WEEK, Gil could shoulder a weapon. So Stuckey gave him that eye patch and put him in a trench a few hundred yards in front of the dirt walls.

By now, the British had left off chasing Washington and were turning their attention to this fort, the last American outpost on Manhattan Island.

On the morning of November 14, Gil was in his trench when the British and Hessians began their attack. By afternoon, the enemy had taken every defensive position outside the earthworks and driven almost three thousand Americans back into a fort meant to hold a third of that number.

Gil Walker and the Bookworm stood shoulder to shoulder in the mass of men and smelled fear and saw fear, even in the eye of Bull Stuckey, because once the British brought up their fieldpieces and began to lob cannonballs into that mob, Fort Washington would become a slaughter pen.

Instead, the Americans surrendered.

BY DAWN THE next day, a great scar of homespun and hats, of brown breeches and tan hunting shirts, of tattered coats and worn shoes, cut across the cold November fields and slashed down the Bloomingdale Road.

Twenty-eight hundred prisoners marched to the slow, thumping cadence of the British drums. If there had been music, it would have been a dirge, because these men were going to the prisons, and once the prisons were full, to the prison ships.

Gil and the Bookworm went together, near the middle of the two-mile-long column. They positioned themselves on the right side of the line, in the hopes that the girls would show themselves at Woodward Manor.

"It takes two hours for the column to pass a single point," said the Bookworm. "It'll be hard for the girls to stay outside that long."

"Maybe so, but when you see them, don't go runnin'. It'll only make things harder for them, especially if the squire is watchin'."

Up ahead, they saw the cupola atop the Woodward house and the winter-bare arms of the great oak that grew before it. And there were the girls, wrapped in shawls, leaning against the trunk of the tree, as if trying not to attract the attention of the British guards.

Loretta's shawl was green, Nancy's was gray. As soon as the girls saw Gil and the Bookworm, they cried out their names and began to walk along beside the column, though they were separated by a split-rail fence.

And the Bookworm couldn't control himself. He stopped and tried to step out of the ranks to go to Nancy.

But one of the Hessians growled and poked him with a bayonet.

And Gil pulled him back into line.

It was then that Loretta must have seen Gil's face, the eye patch, the raw, bruised flesh that seemed to be oozing out from under it. She gasped and cried, "Oh, Gil—"

"Don't worry, miss," he said over his shoulder. "Just a scratch. It'll be fine, miss."

And she seemed to understand, because even though she and Nancy kept walking on the other side of the fence, her voice took on a more formal tone. "I shall pray for you, sir. And I shall pray that you keep your faith. We ladies will never forget you."

"Never," cried Nancy.

Finally, a Hessian guard stopped the girls with the tip of his bayonet.

The Bookworm said, "Good-bye, ladies. Good-bye and thank you for your good words."

Gil allowed himself a last lingering look over his shoulder at Loretta. He wanted to say that he loved her, that he would survive for as long as it took, that he would come riding in under the oak branches one fine day and take her away to the life that they dreamed of. But all he could say was, "Do somethin' good with your gifts, miss. Do somethin' good for your country."

"I will," she answered. "The Lord seeth all and loveth all! So don't despair!"

"Despair? No, ma'am. That would be a sin against the gift of life that God give us!" And Gil Walker felt the tears sting bitterly in his ruined eye.

FIVE

Tuesday Midday

Peter and Evangeline came up out of the subway at Broadway and Seventy-ninth at about eleven thirty.

After St. Paul's, they had gone to Delancey's, but no Delancey. Not in his store on Book Row, not answering his cell.

So they had come back uptown, because the New-York Historical Society was in Evangeline's neighborhood, and Peter was planning to pay a visit, once he heard from Fitzpatrick. Besides, computer research was a lot easier on a laptop than an iPhone. And it was plain that they were onto something.

But whenever he rose from that subway, Peter could think of only one thing: "Zabar's."

"Zabar's?" Evangeline started down Seventy-ninth. "You've just been tailed by a guy named Boris—"

"Or Mary—"

"On the uptown number 4. You've gone to a bookstore that's always open and it's closed—"

"Maybe Delancey took the day off."

"And some guy you never heard of has asked you to help save America. And all you can think of is food?"

"Food from Zabar's." He took her by the elbow and turned her up Broadway, toward the gourmet supermarket at Eightieth. *NEW YORK IS ZABAR'S . . . AND ZABAR'S IS NEW YORK. SINCE 1934.* It said so on the sign. "How about a Zabar's kosher salami and a nice cheese, like a Drunken Goat, maybe?"

"I have one at home."

"Drunken Goat? You like Drunken Goat?"

"I've dated enough of them. I've also visited the Spanish village where they make it. I've even written about it."

"So let's get a baguette and a salami to go with it."

"Only if you admit there's nothing like Zabar's in Boston."

"Sure. I'll admit that."

"And if you admit that"—the light turned and Evangeline started across Broadway—"you'll admit that we should live here instead of there."

"Fight fair, Evangeline. Don't start when I'm hungry."

"But you can run a business—or save America—just as easily from New York as you can from Boston. And you love this neighborhood."

"Love is a strong word," said Peter, "but—"

It was one of those sparkling spring days that made every building look as if it had been power-washed and squeegeed. They'd practically invented the luxury apartment house around here, so even at the edge of a low-rise block with a CVS and a Best Buy, with the traffic thrumming the New York baseline that played day and night, with hundreds of people hurrying along, all of them doing the most important thing in the world (at least in their own minds), you could still lift your eyes toward the beautiful detailing of the Ansonia or feel the magnificent bulk of William Astor's Apthorp and know that you were part of the parade that had been rolling since the Dutch made a deal with the Indians and started cutting in *De Heere Straet.*

"Okay," said Evangeline. "So you *like* the neighborhood."

"And there are some things I like a lot."

"Like what?"

"Zabar's, the museums, the Historical Society, the history."

"I thought all the history was downtown."

"There's history all along Broadway. Up here, it used to be called the Bloomingdale Road. It ran through fields, forest patches, and orchards, until it just petered out a few miles north of here. A place called Woodward Manor was right about where Zabar's is today. It was one of the big estates."

Sometimes she thought Peter had a pair of extra lenses in his sunglasses and whenever he wanted, he could flip them down like polarizing filters to remove the modern world, so that he could see the shadows of the past as if it were still unfolding.

"If you were here in November of 1776," he said, "you would have seen three thousand Americans marching to the prison ships after Fort Washington fell. And most of them would die. Three times as many men died in the prison ships as on the battlefields. Something like eleven thousand."

"No Zabar's back then," she said.

"Just disease, exposure, and starvation."

The faux siding on Zabar's was supposed to make it look like a European food emporium. But the siding was the only phony part of this place. They stepped inside, inhaled a symphony of aromas—coffee, cheeses, pickles, salamis, fruits, pastries, chocolates, bread. And they forgot about the Continental Army and the prison ships.

Then Peter's iPhone vibrated. Another text message:

Have you considered my invitation? Avid Austin

IT WAS A short walk to Evangeline's building.

At the desk, they asked Jackie if there had been any visitors or messages.

"Nope. Nothin'. Nobody." Jackie glanced at the bag. "You been to Zabar's, eh?"

Peter held up the bag.

Jackie grinned. "A loaf of bread, a Zabar's salami, and thee."

"Thou," said Evangeline.

"Pah." Jackie looked at Peter, "A broken-down old pug don't just quote *The Rubaiyatt of Omar Khayyam*. He *paraphrases* it. And *she* corrects him."

"I only correct the people I love." Evangeline pressed the elevator button. "I want to make you look good."

"Miz Carrington"—Jackie pasted a grin on his face—"you make me look good just by standin' there."

"You're too kind." She batted her eyes to tell him she didn't believe a word of it.

Jackie gave Peter a wink. "I gotta work on my Christmas tips year-round."

"You got your pocketknife?" Peter asked him.

"Now, don't go stickin' her, just 'cause she's correctin' me."

Peter pulled the salami out of the bag.

Jackie pulled out a pocketknife, pressed a button, and a three-inch blade appeared.

Peter took the knife and cut off a chunk of salami.

"I think I'm gonna like this guy," Jackie said to Evangeline.

The elevator *bonged* and the doors popped open.

Peter handed the knife back to Jackie. "A Buck knife, Right?"

"Buck Bantam BLW." Jackie sliced a piece of salami and popped it into his mouth. "Small, convenient, one-hand operation. A fine blade for a lot of purposes."

Peter lowered his voice. "If anybody comes around lookin' for us, someone who looks a little dicey—"

Jackie stopped chewing. "Dicey? How?"

"Neck tattoos, maybe, or a bulge under the windbreaker."

"Heat?"

"Peter," called Evangeline from the elevator.

Peter kept his eyes on Jackie. "Yeah. Heat. If somebody like that comes 'round wanting to see us, call upstairs and say, 'Hello, Buck, there's a gentleman here—' "

"You mean, 'Buck' like the knife?"

"That'll be our signal."

Jackie squared his shoulders as if he was answering the bell. "About time we got a little excitement around here."

"Very little, I hope," said Peter, then he stepped onto the elevator.

The door thunked shut, and Evangeline said, "Buck?"

"Now Jackie can send a warning without saying it out loud."

"Okay, *Buck*. Press eight."

THE MIDDAY SUN flooded Evangeline's apartment.

She never pulled the curtains because the shades in the apartment across Seventy-ninth were always drawn. And the view out the front reached to infinity.

She called her decorating taste "New York eclectic." Oriental carpets, a slim modern sectional in chocolate brown, Eames leather chairs in a complementary earth tone, mirror over the mantel, watercolors and oils from places she had visited, along with African masks, framed Fijian stencil paintings, wood carvings, and in the dining area, a Stickley mission-style table, chairs, and sideboard.

It was all a bit like her, thought Peter. The facets fit, even if they didn't quite seem to work on first glance.

She grabbed her laptop and opened it on the dining-room table.

He set out the lunch—sliced salami, Spanish olives, Drunken Goat, bread.

While he poured sparkling water for her and a glass of Rioja for himself, she Googled Austin Arsenault and came up with about twenty thousand references.

"That should keep us busy." Peter set his computer next to hers, and as they ate lunch, they worked through the list.

For the next hour, it was salami and *The Economist*, olives and *The New York Times*.

Rioja for Peter. Seltzer for Evangeline.

Drunken Goat, a bit of bread, and the *Boston Business Journal.* More salami and the Web site of the Paul Revere Foundation.

"Drink to Revere," said Peter. "The man who brought us together over a lost tea set all those years back." And he filled her wineglass.

"Oh, what the hell." Evangeline had some wine.

"Another drink or two, maybe I can convince you to squeeze in a nooner."

"This is a working lunch."

By the time the wine was half gone, they had a clear picture of the man in question:

Harvard Business School, '75. Major player on Wall Street. Exclusive broker who only handles "high net-worth" clients through his company, Avid Investment Strategies. Twice-divorced fixture on the New York charity circuit, occasional subject of Page Six boldface. Fashions himself as Mr. Triple A, the *Avid* Austin Arsenault. Collector of scripophily, current plaintiff in a lawsuit against the United States Government over the redemption of two-hundred-and-thirty-year-old bonds.

"And he's the broker that Delancey is always trying to get me to put my money with," said Peter.

People Magazine had done a profile that explained the nickname:

"Be avid about everything," he says, "in both senses of the word. Be eager and greedy. Be eager for experience, from diving on the Great Barrier Reef to dining at Le Cirque . . . for relationships of all kinds, with politicians, celebrities, ballplayers, power brokers (of either sex), and with the most beauteous members of the opposite sex, too . . ."

"Beauteous?" said Evangeline.

"It means nice tits and long legs."

"Keep reading . . . *Buck.*"

". . . and for things, for possessions, for art and furniture, cars and carpets, wine and rare books and all the other aesthetic objects that enhance a man's enjoyment of his own existence. And be greedy, too, because without a bit of healthy greed, none of the above would be possible."

Sporting a deep tan offset by a mane of silver hair, Arsenault seems a man who drinks deep from every stream, in the hope that one of them might just be the fountain of youth.

"A man after your own heart," said Evangeline.

"The heart, maybe," said Peter. "But what about the soul?"

"You score points for asking," she said, "even if what you're really thinking is, 'This guy sounds like a buyer. What can I sell him?' "

The *People* piece had been written at the launch

of the Paul Revere Foundation. And however greedy he was, it seemed that Avid Austin was also a patriot:

> *For all of his personal self-indulgence, he says that we are watching our wealth and the wealth of our children disappearing, sucked up into the giant hot-air balloon called the National Debt, and one day we will regret our lifestyles of me-first consumption and profligate spending.*

"It sounds like some editor at *People* was asleep at the switch," said Peter. "Most of their readers love stories about me-first consumers and profligate spenders."

"Pour me some more wine." She held out her glass. "And read this from the Paul Revere Web site:

> *The Foundation seeks to do what its namesake did: warn every American village and farm, every household and legislature, every thrifty child of the Depression and every free-spending baby-boomer and all their kids, too, about the dangers ahead. These dangers can be reduced to one word: DEBT . . . national debt and personal debt, the crushing burden of debt that threatens the happiness of every American man, woman, and child. We started borrowing in the Revolution because we needed money and there were nations—and individuals—ready to lend. We paid those debts, proving the maxim of Alexander Hamilton: "A*

national debt is a national asset. . . . If properly handled."

Do you think we've handled the current national debt properly? Well, do you?

If not, click the link and join our crusade to save America.

"Let's click the video link instead," said Evangeline.

The foundation Web site was classy, colorful, not too heavy on the text. But it had plenty of links, blogs, widgets, and ways to wind through the information pile. Book readers moved in a straight line toward truth. A good Web site let you bore holes into it. Peter called it learning in three dimensions.

He preferred books. Whenever he opened some fancy Web site, he felt like the defender of a dying faith, a Roman pagan before the glowing presence of Christianity. If the march toward the electronization of everything from novels to newspapers continued, he'd have to start calling himself an antique dealer instead of a rare-book dealer, because the book would finally go the way of the buggy whip.

Evangeline didn't see things quite so starkly. She just clicked the link that took them to a taped interview on the MarketSpin.com business Web site.

The logo appeared, and there he was: Avid Austin Arsenault, looking just as tanned, silvered, and sleek as *People* had promised. He was sitting on the set of a Manhattan television studio with Columbus

Circle in the background, while off-camera, a female voice was introducing him.

Peter's iPhone buzzed again. "Speak of the devil," he muttered as he read another text from Avid Austin:

> Now that you have considered my proposal and researched me (no doubt), allow me to invite you and Ms. Carrington for lunch tomorrow, 12:30 P.M., 145 CPW. And put on CNBC if you are near a television. It will give you a bit more background.

At the same moment, Peter heard Evangeline say, "Jesus Christ."

He realized that the female voice coming out of the computer speaker sounded familiar. Very familiar: Kathy Flynn, posing a softball question for Avid Austin Arsenault. In an instant, Peter remembered the red hair, the creamy complexion, and that voice that flowed like honey. He remembered other things, too.

So did Evangeline. She glared at the screen and said, "Of all the info-babes on all the financial Web sites in all the world, and *she* has to show up on this one."

"We both knew that she worked in New York as a financial reporter."

"But I thought she was a writer. Who's putting her on a Web site?"

"Someone who likes her reporting. Or someone who thinks she looks good."

"Do you think she looks good?"

Peter shrugged.

"Well, whatever you think, don't even think of going near her again."

Peter closed the window on the computer screen. The sound of Avid Austin's voice clicked off. Peter said, "Kathy Flynn is in the past. Let's leave her there. It's been over twenty years. She's probably married by now, with three kids and stretch marks."

Evangeline turned to the window. "Yeah, well, she *does* look good."

Peter poured them both more wine. "So do you."

"You better say that."

"So let's put on the TV. Arsenault says that I should watch CNBC."

Evangeline took her wine glass, stalked over to the sofa, found the remote between two cushions, and aimed it at the flat-panel on the inner wall. "Your ex-girlfriend better not be on when the picture comes up, or—"

"Or a nooner is out of the question?"

"We're too old for nooners." She flopped onto the sofa and kicked off her shoes.

"You're never too old for a nooner." He sat next to her.

And there was Arsenault again, on a split screen: silver hair slicked back and curled slightly at the collar, silver-gray suit, blue shirt, darker blue tie, matching pocket square. He was talking while, at the top of the screen, in orange "alert" mode, the stock averages were flashing: S&P: *DOWN 31.* DOW: *DOWN 350.* NASDAQ: *DOWN 29.* A horrible day.

And Arsenault was putting it all into perspective: "This is the Wall Street response to China's announcement that they are not going to purchase United States Treasuries at the Thursday auction."

The other talking head was Robert Lappen, secretary of the Treasury.

The moderator, Maria Bartiromo, asked Lappen, "Is this all about Taiwan, then?"

Lappen measured his response, which was not surprising: "The Chinese have legitimate security concerns. To say that they are unhappy with our sale of technology to Taiwan would not be an exaggeration, so—"

"So they plan to stop buying our debt," said Arsenault, "and at least for this week, stop financing our profligate ways so as to influence our politics and . . ."

"Pretty arrogant," said Evangeline. "Thinks he knows more than Lappen."

"When it comes to money," answered Peter, "he probably does."

Arsenault plowed ahead, ". . . and they can do it because every administration since Reagan has been auctioning our sovereignty in the form of United States Treasuries to fund everything from missiles to Medicare to pieces of pork with their ears marked. The Chinese, along with the oil sheikhs, have been buying our debt for years. And now, what some of us have always feared is coming to pass: the Chinese are reminding us of the Golden Rule: he who has the gold makes the rules."

"And the Chinese have the gold?" asked Ms. Bartiromo.

"Correct," answered Arsenault. "We can no longer impose our will on the world or take care of our obligations to our own people without fearing financial repercussions like this."

Lappen said, "That's a rather simplistic spin to put on international relations."

"But accurate, sir," said Arsenault. "Perhaps you should join our crusade."

"Perhaps," said Ms. Bartiromo. "But I'm afraid we'll have to leave it there."

"I don't know what's worse," said Peter. "That the Dow is down by that much, or that Arsenault is probably right about the reason." He clicked off the television.

"Add all that to the streaming video appearance of an old girlfriend," said Evangeline, "and . . . it's enough to kill the mood."

"For a nooner?"

"Like I said, we're too old for nooners."

"Look at it like the five thirty dinner special at Denny's. Have a nooner, then you don't have to worry about staying up late."

She looked at her watch. "It's one thirty."

"So time is running out."

"But there's a worldwide financial crisis, and—"

He refilled her glass. "All the more reason for a nooner."

She took the glass, took a sip, leaned back and put a bare foot on the sofa.

A promising gesture, he thought, but no fast moves. Just set the wine bottle down.

She stretched her leg. "I have a deadline. And you have to get about the business of saving America. Besides, there's no word for doing it at one thirty in the afternoon."

He shrugged. "One thirtyer?"

She rolled her eyes. "That's weak."

"Maybe, but life is short." He reached over and put his hand on her bare foot and stroked the arch with his thumb. "Time is slipping away."

She looked at her watch. "One thirtyer. I guess it works. And I suppose a man needs to be inspired if he's going to save America."

THEY WERE IN bed an hour later when the telephone rang.

Peter was closer. He grabbed for it.

"Hello, Buck?"

Peter popped up. "Jackie?"

Evangeline popped up, too, rolled out of bed and began to dress.

Jackie was saying, "There's a gentleman here, he says his name is—oh, shit—"

"What? What is it?" Peter held the phone with his shoulder and hopped into his pants. "Jackie!"

"Hang on a minute. The guy was here a minute ago, now he's disappeared."

Peter told Evangeline, "Stay here. Don't let anyone in. If this guy slipped past Jackie, he might—"

"Nobody slipped past me," shouted Jackie into the phone. "The guy went outside. He's headed toward Columbus. You want I should follow him?"

"No. Don't leave the desk. I'll be right down."

Jackie was waiting when Peter stepped off the elevator.

"What was his name?" asked Peter.

"He said it was Delancey."

"Delancey? About fifty-eight, Vitalis comb-over?"

"Yeah. That's him. Is he trouble?"

"I think he might be *in* trouble. Where did he go?"

"He come in and asked for you, then somethin' spooked him. I don't quite know what it was. I was on the phone."

Peter ran out onto Seventy-ninth Street.

Jackie followed him to the door. "He crossed Columbus and turned south. Maybe you can catch up to him."

Peter peered down Columbus, looking for Vitalis shining in the sun. Delancey lived downtown, so it made sense that he'd be heading south, unless he'd already hopped a cab. But Peter had been doing business with him for a long time, and never once had Delancey picked up the check or paid for a cab, so Peter decided he had to be on foot and heading south, unless he had doubled back around the block to the Eighty-first Street subway station.

Peter took out his cell phone and called Delancey's. Four rings, no answer. So he crossed Columbus at Seventy-seventh. And his phone rang. He answered without checking the caller ID.

"This is James Fitzpatrick speaking."

"James. Thanks for getting back to me." Peter decided to head toward Central Park West while he talked. "What do you know about the crown finial?"

"Disappeared about three months ago from the New-York Historical Society."

"I'm walking along Seventy-seventh right now, right next to the society."

"Handsome building. Fine library."

"What else was in the stolen box?"

"Some letters, some news clippings, a few personal possessions that belonged to a guy named Gil Walker."

"Who was he?"

"Just one of those tiny grains of sand in the great machinery of history."

Peter imagined Fitzpatrick leaning back in his oak-paneled Boston office and plucking that image out of the air. He said, "Not only are you a fine librarian and a brilliant scholar, James. You're a philosopher, too."

"Go see my friend, Karen Richards, in the historical society library. Use my name. In the meantime, I'll e-mail you a few things."

"Good, but I have to run."

Peter clicked off and began to quickstep ahead, because he had just seen a tall, skinny guy cross Central Park West and go into the park by the Seventy-seventh Street entrance: Mr. *Daily News*, aka Boris.

But where was Delancey? And why had he come uptown to talk to them? What was wrong with telephones and e-mails?

And why was Boris heading into the park?

Following Delancey? Then Peter remembered that in addition to being a cheapskate, Delancey was a bird-watcher. So he must have headed for the Ramble, thirty-eight acres between the Seventy-ninth Street transverse and Sixty-fifth, one of the most important birding areas in urban America. Peter knew this because Delancey had told him about it when he was trying to sell an Audubon Elephant

Portfolio. In the Ramble, a man could get as easily lost as he could in a dense fog on Long Island Sound. Peter knew this because he had gotten lost in there himself.

From the sidewalk, Peter watched Boris head toward the Ramble. Should he follow, or let Delancey fend for himself? Why should he help Delancey out of trouble? Delancey had put Evangeline hip-deep in it the night before. But tracking Boris might lead back to his handler. Or maybe even to the bag lady.

So Peter started into the park, but he was wearing the same khaki slacks and blue button-down he'd been wearing that morning. Even without the blue blazer, that would make it easier for Boris to notice him. And if Boris noticed Peter . . .

Then, just above the traffic noise, Peter heard a rattling, a thumping, a grunting.

He turned and saw a big pushcart rolling toward him. It was loaded down with souvenirs—balloons, Empire State Building paperweights, miniature Lady Liberty statues, stacked T-shirts, piles of bumper stickers, and—yes—baseball caps. Yankees, Mets, the old Brooklyn Dodgers.

Peter went up to the guy pushing the cart, but the guy kept going, as though he finally had some momentum and wasn't going to stop.

"How much for a hat?" Peter began to walk along beside him.

"Twenty bucks, but I'm closed," said the guy, a bulky young Hispanic with a healthy stream of sweat pouring down his cheeks. He had pushed the cart a long way, probably from somewhere well north of the park. "My permit's no good above Fifty-ninth Street. They catch me sellin' here and—"

Peter usually carried his cash in his wallet, but when he was in New York, it went into his pocket. Easier to get at, because New York was a cash town: cabs, tips, sidewalk vendors. Cash was quicker, and fumbling with a wallet was never a good idea in a crowd. He pulled out the wad and peeled off a twenty.

The guy said, "I told you, man, I'm closed." And he kept pushing.

So Peter slipped a C-note from the middle of the roll and curled it over a finger.

The guy stopped, looked around, and said, "Which team?"

"Yankees."

The guy handed over a hat. "I'm a Mets fan myself."

Peter put on the navy blue hat with the white *NY* on the front and pulled it down over his eyes. "I'm from Boston."

"Boston? So what's this, some kind of initiation?"

"No. It's a disguise." And he put on his sunglasses.

"Yeah, well, nobody from Boston gonna reco'nize you."

Peter gave the guy a wave and went into the park.

He had to dodge the bicycles and Rollerbladers speeding along the West Drive. Then he went up a rise, with the lake on his right, took a few turns onto the paths that he thought Boris or Delancey might have taken, and suddenly found himself in the midst of dense plantings and tall trees, as isolated as if he were in the Adirondacks.

That, of course, had been the idea in 1857, when Frederick Law Olmstead and Calvert Vaux looked at a shantytown on some rock outcroppings and imagined this maze of interlocking pathways, like trails in a forest. They had not designed it for a foot chase, or at least not for the one doing the chasing.

So, after a few minutes, Peter stopped, stood, and listened. He thought he might hear footfalls. All he heard was the dull hum of the city traffic and the nearby birdsong

Then he got an idea. Delancey might have turned his telephone on. So Peter called him again and started walking and listening. If he heard a cell phone ringing somewhere in the maze of paths, it might lead him to Delancey.

The phone rang a dozen times, then Delancey's voice came on: "Not available. Out looking for books or birds (pronounced *boids*). Leave a message."

"Delancey, it's Fallon, I need to talk to you. Please—"

He came around a bend and walked into two people: an Asian man in a white sun hat who was pointing a pair of binoculars into the trees, and a New York woman in a kerchief and Birkenstocks who held a camera. Peter knew the woman was a New Yorker because she looked at him like he was bird dung and started scolding him. "For chrissakes will you turn off the goddamn cell phone?"

"Sorry," said Peter.

"Can't you see we're birding? We got a Wilson's warbler up there and you're scarin' the shit out of him."

"He gone," said the Asian man. "Bird gone."

"See?" the woman snapped at Peter. "A man comes all the way from Japan to see a Wilson's warbler on its spring migration, and you scare the damn thing off."

"Sorry," said Peter, "but did either of you happen to see a man go by?"

"No," said the woman, "we *were* looking at one of the rarest birds on the continent."

Peter tugged on the Yankees hat, just to let her know he was one of them, and kept talking. "There was a small man with a comb-over and a tall guy in a leather jacket."

"I see," said the Japanese man. "With tattoo. Heart and arrow." He pointed to his neck, then to the path that the man had taken.

"Thank you," said Peter.

"Go Mets," said the woman.

Peter pushed on into that urban wilderness and tried not to remember the stories about the muggings and gay-bashings that used to happen in the Ramble. New York had changed a lot since he first started visiting in the seventies. Back then, it had all been kind of scary. Now there were only a few pockets of scary. And this surprisingly dense bit of forest was one of them, at least for the moment.

Especially when he rounded a bend and saw a body.

He stopped. No shiny comb-over. But—

He took a few more steps and saw the tattoo. *Boris loves Mary.*

He could not see blood, but from the look of things, Boris would not be having supper or sex with Mary or anyone else that night.

Peter bent closer, to touch Boris's jugular, and his cell phone rang. It was as startling as if Boris jumped up and grabbed him.

Number blocked.

"Fallon here."

"Just keep moving," said the voice.

"Delancey?"

"Just keep moving."

Peter stood. "Joey Berra?"

"Don't look for me because you won't see me. Just move out now. Walk straight ahead and turn left on the next path. It'll take you to the Seventy-ninth Street transverse. Go home from there. And . . . nice hat."

Peter looked around once more. Then he did as he was told.

When he reached Central Park West again, he tried calling the number that Joey Berra had given him on the business card.

A generic female voice: *The party is not available. Please call later.*

"WAS HE DEAD?" asked Evangeline.

"I couldn't tell," said Peter.

"Well, one thing's for certain."

"What?"

"My instincts were right about this being . . . *something.*"

"Yeah," he said. "*Something*."

"Should we call someone? The police?"

"Let's not wave red flags," he said. "Let's see what happens."

Peter heard police sirens down in the street. He went to the window and peered across the tops of the trees surrounding the Museum of Natural History.

"Were there witnesses?" asked Evangeline.

"Two bird-watchers. If the police are interviewing them—"

"Could they finger you if you weren't wearing the Yankees hat and sunglasses? Pick you out of a lineup, maybe?"

"A lineup?" Peter took off the hat and threw it on the sofa. "Let's not find out."

He went into the bedroom and changed into blue jeans, a green golf shirt, and running shoes that he kept in her closet. When he came out, he felt better.

Evangeline had clicked on the television. "It'll be on the all news station." She went into the kitchen and made an afternoon pot of tea. "I can see it now. A police sketch of Peter Fallon in the paper . . . in a Yankees hat. If they ran it in Boston—"

"They'd make me give up my season tickets." He went over to the dining-room table and opened his laptop.

"And breaking news—"

That got his attention.

"A body has been found in the Ramble in Central Park," said the announcer. "Police are on the scene. More as information becomes available. And speaking of Central Park, Manhattan dog walkers have a new space for off-leash canine hijinks—"

Peter grabbed the remote and turned off the TV.

Evangeline put two cups of tea on the table and sat. "Now what?"

"We see where things take us. Starting with this—" Peter opened his e-mail and clicked on the name James Fitzpatrick.

> Afternoon Peter: I had NYHS librarian Karen Richards e-mail me the text of some of the material that was in the mahogany box. She said to come see her in the A.M. She knows your work and says any friend of mine is a friend of hers.

Peter clicked on the icon that read: Newspaper Article.

A scanned image appeared: an article from Rivington's *Royal Gazette*, dated March 21, 1780.

"This paper was published throughout the Revolution," Peter explained. "Read by all the loyalists in New York, which was the British capital for most of the war."

"So they spread British propaganda?"

"True, even though the publisher turned out to be an American spy."

> HOPELESS ATTEMPTS TO FINANCE REBELLION
> *The rebel government of New York, seated at Poughkeepsie, has joined with rebel governments in the other twelve colonies to recapitalize their obligations and replace the all-but-worthless rebel currency now in circulation.*

This plan, hatched by Robert Morris and others, encouraged by the likes of financier Haym Salomon, a Jew, asks holders of Continental dollars to turn them in at specified sites of redemption. For every forty dollars, they will receive one dollar's worth of so-called New Emission Money, state currency that will be backed—so they say—by the full faith and credit of the Continental Congress which is, if you'll pardon our opinion, a joke.

It is a testament to how deep the rebel fortunes have sunk. Their money is all but worthless, their leadership is bereft of ideas, and their hope of victory dims with every new "emission."

Those of our readers unlucky enough to hold Continentals may decide to make the trip north to Poughkeepsie. If so, remember two things: As the roads above Kingsbridge are not protected by the Crown, beware of highwaymen. And undertaking such a journey means that instead of holding forty pieces of worthless paper, you will hold only one, because currency not backed by gold is "as worthless as a Continental."

And the rebels have no gold. So they will not defeat the Crown.

"New Emission Money," said Evangeline.

"In debt now," said Peter, "in debt then."

"Could these be the bonds that Delancey sold to Arsenault?"

They looked at each other and a tumbler clicked.

This kind of work could be like safecracking. Spin the dials, test the theories, read the articles, and then something would fall into place. And they would take a small step toward figuring out . . . something. Debt was part of this story. And old money. New Emission Money.

"Let's read the letter." Peter clicked on the second attachment.

Woodward Manor, March 25, 1780

Dear Gil, The Lord still seeth all and loveth all. I have waited four years to do what we talked of. And now 'tis done . . . because men like Mr. Salomon have spoke of the country's need. Our good deeds will come back to us many times over in the blessings of freedom, stored safe and sound in a mahogany box. I await your return to show you our investment in the future.

Love, L. R.

Evangeline read over her shoulder. "A love letter . . . about money?"

"Looks like. And a promise kept, too."

And another tumbler clicked. With almost every item Peter had ever tracked, from the lost tea set to the first draft of the United States Constitution, there was an overarching tale of politics, business, and occasionally war, but there was a human story, too. It might be about a love affair or dream, a dream deferred or a dream fulfilled. It might have a happy ending or it might be a tragedy.

"I wonder who L. R. was," said Evangeline.

"A patriot, it would seem."

"A patriot who lived in the house on the site of Zabar's."

"As I said, there's a lot of history in this neighborhood."

"I wonder who Gil Walker was."

"Fitzpatrick called him one of those tiny grains in the great machine of history."

SIX

April 1783

Gil Walker stood at the side of the *Jersey* and stared down at the cutter that would carry him to freedom.

He was thirty years old, but any who looked on him would have said he was forty . . . or fifty . . . or more. And he carried in his mind more horrible images than a man could conceive if he lived to a hundred.

He did not even glance at the faces around him, not at the guards whose contempt had evolved into sullen anger because their war was lost and a few prisoners still survived; not at the oarsmen in the cutter, who may have heard stories of prison ship horror but now saw evidence in the flesh; and not at the faces of the other survivors.

Gil seldom looked at faces because someone might look back, and if that happened, Gil might smile, and if he smiled, he might make a friend, and making a friend would bring only more pain when the friend died . . . as all of them did, as all of them had.

One of the guards said Gil's name.

They all looked alike to Gil, all took their orders from brutes and were all brutes themselves. They had determined what little food the prisoners would be fed, what little warmth they would have in the freezing hulks, what little ventilation they would have in the summer heat, what few rags they would wear when their clothes wore out, what little succor they would enjoy when the dysentery came and they shit their guts out and died, or the pneumonia came and they coughed their lungs out and died, or the smallpox came and they fevered and shivered and erupted and died.

Gil hated the guards, every last one of them.

"So," said this one, "you've lasted six and a half years in a place that killed most men in six months. Must make you proud."

"I was cursed."

"We're all cursed, mate."

"No"—Gil put his foot on the ladder to freedom—"I was cursed for robbing a house. My curse ends when I die. You and your friends, you're damned for all time."

It would not have surprised Gil Walker if the guard had thrown him overboard for that. A few years earlier, he would have hoped for such a fate. But no longer. Now that he had survived the ship, he expected that he would live a long life. He hoped only that there would be less pain ahead of him than there was behind.

He took a seat in the bow of the cutter, heard a few words of warmth from one of the rowers, and watched the shit-colored hulk of the *Jersey* grow smaller and smaller against the backdrop of Brooklyn's greening landscape.

And he felt . . . nothing. He had felt nothing for so long that it seemed the only way to feel.

But in the middle of the East River, a breeze skittered over the water. It came out of the southwest and carried the rich smell of turned earth warming in the sun. And it reminded Gil of . . . something. He thought it was hope. He was not sure.

WALKING THROUGH NEW York that day, he tried to remember the city that he had left. He remembered fences along alleys and in front of houses. He remembered trees in yards and along streets. He remembered shutters on windows and paint on clapboards. But most of the fences had been stripped for firewood, most of the trees cut down. The shutters had fallen off, and there was not a house that had been painted in seven years.

As for the streets themselves, there was little garbage because the pigs that ran loose rooted it up before it rotted. And the defenses that the Americans had dug seven years before were now no more than ugly piles of dirt or trenches filled with stagnant water. And the wagons and carts now made deep ruts in streets that had not been rolled or oiled for years.

Military governors in occupied cities cared little for civil works, only civil order. And until the treaty was signed, New York remained an occupied city.

Still, there was familiarity on every corner. So Gil

allowed himself to look for familiar faces, but he saw none. Then he looked for happy faces, but he saw few, because the population was mostly loyalist, and most of them were preparing to leave on British transports bound for the Indies, for Nova Scotia, or for England itself.

As he walked west on Wall Street, he could see that Trinity Church still lay in blackened ruins. And the Burnt District beyond was not much more than a field of charcoal. So he turned instead at Broad Street, which would lead him past Haym Salomon's shop and down to Fraunces's Tavern.

Men who had come aboard the *Jersey* a few years earlier had brought news that Salomon had been arrested in 1778. The provost marshal had condemned him to death for helping prisoners to escape, but somehow, perhaps with the help of a Hessian guard, Salomon himself had escaped and fled to Philadelphia. He lived there now with his wife and children and served as broker for the Congressional Office of Finance.

That, at least, was good news.

But there had been none about Loretta.

Twice in the first month, guards had shown Gil the gold guineas that she had paid them, just so that she could gain a glimpse of him.

"And you took the money, even though we never saw each other?" Gil had asked.

"Oh, she saw you. She stood on the Brooklyn side and we pointed you out. Saw no reason to tell you, though. Maybe next time we'll let you wave to her. Then she'll pay even more."

Gil had wondered about this for a few days,

unsure if he would be happy to see her or angry that she was paying out their future to redcoat vultures. But thoughts of Loretta had soon faded before the stark reality of the smallpox.

Gil had noticed it first when a prisoner who slept nearby erupted in red sores.

"Best move away from him," Gil had told the Bookworm.

"No use," the Bookworm had said. "It'll go through the whole ship. Any man who hasn't had it will get it. And I never had it."

"Me neither," said Gil.

"Best inoculate ourselves, then."

"Inoculate?"

"I read about it," the Bookworm had said.

"You read too much." Bull Stuckey had left off complaining about the poor condition of the ship and spent most of his time staring one-eyed into space.

So the Bookworm had explained that a third of the men who got the pox would die. Nine of ten who were inoculated would survive.

"I still don't like the odds," Stuckey had answered. "You ain't doin' it to me."

But the Bookworm had convinced Gil that it was better than waiting to get sick. Then he had taken out the sewing needle that he kept in his hatband and pulled a string of thread from his shirt. With the pin, he had opened one of the pustules on the sick man's arm and passed the thread through it to collect some of the "matter."

Gil had rolled up a sleeve so that the Bookworm could introduce the "matter" into his arm with small pinpricks. Then Gil had done the same for the Bookworm, who had laughed nervously and said, "A hell of a way to get rich."

Gil had sickened first, shivering through a fever, showing a small rash, but feeling better within a few days.

Soon Bull Stuckey had begun vomiting, then shivering, and he had admitted that he should have listened to the one who read the books.

But a day later, the Bookworm himself had exploded with all the symptoms, including the hideous pox. For him, inoculation did not work.

Gil had stayed at his side, as the Bookworm had stayed with Gil in Fort Washington. And Gil had done what he could to see that the Bookworm had water, though the water on the *Jersey* was something no free man would drink; that he kept his place in the eight-man mess, though the Bookworm had no appetite and the food was unfit for a rat; that there would be cool rags to bathe the agonizing pustules soon covering the Bookworm's body; that there would be someone to mourn when Gil awoke and realized that he was staring into the open mouth and dead eyes of his friend.

Bull Stuckey had died an hour later, so he and the man he had derided as pukin' Mary rode the dead-boat together.

Gil had envied them.

And every day, the guards had reminded Gil that his girl had not come back to the tavern where she first bargained with them.

"Guess we got all she had, or maybe she spent the rest on somethin' good."

Maybe she had. Maybe she hadn't.

But Gil meant to find out. If anything had kept him alive, it was finding out.

He stopped for a moment in front of Salomon's old storefront. An unfamiliar merchant was bent over a ledger in the office where Gil had learned so much. Now Gil could barely remember the features of Salomon's face, let alone his tutorials on bills of exchange, debt, and credit. Times changed, people changed, but business went on.

And one place where business never ceased was the Queen's Head, Sam Fraunces's tavern.

Gil stopped out front for a few moments and watched in the warm April sunshine as men wobbled out with bellies full of more food than a *Jersey* mess crew would have seen in a week. He considered going around to the back. But the cooks might think he was a beggar, with his rags and eye patch and scrofulous beard. Besides, he had earned the right to go in by the front.

As the tavern door closed behind him, the bright sunlight faded to darkness. It relaxed him, because darkness had been his only comfort in the tweendecks. Then he felt the eyes turn toward him, from the dining room and the taproom. And he heard people sniffing, as if someone had dragged something foul into the room. And he realized that what they smelled was himself.

A British officer at the bar put down his brandy and said, "They may have forced us to accept a Cessation of Arms, but they can't force us to accept the stink of rebels in the Queen's Head. Remove that thing at once or I shall be forced to bloody my sword."

A black servant hurried up to Gil. "You better get out, mister. That feller ain't in a mood for"—the servant stepped back as though he had seen a ghost—"ain't you one of them Waterfront Boys?"

"The *only* one. Where's Black Sam?"

THAT AFTERNOON, GIL Walker experienced pleasure such as he had not expected again until the rapture: a bowl of beef stew.

And then he slipped into a tub of hot water behind the tavern. He had boils and lice and the itch called impetigo, so the water stung as it struck, but it soothed him soon. Then it turned gray, then black, and then bugs floated to the surface and began swimming for their lives. The sight of them made Gil laugh, and he realized that he had grown so used to pain that he had forgotten what its absence felt like.

Sam Fraunces, who had been captured by the British and brought back to run the tavern, put a pile of clothes next to the tub, then he pulled up a stool. "Sittin' so long in warm water ain't natural, but you have to get all that dirt off you . . . and all that death."

Gil looked into the face of his old friend.

They called him Black Sam because his complexion was swarthy and the hair beneath his white wig had a tight curl. Some said that he was a mulatto, or perhaps an octoroon. He had been born in the West Indies, so no one in New York knew his parents or grandparents, so one of them might easily have been carrying black blood.

But Fraunces himself kept slaves, and he was a Freemason and a pewholder at Trinity, so Gil was not sure about Sam's blackness. And he was not sure he cared, either.

"The dirt's goin'," he said. "The death may take a while."

"You can have your old job back, once you're strong enough," said Fraunces. "And you can get strong sleepin' in your old attic room."

"Thank you, Sam." Gil worked the soap into a lather and rubbed his neck. "Do you remember a girl, used to work for Fanny Doolin, by the name of Loretta Rogers?"

"Now, Gilbert, I'm a family man. The frequentin' of brothels—"

"I was in love with her," said Gil.

"The girl? Or Fanny?"

"The girl."

"That's good, because Fanny's dead. Leaner McTeague strangled her over money, then he went to strangle the old slave. The slave couldn't see but he kept a knife in his boot, and he knew right where to put it."

"And the slave?" Gil hoped that at least Ezekiel might be alive to tell about Loretta.

"They hanged him. Damn shame. He sure could play the flute."

Gil took a pair of shears, grabbed a handful of wet beard and cut into it. "I don't know why I lived when so many died. But thinkin' of that girl kept me goin'."

"Did she ever work elsewhere?"

Gil made a few more cuts and dropped the hair on the ground next to the tub. "After the fire, she went to work for John Woodward."

"Woodward? Of Woodward Manor? If you want answers from any who live there, best hurry."

"Why?"

"When 'twas plain the war was over and the rebels had won, the old squire went out to the barn and hanged himself. Not the only one to do it, but . . . but they're auctioning everything and sailing for Nova Scotia."

ii.

The next day, Gil Walker headed north on Sam Fraunces's horse.

He wore his best coat and breeches, which had been sitting in a trunk since '76. Aboard the *Jersey*, he had grown dextrous with needle and thread and worn-out rags, and his skills now gave a bit of shape to the garments that hung on his broomstick frame.

The orchards were budding, and the fields north of the city were greening. But where Gil had expected to see woodlots and forest patches fringed with new growth, stumps dotted the landscape. Seven winters had passed since he went to the prison ships, and every one had left Manhattan with fewer trees the following spring.

As Woodward Manor came into view, Gil pulled up on the reins and dismounted. He had not been afraid for a long time. But he stood there, unable to move, because the memories rushed back, memories of moments that unfolded within sight of that house.

The wounded Rooster falling to his knees.... Nancy Hooley rising naked from the river.... Loretta loving him on a blanket and afterward, telling him that he should complete his mission because they were doing good work and their gold would never tarnish.... Loretta and Nancy urging him and the Bookworm not to despair on their march to the prison ships....

Then he heard someone clopping up behind him.

"You here for the auction?"

Gil turned to a skinny fellow driving a cart. "Auction? Today?"

"Auction tomorrow. Walk-through today. We kept our head down long enough. Now it's the Tory's turn. Say, what happened to your eye?"

"I didn't keep my head down."

The man leaned closer to him. "Well, you'd best keep it down when the auction comes, because I mean to buy this property, lock, stock, and barrel. I've saved every sovereign and guinea and copper I could for this whole war. Hard money. And nothin's so good these days as hard money."

"I got no interest in buyin' a house," said Gil.

"In that case"—the man offered his hand—"the name's Daggett. Erastus Daggett. Enjoy your tour." Then he snapped the reins and his cart went clopping ahead.

Gil sucked up his courage and walked on.

The house was still shaded by the great oak that had survived the British ax. Two soldiers stood at the gate. Black crepe hung around the door, proclaiming a house in mourning. Even if the squire had not hanged himself, it would be a house in mourning, as all Tory houses were.

Still, it was a fine house. A center hallway led to French doors that overlooked the back acreage, the servant's quarters, and the distant river. Off the hallway were parlor, library, dining room, receiving room. And people were moving about, examining furniture, paintings, carpets, all as if they were back at the Fly Market.

The chief auctioneer stood in the foyer and peered over his glasses at Gil, "You may examine the materials today, but to participate in the auction tomorrow, you will need to demonstrate an ability to pay."

"Don't worry," said Erastus Daggett, who was inspecting a mahogany-framed mirror in the hallway, "he said he won't be biddin'."

The auctioneer glowered at Gil. "So what are you here for?"

Gil simply looked the auctioneer up and down. His glare—even with one eye—was still good enough to speak without words: I have endured things that ordinary men could only imagine. Best not to push me.

The auctioneer gave a jerk of the head, as if to say, all right, then, have a look.

Gil glanced into the dining room: a long cherry table, heavy ball-and-claw chairs, sideboard, silver, fireplace, a painting of the Hudson hanging above the mantel.

Then he glanced into the library, where several men were pawing the leather-bound books. And through a window, he saw her.

She was out by one of the sheds. A pile of clean laundry lay in a basket on one side of her. A pile of dirty laundry lay on the other. And she was scrubbing a sheet against a washboard in a tub.

He went down the hallway, through the French doors, and out into the sunlight.

She glanced up and blew a strand of hair from her forehead. "There's nothin' for sale out here, mister. It's all in the house." And all the while, she kept washing . . . until he said her name. "Nancy."

The water splattered over the top of the washtub. The arms stopped moving. She looked up again. "Gil? Gil Walker?"

He came closer. "In the flesh."

She looked over his shoulder, as if searching for another face. "Augustus?"

He shook his head. "Loretta?"

"Gone now . . . three years."

Gil looked out toward the river and tried to call forth the numbness that had protected him from so much over so many years. It came, if a bit more slowly than usual.

And Nancy began again to scrub, and once her hands were moving in rhythm, she asked, "What killed the Bookworm?"

"Smallpox. . . . Loretta?"

She dried her hands and told Gil to follow her.

She led him down to the long wharf that planked across the mudflats and ended at the river. A rowboat and a cutter bobbed on the current. The breeze was gentle and warm from the west. They sat on a bench and looked out at New Jersey.

"Won't you be missed from your chores?" he asked her.

"Chores don't matter anymore." Nancy said that the squire's wife no longer cared about the household. The squire was dead. Her goods were bound for the auction block or the hold of a ship. Those servants who were not leaving with her would be out of work soon enough.

"Loretta tried to find you," said Nancy. "She came up with two gold guineas—she never told me where—and she visited every tavern till she found the one where the prison ship guards did their drinkin'. She paid so that we could see you and the Bookworm. But she figured out soon enough that we was bein' cheated."

Gil did not say so, but he was glad that Loretta had not wasted more gold.

"We tried other things. When we heard that Washington was sendin' a man to New York to see about the treatment of the prisoners, we tried to see him. But . . . we was just housemaids, workin' for a Tory. . . ."

A breeze puffed across the water.

Gil said, "It wouldn't have mattered. The pox took the Bookworm in six weeks."

After a moment, she wiped a tear from her eye and continued: "Bein' that we needed a roof over our heads, we stayed here and worked. And every week, Loretta snuck down to the city to tell what we heard when British officers talked at the table."

"Did she ever say who she told?"

"Sam Fraunces collected information and passed it on. And there was a Jew named Salomon. She begged him to help get you out. He said he'd do what he could but . . . he had problems of his own."

"What happened to Loretta?"

"The squire found out. We always thought one of the other house girls told him what she was doin' . . . and what she used to do at the Shiny Black Cat. So the squire told Loretta he would not turn her in, so long as she brought the Shiny Black Cat to him."

"You mean . . . she started givin' him favors?"

Nancy Hooley nodded. "It was that or a visit to the provost marshall."

"Why didn't she run?" asked Gil.

Nancy stared across the river for a time. Then she said, "The squire was good to us, especially after Loretta started . . . *favorin'* him. He even took us into the house to live in the attic." Nancy looked at Gil, as if to see if her story was angering him, but Gil was simply staring at the river, so she went on. "At night, the squire would visit Loretta. And so long as she give him what he wanted, he never asked what she did when she went sneakin' into the city . . . or up to Poughkeepsie."

"Poughkeepsie?"

"The Provincial Capital. She went up there about three years ago this time. Left at night on a rowboat. Took a heavy bag. I asked her what was in it, but she wouldn't tell. I asked her what she was doin' and she said, 'Somethin' good for the country, like Gil and the Bookworm would've wanted.' "

And Gil knew what was in the bag.

"She come back a few days later, without the bag. Just said she done somethin' to help the American cause."

"Then?"

"About two weeks later, she was servin' at table. The missus and the squire was eatin' alone. Otherwise I don't think that the missus would've said nothin', but she looked up and as sweet as you please, she said, 'Why, Loretta, what are those sores around your nose? I do hope it's not catchy.'

"Loretta brung a hand to her face, and the squire looked up like a man whose wife just caught him with his finger in . . . well, I won't say where his wife was thinkin' he'd had his finger. Bye and bye, Loretta told me that in two years of workin' for Fanny Doolin, she'd never once been sick, never once had the itch, but those sores looked mighty damn suspicious."

"Did she die from the syphilis?" said Gil with sudden impatience. "Yes or no?"

Nancy took a deep breath then stood and walked to the edge of the dock. " 'Tis a beautiful day, Gil Walker. Can you smell the springtime blowin' in?"

Gil stood. "Just say what happened to her, Nancy."

"A few mornin's later, I found her floatin' right here." Nancy looked at the water.

"Did the squire kill her?"

"It was an accident . . . or so said a British officer who come round investigatin'. But I always figured the squire done her in. Maybe she give him a dose and . . ."

And they were silent for a time. And then Gil turned toward the house.

There was more to tell of the war on Manhattan Island, but for Gil, the story was finished. All that remained was for Nancy to fetch a package from her room. It was wrapped in brown paper and Gil's name was written in the upper right corner.

"I don't think she ever lost faith that you was alive," said Nancy as they stood under the big oak in front of the house. "That's the true reason she stayed. She said she wanted to be here the day you come ridin' up."

Gil took the package, held it, ran his hand over the paper and string, as if by feeling something that Loretta had felt, he could feel her. Then his fingers fumbled with the string and he felt Nancy's hand on his.

She said, "Don't open it now. Wait till you're alone, then come back and tell me what was in it."

"Thank you. You . . . you have a good heart, Nancy Hooley."

"So did Loretta."

THAT NIGHT, GIL Walker sat on his bed under the eaves of Sam Fraunces's tavern and unwrapped one of the mahogany boxes. Inside was the crown finial and an envelope addressed: Gil Walker, Prison Ship Jersey, Brooklyn, New York. And written below it, in parenthesis and pencil, the words "not sent—too dangerous."

He opened the envelope and read the note:

Woodward Manor, March 25, 1780

Dear Gil, The Lord still seeth all and loveth all. I have waited four years to do what we talked of.

And now 'tis done . . . because men like Mr. Salomon have spoke of the country's need. Our good deeds will come back to us many times over in the blessings of freedom, stored safe and sound in a mahogany box. I await your return to show you our investment in the future.

Love, L. R.

And inside the envelope was a page torn from Rivington's *Royal Gazette*, dated March 1, 1780. It was entitled, HOPELESS ATTEMPTS TO FINANCE REBELLION. And when he was done reading, Gil knew two things. The attempt had not been hopeless, because the Americans had won. And Loretta had used their gold to help. And that made him proud.

He imagined her slipping down to the landing and taking a rowboat north. It would have been the safest way to get past the British guards at Kingsbridge. She would have stayed close to the shore, moved at night, muffled the oars . . . all things that he had described to her about Farmer Dibble's night trips in '76. She may even have carried a pistol for protection.

And he imagined her arriving at the courthouse in Poughkeepsie to present her money: almost two hundred gold guineas, more than worth their weight in gold, a contribution to the faltering finances of a government that had no money.

He hoped that she had met up with an honest government trader—someone like Salomon—a man who would give her a fair price. He reckoned that by then a gold guinea coin would have been worth a hundred dollars, because by the end of the war, he had read that a gold guinea was worth a hundred and sixty-seven dollars. So if she had traded near two hundred guineas, she would have returned from Poughkeepsie with near twenty thousand dollars worth of New Emission Money.

But where was it? He would ask Nancy.

So he went back to Woodward Manor the following week but was met at the door by Erastus Daggett and two huge, barking mastiffs.

Daggett called for his wife, who came and pulled the dogs away, then he turned back to his visitor.

Gil removed his hat. "I'm—"

"I remember you," said Daggett. "You was a damn suspicious one the other day, and you're even more of it now. Don't seem right, a man comin' to an auction preview, then he don't come back for the auction, but here he is nosin' around a week later. Strikes me you're up to no good, mister."

"I'm lookin' for Nancy Hooley, the maid."

"She's gone. Gone off to Nova Scotia with her mistress. And if you come sniffin' around here again, I just might introduce you to my dogs."

Gil could hear them growling.

Daggett said, "I let 'em tear a Tory informer to pieces one night. So—"

Gil backed off the porch, got on his horse, and left.

He could not believe that Nancy would have sailed away without a word. She had mentioned nothing of those plans to him. He could not find her in the city, though he asked after her in boardinghouses and taverns and walked the Burnt District looking for her among the prostitutes and trash pickers. His last link to Loretta was gone.

iii.

A man broken in health, in pocketbook, and finally in the heart may repair the places where life has broken him, or he may surrender to the broken things. Ambition may fade and mere comfort become his only goal.

A place to labor, a place to sleep, a full belly, a few friends . . . for a man who has lost everything, these are a currency of high value.

Simply surviving on the prison ships had taken a lifetime's worth of resolve, and if there had been a wellspring from which Gil Walker might have renewed his soul, she was gone. So he consoled himself by breathing the free air of a new nation and by doing his job for Sam Fraunces, which meant playing a small role in a scene of high drama.

In November, the American army paraded down Broadway. A few nights later, fireworks lit the sky. A few weeks after that, George Washington prepared to leave New York and the army he had led for eight years. So he called his officers together in the Long Room of the Queen's Head, now known as Fraunces Tavern.

Gil Walker poured the brandy with which Washington toasted, then he stood by, bottle at the ready, as one officer after another came up to Washington and spoke a quiet farewell. And as he refilled Washington's glass, he saw tears in the general's eyes.

Gil knew that he was living something that men would speak of a century hence.

BUT GIL HIMSELF never wept. As a boy he had learned that weeping was a sign of weakness, and showing weakness was no way for an orphan to survive in New York or for anyone to survive on a prison ship. Aboard the *Jersey*, men who wept at night were dead by daybreak.

Instead of weeping, Gil kept on.

He worked hard for his old friend. And sometimes he visited what was left of the Holy Ground and spent a few coins. And on occasion, he tried to talk with young women in the back pews at St. Paul's, but he found that his eye patch put most of them off.

Then, about a year after his release, he felt ambition beginning to stir again, so he wrote to Haym Salomon in Philadelphia.

Salomon wrote back that, though he had invested much in the Revolution and received little in the way of profit, he was still hopeful for the new nation. He added that he was considering a return to New York. "Perhaps we can pool our strengths. Your miraculous constitution and my knowledge of money may yet help us turn a profit." But between the lines of that letter was a sad truth. Salomon's constitution had failed. He died of consumption in early 1785.

But Gil never stopped thinking about the New Emission Money, which paid 5 percent interest to the bearer. Nancy Hooley might have lied and kept it herself. Or it might still be hidden. Such thoughts kept Gil awake many a night.

So once a month, under a full moon, he would travel up the island to what was now called Daggett Manor. And he would poke about near the riverbank—under rocks, in tree hollows, beneath the foundations of the now-vacant outbuildings—for places where Loretta might have hidden the other mahogany box. But he never tried the house, because he did not break into houses any longer, especially houses guarded by big dogs. And he did not think that knocking on the front door would get him anywhere, because the man who now fashioned himself as Squire Daggett did not appear to be one who would forget a face.

THOUGH THE FRAGILE collection of American states was dead broke, New York burst back to life.

It began when Alexander Hamilton and a handful of friends started the Bank of New York and brought order to the chaos of dollars and pounds, paper money and specie, state money and Continentals flooding the city. Merchant ships sailed in again. Men conducted business in the coffeehouses once more. And the old trenches were filled and the earthworks smoothed and the Burnt District rebuilt. And Second Trinity Church rose from the ashes.

When Americans realized that the government they had created under the Articles of Confederation did not work, they ratified a new constitution, named New York as the capital, and inaugurated a president.

On a warm April morning in 1789, Gil Walker joined the crowd in front of City Hall, which had been gussied up and renamed Federal Hall, to watch George Washington take the oath of office. Gil had seen Washington weep. Now he saw him stand as a god in a simple brown suit of American cloth. When Washington said, "So help me, God," the roar was so powerful it made the glass vibrate in the windows of Wall Street and echo down Broad Street all the way to the water. Then the church bells rang. And a moment later came a thunderous *feu de joie* from all the cannon on all the ships up and down both rivers.

America had traveled far, thought Gil, from the last time that a New York crowd had roared as loudly, on a July evening in 1776.

Now there was something called a Federal government. And Sam Fraunces, named chief steward to the president, had already sold his tavern to house most of it.

Within a few months, the departments of State, Treasury, and War had moved in. And Gil Walker, who saw to the physical care of the building, played unofficial steward to those who labored late in service to this new government.

So it was that on a fall night, as Gil was going up to bed, he noticed a light in the Treasury office. Thinking someone had left a lamp burning, he followed the light through the outer office to find Alexander Hamilton leaning over his desk, surrounded by books and ledgers that rose like ramparts on all sides of him.

Gil knocked and asked if His Honor would

like anything. Hamilton requested a pot of strong coffee.

Fifteen minutes later, Gil returned with the coffee and ginger raisin cake and placed them on the table. Then he stepped back, waiting for some acknowledgment.

But Hamilton was hunched over his work, as if rooted to it by the tip of his quill.

Finally, Gil spoke: "There's folks say coffee at night will keep you awake, sir."

"That's the idea." Hamilton did not raise his head.

Gil listened to the scratching of the pen for a few moments. Then he took the coffee and poured. It gurgled into the cup and sent up a little cloud of steam. Then he stepped back and cleared his throat.

Hamilton finally looked up. "What? What is it?"

"Some coffee, sir . . . to keep you awake."

"Very good. Thank you. Thank you and good night." Hamilton turned again to the page.

"Sorry, sir. But I was just wonderin' what it is you're writin'—"

"It's called *Report on Public Credit*, if you must know."

And Gil felt something stir in his mind or his soul. He was not sure which. He said, "There was a time when I tried to learn about credit."

"Did you, now?" Hamilton dipped his quill and kept his eyes on the paper.

"Credit, a man once told me"—Gil strained to remember the words exactly—"is a lender's faith in his fellow man and a debtor's faith in the future."

Hamilton stopped writing, looked up, and said, "I like that." Then he jotted it down on a piece of scrap paper. "Who was this wise man?"

"A Jew named Salomon."

"Haym Salomon?" Hamilton set down the quill. "You *knew* him?"

"Yes, sir. He got me out of the Provost Jail . . . and I went to work for him."

"Do I know *you*? Where did you serve?"

"With Stuckey's company, then on the *Jersey*. Six and a half years."

Hamilton stood and raised a lamp to Gil's face. "You must have a powerful constitution to . . . I remember you now. You're one of the Waterfront Boys."

"You once saved us from a floggin', but that was a long time ago, sir. And my constitution got used up survivin'. Otherwise, I might've made somethin' of myself."

"You were in the rearguard on the retreat from New York. One of the Boys took a bullet, didn't he?"

"Rooster Ramsey."

"Yes. I remember. A cocky fellow. . . . The stand you lads made that day . . . it helped me escape with my two fieldpieces. Come December, I used those guns to hold off the British on the Raritan and cover Washington's retreat. So you could say that your friend's sacrifice saved the army. Take comfort in that, at least."

Gil had heard stories of Hamilton. Men said that when he smiled at you and asked a question, he made you feel as if he truly meant the warmth and truly cared about your answer. In that moment, it seemed to be so.

"Tell me," Hamilton went on, "how's—what *was* his name?—my old friend from King's College. Augustus, Augustus the Bookworm?"

"I'm afraid he—"

"He didn't make it?" said Hamilton.

"None of them did, sir, 'cept me. We joined on a whim, but we showed what courage we could. We done our best." And Gil Walker began to cry. In all his life, he had never cried for any of them. He had tried instead, when he lived the horrors and when he thought about them, to harden himself. Why his emotion burst forth at that moment was something he could not understand.

Hamilton slid his chair out and told Gil to sit. Then he took the cup of coffee and put it into Gil's hand. Then he slipped a bottle of brandy from the drawer and poured a generous shot into the mug.

"The secretary of the Treasury fills my cup." Gil dragged a sleeve across his nose. "Life still has its wonders."

"You're a veteran. You've earned it. And if you've held onto your pay certificates, I intend to see that you're recompensed in full."

Gil took a sip and felt the warmth of coffee and brandy both. "Not my pay certificates I'm worryin' about, sir."

"Did you sell them for pennies on the dollar, like so many other soldiers?"

"Not exactly. Mine's a long story, and seein' as you're busy with figurin' out the finances of the country and all. . . ."

But Hamilton insisted he had the time.

So Gil Walker, in the quiet of that warm room on the second floor of Fraunces's old tavern, decided to tell the story. He reached into his shirt and took off the crown finial that he wore on a leather lanyard around his neck. "This is where it begins."

The fire crackled on the grate. The oil in the lamps silently turned to light and smoke. And the two men drank more brandy.

When Gil was done, he drained his cup and stood. "A long story, sir. As I said."

Hamilton picked up the finial and turned it over in his ink-stained hand. "Why did you want to tell me all this?"

"Well . . . just seein' you up to your elbows in the business of money . . . it reminded me of the things I tried to learn from Mr. Salomon, back when I dreamed big dreams, back when my friends and me were the top men in town. I dreamed of understandin' credit and debt and how to make them work."

"I've dreamed of putting my understanding into action." Hamilton gestured to the sheets on his desk. "I'd convince Congress that a national debt can be a national blessing. As Salomon said, it reflects our belief in ourselves and our faith in the future."

Gil stood for a moment more, then said, "Thank you, sir. Thank you for listenin'." He took the finial and turned to leave.

"Do you still have your dreams, Gil Walker?"

"It's been a long time since I dreamed much of anything."

"Since you learned that your Loretta had died?"

"I loved her sure enough, and she loved me." Gil shrugged. "We came from hard times, hard places, but we tried to do our best with the gold—"

"Once you'd stolen it, that is," said Hamilton with no hint of disapproval.

"Ill-gotten gains, yes, sir. But I'd feel better about stealin' it if I thought that it helped America. So I'd love to know for certain if she really swapped it for New Emission Money."

"That may be a question I can answer." Hamilton took the lamp and went over to a huge ledger on a stand in the corner. "You say her last name was Rogers?"

"Yes, sir."

"And she conducted her transaction in Poughkeepsie?"

"As I understand, sir."

Hamilton flipped through several pages, back and forth, until he found it. "Aha. Here. Come over here."

As Gil looked over his shoulder, Hamilton explained that some of the states had left master lists of their large sales. Each New York bill had been numbered and duly entered. And there—he jabbed a finger—was the name Loretta Rogers. "Twenty thousand dollars. Two hundred bills issued in hundred-dollar denominations, numbered from 2510 to 2709.

"And," said Hamilton, "as of a month ago they had not been redeemed."

"They're still out there?" said Gil.

Hamilton's eyes reflected the lamplight, though the light seemed to be pouring from that powerful brain. "Still out there, still accruing interest. So bring them in, whenever you can, and unless some other disposition has been made in the interim, they will be redeemed. There are some who would fold this debt into state debts to be assumed by the new Federal government, others who would put the responsibility directly onto the states for redemption, but I take this very seriously, Gil Walker. The New Emission Money helped to win the Revolution. It's a debt of honor. And if I have anything to say, it will always be backed by the full faith and credit of the United States government."

A DEBT OF honor . . . full faith and credit . . .

Gil Walker fell asleep with those words rattling in his head, and his dream revived.

For weeks after, he schemed to get back into the house where the bills might have been hidden. But whenever he rode up the Bloomingdale Road, day or night, Squire Daggett or one of his family or his dogs were there.

Once, Gil saw Daggett at the Fly Market, so he hurried back to his quarters, collected a box of books, put on his best breeches and deerskin waistcoat, and rode the six miles to Daggett Manor, planning to present himself as a traveling book salesman, just to get inside.

But Squire Daggett had somehow arrived ahead of him.

And so, he went back to work. And in time, he

tamped down his ambitions, as he had tried for so long to tamp down his pain.

iv.

In January, Hamilton delivered his *Report on Public Credit,* a work of enormous detail and depth that laid out the principles for creating an economy, a credit system, and a plan for paying back those who had purchased America's debts during the Revolution. While the Congress debated Hamilton's recommendations, Americans indulged in great flurries of speculation. Men made markets in Continental dollars, pay certificates, and bills of exchange, because if Hamilton's plan went through, the new government would cover the debts of the states as well as the Continental Congress.

Gil Walker read the report when it was published, did his best to understand it, and found himself dreaming again about finding that mahogany box.

Then he found the next best thing: the only woman who might lead him to it.

He and one of Black Sam's slaves were at the fish market to buy spring shad for the president's table. Whenever he went to the fish market, Gil stopped at Blue-Point Charlie's, a vendor who pitched his tent at the edge of the market and shucked oysters on the spot. Gil would buy a dozen oysters, look out at the place where the *Jersey* had finally sunk into the mud, eat the oysters, and congratulate himself that he was still alive.

It had taken years before he could look at the

Brooklyn Flats without feeling guilt's burden at surviving when the Bookworm and so many more had died. But now . . . every oyster tasted like the sea breeze that for all those years had taunted him with the scent of freedom.

As he tipped his head back and let the cool, juicy creature slither down his throat, he heard a woman say his name.

He almost choked on the oyster. "Nancy? Nancy Hooley?"

"I'm back."

"Since when?"

"There's a general amnesty. Tories who was expelled can come back, so long as they don't lay claim to their confiscated property. And after seven years, the mistress hated Nova Scotia—"

"How long have you been back?"

"A month," she said. "I . . . I meant to come down to the tavern, but it looks so official now, with the sign out front that says, 'Departments of State, Treasury, and War.' I didn't think you'd even be there."

He offered her an oyster, sea-fresh and succulent, with a dash of West Indian hot sauce. "It's a fine thing to see you."

She tipped back her head, let the oyster slither into her mouth, and licked the juice from her lips. "You look better than the last time I saw you, Gil Walker."

"I been survivin'."

She patted the stomach beneath his waistcoat. "Seems like more than survival."

"And you, miss—it's still 'miss,' isn't it?"

"Still 'miss.' Never met anyone to match the Bookworm."

Gil said, "You look as beautiful as the night I first laid eyes on you."

"Naked in the river, you mean?"

"Beautiful in the moonlight," he said.

" 'Twas drizzlin'."

"Then you were beautiful in the drizzle."

She looked into his eyes and said, "May I have another oyster?"

They shared oysters, and a long walk back to the Woodwards' new home on Vandewater Street.

THEY MET EVERY week after that and walked the city and visited the reopened theaters and attended services at the new Trinity together.

And on a Saturday night after they had enjoyed a performance of *The Beggar's Opera,* they went back to Gil's bed under the eaves. And for the first time since he lay on a blanket with Loretta, he felt sweet lips on his lips, soft breasts on his chest, smooth legs around his waist . . . without paying for any of it.

They awoke the next morning to the chiming of the Trinity bells.

"Those could be wedding bells," said Gil, "if you agree."

She rolled against him and wrapped an arm around him. "I will agree to be with you whenever you want, Gil Walker, so long as you agree never again to frequent places where you pay for what I'll give free of charge. But marriage? What would two servants do for money? And what better job is there for two old dogs like us?"

Gil stared up at the roof boards. "Loretta left something for me I never found."

"What she went to Poughkeepsie for?"

"A stash of money. She must have hid it in Woodward Manor."

She rolled off of him.

"In the room you shared with her . . . do you know was there any hidin' places?"

Nancy pulled the sheet up around herself. "Is that why you've been romancin' me? To find out—"

"I love you, Nancy. I never thought I'd say that to anyone again. But . . . if we need money, and we know where to find twenty thousand dollars . . ."

And she relaxed. She lay back on the bed. She stared up at the eaves, too. And finally she said, "There was a loose floorboard . . ."

SO . . . PERHAPS THE adventure of his life had not yet been lived. Perhaps there was something more ahead of him than a slow bending to the wind of time.

That's what Gil Walker was thinking all that Sunday and all the next morning, as he awoke too early and dragged himself down the stairs to stoke the fires and dreamed of staying in a warm bed with a warm Nancy Hooley beside him.

He did not ask her for help. Now that he knew exactly where to look, this was something he would have to do himself. Another person would only make it more dangerous. And his adventures had cost the lives of too many people he loved.

So every night for two weeks, he rode the six miles to Daggett's house. He never arrived before eight or nine o'clock. He tethered his horse in a field on the east side of the Bloomingdale Road, then he sneaked across to the front yard.

He brought two chunks of horsemeat for the dogs. But they did not run loose on cold nights. They stayed in the house, warming their master's feet.

For the first week, Gil watched the windows and tried to determine the movement of the family by noting the movement of lanterns through foyers, up stairs, into bedrooms. And he wrote down the exact time each night that each lantern went out. During the second week, he worked his way around to the back of the house, to time their visits to the privy. In all things, people were creatures of habit. Even on prison ships, men ate and slept and shat at the same times.

He grew bolder as the nights passed. He sneaked closer to the house. He peered in the windows. Daggett read a book each night. His heavyset wife worked at her knitting. The dogs lounged by the fire.

Gil counted three Daggett children, all in their mid-teens. They concerned him because it was possible that one of them was living in a third-floor attic room.

And sneaking past the dogs might not be easy, despite their evening languor.

But there was the great oak. It extended its branches onto the sloping roof. And atop the roof were two dormers and a glassed-in cupola . . .

He found a pruning ladder in a shed in the orchard across the road. It would get him to the lower branches of the oak. Then he could climb.

On a moonless night, he decided to move. The starlight, so much more brilliant here than in the city, would guide him.

He waited thirty minutes after the lights in Daggett Manor had gone out. Time passed slowly. Three minutes seemed like thirty, ten like two hours. And it was cold, as only March nights can be cold, when the snow is gone and the hope of spring is in the air, but the frozen ground still feels like ice underfoot.

Somewhere nearby, an owl hooted. It reminded him of nights when he had done good work for the cause. Now he was doing good work for himself and Nancy.

He moved closer. He tethered the horse to the fence some hundred feet in front of the house. Then he shouldered the ladder and slinked forward.

At the base of the tree, he waited a few moments. But there was no sound, no barking from the monstrous dogs that probably slept with their master. Even the owl had stopped hooting.

He looked up at the roof. It seemed much higher from here than it had from across the road. But the shadows of the tree branches twined tight around the trunk, so he knew that once he found his footing, it would be easy to reach the top. Then it would be a simple matter to work his way out along the branch that overhung the roof.

He took two or three deep breaths, ignored the chill of cold sweat on his flanks, and began to climb. Off the ladder he boosted himself to the lowest branch and lifted. He had solid muscles from hard work, and he did not fear heights because a man who had survived the prison ships feared nothing.

Five feet, then ten feet he rose, always careful, always using one hand to climb and one hand to hold.

He paused as he went past the second story and peered into the master chamber.

If he had any doubt that he was doing the right thing, the sight of Erastus Daggett and his wife, buried in bliss beneath a mountain of blankets, kept him climbing.

He decided it would be best to put the tree between himself and the window. So he swung a leg around the trunk then reached with an arm, and as he did, something burst from a hole in the side of the tree, a hole that Gil hadn't seen because it was on his blind side: the owl, frightened from its nest.

It struck Gil in the face, knocking him off balance. He slipped and lost his grip.

Then he was falling. He dropped five feet in an instant and slammed his belly against a branch. It levered him over, so that he hit the next branch on his back. Then he flipped again and slammed his outstretched arms off another branch and then he was on the ground, on his back, looking up into the tree.

He let out a long, low groan of pain and shock.

In all the things that had happened to him, he had never once said that he could not believe what was happening to him, until that moment. He could not believe that he had just fallen forty feet and was still conscious.

He moved his legs, then he raised his hands to look at them. Nothing seemed to be broken. But he felt a pain in his gut, a pounding, throbbing thing that seemed to grow with every beat of his heart.

And then he heard a window open above him.

Erastus Daggett said, "I don't see nothin'."

From within, the wife said, "I heard *somethin'*. A flutterin', a fallin', a groanin'."

Stay still. Stay silent.

"The damn owl is what you heard."

"It was bigger than an owl."

The pain . . . the pain. . . . Stay still. Stay silent.

He heard Daggett say, "Maybe the coons are wakin' up. Early March . . . big coon falls out of a tree . . ."

The voice faded.

Gil looked up at the shadow of the house and the black, star-glittered sky above it.

Then a white chamber pot appeared from the second-story window, and the Daggetts' night piss hit him in the face.

DAWN CAME EARLY in March. By five o'clock the sky was bright.

That, thought Gil, was a small mercy. He slumped in the saddle, his hands on the pommel, the reins trailing, his head bobbing.

The horse did not move at a gallop or a trot but a simple walk. And it stopped to nibble whenever it saw bits of winter straw grass. So it took its own sweet time to pass the Common.

Then Gil heard hooves coming toward him on Broadway.

Then he heard voices: "I'm telling you, sir, debt assumption means everything. We must give investors and creditors confidence in our ability to cover *all* American debts if we're to be a truly federal government. It's the only way to guarantee that the economic system—and the government itself—will work."

"I agree," the bigger man said, "but let us ride in peace and speak of all this at breakfast—"

Gil raised his hand and said good morning. But he could not quite tell who the two men were until one of them rounded back on him and pulled up his horse.

"Gil? Gil Walker?"

Gil recognized the voice more than the face. "Mr. Hamilton?"

"Are you all right, man? You look—"

"He looks blue," said the other man.

"So he does, Mr. President," said Alexander Hamilton. "What happened, Gil?"

"I like to ride in the dawn, like Mr. President here."

"It's good for the constitution," said George Washington.

"Except when you . . . you . . . fall."

"You fell? Are you hurt?" asked Hamilton.

"I fear somethin' burst inside of me. I . . . I . . ."

And in the bright light of a cold March dawn, the last two faces that Gil Walker saw were the faces of the Revolution and the federal government: George Washington and Alexander Hamilton.

His last thought, as he passed from consciousness, *a hell of a way to get rich.*

He did not feel anything when he struck the ground in front of St. Paul's Chapel.

SEVEN

Wednesday Morning

A headline caught Peter Fallon's eye: FEDERAL STEWARD DIES IN PRESENCE OF GEORGE WASHINGTON.

Peter was sitting in the New-York Historical Society library, a room that honored the scholar's art with two-story columns supporting a vaulted ceiling and stained-glass windows celebrating New York history. It reminded him of a small chapel. So he was praying over a thin folder of material about Gilbert Walker.

The article from the *New York Daily Advertiser* for March 12, 1790, described Walker's service in the Revolution, his six and a half years aboard the *Jersey,* and his death after a fall from a horse, all in the typically florid style of the era:

> *If the time and place of a man's passing, and those who attend upon it, reflect the significance of his life, then the death of Gilbert Walker must bear witness to a life of importance, despite his station as a simple steward, for he expired at sunrise, on Broadway, in front of St. Paul's Chapel, the only witnesses being the only witnesses a man would want, aside from the Savior himself, namely the president of the United States and his secretary of the Treasury.*

Peter wished that the writer had done more reporting and less stylizing. Where had the decedent been coming from? What did Washington say when he . . . deceded? Did Hamilton help him? A little CPR, maybe? A few chest compressions?

Gilbert Walker's funeral service in St. Paul's Chapel was also attended by men of importance: Secretary Hamilton, Sam Fraunces, and numerous others who had known him. Mr. Walker died without wife or issue. His body and belongings were claimed by Nancy Hooley, housemaid. He was buried in the chapel graveyard.

So, thought Peter, Gil Walker's grave site had been covered by the rain of death on that September day in 2001.

He flipped through the rest of the folder, looking for the identity of "L. R.," perhaps, or another mention of Nancy Hooley. It did not take long:

WOMAN MAULED TO DEATH ON BLOOMINGDALE ROAD!

Nancy Hooley, housemaid to former loyalist Abigail Woodward, was last night attacked by two mastiffs belonging to Erastus Daggett, owner of Woodward Manor. By the time that Squire Daggett heard the dogs, they had torn loose the veins in the poor woman's throat and savagely chewed on her limbs. She expired on the scene. The constable says there will be no further action, as the dogs were protecting their property, Miss Hooley having been found trespassing inside Daggett's fence.

When Peter sat back, Karen Richards materialized from somewhere in the stacks. "Find anything that helps?"

"Everything helps." Peter did not whisper, since there was no one else working in the library that morning. "The woman who stole the box, did she give a name and address on the call slip?"

"She said her name was Erica Callow."

Ms. Richards looked to be in her late fifties. No wedding band, reading glasses on a loop around her neck, hair pulled back and graying all over, a nervous laugh, and a story to tell: "She said she was researching the history of Fraunces Tavern. She called it the beating heart of the city from 1774 to the day that the federal government left."

"What did she look like?" asked Peter.

"Very pretty. Tall. Blonde. Late forties. Nice shoes. Jimmy Choo, maybe."

From tall blonde to bag lady in eight months? Peter wondered. And Jimmy Choo's?

"She had worked a lot with our Revolutionary War material. She had read the folder you've just read. Then she asked for the actual box left behind by Walker."

"How had the box come to you?"

"We were in existence long before the Sons of the Revolution opened their museum at Fraunces. And one of our early benefactors was Abigail Woodward, wife of a loyalist who hanged himself. She found the mahogany box in Nancy's things. She donated it when we opened. It contained the only finial known to have survived."

"What about this Hooley woman?"

"The one who was mauled to death? She doesn't leave a lot of footprints on the sands of time. Ditto the one called L. R."

"How do you think the theft was accomplished?"

"We follow the security procedures of any rare book library, but Erica Callow had established a relationship with us, so our guard was down. I was in the stacks, and my assistant took a call from a gentleman asking a stupid question about the external architecture of the building, a question that my assistant could answer simply by getting up and looking out the window."

"Do you think the caller was an accomplice?"

"Erica Callow disappeared in the few seconds we were distracted, so I'd say yes."

"So . . . what's your take?" asked Peter. "Why would the blond scholar in Jimmy Choo's steal a finial and a few pieces of printed material in a box?"

"Maybe she liked the story it tells."

"Of what?"

"A rebellion born in a burst of optimism. A freedom won by great exertion at great expense. An expense that put a government in great debt. A government that decided there was no recourse but to print money."

"Sounds like us."

"Either that," said Ms. Richards, "or she just liked finials."

AFTER PETER LEFT the Society, he crossed Central Park West, so he could walk along the wall of green and not have to wait at every corner for the lights. Then he pulled out his cell phone and called Evangeline.

She was working on a deadline for an article to run in the *Times* travel section: "Honeymoon in New England," off the notes from their last adventure, which had been anything but a honeymoon.

Peter could hear the *click-tick-click-tick-tick* of her keyboard. He told her what he had learned, which wasn't much, but it did prompt a question:

"Your bag lady, was she wearing Jimmy Choo's?"

"Orange Chuck Taylor high-tops. Now I have to finish this piece. Can you entertain yourself until lunch?"

"I have a few other things planned. They don't call it fun city for nothing."

"Good. And Peter, I'm sorry for sticking my nose into this."

"I would have been disappointed if you hadn't."

"Be careful." Evangeline hung up and went back to work. She was writing about the Mount Washington: ". . . the most beautiful hotel in New England, where . . ."

She stopped writing, looked up, looked out the window. *A few things?* What things? A visit to Kathy Flynn, maybe, the red-headed correspondent for MarketSpin.com, once a graduate student at Southwestern Iowa State?

Peter had gone out there to begin a career as a history professor. Evangeline had gone with him. They had been in their twenties. They had lasted two years before they grew bored with the place and each other and Evangeline applied to Columbia School of Journalism. She had always given Peter the benefit of the doubt about Kathy. He insisted that Kathy had *not* slipped off her underpants during office hours in his carrel, at least not until after Evangeline said she was leaving. But she *had* slipped them off.

Still, as Peter said, it had been a long time ago.

So Evangeline got back to writing about the Mount Washington Hotel.

PETER WAS WALKING south, enjoying the day and doing business, too.

He called his office, and Antoine Scarborough answered. "Fallon Antiquaria."

Antoine had begun a history Ph.D. program at Boston College, but he still worked two days a week for Fallon, while Peter's Aunt Bernice, a family fixture for four decades, handled the desk the rest of the time.

"I like the way you answer my phone," said Peter. "Bernice always sounds like . . . Bernice. You sound like—"

"Go ahead, say it. James Earl Jones. I don't mind."

"I was thinking Chris Rock."

"My dad was right. I should've gone to law school and gained some real power. Then I wouldn't have to take this abuse from the man."

They talked like that, because the Fallons and the Scarboroughs went way back. Antoine's father had worked for Fallon & Son Construction. And when Antoine and his father had the same argument that Peter had with his father—law school or a history Ph.D.—Peter had given Antoine a chance to see the practical side of the history business.

"Do you need something," said Antoine, "or can I get back to reading for my three o'clock?"

Peter told Antoine about Gil Walker, Nancy Hooley, a love letter from "L. R.," and a newspaper article about New Emission money. "Check them out. And see what you can find about a place called Woodward Manor."

"Where was that?"

Peter could hear him jotting notes. "It was on the old Bloomingdale Road, aka Broadway. Find out when it was torn down, who lived in it, stuff like that."

"How soon do you need this?"

"Yesterday."

"Like always. What are you on to?"

"Not sure yet. I'll tell you more later."

"Like always. Is it big?"

"Not sure yet."

"Dangerous?"

"Unh . . ."

"Sounds like somebody already chasin' your ass around the Big Apple."

"Let's just say that I had to put on a Yankees hat as a disguise."

"That's like me puttin' on a sheet."

"Just put on your computer and get to work."

At the Sixty-fifth Street transverse road, Peter stopped for a red light.

Cabs roared past on their way over from the East Side. A few people hurried along. A police cruiser rolled past, but the officers didn't even look at him. That was a good sign. The Yankees hat and sunglasses must have done the trick.

The red Stop hand changed to a little walking white pedestrian. As Peter crossed, a voice came behind him. "You seen the papers?"

Peter kept walking. He knew the voice. Joey Berra.

"The *Daily News* got a nice sketch on the front page," said Joey. "Guy in a Yankees hat and sunglasses. Japanese guy and some lady bird-watcher fingered him."

"Was Boris chasing Delancey?" asked Peter.

"Don't know."

"Why did Delancey come to our apartment?"

"Don't know."

"Don't you know anything?"

"I know Boris won't be down for breakfast. But I did a few things that'll make it play like a drug overdose, once they get the toxicology report. So we'll both be in the clear." Joey did not look at Peter. He simply walked ahead, eyes on the sidewalk.

"You killed him? Why? To protect Delancey?"

"I'd like Delancey alive, and it was time to pick off one of those motherfuckers."

"What motherfuckers?" Peter stopped on the sidewalk. "And who's *we*?"

"*We,* like I told you, is the American people. And keep walkin', numb nuts. You don't know who could be watchin'. Neither do I."

Peter gave a look around, then he kept walking.

"Now, listen," said Joey. "I'll give you a chance to get out of this. Delancey led Boris right to your girlfriend's door, but her address died with him. That stupid fuckin' Russian hadn't called his handlers to tell them where he was. I checked the phone."

"His handlers? Russians?"

Joey didn't answer. They were coming up to the light for the eastbound transverse entrance off Leonard Bernstein Way.

"Have you met Arsenault, yet?" asked Joey.

"Lunch, today. At his place."

"Don't be impressed by the fancy-schmantzy."

At the corner, the light was green for the eastbound traffic.

"I'm peelin' off here," said Joey. "Keep walkin' south. If you follow me, I'll stick you with the same needle I used on Boris. You'll drop right in the middle of Central Park West and some fuckin' Arab cabbie'll turn you into Boston roadkill."

Peter took that as fair warning and stopped.

From the middle of the street, Joey said, "Stay in or out. It's up to you. But I can't keep protectin' you and your girlfriend. And don't put on that Yankees hat again. Every time you do, I can hear Joe DiMaggio turnin' over in his grave."

"Yeah . . . Ted Williams turns over, too."

"Nah. He don't turn. He just melts a little."

SO PETER HAD even more to think about as he came into Columbus Circle.

And he was going to have to make a decision. To avoid it, he stopped for a moment at the place where Broadway met Eighth Avenue.

The sun was high, the traffic was swirling, and

the surfaces of the city sparkled like a windblown sea on a running tide.

To the west, the Time Warner Center formed the newest and biggest development in New York. But not for long, because the "City that Never Sleeps" was also the "City that Never Stops . . . Changing." Every newest and biggest gave way to something newer and bigger, sometimes in a year, sometimes in a decade, almost always in a generation.

After the Revolution, New Yorkers rebuilt the ruined city. By 1800, they had extended the tangle of streets another mile north of the Common. And the city fathers decided to bring order to the growth, because twenty-four square miles of island remained between Houston Street and the Harlem River.

So, in 1811, a board of commissioners conceived of a grid, twelve avenues running north to south, a hundred and fifty-five streets running east to west. They prescribed lot sizes, block sizes, street widths. Some people thought the plan was a waste of time because they couldn't imagine the city extending farther north. Some said the grid was about as imaginative as a plowed field. But most knew it was plain prophesy.

The lines were drawn with pen and ink on a map, and then the streets were cut with pick and shovel across the fields and outcroppings, through the grand estates and shanty farms. Only the diagonal of Broadway defied the plan, and each time it crossed an avenue, it forced an open space into the unrelenting density—Union Square, Madison

Square, Herald Square, Times Square, and the traffic circle with the statue of Columbus. Once the building began, it moved north at the rate of more than a mile a decade.

By 1910, the city had reached all the way to the top of the island, so they went back to the bottom to build again. But this time, they built *up,* which was easier in New York than in most cities, because Manhattan Island was really a sliver of granite, solid bedrock to support the biggest buildings that technology could invent or money could buy. And since the city by then had become the center of American commerce, finance, and culture, there was plenty of money to buy the technology, and plenty of competition to be the biggest—and the best—in everything.

So the skyscrapers rose: the New York World Building, eighteen stories in 1890; the Flatiron, twenty-one stories in 1902; the Metropolitan Life Building, with the lantern on the roof, fifty stories in 1909; the Woolworth Building, an amazing sixty stories in 1913; and on up the island, to the Chrysler Building and the Empire State.

And then, another generation went back to the bottom to start again with the World Trade Center in 1970. And then . . .

The offices of MarketSpin were in the Time Warner Center.

That's why Peter Fallon was standing there ruminating about New York.

He had Googled Kathy Flynn the night before. He had debated whether he would send her an e-mail, but he knew it would annoy Evangeline, so he hadn't.

Kathy had e-mailed him instead:

> Peter: Long time, no see. Hope all is well. The ever-observant Austin Arsenault noticed that you and I were at Southwestern Iowa State together. He asked me about you. I told him you were very smart and very handsome. But I didn't tell him everything. A girl should have a few secrets. Any time you want to know about him, contact me. Come by the office. We can talk. Kathy, www.marketspin.com.

So there it was. She was offering him the kind of knowledge that he should have before he ventured into a meeting with Arsenault, even if she was flirting with him.

And business was business. So he sent Kathy a text. "Do you have some time? I'm in Columbus Circle."

He told himself he would wait five minutes for a response, then head downtown.

His phone buzzed as soon as he put it back in his pocket. "Come on up."

HE STEPPED OFF the elevator on the fifteenth floor: MarketSpin.com.

He didn't want to admit it, but he was nervous . . . meeting an old girlfriend . . . an image of his youth that still from time to time danced naked through his imagination.

He remembered one of the first things she ever said to him, about how pleased she was to have such a tall advisor. Pretty cheeky for a master's candidate to be talking like that in her first graduate meeting, walking the fine line between forthright and forward. But her beauty had been enough to make him catch his breath. So he had said, "I'm not *that* tall."

"You're taller than I am," she had answered, "which I like."

She was waiting for him in the reception area.

He was still taller, though the heels she was wearing made her taller, too.

"Peter Fallon"—she offered her hand—"it's been a long time."

His eyes flicked to her left hand. No hardware. Still single.

"As beautiful as ever," he said.

"As? *More*. Come on." She turned and walked ahead of him with that loping stride that he remembered as soon as he saw it.

She was wearing a green silk blouse, black skirt, black stockings. And the black pumps looked pretty expensive. Manolo, maybe, or Jimmy Choo. *Jimmy Choo?* The green complemented her auburn hair and popping red lipstick. The skirt did the same for her ass. The shoes gave her legs all the shape they would ever need.

As she led him past the studio, he glanced onto the set where she had interviewed Arsenault. The control room door was open. Somebody was rewinding a tape of Kathy. Playing and rewinding, playing and rewinding, and each time she said,

"Whether this is the beginning of another stock market crash or just a correction . . . Whether this is the beginning of another . . . Whether this is . . ."

"Pretty weird to be hearing your own voice like that," she said.

"You always had good pipes." He tried not to sound like he was flirting.

She turned and gave him that smile. "Do you mean my legs or my voice?"

"Both." What else could he say? It was the truth.

"Peter, sometimes I wonder why we ever broke up." She took a right into her office. The furnishings were sleek, modern, lots of glass, chrome, leather. And the windows overlooked Lincoln Center.

"You've done well," he said.

"Our network has done well. I'm one of the stars. You could call me one of the Money Honeys, but that term is taken. So call me one of the Bucks Babes, one of the Stock Market Sweeties, one of the Cash Queens."

"Just so long as no one calls you a cash cow."

"That would be sexist, but I'm that, too."

He was glad that she sat behind her desk and not beside him on the sofa.

She leaned forward and put her chin in her hands and fixed him with her gaze. It had been her favorite gesture when she wanted to interest him. "What about you? No wedding band. Married? Divorced?"

"Divorced, soon to be married. To Evangeline."

"Shucks." She rocked in her chair and said, "Speaking of marriage, I hear you're getting in to bed with Mr. Triple A."

"Maybe. What's it like?"

"I wouldn't know. But you won't be the first. What has he said to you?"

"He's asked me to save America."

She laughed. "He asks everyone that. He asked me when he pitched the interview for his Paul Revere Foundation."

"So he's the messiah type."

"More like the narcissistic personality disorder type . . . pervasive pattern of grandiosity, need for admiration, lack of empathy, all the usuals."

"Does this mean I *won't* be saving America?"

"Hard to say. Men like that can sometimes work miracles. Who ever thought he'd push this New Emission Bond business all the way to the Supreme Court?"

Peter didn't say much to that. He didn't know enough yet. So he tried a lame joke: "New Emission . . . do I have to change my pajamas afterward?"

"Ha-ha. Still the smart-ass. But what do you think? Pretty interesting."

Peter didn't know what to think, except that she wasn't really offering much. Maybe she was just trying to find out what *he* knew. He shrugged and said, "Whatever . . . the Chinese crisis has him all upset."

"It should," she said. "They're not going to buy at tomorrow's T-bill auction, so the Dow was down three hundred yesterday. And it's down"—she glanced at her computer—"another fifty today. It looks like it's hitting some technical resistance, but—"

"Why the obsession with China?"

"They hold over a trillion dollars worth of our twelve-trillion-dollar debt."

"Trillion? A thousand billion?"

"With a capital T. We buy everything from China, from baseball bats to computer parts. They take our dollars, then they buy our debt, so that we'll have the cheap credit to buy more of their cheap goods, so they can take more of our dollars, so . . ."

"Economic symbiosis," he said.

"More like the cycle of condensation to evaporation to rain. They have to stay in business with us because if we go down, their system dries up. But if we keep printing money, flooding the market in order to fight a recession or fund our pet projects or build a missile defense system to protect us from a Chinese attack that will never come, the dollar loses too much value against world currencies—"

"And the Chinese have to take a hard look at whether they want to keep buying?"

"Right. The immediate crisis comes as the Chinese make a political point by sitting out the auction tomorrow. And of course, the Supreme Court delivers their decision on the New Emission Bonds the day after tomorrow."

"How does one affect the other?"

"Let Avid Austin tell you."

"I guess this will be an interesting lunch, then," said Peter.

Kathy leaned forward on her elbows. "Since you're busy for lunch, how about having drinks with me later?"

"I'd love to, but—"

"I'm not coming on to you, Peter. Evangeline would find me and kill me."

He laughed. "You got that right."

"But come to the Harvard Club. Five o'clock. I'm meeting Arsenault's accountant. Deep background."

"On what?"

"Stay tuned." She stood. They were done.

They shook hands. He considered giving her a hug but thought better of it. At the very least, he didn't want Evangeline smelling someone else's perfume on his lapel. That would mean way too much explaining.

THE SAN REMO on Central Park West: famous for the movie stars, fashion designers, and business celebrities who lived there, famous for the silhouette of two graceful towers rising ten stories above the main structure, famous as the place where the Ghostbusters fought the Stay Puft Marshmallow Man.

Austin Arsenault lived in the south tower.

"How do you want to work this?" Evangeline said as the elevator doors closed.

"By pushing the button?" said Peter.

"How do you want to work it with Arsenault? Sometimes you do the analysis and I do the emotional context. Sometimes, you pick up on the emotions while I'm the cold-eyed one."

It was true, he thought. They really did complement each other, even in the wardrobes: he was wearing his blue blazer with a clean shirt and yellow tie. She had put on a sleeveless form-fitting yellow jersey with a matching sweater, blue slacks, pearl earrings, pearl necklace. Complementary, whether they'd planned it or not.

He said, "How about, you try to figure out what's going on below the surface—"

"Okay. And you'll—"

"I'll just be as superficial as usual."

The elevator stopped and the door popped open.

A butler greeted them in striped trousers and morning coat. He led them through an inner foyer, past a spectacular staircase that led up to the bedrooms, down a hallway to the living room.

Windows faced east across Central Park and south toward Midtown, but heavy drapes forced the eye from the view to the furnishings—the wing chairs, the antique mahogany side tables, the Oriental carpet, the paintings on the wall, including one that looked like an original Renoir.

Arsenault rose from a chair by the fireplace. "Mr. Fallon and Ms. Carrington. The man and woman of the hour."

He seemed even sleeker in person, thought Evangeline. Silvered hair, smooth pink skin, double-breasted blue blazer, ascot. As he shook her hand, she felt the male energy, the confidence, the *smooth*, as she liked to call it.

Peter didn't. He was looking at the monogram on the blazer. New York Yacht Club? And how much money did he spend for the Renoir? And why was he at home in the middle of the day, in the middle of a financial crisis?

Then another guy got up to greet them, a guy in a gray suit.

Evangeline shook his clammy hand, felt less energy, but she felt something. Doggedness? Relentlessness? The stooped posture said this one wasn't afraid to hunch over a desk for as long as it took to get a job done. The widow's peak showed he would comb his hair as he always had, male-pattern baldness be damned. The thin line of perspiration across his upper lip suggested he was a detail-sweater, even in the air-conditioned splendor of Arsenault's co-op.

Who did he remind her of? *Nixon.* She had once shaken hands with Nixon, when he was living in New York after his exile: clammy hand, sweating, slouching a bit, and—

"This is Owen T. Magee, my attorney," said Arsenault.

"Mr. Magee," Peter offered his hand.

"Owen *T.* Magee," said Arsenault. "Owen says the 'T' that rhymes with 'Magee' gives his name a meter that plays like a song in people's heads."

Magee laughed as if he didn't especially like Austin's joke. "Either that or I give them my card." He pulled one out and offered it to Peter: *OWEN T. MAGEE, MAGEE & MAGEE, ESTATES, TRUSTS, AND TAXES, FLATIRON BUILDING, 175 FIFTH AVENUE, NEW YORK.*

"What the card doesn't mention," added Arsenault, "is a reputation for probity and discretion, fanatical attention to detail, glacial calm in the presence of the IRS, and stoic refusal to cede a nickel of a client's money without a fight."

"I also hear that he's suing the government on your behalf," said Peter.

"I told you he was thorough," Arsenault said to Magee. "Now then, we have a very nice lunch, but first"—he snapped his fingers, and the butler came in with a tray, four glasses of white wine—"Chassagne-Montrachet 2006. I always like a good wine when I show off my money collection."

"Money collection?" said Peter.

"I thought people kept their money collections in banks," said Evangeline.

"I'm talking about money as art, Ms. Carrington. Money as history. Money as the physical expression of our national aspiration."

He led them down the hall to the library. The heavy drapes were drawn tight, blocking the view, darkening the room, muffling the voices. He had installed UV-filtering glass. "But I still keep the illumination low to protect the treasures."

He flipped the switches by the door. Spotlights hit framed certificates on the walls, items in glass cases, notebooks on the shelves.

Peter and Evangeline scanned the room but said nothing.

Arsenault, however, liked to talk about himself. "I may be the world's most prominent scripophilist, which means I collect old money—stock certificates, bonds, currency—not for their face value but for their historic and artistic importance."

And in the next few minutes, Arsenault introduced them to a new way of seeing American history: not as a string of events or inventions or political decisions, but as a series of financial investments in the future. It was all there: a 1782 French debit note for 500,000 livres, signed by Benjamin Franklin in Paris . . . an 1893 share of General Electric, the only stock of the original Dow Thirty still trading today . . .

a 9½ percent Enron bond, face value $10,000, worth a bit more than three hundred bucks to a collector.

"The march of a great nation," said Arsenault, "mirrored in the instruments of capitalism . . . the expansions, the collapses, the dreamers, the scoundrels, the Bulls charging from one coast to the other, the hibernating Bears living off their belly fat—"

"Or someone else's," said Owen T. Magee.

"Always better to live off someone else's belly fat," said Peter.

"A lesson that brokers and lawyers learned early," cracked Evangeline.

Arsenault gave her a look. "Watch out for her, Owen T. She's the sarcastic one."

Evangeline sipped her wine. "Peter can be sarcastic, too. We're a tag team."

"Allow me to impress the sarcasm right out of you." Arsenault pulled down a leather-backed ring binder with the dates 1775–1783 on the spine. He laid it on a table and flipped it open to reveal archive-quality plastic sleeves containing bills, bonds, certificates, and primitive scrip. "Some people collect swords and pistols from the Revolution, but these were the *real* weapons of American independence."

He unsnapped the binder and took out one of the sleeves.

Inside was a bearer bond, issued in 1780. It did not look like much, about half the size of a modern dollar bill, rudely printed on thin paper.

"Picture a fledgling nation at war, a nation with no industry, no trade, a treasury in name only. They start printing money, but there's nothing to back it up. No gold, no revenue, no promise of taxation. So it inflates faster than a dead horse in the hot sun. By 1780, a man needs forty dollars to buy what he bought with a buck in 1776. So Congress tries to get all that old currency off the market and replace it with a fresh issue."

"The New Emission Bonds," said Peter.

"We call them bonds today," said Arsenault, "because in essence, that's what they were. They had fixed rates of interest and dates of maturity."

"But in Hamilton's time," said Owen T. Magee, "the term 'bond' referred specifically to bail and to notes put up by men handling public money."

"Hence the term New Emission Money. But you can call them bonds." Arsenault slipped one from its sleeve and placed it on the table. Then he swung a magnifying lamp over it and invited them to have a look.

Across the top were the words "State of New York," the number of the bill, handwritten by the clerk who had sold it, and the words, "The Possessor of this Bill shall be paid One Hundred Spanish Milled Dollars by the Thirty-first Day of December One Thousand Seven Hundred and Eighty-five, with INTEREST in like money at the rate of five per centum per Annum, by the State of New York." At the bottom, in handwriting as graceful as calligraphy, an ancient signature attested to the purchase.

"Each state issued bonds as needed," said Arsenault, "but here's the cool part—"

With tweezers, he turned the bond over to reveal more engraving, the words "The United States" in black ink, blocked with red, and this: "The UNITED STATES ensure the payment of the within BILL and will draw Bills of Exchange for the interest annually, if demanded, according to the Resolution of CONGRESS of the 18th of March, 1780."

"The bonds were backed," said Owen T. Magee, "by the full faith and credit of the United States government."

"A government operating under the Articles of Confederation. Look here"—Arsenault picked up the bond and held it above the light, to show them the watermark, the word "Confed—eration," in two lines.

"And you're suing the government to collect on these bonds?" said Peter.

"Under Article Six of the Constitution," said Owen T., "which says that even the debts of the Confederation Congress will be honored by the new government."

"If we win on all counts," said Arsenault, "one hundred dollars from 1780 will render seven-point-four million. And I have two of these bonds."

Peter whistled softly.

Arsenault turned to Evangeline. "He's impressed. What about you?"

"You had me at Chassagne-Montrachet."

Arsenault looked at her, as if deciding whether to be annoyed or amused. He chose amused. "Good answer."

"Why are these bonds still uncashed?" asked Peter.

"Because Hamilton settled most federal obligations when he recapitalized the debts of the Revolution," said Owen T. Magee. "But the New Emission Bonds had been issued by the states, and they issued them at different times, for different purposes and different funds, which caused confusion and not a little controversy."

"So some states honored the bonds," said Arsenault, "but some only honored them if you lived in the state. Some, like Rhode Island, wouldn't honor any. That's one of the reasons that the other states called it *Rogue* Island."

The lawyer leaned close, so that the perspiration on his upper lip glistened politely in the light from the magnifying lamp. "Some states sent the bondholders to the federal government for redemption. And the feds sent them back to the states."

"A literal case of buck-passing." Arsenault returned the bond to its envelope. "Nevertheless, Hamilton called these bonds a debt of honor in his *Report on Public Credit*. But he put off the fight over them to win other points in 1790. When he brought up the subject again in 1796, Congress had other things to do. So the bonds fell between the cracks. Messy. Very messy."

"Why hasn't anybody fought this case before?" asked Evangeline.

"People have. But the government always stonewalls, saying that they determine who can sue them and who can't."

"Sovereign immunity?" said Peter.

"Correct," said Arsenault. "But none of them ever had Owen T. Magee."

The lawyer flashed a quick smile. Nixonian, thought Evangeline.

"We believe that these bonds have a prior claim on the credit of the United States," said Owen T. Magee. "While we lost in the lower courts, we have an originalist Supreme Court, and my argument about Article Six struck a note with them. So, too, did our position on compound interest."

"Yes," said Arsenault. "While the bonds have five-year maturities, the bearers were denied the opportunity to reinvest and hence lost the use of the money for all those years. So the interest should be compounded."

"It's the same position that the IRS takes when they penalize you," added Magee. "We expect that when the decision is rendered on Friday, we will win."

"Which brings us," said Austin Arsenault, "to the subject of yourself . . . or yourselves. We want you to help us find as many of these bonds as possible."

And luncheon was served.

SO THEY SAT in the dining room, in shafts of sunlight that reflected off the mirrored walls. They ate Dover sole flown in from Arsenault's English supplier and washed it down with more Chassagne-Montrachet '06.

Peter thought the mirrors were appropriate, considering what Kathy Flynn had said about Arsenault. But there was something genuine about his enthusiasm. Owning two bonds worth seven and a half million dollars each would make anyone enthusiastic.

Evangeline tasted the fish and said it was as good as the wine.

Arsenault accepted the compliment as if he had caught and cooked it himself.

Peter let the small talk fade, then he dove back in. "So, you want me to find as many bonds as possible? Aren't there a lot of other people looking for them, too?"

"Most of the bonds are held by institutions like your Massachusetts Historical Society," said Owen T. Magee. "They've kept them for their historical value. Until our suit, these bonds retailed as historical paper for fifteen hundred to three thousand apiece. But everything that's on the market has been snapped up."

"Then why are we here?" asked Evangeline.

"Or more directly," asked Peter, "why didn't you contact me earlier?"

"For starters"—Arsenault took a taste of fish—"New Yorkers usually don't turn to Boston for help. We have a lot of good rare document people right here in the city."

"But I'm the best at it," said Peter.

"We were working with Oscar Delancey," said Owen T. Magee. "How could we not, with a great old New York name like that?"

"Oscar Delancey is Jewish," said Peter. "His ancestors came from Poland three generations ago. They just thought it was a good name if you wanted to get by in the big town. Have either of you seen him recently, by the way?"

Arsenault and Magee exchanged glances.

Peter and Evangeline did, too.

"Wherever he is or whatever he's up to," said Arsenault, "he's not giving us much help at the moment, which means he's doing America a disservice"—Arsenault set down his knife and fork—"because we aren't in this for the money."

"Not in it for the money?" said Evangeline, with the I-don't-believe-a-word-you're-saying deadpan that Peter loved.

"Then why *are* you in it?" asked Peter.

"I believe I told you," said Arsenault. "To save America."

"How," said Evangeline, still deadpanning, "are you going to do *that*?"

Arsenault laughed, though it did not sound genuine. It was more like one of the repertoire of sounds that a man of stature makes to express an opinion without words. This one sounded—what—amused? Condescending? Condescendingly amused? "By spreading the alarm about the deficit, of course. What do you think the Paul Revere Foundation has been doing?"

"Hamilton spoke of a national debt being a national asset, if properly managed," said Owen T. Magee. "We stopped managing our debt in the Reagan years."

"I thought all you rich Wall Street types were Republicans," said Evangeline, "and you're criticizing the rightie Jesus?"

"History will be kind to Reagan," said Owen T. Magee. "He pulled us out of a recession and raised the standard of living for a generation. The supply-siders told him he could cut taxes and increase military spending and with a few bumps along the way, we'd still have thirty years of prosperity."

"He only got twenty-eight," said Peter.

"In American politics, twenty-eight years is like an ice age, a temperate period, and a century of global warming, too. By the 2008 meltdown, it was somebody else's problem. Now our grandchildren are up to their eyeballs in debt before they're born. You heard me say all this on CNBC yesterday. And I'm told that you heard Kathy Flynn's condensation-to-evaporation-to-rain speech this morning."

What Peter heard was the sound of Evangeline's fork hitting the plate. Though the Dover sole was nicely filleted, he suddenly felt as if he had a bone in his throat.

He saw the eyes of Arsenault and Magee shifting to Evangeline, then to her fork.

So he made only the briefest eye contact with her. A clanging fork, a tightening of her features . . . but she was not the sort to show anything to outsiders. She simply put her fork back to work on the fish and acted as though it had just slipped from her hand.

After another mouthful, she recovered and said, "Most people aren't paying attention to stuff like this."

"True," said Arsenault. "They're too busy voting for the next American Idol. We need to shock them, wake them up with a tangible symbol of the national debt."

"The two bonds."

"Not two bonds," said Arsenault. "A *box* of bonds."

"A box?" said Peter. "Nobody said anything about a box of bonds."

"A box of two hundred," said Arsenault, "worth twenty thousand dollars in 1780, now worth one-point-four billion. The unretired debt of the American Revolution. What better symbol could there be of the consequences of kicking your troubles down the road? How many stories would that spawn on cable news, in newspapers, in books?"

"And of course, you're planning to redeem them," said Peter.

"If we find them, we cash one a week, and we keep the story going for years," said Owen T. Magee.

"That's what it's going to take," said Arsenault, "to get people thinking."

"To save America from itself," said Owen T. Magee.

Evangeline said, "If you really cared about that, you wouldn't cash them at all."

"A few years ago," said Arsenault, "hitting the government for a bill for one-point-four billion would have seemed excessive. Now, we're bankrupt anyway. So what's the difference?"

"So"—Peter looked from Arsenault to Magee—"you want me to find a box of bonds? In twenty-eight square miles of Manhattan? Any idea of where I start?"

Owen T. Magee pulled a sheet of paper from the briefcase on the floor beside his chair. "Before we go further, a signature."

"Signature?"

"We're about to offer you sensitive information.

So . . . a contract to outline your responsibilities, including a nondisclosure agreement."

"Nondisclosure? Of what?"

"Of your activities. You will use your skills and the information we've gathered to find the bonds, take your pay, and stay out of the press."

"So Kathy Flynn doesn't count as a member of the Fourth Estate?" said Evangeline.

Arsenault gave her that smile again. It was more like looking down his nose. "Don't you worry about Kathy."

Peter almost laughed. He knew that Evangeline was worrying more about Kathy than the box of bonds. He picked up the contract and looked at it briefly. "Usually, if I go after something for a client, it's a partnership. I get half, once we broker the sale."

"Or you take a thousand dollars a day and expenses." Owen T. Magee offered the pen. "We've researched your fees."

Peter began to read the contract.

"Don't worry," said Magee. "It's taken from the standard agreement on your own Web site, with the nondisclosure clause and a few other things added."

Evangeline threw her napkin onto the plate. "Don't do it, Peter."

He knew she was still angry about the other things, but she was right. He put down the contract. "If I take on a client, I reserve the right to negotiate any fee."

"So what do you want?" asked Arsenault.

"Fifty percent of what I find. As I said, I'm the best."

"Seven hundred million? Not likely."

Evangeline looked around at the furnishings and the art. And she knew exactly what to say to Peter. "Think of the treasures you could save with that kind of money."

"True," said Peter. "Unless the Supreme Court ruling goes aganst the bondholders. Then this whole thing falls apart." He stood, walked around the table, and slid out Evangeline's chair. "I'm interested, gentlemen. I'll read the contract. You reconsider your offer."

"You have until four o'clock to accept," said Owen T. Magee.

"Otherwise," said Arsenault, "we may have to withdraw protection."

"Protection?" Peter didn't like the sound of that. "From whom?"

"The possibility of making one-point-four billion dollars in an afternoon tends to bring out all sorts of people."

"Who's protecting us? Joey Berra?"

"I have absolutely no idea who that is," said Owen T. Magee.

Yeah, thought Evangeline, and Nixon didn't know anything about Watergate.

"If we don't hear from you by four," said Owen T. Magee, "watch the four thirty news. The police may learn the identity of the man in the Yankees hat depicted on the cover of today's tabloids. We see a distinct resemblance to you, Mr. Fallon."

* * *

THE RIDE DOWN the elevator was passed in silence.

So was the walk back to Evangeline's apartment. And the passage through the foyer didn't generate the usual jokes with Jackie.

In the apartment, Evangeline went into the bedroom and slammed the door.

So Peter poured a cup of coffee and sat down to read his e-mails.

There was one from Antoine, with an attachment. He opened it immediately, read it, then went to the door of her bedroom and said, "I'm sorry, Evangeline."

"I'm being pissed at you, Peter. Come back later."

He waited a moment and said, "It was business. She offered information about Arsenault. I had to have it. Business is business."

She pulled open the door and glared at him. Her eyes weren't puffy. She hadn't been crying. That wasn't her style. "Did it help?"

"Seeing her?"

"No. The information. Did it help this business?"

"No, but Antoine did. Let me show you." He walked back to the computer.

She stood in the doorway a moment, then she decided that she had made her point. "All right. What do we have?"

"The site of Zabar's, as it looked in 1893."

On the screen was a picture of an ancient wood-frame house with pillars, cupola, and tall oak tree shading the dormers. There was trash strewn about. A scruffy dog was looking at the camera. And the headline: OLD DAGGETT TAVERN TO BE TORN DOWN.

The article described the growth of the Upper West Side, and the plans for the Broadway block between Eightieth and Eighty-first. The owner had hired a company called Riley Wrecking.

"You really think this house is important?" she asked.

"Someone called L. R. writes a letter from this house to Gil Walker, the guy who ends up with the finial, about a mahogany box containing the blessings of freedom. And his girlfriend is mauled to death outside this house a few weeks after he dies."

Evangeline told Peter about the picture the bag lady showed to Delancey. "He said it was of an old house on the West Side . . . a fancy estate in Washington's time, an eyesore in Lincoln's, torn down in Teddy Roosevelt's."

"Could be the same one," said Peter. "I think I'll have Antoine look into Riley Wrecking."

"I think you should still be trying to find Delancey . . . or the bag lady."

"They'll find us, if they want to."

"If they're alive, you mean." Evangeline went into the kitchen and poured herself a cup of coffee.

Peter said, "I also don't think she's a bag lady. Based on what the Historical Society librarian told me, she's probably tall, blond, and has a taste for Jimmy Choo."

"The bag lady was stooped over."

"It could have been an act."

"But she wasn't blond."

"It could have been a wig."

Evangeline came in and sat at the table next to him. "She might even have been covering red hair."

"Red hair as in Kathy Flynn?"

"Mmm-hmm." Evangeline looked into her cup.

"Come to think of it, Kathy *is* tall, and she wears Jimmy Choo's."

"So you looked at her legs?"

"I looked at her shoes . . . and her legs."

"If I catch you looking at her ass, I'll close the bedroom door and lock it"—Evangeline brought her lips close to his ear—"on your dick."

"How about, I won't go near her unless you're with me?"

"Can I bring my gun?"

"Carrying concealed gun without a license is illegal in New York City. Otherwise, I might be carrying myself right now."

He typed a message to Antoine, telling him to research Riley Wrecking, which according to the old newspaper article, operated out of the livery stable at Eleventh Avenue and Forty-third Street.

She looked over his shoulder. "The old Hell's Kitchen neighborhood."

EIGHT

July 1893

Timothy Riley once asked his father how Hell's Kitchen got its name.

His father said that no one quite knew, but there were plenty of stories.

Some claimed that a newspaperman coined the term for a tenement on Fifty-fourth Street. Others believed that two cops on a bad corner came up with it. A few even credited Davy Crockett, who once said that the Irish he had met across America were all fine upstanding folk, except for the Irish of New York, who acted as if they all ate their dinner in Hell's Kitchen.

The truth was that after a walk from Thirty-fourth Street to Fifty-ninth, anywhere between Eighth Avenue and the river, past the rat-infested tenements and shanties, past the warehouses and train yards, the docks and slaughterhouses, the dram shops and clip joints and gang hangouts where a hundred crimes were planned or committed every day, a Hindu from Calcutta could have come up with the name.

And yes, Hell's Kitchen was mostly Irish, but Italian and German immigrants lived there, too. So did a few Jews. Even the Negroes had their corners.

And the worst of them engaged regularly in the robberies, beatings, riots, extortions, turf wars, and general troublemaking that made Hell's Kitchen what it was. But most who lived there lived lawfully and worked hard and could not afford to live anyplace better.

Timothy Riley lived with his family on the top floor of a tenement on Forty-eighth Street, half a block from the Ninth Avenue El.

His mother, Mary, kept house and took in sewing.

His father, Richard, known as Six-Pound Dick, ran a salvage company called Riley Wrecking, comprised of a wagon, two horses, and a beer-drinking brother-in-law.

Timothy shared a bed with his brother, Eddie, who had lost a foot to a moving train on Eleventh Avenue and now spent most of his time playing the harmonica and looking out the window.

They were Irish twins, siblings born within a year to Irish Catholic parents who were supposedly too ignorant—or too religious—to protect themselves from their own urges. Timothy was a month shy of his fourteenth birthday. Eddie had just turned thirteen.

And every morning, the Ninth Avenue El woke them up.

To Timothy, a track that ran two stories above the street, all the way from the tip of the island to the top, was not one of the wonders of the age, as it had been to his father, but a necessary thing that blocked the sun and spread coal smoke and noise every time a train passed.

And the tenement in which he awoke was not a horrible place where families of five or six lived in two tiny rooms and a kitchen, where three outhouses and a single water spigot served a whole building, where a single case of typhoid could wipe out a whole family and then a whole block. It was home.

And when he was at home, Timothy liked to read. He did not reveal this to friends, since it might make him appear weak, and in Hell's Kitchen, appearing weak was worse than being weak. But every Thursday, he would go down to the New York

Society Library, take out as many books as he could, bring them home, and read beside the front window. Whether he read Sir Walter Scott or Ned Buntline or Shakespeare, he would always be carried to another world.

But he also read the newspapers, to know what was happening in his own world. So he knew about the great panic.

For twenty years, Americans had been building railroads. They had built them across every state and into every city, and then into every small town, farm town, mill town, and mining town from Maine to California. They had built and built until one day, they had built too much. There were simply too many railroads.

So one of them went broke, the Pennsylvania and Reading. "And like a train whistle echoing across the prairie," the paper said, "the warning rolled from coast to coast. The boom was over. The bubble had burst." Depositors rushed their banks, investors sold their stocks, Europeans redeemed their dollars for American gold.

They called it the Panic of 1893.

Times got tough, then tougher.

That was the story on Wall Street and all over America.

But in Hell's Kitchen, New York, Timothy Riley hardly noticed, because in Hell's Kitchen, New York, times were always tough, and the facts of a boy's existence were usually simple, sometimes stark.

If Timothy's life had any complication, it was this: he awoke every morning with a dick as stiff as the handle of a ball-peen hammer. He had heard enough talk among his friends and watched enough dogs doing the dance in the street to know what this was all about. And it was not unpleasant, but it could be embarrassing, especially if it happened during the day, or whenever he thought about Doreen Walsh, the neighbor girl whose chest had recently expanded so nicely. And sometimes, it even happened at Mass, because Doreen sat in the next pew, where Timothy's mind might easily wander into what the priests called an occasion of sin.

But every Sunday, Timothy and his family dressed in their best and walked up to Fifty-first Street, to Sacred Heart Church, the finest building that any of them had ever been allowed to enter through the front door . . . without paying an admission.

The church, said the boy's father, was where the rich and the common mingled as nothing more than men, for the Lord saw little difference between them.

THE PEOPLE OF Hell's Kitchen, however, saw plenty of difference between themselves and the Rileys, because Dick Riley had a reputation. He had earned it five years earlier, when a gang set themselves up around Forty-sixth Street and Ninth Avenue just as he was setting himself up in business.

The leader of the gang, a scrawny little miscreant by the name of Slick McGillicuddy, told Dick Riley that it would be in his best interest to pay protection money to the Irish Niners, or the Niners would make life miserable for the Riley family.

The father later told his son that he considered

going to Tammany Hall for help but decided instead that a man should look such a problem straight in the eye. So he told Slick McGillicuddy to go to hell.

The next morning, Dick Riley went down to the livery stable and found his horses dead in their stalls, their throats cut and a river of blood flowing out onto the street.

He swallowed down his anger because, as he told his son, anger was the enemy of a clear head. Then he took the six-pound sledge from the back of his wagon, lay it over his shoulder, and set out as if he were simply walking to work. He followed the Eleventh Avenue railroad tracks to Forty-sixth Street, then he turned east and went two blocks along the row of tenements, until he came to an alley protected by a gate.

On the other side of the gate, in a little dooryard, half a dozen Irish Niners were playing poker. The pot in the middle of the table was piled high with coins and bills. A whiskey bottle stood next to the pot. It looked as if they had been playing all night.

At the squeak of the gate, Slick McGillicuddy glanced up from his cards, and a six-pound hammer struck him square in the face. Teeth, blood, and Slick himself went flying.

No one knew how many times Dick Riley swung his hammer that morning, but when he was done, all the Irish Niners lay like corpses, which some of them were. Then Dick Riley swept the poker money into his hat as payment for his horses and took a drink from the bottle. He swung the hammer one more time to smash the table . . . and left.

Word of his deed traveled quickly through Hell's Kitchen. Men spoke of it in awestruck tones. Who would be so brave—or so insane—as to take on a gang, not with a gun or a gang of his own, but with a six-pound hammer, a clumsy weapon when compared to a good ax handle, but capable of the kind of damage that could make myth out of simple mayhem?

The Irish Niners were finished. No self-respecting gang could survive the beating that Dick Riley gave them. And the police didn't much care, so long as it was only a few gangsters who took the beating. And the other Hell's Kitchen gangs actually appreciated the favor that Riley had done them, especially since he showed no interest whatsoever in making any trouble whatsoever for anyone else on any side of the law.

People left Dick Riley and his family well alone after that, except to give him his nickname: Six-Pound Dick. As someone said, a man with balls that big surely must have a six-pound dick between 'em.

ii.

The hot morning of July 3 found Six-Pound Dick and Timothy taking the Riley Wrecking wagon north on Ninth Avenue.

The boy was now five foot seven, an inch taller than his father, so it was time for him to spend a summer building his muscle in the family business. For his first day on the job, he wore a T-shirt, new denim overalls so stiff that they chafed between his legs, and a black visored baseball cap like those worn by the New York Giants, his favorite team.

Winter and summer, Six-Pound Dick wore hob-nailed boots, twill trousers held up with heavy sus-penders, a red union suit, and a black derby.

They were plainly father and son. In the close-set eyes and the quick smile and the cock of the head, the boy resembled the man. And as they went, the man did the fatherly job of explaining all that passed.

They traveled under the El he said, "Because there's good shade and less traffic."

And whenever ladies crossed in front of their wagon, the father lifted his derby. "Always tip your hat to a lady," he told his son. "It's good manners. And tip your hat when you pass a church. It's good for the soul. And show respect to every man, until he proves he don't deserve it."

At Fifty-ninth Street, the names of the avenues changed. Eighth became Central Park West. Ninth became Columbus. Tenth became Amsterdam. Elev-enth became West End. The father explained that real estate men were hoping to give the neighbor-hood a bit of a shine by changing the names. "It's a fine idea, but there's still too many old farms and shanties mixed in with the fancy new places, and changin' the names won't keep the stockyards on Sixtieth from stinkin'."

At Seventy-second, the Riley wagon turned onto Broadway, which followed the path of the old Bloomingdale Road. The city had widened and improved the road just after the Civil War but had only recently gotten around to paving it, so the macadam ended somewhere in the Nineties, where a dust cloud marked the work.

The Rileys had come to tear down a house. They had put in a bid and were hired by the man who had bought the block. Tear down a house, salvage the good parts, and leave the lot ready for construction. Dick Riley had done it dozens of times.

But this house was one of the last remnants of old New York. It had been known as Woodward Manor, seat of a famous Tory family. It had later become the Daggett Tavern. And it had ended its life as a flophouse for day laborers.

But there was still something dignified about the old place, thought the boy. Perhaps it was the pillared front porch . . . or the ancient oak that shaded the roof . . . or the carriage drive that still formed a grand semicircle off of Broadway. Or was it the way the house just sat there staring out at a world changing so rapidly around it?

"Washington ate here," said the father.

"Then how come we're tearin' it down?"

"Because New York is growin'. Besides, after the squire fed Washington, he fed the British officers *chasin'* Washington." The father pulled the brake and jumped off the wagon. "That makes the tearin' down easier."

"How come you don't like the British, Pa?"

"I have no argument with your dagoes or your darkies, and Jews is hard businessmen, just like the Irish, so we understand each other. But the Brits"—Six-Pound Dick gave a shudder—"they sent my father scurryin' for America over forty years ago. So you just might say they killed him."

"But he died with the Irish Sixty-ninth at Fredericksburg."

"He left Ireland on account of rotten potatoes and rotten British landlords. It's just good for us that he come here. And now that we give our blood for this country and our sweat for this city, it's time we got somethin' back."

"Yes, sir."

"So my son'll work with his head, not his hands." The father went to the rear of the wagon and pulled out a tool belt and strapped it on. "Just do me one favor. When you read, read about money. Enough with history and novels. George Washington and Will Shakespeare and all them fellers had a fine run when they was alive, but we're in modern times now. And a boy with a good head can go far, so long as he don't fill it with silly notions. Besides, Shakespeare was British."

"Yes, sir." The boy climbed down.

"Now then"—the father gave him a pinch bar—"good head or not, let it never be said that a son of mine don't know how to work with his hands. If you can work with your hands, you'll never go hungry."

AS SOON AS the father removed the padlock and opened the front door of the old house, the boy smelled must, stale beer, and dead animals.

Inside, it was dark and clammy. A center hallway led to French doors at the back. Beyond was a patch of grass, a few fallen-down outbuildings, and a stretch of new row houses on West End, blocking what must once have been a fine view of the Hudson.

"Before the Revolution," said the father, "this spread covered a hundred acres."

"In New York?"

"Ain't nothin' compared to the Apthorp spread. We took their house down on Ninety-first last year. They owned *two* hundred acres. But that was back when New York had twenty-five thousand folks. Now there's two and a half million." The father cocked an eye at his son. "That's an increase *times what*?"

"A hundred, sir."

"See that? A fine head for figures you've got."

The boy did not tell his father how easily the math came to him. He liked his father's praise and did nothing to deflect it.

"Get out your notebook and write it down to take these French doors," said the father. "I know an old Jew who's lookin' for a set, and these are as fine as any I've seen."

In every dusty room, there were things to salvage—doors, moldings, bits of furniture that might bring a price, and things to avoid—rotting food, empty whiskey bottles, clumps of old newspapers that squatters had used for bedding. The boy made notes and followed his father from the hallway through the dining room into a parlor that had become a taproom. They went up the grand staircase, surveyed the second floor, then took a smaller staircase to the attic and heat so strong that the boy could smell the century-old dust baking into the floorboards and rafters.

The father looked around at the four roughed-in rooms. "Servants would have lived up here. Cold in the winter, hot in the summer."

The boy pointed to the trapdoor and the spring-loaded ladder attached to the ceiling. "What's up there?"

"What they call a cupola, a little glassed-in turret." The father pulled down the ladder and dropped the trapdoor. Light flooded the ancient attic. "Let's have a look."

As the boy climbed, a startled pigeon exploded from the rafters, flapped around, found a missing pane of glass, and was gone. The boy, as startled as the pigeon, took a breath, then levered himself up into the little space, only to be startled again by the view.

"There it is." The father popped up behind him. "The city of dreams."

It lay in a thick haze of July heat, like an army uniformed in redbrick and brownstone, its forces massed below Fifty-ninth Street, but its columns advancing quickly up the avenues of the West Side.

"Men come here from all over world, son, just for a chance. And the city don't ask where you was born or what you done in the old country. It just says 'Be smart and work hard and you'll be rewarded.'"

"We work hard, don't we, Pa?"

"We do for certain."

"Is Hell's Kitchen our reward?"

"It's a roof over your head and food on your table and a family who loves you in a parish that cares. That's some reward, if you ask me. So's a view like this."

From up here, the streets looked as if they had been drawn with a straight edge, and the land west of Central Park was filling fast with apartments, hotels, row houses. But vegetable patches still grew behind tar paper shanties, and clumps of trees still caught the sunlight, as if to remind New Yorkers of what once had been.

The boy tried to pick out some of the landmarks to the south. The twin steeples of St. Patrick's rose as clear as the cross of Christ. Other steeples etched the horizon, too. From a distance, New York seemed a much holier place than it was. But the steeples were disappearing behind new buildings like the Savoy Hotel, which towered twelve whole stories above Fifty-ninth Street. And soon, said the father, there would be skyscrapers of forty, fifty, even sixty stories. But the boy found that hard to imagine.

So he turned and looked past the new All Angels Church on West End, out over the stockyards and steaming train yards, out to the river itself, to the hundreds of boats skittering along, their smokestacks belching exhaust that formed what his father called "the great cloud of commerce that rains money like water on the city of New York."

Then he looked north, past Morningside Heights and the orchards of the old Bloomingdale Insane Asylum, up toward the rising new row houses of Harlem. And somewhere beyond lay the Polo Grounds, home of his beloved Giants.

When he turned east, an owl stared up at him from a hole in the side of the old oak, but the boy barely noticed. His eye went to a train puffing smoke along the Ninth Avenue El, then to an apartment building on Central Park West. At its opening nine years earlier, people had nicknamed it the Dakota, because it stood so far from the city that it might as well have been *in* Dakota. Now a hotel called the Majestic would soon block its view to the south. And another grand structure was rising to the north.

But its easterly view reached out over the green expanse of the park itself. Somewhere beyond lay Fifth Avenue and the fabled row of rich men's mansions, one after another, side by side, all filigreed and buttressed and gargoyled, like the ancient cathedrals and castles that the boy had read about in his novels.

"Son, in the circle you just drew with your two eyes, a man with a dream has a better chance than in all the principalities of Europe."

"Yes, sir."

"But there's never been a dreamer yet who got anything out of life without hard work. So"—his father snapped at his suspenders—"let's get to it."

THEY STARTED IN a servant's bedroom under one of the dormers.

The father took out a pair of cotton work gloves with leather palms and told the boy to put them on. The gloves were new and stiff and a little big, but the boy liked the way that they came up around his wrists. He thought of Ivanhoe pulling on his gauntlets before a joust.

Then the father took a thick chalk from his tool

belt, crouched, and drew an X on half a dozen floorboards.

"What's that mean, Pa?"

"You put an X on what you want to save. You don't see floorboards like these too often. Twelve-footers, fir, eight-inch wideboard, never waxed. We'll sell 'em to Squints O'Day. He's buildin' water tanks these days."

"Water tanks? To go on roofs, you mean?"

"It's the comin' business. With buildin's gettin' taller, they need tanks to keep up the water pressure above six stories. They pump water up to a tank on the roof, then—"

"We don't have water pressure, do we, Pa?"

"No, son, we don't. We don't even have runnin' water. We get our water from the spigot in the yard."

The boy knew that his parents talked about moving to a place with a spigot on every floor, especially now that Eddie had to hobble up and down the stairs on a crutch. But those tenements cost more. So did tenements on the lower floors. And money was tight. Money was always tight.

"Now, then"—the father made a few more X marks, as if to change the subject—"we'll load up on these and take 'em to Squints."

"Didn't you used to work for him?"

"Still do, when the demo jobs get slow. I learned cooperin' at the age of fifteen. Squints used to call me the best barrel-bottom man in the business. And whenever I do a bit of part-timin' for him, he's after me to stay. Tells me now I'm the best *tank*-bottom man in New York, which means I can cut a lot of fitted boards into a neat circle. But I like workin' for myself. So"—the father took the pinch bar—"let's work."

"Yes, sir."

"Now, tearin' up rough floorin' is easy, 'cause the boards is face-nailed. Just find a line of nails, then . . ." He jammed the pinch bar down between two boards and levered.

Nails and wood gave out with a yelp.

Then he moved to the next line of nails, levered and lifted, then a third and fourth time, and the board came free. Beneath was a latticework of lathe and ceiling plaster.

And from somewhere downstairs came a voice: "Hello! Hello!"

"Your uncle." The father rolled his eyes. "Pray that he's finished his beer fartin' for the mornin'."

The boy laughed. He liked it when his father let him in on a joke.

The father handed the boy the pinch bar. "Use the straight end."

The boy slid the bar along the top of the newly exposed floor joist until it ran into a row of nails. He twisted and pivoted, and another board lifted.

"Funny," said the father, "that board's only been nailed in at the ends, like somebody didn't want to bother renailin' the middle. Give 'er a pull at the other end."

So the boy did, and with barely any levering at all, the board popped up, revealing more lathe, more plaster, and fitted neatly between two of the joists, a wooden box about ten inches by seven inches by four inches high.

"What's that, Pa?"

The father crouched down. "*That,* Timothy Riley, is why I love my line of work."

"Hello! Hello!" The voice echoed up from the second floor.

The father glanced over his shoulder, then lifted the box. It was dark wood, mahogany, hinged, held shut with a little padlock clasp. The father probed the clasp with his screwdriver. The little nails holding it pulled away, and the box popped open: empty.

"Too bad," said the boy.

"Not so fast." The father tapped the bottom of the box. "You hear that? Sounds solid. Too solid." Then he turned the box over, looked at the sides, ran his fingers along the little molding strip around the bottom. And then he found it, a fitted piece of molding that moved, and he slid it all the way off the side of the box.

"Hello! Hello, Six-Pound! Where the hell are you?"

The father glanced again toward the sound of his brother-in-law's voice, then gave the boy a grin. "Many's the box I've found with a false bottom. Now . . . watch." He slid the bottom out through the space left by the molding to reveal—

"What the hell is this? Paper? Paper notes?" The father picked one of them up. It was a small thing covered in small print on paper yellowed from the heat of decades beneath the attic floorboards.

The father read the words at the top: "'One hundred dollars.' It says 'One hundred dollars.'" Then he held it up to the dormer light. "And a watermark."

"Watermark?"

"A kind of shadow writin' that tells who made the paper." The father squinted. "It says, 'Confed . . . eration.' "

"*Confederate* money?" The boy looked closer. "But 'State of New York' is printed right under the 'Hundred Dollars.' "

"Well, New York wasn't in the Confederacy. We know that."

"Are you up there, Dick? Who's with ya?" The uncle was climbing to the attic.

The father made a gesture to the boy: Quiet. Don't say anything. Then he took off his derby, put a few of the notes into the crown, and put the hat back on. He closed the box and slid it far under the floorboards.

"I got some bad fuckin' news for you, Dick." Uncle Billy Donovan's brogue entered the room, followed by his beer belly, then Billy himself, all out of breath.

Dick Riley stood and turned. "The bad news is you're late, and jobs is gettin' tougher to come by."

"Ah"—Billy made a wave of his hand—"you mean that panic thing the papers is talkin' about? I wouldn't worry too much about that."

"I would," said Six-Pound Dick, "and watch your language."

Uncle Billy looked past his brother-in-law at Timothy. "Come to work with the men, have you, boy-o?"

"Yes, sir," answered the boy.

"Now what's this bad news?" asked Six-Pound.

"I'll keep it under me hat, so's I don't scare

Timmy." Billy smiled. He had one of those pushed-up noses that always seemed to be pulling on his upper lip, so that a smile revealed his front teeth and gave him the look of a rodent . . . a large, beer-drinking rodent.

Six-Pound looked into his eyes. "I'd say you was drunk last night. Are you still?"

Billy farted. "As sober as a judge I am. And it was with these two sober eyes that I seen Strong McGillicuddy in his mother's saloon."

"You was drinkin' in Mother Mag's? I told you to stay out of there."

"Ah"—Billy made another wave of his hand—"I go where I want, when I want."

"And you mean *Slick* McGillucuddy, don't you?"

The boy sensed a change in his father's voice.

"Not *Slick*. Since you took the hammer to Slick, he's good for nothin' 'cept washin' beer mugs or drainin' 'em. Strong's the older brother. He's bigger and meaner, which is the reason for why he been up the river these last ten years. He—"

Six-Pound put up a hand. "Enough."

"Just a word to the wise, Dick. You know you can count on me."

"They won't touch me, Billy. Been too long."

"Ah, but some of these boys has long memories, Dick. So keep an eye out, and I'll watch your back." Then Billy looked again at Tim. "What you got there, lad?"

The boy held up the pinch bar.

"Not that. You two was kneelin' down there like you just found the crown jewels in the floor-boards of an old tavern."

"There's nothin' here," said Six-Pound Dick. "Not a thing."

"Nothin' valuable, then?" asked Uncle Billy suspiciously.

"To a man who likes beer as much as you do, Billy, the most valuable thing in this old place is the fumes in the taproom. So"—Six-Pound Dick turned his brother-in-law toward the stairs—"let's go down and take a deep breath. It'll be as good as the hair o' the dog."

THAT NIGHT, THE Rileys ate dinner to the sound of firecrackers.

Boiled beef, boiled potatoes, boiled carrots, and explosions, some like cannon blasts right under their windows, others like the familiar sound of far-off gunshots.

It was the night before the Fourth, and kids all across Hell's Kitchen were firing off bottle rockets or cherry bombs or Chinese stringers.

As soon as the boys were excused, Eddie and Timothy went to the front window. Eddie looked down into the street. Timothy peered into the windows of the third-floor tenement diagonally across from theirs.

That was where Doreen Walsh lived.

And there she was, standing beside the piano in her front room. Her voice rose along a simple scale—*do-re-mi-fa-so-la-ti-do*—as her mother played. Her strawberry blond hair shimmered in the evening light.

"Ma, Timmy's peekin' at Doreen again," said Eddie.

"I ain't peekin'. I'm listenin'. When the teacher asked us kids what we wanted to be when we grew up, Doreen said she wants to sing in Tony Pastor's show."

"Vaudeville"—the mother gave a snort—"a fine dream for a young girl."

Timothy pretended not to hear the sarcasm. "I told her if she sang by the—"

"She sings like a rusty gate," said Eddie.

The mother ignored Eddie and asked Timothy, "If she sang by the *what*?"

"By the window, Ma. If she sang by the window, I'd be her audience."

The mother craned her neck to see out without being seen.

Doreen Walsh was launching into a Tony Pastor song, "The Fourth of July."

Once more fellow freemen, we've met on that day,
That reminds us of times that have long passed away . . .

"I recognize that air," said the mother. "'Sprig of Shillelah.'"

"But different words," said Timothy.

"She has a nice voice, just the same," said the mother.

"I say she sings like a rusty gate," said Eddie, then he turned to his father. "Hey, Pa, can we buy some firecrackers?"

"In a few minutes, Eddie. Your mother and me needs to have a talk."

"A talk?" The mother turned to her husband.

In most families, having *a talk* meant trouble.

See Jefferson's pen Independence declare.

Dick Riley raised the lid of his wife's sewing machine, took out the mahogany box, and set it on the table.

"What's this, then?" asked Mary Riley.

Meanwhile to support it our forefathers swear,
In Seventy-six on the Fourth of July . . .

Timothy had not seen his father take the box from under the floorboards or carry it out right under Uncle Billy's nose. But there it was, polished and shining.

Dick Riley nodded for his wife to open it.

She wiped her hands on her apron.

And Washington, prompt at his country's call,

Timothy drew closer.

Both parents shot glances at the boy, then at each other, and an agreement passed between them. *He's old enough*. The father pulled out a chair and told him to sit.

Unsheathed the bright sword and urged on one and all,

Like her husband, Mary Donovan Riley was nearing forty. But where Six-Pound was skinny and solid, Mary carried extra weight through her hips and across her chest. And where he was a talker, she had little to say, so that what she said carried extra weight, too. And it was tinged with the brogue she had brought from Donegal as a girl. Six-Pound, for all his Irish sentiment, was all New York with a New York accent.

The mother raised the lid, and there were the small paper notes.

Pop-pop-pop-pop-pop!

"Wow!" cried Eddie. "A whole string, right down on the street. Let's go, Pa!"

"In a minute, son."

While we chant in full chorus on the Fourth of July . . .

Timothy listened to his parents talk their way toward understanding what they had found: twenty thousand dollars worth of old bonds, bearer bonds, which meant that whoever held them could cash them, if they were still good. The bonds had been issued during the Revolution with five-year maturities at 5 percent interest.

The father asked the boy, "What's twenty thousand at five percent for five years?"

"Twenty-five thousand." Timothy didn't need a pencil. "Simple interest."

"Did you tell Billy about this?" asked the mother.

"No," said the father. "He'd blab."

"True enough," she said.

"But if there's somethin' here," added the father, "he'll get his share. Whether he banks it or drinks it is his own business."

She fingered the bonds. "This looks like a considerable lot of money."

"If it *is* money," said the father, "and even more considerable if it's what they call compound interest."

"Well, I don't know nothin' about compound interest," she said. "My bank has a snout on its face and a slot in its back."

Columbia will honor the Fourth of July.

Timothy had all but forgotten the angelic sound of Doreen's voice, which was still shimmering in the air above Forty-eighth Street.

The father said to him, "Do the compound interest for five years."

Timothy took a pencil and paper and wrote a few figures. "Twenty-five thousand five hundred twenty-five dollars and sixty-three cents."

"You know, Dick," said the mother softly, "with this kind of money, we could move to a first-floor flat with runnin' water."

The father pulled out a red handkerchief and mopped his brow.

The mother picked up a bond. "But how could things so flimsy be worth so much?"

"Don't get all excited just yet," said the father. "They could be as worthless as—"

The mother raised a finger. "Don't say it, Dick!"

Timothy had often heard his father call something "as worthless as Billy Donovan." And while his mother generally agreed with the sentiment, she did not like it spoken aloud.

"I was going to say they could be as worthless

as a Continental. Ain't you ever heard that expression about money from the Revolution?"

"No, I ain't." She put the bond back, studied the box, drummed her fingers on the table, and finally said, "I think you should talk to himself."

"The sachem? I could. I could do that. I could talk to him tomorrow."

"On the Fourth?" she asked. "Can you get close to him on the Fourth?"

"I've been wantin' to introduce him to Timothy—"

"You're bringin' the boy to Tammany Hall? To hear all that windy speechifyin' and witness all that hard drinkin'?"

Timothy immediately said he'd love to go.

"See that," said the father. "He'd love to go. And it's good for the local boss to see that your son's growin' straight and tall."

By the Union we live, for the Union we'll die;
We'll remember our sires of the Fourth of July—

iii.

Father and son dressed in their Sunday best—jackets, celluloid collars, ties, clean trousers. The boy was wearing mostly hand-me-downs from his father, so his tie was stained and his trousers did not reach to his ankles. He refused, however, to wear knickers and kneesocks to his first Fourth of July at Tammany Hall.

And the father agreed. "He's a workin' man now. And he's got Doreen Walsh on the brain." The father winked at his son and poured coffee. "So I'd say he's growin' up. And Doreen is . . . *developin'* . . . quite nicely."

Eddie gave out with a guffaw. "Timmy says she's growin' nice bubbies, too."

"None of that talk, now," said the mother. "Not at the kitchen table."

She fed them bacon and eggs and after a warning about imbibing too much Tammany spirit or saying the word "bonds" too loudly in public, she sent Dick and Timothy on their way.

The father asked Eddie to come, too. But Eddie said he would stay home to keep his mother company and play his harmonica, because Eddie hated going into crowds on his crutch.

A THUNDERSTORM HAD blown through overnight and scrubbed the air clean. So everything glimmered, every brick on every building, every cast-iron pillar and plate glass window, every length of trolley track and every horse turd, for as far as they could see.

A walk down Broadway, the father said, led through the heart of his city, "where the fine folks shop and eat and play." And on a day like that, it would be a sin not to walk what he called the greatest street in the world. So down Broadway they went.

They passed through Madison Square, home of the famous Garden, and the boy gazed up at the yellow brick mass, the arches, the tower, the weathervane statue of Diana. As always, he slowed to admire the huntress, who happened to be naked.

"Come on, Tim. We need to see the sachem before he goes into the hall, because afterward, the high mucky-mucks have a private lunch and you can't get near them."

South of Madison Square was the Ladies' Mile, a stretch of expensive shops and giant retail emporiums called department stores, where pennants fluttered from rooftops, colorful awnings shaded the street, and anyone—lady *or* gentleman—could buy almost anything from almost anywhere in the world. It was an easy walk from Hell's Kitchen, but this magical neighborhood seemed to the boy as if it existed on another planet.

At Twentieth Street, the father pointed out the façade of Lord and Taylor's, wrapping the southwest corner in five stories of shimmering glass, cast-iron pillars, wrought-iron trim work, and a shiny coat of beige paint.

"There's the handsomest building in New York," he said, "and a sad thing it is that your mother never come here to shop. But if them bonds is worth anything, I'll have her down here faster than a nun can say Hail Mary. She can ride the steam elevator all day, and buy herself a bustle and a parasol and the fanciest hat in the window."

"I think she'd just like a new sewin' machine."

"Well, she won't need to be takin' in sewin', either. Money'll make her a fine lady. Money's the thing, son."

"But you said *respect* was the thing."

"I said every man deserves respect till he proves he don't. But not every man thinks like me. In this world, you have to earn respect. Better to get it by usin' a good brain to make money than by usin' a six-pound sledge to beat fellers senseless."

As they passed Brooks Brothers and Bonwit's, the crowd began to build. Then the boy heard music thumping up Broadway, something by Sousa, and it made his heart pound. The spectacle was near.

At Union Square, the father headed straight for the statue of George Washington, where the trumpeters of the Sixty-ninth Regimental Band were playing a flourish, calling the sachems and braves to take their places for the parade down Fourteenth Street to the wigwam.

Sachems, wigwams, braves . . . this Tammany organization, which had been taking care of New York Democrats for over a century, took its name from the famous Delaware Indian Sachem, Chief Tamanend. And to its "braves," it was a true tribe.

That's what the father said as he jostled and glad-handed his way across the sun-drenched square. Clustered around the statue were the twenty-four top hats worn by the sachems of the twenty-four New York assembly districts. Some of them were ceremonial figures, but most were also district bosses, the ones who could always help, no matter the problem, because they knew everyone in their districts and had done favors for most of them. And if their top hats were not enough to identify them in a sea of derbies and straw boaters, they all wore white aprons over their swallow-tail coats, aprons edged in gold-threaded fringe and bearing an image of the chief himself.

"Mr. Plunkitt! Mr. Plunkitt!" cried the father.

At the sound of his name, a man with gray hair and a black mustache turned and pasted a smile onto his face.

At the same moment, the boy thought he saw Uncle Billy pushing toward them. But then the crowd shifted and Uncle Billy disappeared.

The sachem took Dick Riley's hand. "How's the best salvage man in Hell's Kitchen, and his handsome son, too?"

Timothy Riley took off his New York Giants hat and said, "Hello, Your Honor," just as his father had coached him.

"We're fine, sir. Fine," shouted Six-Pound Dick over the noise. "I've brung Timothy to meet you. This is his first time celebratin' the glorious Fourth at the hall."

George Washington Plunkitt offered his hand to the boy. Though the sachem was shorter than the father, his grip was even stronger.

"Are you marchin'," asked Plunkitt, "or goin' ahead to get a seat?"

"We're after seats down front," said Six-Pound. "I want the boy to hear every word of the Declaration."

"Well, that's just grand. Every boy should know it by heart." And the sachem began to turn away.

"Mr. Plunkitt, sir," said Six-Pound, "I need a bit of advice."

The trumpets played another call, and the bandleader urged the sachems to fall in.

Plunkitt's smile dropped off his face. "Now,

Six-Pound, this ain't the time or the place for business. If it's a job you need—"

Six-Pound Dick took off his hat, looked around to make sure that no one was paying attention, and pointed into the crown. "It's this."

Plunkitt looked in, then reached in and lifted out a small piece of paper.

Six-Pound said, "I was hopin' you'd know what I should do with it."

Plunkitt read the bond, front and back. "Where did you get this?"

"Well, let's just say—"

"Now, Six-Pound," said Plunkitt, "you're workin' in the old Daggett Tavern. Is that where you found this?"

"How did you know I was workin' up there? It ain't even in the district."

"Who do you think put in a word with the owner?"

As the men talked, the boy was looking around at the crowd and up at the statue, and for a moment, he thought that he saw Uncle Billy peering down from the base of Washington's pedestal. But the crowd shifted again, and Billy was gone.

Plunkitt slipped the note into his jacket pocket. "Come and see me at my office on Monday and we'll figure this out." Then he turned to the boy. "You know where my office is, son?"

Timothy shook his head.

"Afternoons, I'm in the district at Washington Hall. But every mornin', you'll find me down at the County Courthouse, at the bootblack stand. That's where a man of the people does the people's business, out in the open, out where the people can see him."

"Yes, sir," said the boy.

"Oh, and Dick, do you have more of these things?"

"Unh . . . just a few."

"Well, hold onto 'em till Monday," said Plunkitt. "And don't show 'em around."

"One, two, three!" cried the bandleader, then the brass strains of "Washington Post" all but blasted the boy's hat off.

As the parade began to move, the father just stood there in front of the statue of Washington.

So the boy asked, "How come you didn't tell him there was two hundred bonds?"

"Well, son, if the day ever comes that I'm not around to help you, he's the man to go to. But don't ever trust him . . . or any other powerful man."

"Do you think he'll help?"

"Unless there's better reason not to." The father clapped the boy on the shoulder. "Now, then, let's go and enjoy the show."

As they pushed into the crowd, the boy saw Uncle Billy again. He said, "Pa—"

The father stopped and turned. "What?"

"Uncle Billy been watchin' us ever since we come into the square, and whenever I see him, he ain't lookin' happy."

"He won't be happy if he thinks we're goin' behind his back. He's touchy that way. Come on."

FATHER AND SON hurried down Fifteenth Street, slipped down Irving Place, and beat the parade to

Tammany Hall, known to the braves as the wigwam.

This wigwam was no Indian tent, but a handsome three-story building topped with a statue of Chief Tamanend. The domed ceiling and grand chandelier in the auditorium reminded the boy of the medieval halls he had read about, though there was nothing medieval about the flags and bunting that hung everywhere, even from the window shades.

"If you could turn color into gas," said the father, as he jostled toward a pair of seats halfway down on the left side, "we could cut this building loose, and all the red, white, and blue would float us right over to Brooklyn."

The ceremonies began with resounding music as the sachems took their places on the stage and joined in "The Star-Spangled Banner." Then came the resounding words, "When in the course of human events . . . ," followed by the resounding cheers, then the resoundingly boring speeches, first from the long talkers—two politicians who spoke on big issues that the boy did not understand—then from the short talkers. He liked them better because they were, well . . . short.

Still, it was four hours before the Tammany Glee Club launched into the closing anthem, and the boy was swept up by the energy of all those hungry, thirsty, sweaty, cigar-smokey men singing along:

Columbia the gem of the ocean! The home of the brave and the free.

The hungriest and thirstiest began to slide toward the exits.

The shrine of each patriot's devotion.

But the rest continued to sing, though all knew that downstairs there were a hundred cases of champagne and two hundred kegs of beer . . . just waiting.

A world offers homage to thee.

The boy was amazed to hear his father singing, so he joined in.

Thy mandates make heroes assemble,

Then his father stopped singing and looked seven or eight rows ahead.

When Liberty's form stands in view.

A scrawny little man with a bashed-in face had turned and was looking at the Rileys through the haze of cigar smoke. Slick McGillicuddy. And he was whispering into the ear of a big man in a checkered suit. His brother, Strong.

Thy banners make tyranny tremble

Dick Riley tipped his derby to the McGillicuddys and finished the song.

When borne by the red, white, and blue.

Ten minutes later, the Rileys found a spot in the corner of the huge lunchroom, elbow to elbow with braves from across the city. The beer barrels and the champagne cases were rising from the subbasement called "the spring." Negro waiters were sending food flying along all the tables and countertops—knockwurst and beef tongue and pickled eggs and pig's feet and ham sandwiches. And all the booming laughter and big talk and backslapping were making the windows rattle.

The boy had never felt more of a man, especially when the father put a mug into his hand.

"Your first beer, Timmy. Don't tell your mother."

The boy tapped his mug against his father's, watched his father blow the foam off the top of his, and did the same.

That was when Uncle Billy found them. "Dick, I been looking all over for you."

The father's mug stopped at his lips. "Get yourself a beer, Billy, and calm down."

"I already had a beer. With Strong McGillicuddy himself."

"Strong McGillicuddy?"

Again the boy sensed a catch in his father's voice, a note of concern.

"Me and Strong had a fine talk," said Billy.

"About what?"

"This and that." Billy thrust his thumbs into the armholes of his vest and rocked back and forth on his heels. "He ain't such a bad sort. Not like his brother. Not at all."

A big man in a checkered suit came up behind Billy. He had a heavy brow, a broken nose, and a face so pockmarked that it looked like someone had beaten him with a wool card. He said, "So this is Six-Pound Dick?"

The boy felt his father stiffen.

The man thrust out a hand. "I'm Strong McGillicuddy. I been away a while."

Dick Riley angled his body to put himself between his son and Strong.

"C'mon, shake," said Strong. "Slick *needed* a bit of learnin'. If it had to be done with a six-pound sledge, it had to be done. So . . . no hard feelin's."

"Go ahead, Dick," said Uncle Billy. "Give 'er a shake."

"Right," said Strong. "Bygones."

The boy noticed that Strong McGillicuddy raised his voice and looked around, as if to see if anyone was watching.

Everyone was watching, and conversation in that corner of the lunchroom had stopped colder than the beer.

"Right," said Billy. "Bygones." He nudged his brother-in-law, who took the proffered hand.

Then Strong McGillicuddy looked at the boy. "A Giants fan, are you? I'm for the Trolley Dodgers myself." He pulled the bill of the boy's cap down over his eyes. "I'll see you 'round the neighborhood." Then he turned and pushed back through the crowd.

"There, now," said Uncle Billy. "Ain't peacemakin' good for the soul?"

Six-Pound Dick took the beer from Timothy

and put it into Billy's hand. "From now on, when you drink, drink with men you can trust."

"My sentiments exactly," said Billy, then he stepped closer to his brother-in-law and whispered, "So . . . why am I drinkin' with the likes of you, if you don't trust me."

"What damn fool talk is this?" said Dick. "I trust you."

"So what was it you handed to the sachem out in the square? Somethin' I'm thinkin' come out of the attic of that old house yesterday. A little piece of paper. Looks to me like some kind of funny money."

"I'll tell you when the time comes, Billy. Till then"—Dick gently lifted the beer mug toward Billy's lips—"let's enjoy the day the best we know how."

The boy had seen that gesture work often when Uncle Billy's anger started to boil about something. But this time, Billy kept his eyes on his brother-in-law all the while that he was draining the mug. And when he was done, he turned and stalked away.

iv.

The next morning, Timothy's mother woke him at six thirty and sent him to meet his father down at the barn on Eleventh. When he got there, it looked as if his father had been working for hours at something.

"Where you been, Pa?"

"Doin' a little job for Squints O'Day. Fixin' a leaky tank bottom up on a roof." He handed the boy a tool belt. "Let's go to work."

And they headed for Daggett Tavern. . . .

Uncle Billy didn't show up at the job that day.

The father said that was not surprising. Billy often missed work after a holiday, and it was better not to have him throwing up every time he walked out to the wagon.

On the ride home that afternoon, the father told Timothy that if Uncle Billy asked again, they should stick to the story: they had found some curious pieces of paper—don't call them bonds or money—and Boss Plunkitt was simply looking into it for them.

"So long as Billy gets his share, he'll be happy," the father said. "But I don't want him blabbin'. It might get back to the McGillicuddys."

Then Timothy said, "I never saw you take the box out of the house, Pa. Where is it?"

"Hid good, son. Someplace so safe, not even your mother would think of it. And there it'll stay till we're good and ready to bring it out."

"Can you give me a clue anyways?"

The father did not answer immediately because a train came thundering over. Once it passed, he brushed a few bits of coal ash from his son's shoulder, clucked to the horses, and said, "Remember the cloud of commerce I told you about the other day?"

"Yes, sir."

"Well, the clouds are filled with rain to pour down water on the good and the bad alike. Water makes things grow. It washes away dirt and sins, too, if you been baptized. In America, the cloud of commerce pours down money so we can grow better lives. Now, money don't wash away sins like baptism does, but havin' it makes it easier to live the straight and narrow, since you don't always have to be schemin' how to get it. Without water, there's no life. Without money, there's no America . . . or no New York anyway."

"That's it?"

The father chuckled. "You asked for a clue, and I give you a philosophy. Be thankful you have a father so smart."

The boy might have pressed further, but something caught his eye as they came into the block between Forty-eighth and Forty-seventh.

McGillicuddy's Saloon, also known as Mother Mag's, was about halfway down the block on the west side. And there was Strong, leaning against the building with his arms folded—

"Like he owns the street," said the father.

—and he was talking to a burly woman who wore a man's shirt and trousers tucked into cowboy boots.

"Himself and the miserable bitch who whelped him," said the father.

Tim had heard about the woman called Mother Mag. People said she sharpened her fingernails to points, so that if a man didn't pay for his beer, she'd give his face a scratch so deep it would leave a scar. She carried a carving knife in her boot. And she kept a sawed-off shotgun behind the bar.

Then Timothy noticed Uncle Billy staggering up the street. "Hey, Pa—"

"I see him." Six-Pound Dick gave out with a whistle.

Uncle Billy turned to the wagon, waved them away, then lurched into the saloon.

"Damn fool is on a toot," said Six-Pound.

The boy knew what that was. The neighborhood was full of men who went "on a toot" now and then. The word made the deed sound harmless, but a toot often led to a beaten wife, or kicked kids, or spilled beans somewhere in somebody's life.

"Ain't you gonna stop him, Pa?"

"You can't talk to Billy when he's drinkin'. You can't control him, either. If I try to stop him, he's like to take my head off, then tear that saloon to pieces."

And Strong McGillicuddy shouted to Six-Pound Dick, "Don't you worry none. We'll see he don't drink too much."

"You do that," shouted Six-Pound Dick. "And if he ain't in work tomorrow, I'll come and see you."

"You do that." Strong tipped his hat. "But don't bring no hammers. They give my brother the shakes."

Another train came rumbling over, and the Rileys rode on.

THEY TURNED AT Forty-sixth and rode down to Eleventh Avenue, to O'Day's Cooperage, on the west side of the street.

Men were working late in the big dusty yard and in the one-story shop next to it.

"Hello, Squints!" cried the father.

Half a dozen carpenters looked up from sawhorses and workbenches.

But it was easy to pick out Squints. He was the

one with the big belly under his apron and the narrowest eyes the boy had ever seen. They looked like two slits cut into the fat of his face.

"You fellers sure are workin' late on a hot day." Six-Pound Dick jumped down.

"We work late 'cause we got work," shouted Squints. "This is gettin' to be a big business. Water tanks goin' up on roofs all over New York. If stayin' in business means twelve-hour days, well"—Squints squinted at the others—"never a man here afraid of hard work."

"That's the spirit, Squintsy, my boy, the spirit that made America."

"You got more good wood for me?"

Six-Pound Dick began pulling long planks off the back of his wagon, each of them marked with an X. "Take a look at these. Lifted nice and careful by my own son here. Say hello to Tim."

Squints looked at the boy and opened his eyes a bit wider, as if it was something he saved for newcomers. "Hello, son."

Timothy tugged at his hat. "Hello, Mr. O'Day."

"Nice boy, Dick. You're trainin' him right." Squints examined one of the boards, squinted down its length, ran his hand over the surface. "Fir twelve-footers, eight-inch wideboard, never waxed. That's good."

"There's two more rooms of 'em," said Six-Pound Dick.

"Well, it's plenty dry," said Squints, "but I don't like it that there's nail holes."

"They'll swell as soon as the water hits 'em. Use a double thickness, they'll make a fine tank bottom, and remember, Squintsy, my boy, what you call me—"

"Yeah, yeah, 'the best tank-bottom man in New York.' But still—"

While the men haggled, the boy climbed down and walked around the yard. He was curious about the work the men did. His father told him that it was a good trait, curiosity about a man's trade, because it would help him to appreciate his own work.

He noticed that all the carpenters were a bit squint-eyed, as if they were related.

"Come to watch the men work, have you, son?" said one of them.

"You fellers are cuttin' and shapin' and planin'," said Timothy. "But I don't see much hammerin'. And where's all the water tanks?"

"We're coopers," said the man. "Good coopers don't need nails. We cut the wood for the tanks down here, but we build 'em and band 'em in place, right on top of the buildings. We'll cover New York in tanks before we're done."

"That you'll do, so long as we deliver the wood." Six-Pound shoved a few bills into his pocket and called to his son. "See you with another load tomorrow, lads."

THE NEXT MORNING, Six-Pound Dick woke Timothy at five thirty and told him it was settin' up to be another hot day, so it was best that they start work early.

In the front room, Uncle Billy lay snoring. He had come stumbling to their door just after supper, too drunk to find his way to the El. His appearance had calmed the little household, because over dinner, the father had announced that he was thinking of going out for a bit of a stroll, and mother and sons knew that he meant to go looking for Billy, even if it meant walking into McGillicuddy's. And no good would have come of that.

Six-Pound gave Billy a kick that raised a few loud snores. "Let him sleep it off. He'll find his way to the job when his head stops poundin'."

Billy caught his breath in the back of his throat, farted, and kept on snoring.

AFTER AN HOUR of pulling nails from X-marked floorboards on the third floor of the ancient house, Timothy decided to take a break. His father was working somewhere downstairs and had left the boy to his own devices.

So he climbed into the cupola for his daily look at the city of dreams. He leaned against the little interior railing, gazed south, and dreamed.

And the first person to appear in his mind's eye was Doreen Walsh. What would she say if he invited her up here? What would she smell like in the hot little space? What would she feel like if he pressed against her? And it started to happen. And it was not unpleasant. So he leaned a bit harder against the railing and thought of Doreen's pretty breasts pressed against . . . any part of him.

But his reverie ended with the sound of voices in the yard below. At first, he thought Uncle Billy had arrived. He peered down, but the big oak blocked his view. Then he heard one of the horses make a noise. Then he thought he heard something fall, something as heavy as a horse.

He started to climb down.

But his father was rushing up the stairs, looking into the room where Timothy had been working, calling his name.

"Up here, Pa!"

Six-Pound Dick appeared in the shaft of light directly under the cupola. "No matter what you hear, stay there and don't come down."

"But, Pa!"

"And quiet."

"But—"

"No matter what you hear. *Quiet.*" The father slammed the trapdoor.

Then the boy heard the ladder sliding back into place, locking him in.

He dropped to his knees and put his ear to the floor of the cupola. At first, there was silence. Then low voices. Then the voices grew louder. It sounded as if there were three, four, perhaps five. He couldn't be sure. Then he heard the sounds of fighting, thumping, banging, cursing, and raised voices, all but his father's.

His father's voice stayed low and cold.

Timothy thought he heard someone ask, "Where are them little papers?" A muffled response. Then a question he could not understand and . . . did he hear the words, Billy the Drunk? "Where did you hide them little papers? The funny money?" A muffled response. "Then where's the boy?" Another muffled response. Then the sound of more beating. Then a *bang*! As if someone had slammed a six-pound sledge off of something.

Timothy had to get out, get out somehow, get out and get down, get out and get down and help his father. The cupola was six narrow windows creating a glass hexagon. He pulled on the first. Stuck. Then the second. The same. But the third window, the one that faced east, slid open.

He put a foot out onto the heavy slate. If he could skitter down to the little dormer below, he could catch it, then swing a leg around and slide down the side of it and step through the window. Then he'd use that pinch bar like a club and rescue his father.

So long as he didn't wet himself.

He got both feet out of the window and held tight to the sill of the cupola.

The slope was not too steep. He could do it. He could go down ass first, on all fours, down onto the little peak of the dormer, then slowly slide . . .

He touched the sun-broiled slate with the palm of his hand and it felt like a hot stove. He muffled a cry. He lost his balance and began to slip down the scalding roof. He hit the dormer and rolled and kept going, but he grabbed the corner of the fascia board, where the dormer cut into the roof, held tight, and stopped just a foot from the gutter.

A branch of the old oak reached over the roof and shaded this spot, a cool little valley between the dormers.

"Hey, kid!" the voice growled from somewhere. "You up here? Show yourself. We won't hurt you."

Timothy grabbed the rafters of the dormer and pulled himself close against the side of it.

"Kid! Come out. Come out, wherever you are!" The voice came from the cupola.

Timothy did not recognize it and could not see the cupola. So the guy in the cupola could not see him.

"Come on, kid. Show yourself and we'll call a doctor for your old man."

Timothy Riley pulled himself tighter against the wall of the dormer, and a slate began to slide. He stopped it before it went over the edge and gave away his position to anyone who might be down on the ground.

"Come on, kid! Your pa told us you was up here. Quit hidin'. He told us what you found. Just show us where it is and we'll leave you alone."

The bonds. They had come for the bonds. But how did they know? Plunkitt? Uncle Billy?

"Hey, kid!"

Whatever they had done to his father they would do to him. So he lay there on the sloping roof, pulled tight against the wall, half hidden in the shadow of the old oak.

"Fuck it," said the man in the cupola. "He must've stayed home or somethin'."

Had it not been for the shade of the oak tree, the boy would not have been able to stay on that hot roof. But he waited until he was certain they had left, ten minutes, fifteen.

Then he crawled toward the dormer on the south side, but when he tried to raise the window, the stop broke and it dropped like a stone. So . . . slide to the other dormer, the one with the open window? But the tree branches were closer.

He had climbed down the side of the tenement fire escape once, so he was not afraid. He grabbed the big branch, reminded himself not to look down, then shimmied out to the trunk. When he got there, he fit his foot into the knothole and heard the owl stir. Then he lowered himself to the next branch, then the one after that. He was halfway down the tree when he saw the horses.

Both were dead, their throats cut, and a river of blood flowed down the drive toward Broadway. He dropped the last ten feet and ran into the house.

HE FOUND HIS father on the grand staircase.

They had taken a six-pound hammer to him. His face was battered. There was blood coming from his ears. His eyes seemed oddly swollen, as if something was pressing against them from behind.

Timothy could not believe that the pulp he was looking at had been his father's face. He could not believe that any of this had happened. But he was certain that he saw what was left of his father's mouth curl into a smile at the sight of him.

"Pa."

He felt his father's hand close around his, saw his father's lips move.

"What, Pa. I . . . I can't . . ."

"The bonds. They . . . they . . ."

The words faded. Then the father moved his other hand on the floor. He was holding his chalk, and with it, he wrote an X on the step.

The boy shook his head, as if he did not understand.

Then the father managed to get one word out. "Eyes."

"Eyes? Eyes, Pa?"

The father's brows twitched. The lids tried to close, as if there were a bright light, as if he were squinting in a bright light. And then the muscles around his eyes relaxed. And his breathing stopped.

NINE

Wednesday Afternoon

Peter was reading another article that Antoine had e-mailed.

"Listen to this," he said to Evangeline. "'Richard Riley was beaten to death with a hammer by one or more assailants, who left his body on the stairs of the old Daggett Tavern, originally Woodward Manor, one of the great estates of pre-Revolutionary New York. His son, Timothy, aged thirteen, was hiding in the house. The boy found his father holding a piece of chalk in his hand, having just drawn an X on one of the stair treads.'"

"The poor kid," said Evangeline.

"'The son could not identify the murderers. He did not see them and heard mostly muffled voices. Richard Riley was known to have had troubles with Hell's Kitchen gangs, but a motive for the slaying has not been established. He will be buried from Sacred Heart Church on Monday.' "

"That's it?" said Evangeline.

"Too bad we don't have an index for the *New York Post*," said Peter. "The *Times* was already turning into the gray lady. Sensational murder but no sensationalism."

Just then, Peter's phone rang.

"Owen T. Magee here."

"What's your decision?" said Peter Fallon.

"What's yours?"

Peter glanced at the cover of the *Daily News*. "You got the wrong guy in the Yankees hat. So make me an offer or get off the phone." That sounded more impolite than he usually played it, but he didn't like these guys enough to be polite. And he was lying. He always lied better if he did it aggressively.

Owen T. Magee's voice remained neutral. "We'll up the offer. Twenty percent."

"Twenty?" Peter said it out loud and glanced at Evangeline, who was sliding the laptop accross the table. "That's not much to save America from itself."

Peter pressed the speaker button so that Evangeline could hear.

"It comes to two hundred and ninety-six million dollars," said Owen T. Magee. "Not even the handwritten manuscript of a Shakespeare play is worth that much."

"Some things are priceless," said Peter. "Unlike a pile of rudely printed old bonds that won't be worth twenty-five grand if the Supreme Court finds against you."

Owen T. Magee ignored that and pressed ahead. "We'll also pay a thousand dollars a day and expenses."

"There's a load off my mind." Peter noticed Evangeline tapping away.

Owen T. Magee said, "Take it or leave it. But if you leave it, leave town, too."

Evangeline began to gesture for Peter's attention.

Peter told Owen T. to hang on, then he muted the phone and asked her, "Do I take this deal?"

"You want to know what they know," she said. "That's not a bad payday. And like they say, keep your friends close but your enemies closer."

"You've changed your tune."

"I've calmed down. I'm thinking they work with Joey Berra. I'm thinking he's some mafia enforcer they've hired for muscle."

"But he's the one who told me not to trust Arsenault."

"He could make a world of trouble for you, no matter who he works for."

"What makes you so certain?"

"I'm not, but seeing that picture of you in the Yankees hat reminded me of someone else in a Yankees hat." She slid his computer over to him and pointed to the picture she had sent from Fraunces Tavern: the lone male diner. On the seat next to him was what looked like a Yankees hat. And he was stocky like Joey. "I think that's him. I think we stay in this until we get a few more answers. Then you can explain to the NYPD why you were in Central Park yesterday wearing a Yankees hat."

Peter thought of a dozen arguments against what she was saying, then he clicked on the telephone again and said, "All right. We're in business."

"Excellent," said Owen T. Magee. "We would much rather be with you than against you. I'll have the terms adjusted and some of the historical papers collected. I'm in meetings until six. Come down to my law office at the Flatiron Building any time after that. We can formalize all this and put you to work."

"Am I protected now?" said Peter. "You threatened to remove your protection."

"We have less power than you think," said Owen T. Magee.

"What about Delancey? What kind of deal does he have?"

"Twenty percent," said Magee. "But a clause in the contract addresses the issue of payment should you join forces. You would split the twenty percent. See you after six."

Peter clicked off and called Delancey. No answer at the bookstore or on Delancey's cell. So he texted:

You have a new partner. Me.

"That's your due diligence on Delancey," said Evangeline. "Now what?"

"We have until six o'clock." He looked at his watch. "It's almost four thirty."

"If you say 'four thirtyer—' "

"I *was* going to suggest drinks at the Harvard Club." He leaned back and locked his hands behind his head. "Put on that black Chanel suit, some pearls—"

"What's up your sleeve?"

"Can't a man ask his beautiful fiancée to have a drink with him?"

She put her hands on her hips. "Who are we meeting?"

"The accountant of Avid Investment Strategies."

She dropped the attitude. "Arsenault's firm? Who arranged that?"

"Oh"—he tried to sound casual—"the chief reporter for MarketSpin-dot-com."

Evangeline gave him a long look, then went into the bedroom and closed the door.

So, he thought . . . that went well.

But a few minutes later, she emerged in the black Chanel and the white pearls, and she said, "Put on a tie."

IT WAS RUSH hour, so catching a cab would not be easy. Instead, they took the subway to Times Square and walked across Forty-fourth Street.

At the corner of Forty-fourth and Avenue of the Americas, Peter stopped. "Look up there."

The National Debt Clock was flashing on the side of a building. A real estate developer had installed it in 1989 to warn Americans of the trouble they were getting into by spending and spending and kicking their bills down the road. Back then, the sovereign debt of the United States had been two trillion dollars. Twenty years later, after the Bush tax cuts, the war on terror, the bank bailouts, the auto bailouts, the stimulus package, and all the rest, it was over twelve trillion and rising.

"A hundred grand a second." Peter watched the numbers spin.

"You could go blind looking at it," said Evangeline.

"They turned it off for two years under Clinton. The economy was thriving, tax revenue was up, spending was under control, so the deficit began to shrink. Now, I'll bet Alexander Hamilton is spinning as fast as the clock in his crypt down at Trinity Church."

"Can Arsenault stop the spin simply by finding a few old bonds?"

Peter shrugged. "Smart people like the Concord Coalition have been on this case for years, and the numbers are still spinning, so—"

"Maybe Arsenault has another motive?"

"That would be?"

"Simple greed? Complicated greed?"

"At least those are things we can understand."

"So let's go drink to greed." She pointed ahead to the American flag and the Harvard H hanging over a crimson awning just beyond the Algonquin Hotel.

"Don't call it greed," he said. "Call it enlightened self-interest."

In a city where enclaves of moneyed exclusivity were as common as Starbucks, the Harvard Club of New York might have been the biggest of them all. But the only real prerequisite for membership was attending Harvard. If you had a degree—and you could pay your bar bill—the likelihood was that you could join.

Once, Harvard had been a bastion of old boys' sons, and their fathers had filled the club. But as the face of the college had changed, so had the club. Now it was exclusivity with a democratic overtone. And that, as Peter explained to Evangeline, was why the son of a Boston Irish bricklayer like him could rub elbows with descendants of the old-money aristocracy like her.

"It's not aristocracy," said Evangeline. "The word is *meritocracy*."

"That means we now have to *earn* our right to keep everyone else out."

"Who says you've earned it?" she said.

"Well . . . I'm marrying you."

And as enclaves went, the Harvard Club was more like an auditorium of exclusivity, a theater to dramatize the rewards of accomplishment.

You walked under the crimson awning, through a vestibule, up into a lobby with leather chairs, newspapers, first-strike prints of old college scenes, cloakroom to the right, bar to the left, stairway leading to library, billiard room, guest rooms. Then you passed through the oak-paneled Grille Room, where well-heeled grads were already enjoying pre-theater suppers.

And ahead you saw a brightening. You went through a portal, beneath a balcony that was part of the second-floor library, and the ceiling suddenly rose three stories. A quarter acre of leather sofas and Persian carpets spread before you like a professor's vision of tenured heaven. High windows poured down the light of a spring evening. Two great chandeliers dominated the airspace. Portraits of gowned Harvard presidents gazed from the paneling. And the huge gray head of an African elephant, immortalized when Teddy Roosevelt shot him, seemed to be charging right through the wall.

"Welcome to Harvard Hall," said Peter. "The club brochure says that some critics consider it, and I quote, 'to be the finest clubroom in the Western Hemisphere.' "

"Just the hemisphere? Why not the whole world?"

"Typical Harvard modesty."

"That's like saying typical New York manners."

Peter looked around. "I'd bet the manners in here are pretty good."

"Not much modesty, though," she said. "Just ask the elephant."

They both scanned the room for Kathy Flynn's hair.

There were a few dozen people scattered across the great space . . . old grads, young couples, businessmen reading their *Wall Street Journals* in the quiet company of Mr. Walker, Black, waiters in crimson jackets moving discreetly, wives waiting for husbands, husbands waiting for wives, and reservations waiting in the adjacent dining room.

But no redheads. So Peter and Evangeline took a grouping of four leather chairs near the entrance, where they would be easy to spot.

Peter wrote down his membership number on a club tab and ordered a New Zealand sauvignon blanc for Evangeline and a glass of New Amsterdam for himself.

As the drinks arrived, Peter's cell phone buzzed. A text message from Kathy Flynn: There yet?

Peter texted her a yes and put the phone back into his pocket.

"Who's that?" asked Evangeline.

"Ms. Flynn."

"You're texting with her? Be careful or I may put 'texting with her' into the same category with 'looking at her ass.' "

The phone vibrated again. Peter pulled it out.

> Stuck in traffic. Watch for tall, skinny guy, horn-rims, nervous. Name Carl Evers.

He typed back, will do. Then he handed the phone to Evangeline so that she could read the message. "Okay?"

She made a face.

He hit the button. Then he drained his beer and ordered another.

It wasn't long before they saw someone familiar entering the dining room, but not anyone they were waiting for.

Will Wedge and his daughter stopped in the doorway and scanned the room.

Will was a hail-fellow from Boston, an old prepster whose blond hair had gone mostly gray and whose belly had expanded until his height had faded into the fat. He was also a principal in Wedge, Fleming, and Royce, a Boston brokerage. A few years earlier, he had enlisted Peter Fallon to find that lost Shakespeare manuscript.

His daughter, Dorothy, noticed Peter and Evangeline and came straight over to play the greeting scene that unfolded in the Harvard club a hundred times a day: hellos and handshakes and how's-the-family chitchat.

"What brings you to New York?" Evangeline asked that.

"I'm here to spend a little time with my baby girl," was Will Wedge's answer. "She's living in the big city now."

"Doing what?" Peter felt that he had to ask that one.

"I've set my sail in the world of publishing," said Dorothy. "I started as an editorial assistant, now I'm an assistant editor."

"Right," said Wedge. "She was making twenty-two thousand, now she's making twenty-six. Did you ever try living in Manhattan on twenty-six thousand dollars?"

Dorothy gave her father a playful slap on the arm. "Daddy."

"Doing any business?" That came from Peter to Will Wedge.

"On the board of the Paul Revere Foundation," said Wedge. "I'm told we're making a big announcement on Friday."

Then Evangeline said, "So you know Austin Arsenault?"

"I'm one of the top brokers in Boston. He's tops in New York. Same class in B-school. So we do business. And we're both committed to securing our national future by reducing the deficit."

"I'm familiar with their work," said Peter blandly.

"Too bad you missed out on that bond business, eh?" said Wedge. "Or did you?"

"If I told you," said Peter, "I'd have to kill you."

Someone caught Dorothy's attention, so she excused herself.

Wedge said to Peter and Evangeline, "I'm here to meet the fiancé who will father the children who inherit my wealth—"

"You'd better be good to him then," said Evangeline.

"I want to be," said Wedge, "but he's from India. And you know what our British cousins called them. 'Bloody wogs.' "

"Well, look at me," said Evangeline. "I'm marrying an Irishman, and you know what our British cousins called *them*."

Wedge gave a big braying laugh, as if he didn't quite get that the joke was on him. Then he said, "Really great to see you both. Hope to see you again soon," and he headed for the far corner of the great hall, where his daughter was embracing a handsome young man with a very dark complexion.

"All those kids coming to New York to make their fortunes in publishing," said Evangeline. "Let's hope the Punjab interloper has an MBA."

They sat again, and Peter said, "We should dig up the 501(c)(3) for the nonprofit Paul Revere Foundation. I'd love to see if there are a lot of Harvard men on the board."

"Why?"

A waiter replaced their drinks, then quietly left.

"Arsenault is Harvard Business School. Wedge is Harvard, too. Just a hunch."

"Your hunches usually get us into trouble." Evangeline took a sip from her second glass and noticed another man stopping at the entrance.

He was tall, skinny, nervous-looking.

Evangeline turned to Peter, whose second glass of New Amsterdam was at his lips. "I think that's him."

The man scanned the room until his eyes fixed on the far corner.

Evangeline glanced over her shoulder and saw Will Wedge looking toward the entrance. Was he puzzled? Surprised? She could not tell, but Wedge began to stand.

She looked back at the man in the doorway. He was looking at Wedge with an expression that said he, too, was puzzled or perhaps surprised.

Evangeline said to Peter, "I know this man from somewhere."

"Somewhere? Where?"

She ran the facts of the man's face through her memory bank: bland features, square, conventional . . . nothing to stand out in a lineup or on a police sketchbook.

Then Carl Evers began to walk toward Will Wedge with a long stride that seemed more frightened than confident.

As he passed Peter and Evangeline, she said, "He was on the Bowling Green the other night."

Evers was moving more quickly now, as if he had made a decision.

And Will Wedge was standing but not—for once—smiling.

Evers had gone about a third of the way across Harvard Hall when Peter thought he heard a champagne cork pop.

An instant later, Evers pitched forward, as if he had been struck from behind. He slammed into one of the waiters, sending a tray of Gibsons and green Heinekens flying into the air and shattering onto the stone floor.

The waiter fell back onto a sofa and landed on an old alum, who jumped up and cried, "Goddamn it! Look what you've done to my suit."

The echo of breaking glass and discord stopped conversation all across the hall.

Carl Evers was standing again, steadying himself with a hand on one of the pillars that supported the grand fireplace.

And the surface of that calm leather sea went choppy. People were turning, standing, looking . . . first toward the alum, then toward the man who was once more lurching forward.

Peter could see the hole in his gray suit, just below the right shoulder blade.

And from the end of the hall, Dorothy Wedge cried, "In the balcony! He's got a gun."

Peter looked up, saw the silencer, the barrel of the gun, then the gunman—white, gaunt, balding, disguised in a crimson waiter's jacket and black bow tie . . .

A woman screamed, so Peter did not hear the pop of the second shot.

But Evangeline was still turned to Evers, so she

saw the shot hit the back of his head. He spun forward, slammed into one of the pillars, and dropped to the floor.

And now, people seemed to understand what was happening. The nervous choppy movements became waves of fear. People were jumping up, diving down, or running for the exit.

But the man on the balcony scanned the room as calmly as if he were choosing a place to sit. Then his eye fell on Evangeline.

Peter grabbed her by the arm. "Come on. If we're caught in here, we may never explain our way out." He dragged her into the stream of people pouring toward the exits.

"But, Peter—"

"And I think we might be targets, too."

In an instant they were rushing back through the Grille Room as diners looked up from their steaks and salads at the wave of frightened people. Peter kept Evangeline moving back to the lobby, where two young black men in crimson sport coats, club security, were hurrying toward the noise.

Peter said to them, "In the balcony. Gunman. Be careful." And he kept going, with Evangeline on his arm, right out onto Forty-fourth Street.

The doorman, oblivious to the scene inside, said, "Taxi, sir?"

"Here comes one now," said Peter. "Thanks."

The door of a yellow cab was swinging open under the crimson awning, and a long female leg was swinging out.

Peter led Evangeline toward the cab, pushed the

female passenger back in, jumped in himself, and pulled Evangeline in right after him.

"HEY!" SAID THE cabbie. "Let lady out!" He was wearing a turban. A Sikh.

"It's all right," said Kathy Flynn. "He's a friend . . . I think."

Peter said, "Take us to the Flatiron Building. Fifth Avenue and Broadway."

"That okay with you, lady?" the driver asked Kathy.

"Wherever he wants," said Kathy.

Peter closed the little slider between the front seat and the back.

As the first police sirens started to wail, the cabbie rolled toward Fifth Avenue.

Kathy leaned around Peter and said to Evangeline, "Long time, no see."

If Evangeline hadn't been shaking, she might have come up with something sarcastic, something cool and cutting at the same time. But all she had was direct, blunt, and cold: "Your accountant is dead."

Kathy sat back. "Dead? How?"

"Somebody just put a hit on him in there," said Peter.

"Jesus Christ! A hit?" Kathy looked out the window. "There goes my source."

"That's all you can say?" demanded Evangeline. "A man's dead and you're worried about your source?"

"This could turn out to be a huge story," she said. "And he was at the heart of it."

Evangeline looked out at the people hurrying along. She felt tears welling, shock and anger. She had been around Peter Fallon long enough that she had seen a few shootings, but it was not something that she ever got used to.

Peter took two deep breaths, trying to get cool and stay cool. As the cab pulled around the corner, he glanced back up Forty-fourth Street. The blue lights were flashing and cars and cabs and delivery trucks were making way. The wail of the sirens was echoing down Fifth Avenue, too.

A shooting at the Harvard Club was no ordinary 911 call.

But Peter wasn't concerned with the police. He was looking for familiar faces, unfriendly faces, anyone he might have seen on the Bowling Green or anywhere else. But he saw no one he recognized on the sidewalk or in any doorways.

The cab was one of those Nissan hybrids that were replacing the city's fleet of gas hogs. It had a little backseat television. It did not have a ton of iron to protect you as you hurtled through intersections and slammed over potholes. So whenever he got into one of these little cabs, Peter put on his seat belt, but it was impossible when he was the buffer between two women so ready to dislike each other.

Kathy pointed to the TV screen. "The Dow went down another two hundred today. The technical resistance didn't hold. And now China is saying that if the American bond market receives any more shocks, they might consider *selling* Treasuries."

"What kind of shocks?" asked Peter.

Kathy shook her head and watched the screen.

Peter answered his own question: "The kind that the Supreme Court would send with a decision that forces the federal government to pay out billions of dollars to individuals and institutions holding 1780 bonds?"

"Billions?" said Kathy. "Arsenault really thinks there's billions out there?"

Evangeline elbowed Peter in the ribs, as if she didn't trust this Kathy Flynn about love or money or anything else.

Kathy didn't seem to notice. She said, "Well, however much money it is, it could be a shock either way."

"How?" said Peter.

"If the court upholds Arsenault's claim, the Chinese may decide it's the straw that breaks the camel's back. And if the court finds against, the buyers of U.S. Treasuries may decide that if we're willing to deny payment on the last debts of American Revolution, what else are we willing to default on?"

"A nice little dilemma," said Peter.

Evangeline leaned around Peter. "That still doesn't explain why you wanted us to have a drink with that guy in the Harvard Club."

"I didn't," said Kathy. "*He* did. Carl Evers did. He was laying low, staying in the club accommodations. He said he hadn't left in five days."

"He might have been laying," said Evangeline. "He was also lying."

"Lying?" said Kathy.

Evangeline decided to throw out a bit of information and see what it attracted. "Carl Evers was on the Bowling Green on Monday night. I saw him there."

"The Bowling Green?" said Kathy. "Did a bag lady have anything to do with it?"

"She got us into this," said Evangeline. "In Oscar Delancey's bookstore."

"Delancey?" said Kathy. "He sold the bonds to Arsenault. Have you talked to him?"

"We've tried," said Peter. "But he seems to have gone underground."

"Permanently?" asked Kathy.

"Hard to say," answered Peter. "So why did Evers want to talk to us?"

"Because I suspect you're doing the same kind of work for Arsenault that Delancey's doing. Evers must have had some kind of information for you. I was facilitating it"—Kathy looked out the window—"to pick up something for my story."

"So you were using us?" said Evangeline.

"This is the big city, honey," said Kathy. "Everyone uses everyone else."

"I'll remember that next time I need to *use* a financial reporter," said Evangeline.

"I do what I have to on a story," answered Kathy. "I work the club rooms. I work the boardrooms. I work the street."

"You used to work the library stacks, too," said Evangeline.

"Hey, listen—"

Peter jumped in. "If Evers wanted to see us, why did he walk right past us and head straight for Will Wedge?"

"Will Wedge?" Kathy pulled out her BlackBerry

and typed something. "There's someone worth an interview. I bet Evers had something for Will Wedge, too."

"Can you speculate?" asked Peter.

"I think that Evers was going to spill whatever he knew about Avid," answered Kathy, "like how much they have under management, where they've been investing, how they do their accounting and monthly statements . . . whether he was just signing off on his audits or actually certifying them . . . stuff like that."

"Are you saying Arsenault is in trouble?" asked Peter.

"It's what I'm trying to find out."

"So . . . you really don't know much about anything," said Evangeline, "but you don't mind pulling us into it."

"I didn't pull you in," said Kathy. "The bag lady did. She came to me, too. She said it was time to investigate Avid Austin."

Evangeline looked down the length of Fifth Avenue. The cab had gone five blocks, so they were already below the angle of the Empire State Building. She laughed and said, "And all this time, I was thinking *you* were the bag lady."

"That does it." Kathy threw open the slider and told the cabbie to pull over.

Peter looked at Evangeline and made a small gesture with his hand—stay calm.

Kathy said to Peter, "Next time we're supposed to have a drink, come alone."

The cab stopped. Kathy stepped out and stuck her head back inside. "On Friday, I run a story on

Arsenault and Avid Investment Strategies. It's about the bonds, the Supreme Court decision, and the board of the Paul Revere Foundation, which includes Will Wedge, another Harvard man. It may also be about you. So take care of yourself between now and then."

"You, too," said Peter.

"You know where to find me." *Slam.* Kathy shut the door and went off.

"I just had a thought." Evangeline watched Kathy stalk off. "She set us up."

"For a hit?" said Peter. "Ridiculous. But she's lying about Evers. He wanted to see her. She wanted to see what he did when he met us."

"What he did was not pretty."

THE FAMOUS OLD Flatiron sat where Fifth Avenue and Broadway intersected to create the triangular lot that gave rise to the wedge-shaped building.

Whenever Peter looked up at it, he remembered something H. G. Welles had written: "I found myself agape, admiring a skyscraper—the prow of the Flatiron Building . . . ploughing up through the traffic of Broadway and Fifth Avenue in the late-afternoon light."

But as they got out of the cab that afternoon, Peter was thinking only of looking around to make sure that they were not being followed.

They hurried in, smiled for the camera at the security desk, then rode one of the exquisite old art nouveau elevators up to the office of Magee & Magee.

Most of the Flatiron was occupied by a publishing conglomerate. There were a few literary and theatrical agents, too, along with galleries and a few artists. But the firm of Magee & Magee had occupied one of the upper floors since the forties.

And who would ever surrender that view, thought Peter as the secretary ushered them into Owen T. Magee's office in the prow of the building, right at the apex, the point of the wedge. The rounded window behind Magee offered one of the best views in town. You felt as if you were standing on a rock as two fast-moving streams of cars and people flowed past. And when the headlights began to blink on, the effect was even more dramatic.

"Thank you for coming." Magee was in his shirtsleeves. He wore blue and red suspenders color-coordinated with his blue bow tie. "As the compliance officer of Avid Investment Strategies, I'm expected to operate out of our Wall Street office, but my father rented this space just after World War II. And there's no better view in New York."

"Did you hear about the shooting at the Harvard Club?" said Peter.

Owen T. Magee shook his head. "Terrible."

"That's it?" said Peter. "Your accountant is killed and that's your reaction?"

"He was the soon-to-be former accountant. We had philosophical differences."

"You mean he knew where the bodies were buried," said Peter, "and he was threatening to dig them up?"

"That's rank speculation. There had been improprieties, failings, oversights," said Owen T. Magee.

"We were there," said Evangeline bluntly.

"There? Where?"

"In the Harvard club," she said. "We saw him shot."

Owen T. Magee gave her a long look, as if, with all the other news, this was something he could not process. "Why were you there?"

"We were thirsty," said Peter. "We had a drink. How much danger are we in?"

"As we told you, there are numerous parties pursing these bonds."

"How much did Carl Evers know about them?"

"Not enough to keep him alive, it seems." Owen T. Magee picked up the television control and clicked on the flat panel against the back wall.

While a reporter did a remote in front of the Harvard Club, the crawl across the bottom offered snippets and details: *AN APPARENT BIG-BUSINESS ASSASSINATION . . . THE SHOOTER, DISGUISED AS WAITSTAFF, ESCAPED THROUGH A SERVICE ENTRANCE . . .*

They watched for a moment, then Magee said, "Killing him in the Harvard Club. That's like putting a hit on someone in Saint Patrick's."

"Who killed him?" asked Peter.

"My answer would be purely speculative," said Owen T. Magee.

Evangeline said, "Does Austin Arsenault have Russian clients? A guy named Boris followed us on the subway. The same guy was chasing Delancey later that day."

"I would not be at liberty—"

Peter flew across the desk and grabbed Magee by the bow tie. "Listen to me—"

"You'll get nowhere by roughing me up. There

are three junior associates in the outer office who would insist that you let go of me if I call for them."

Now it was Evangeline's turn to make a gesture—calm down.

So Peter let him go.

Magee straightened himself and tugged at his bow tie. "We should have gone to you at the start, because of your proven ability to operate in dangerous environments."

"I hate dangerous environments," said Peter. "Give me a library any day."

"Well, you can back out if you want," said Magee.

Peter looked at Evangeline. "Do you want me to back out?"

"You've been asked to save America," she said. "I don't think you can back out."

"That's what I was hoping you'd say." Magee sat again and slid the papers across the table. "You'll find everything in order here. But remember that you will be bound to silence with the media and other legal sources."

"I don't like gag orders," said Peter.

Magee reached into his desk drawer and pulled out another envelope. "Sign and you'll get this. Delancey's research. With this and your skills, you might be able to find those bonds before the whole world goes hunting for them."

Peter watched the envelope swinging between Magee's fingers. Even if the bonds turned out to be worthless, he was now after a bigger truth, about money and business and New York power players. So he signed.

Then Magee said, "The answer is yes."

"Yes to what?"

"There are some disgruntled investors who happen to be Russian."

"Disgruntled?" said Peter.

"As Arsenault would tell you," said Magee, "investing is not an exact science."

Evangeline said, "That means he lost a lot of Russian money."

"Or Russian *American*?" said Peter.

"Russian . . . American . . . what does it matter when we're talking about money?" Magee got up and gestured for them both to come over to the curved window, to admire the Empire State Building and the other giants around Madison Square and the river of cars and people flowing down the streets. "Just look at it all. And think about it."

"What I'm thinking," said Peter, "is how do I find a small box of ancient bonds in all of that? It makes a needle in a haystack look like a fish in a barrel."

"You'd better find it," said Evangeline, "because with metaphors like that, you'll never be a writer."

Owen T. Magee said, "I don't think either of you is approaching this with the proper seriousness."

"The more serious it gets," said Evangeline, "the more I joke."

"Well, this is no joke," said Magee. "Boston is history. Washington is power. L.A. is entertainment. But New York is the center of the universe. And that intersection below us, where the two greatest streets in the world cross, is the center of the center."

"Mr. Magee, I know and love a lot of New Yorkers," said Peter, "but you are the most provincial people in the world."

Evangeline rolled her eyes. She'd heard this one before.

Magee hadn't. "How can you say that people who live in the most cosmopolitan place on earth are the most provincial?"

"Because New Yorkers really believe that they live in the center of the universe. But the center isn't real. It's an idea. In America, it's a lot of ideas."

Magee didn't miss a beat. "And what brings ideas to life, Mr. Fallon? *Money.* And Manhattan is money, plain and simple. It's money growing, money spent, money divided to double and divide again, money tucked and trimmed and shaved so that a penny made on a bid-ask trade is multiplied mathematically, then exponentially, and then again until it's grown into a fortune. It's money from all across the country, from all across the world, money that comes here to work for all those American ideas. Money matters, Mr. Fallon. It always has and always will."

"I know an old Boston bond trader who says that when you send your money to New York, nobody cares. It's just more gas to run the greed machine."

"He's wrong. Money's the gas, but it's also the grease, the oil, the fine lubricant without which nothing else works. Every big idea, every invention, every advance in science, art, and the way we live . . . it's all needed money to turn it from an idea to a reality. When Edison invented the electric light, the illumination of great cities was a dream.

It wasn't until he met J. P. Morgan and Morgan's money that they formed General Electric and lit lower Manhattan. Now the whole world glows at night. Why?"

"Because of Edison."

"Because of money. That's why New York is the center of the universe. Because we use money to fashion reality out of ideas."

Evangeline actually thought his voice cracked as he spoke.

"Money matters." And Magee dropped down into his chair, as if all that talk about his favorite subject had exhausted him. He took two or three deep breaths.

Evangeline said, "If I smoked, I'd offer you a cigarette."

Magee straightened up, smoothed his hair, and said, "Of course, we sometimes make mistakes, even in New York. And some clients don't understand. If all they wanted was a sure thing, they should have put their money in a bank."

After a moment, Peter asked if they could see the envelope of research.

Magee handed it over.

Peter pulled out a pile of papers. First was a page copied from a ledger from the New-York Historical Society. It showed state bond sales from 1780 to 1783, including the purchase of two hundred bonds, numbers 2510 through 2709, by a Loretta Rogers.

Peter looked at Evangeline. "That's L. R."

"That's what we've always believed," said Magee. "The one who wrote the letter that was stolen with the box. Read the next page."

Peter turned to a bill of sale recorded in a ledger at the Morgan Library.

Purchased of Timothy Riley of 436 W. Forty-eighth St., one New Emission Bond, number 2510. Face value $100. No redemption value. For the sum of ten dollars. J. P. Morgan.

Beneath that were two more entries, two later transactions between the boy from Hell's Kitchen and the financier.

Just then, Peter's cell phone vibrated in his pocket. Another text:

We have plenty to talk about. Can you come to the store now? Call from outside. I'll let you in. Delancey.

Peter texted back:

Ten minutes. Where the hell have you been?

Delancey's answer:

Trying to save America.

TEN

July 1893

From the moment Tim Riley knew that his father was dead, he resolved not to cry.

He held himself together all that hot afternoon, so that he could tell the police what he had seen. But he was an honest boy, so he admitted that he had not seen the killers' faces or recognized their voices. He could not even say how many there were because the oak tree that shielded him also blocked his view.

And he held himself together at the wake, when his father's body lay by the windows in the front room, beneath the framed picture of Jesus that his mother had cut from a calendar, and people climbed the narrow stairs and packed the stifling flat and brought buckets of beer and food, and all told him to be brave because he was now the man of the house.

That night, he and his brother tried to sleep in their parents' windowless bedroom while their mother kept vigil with the keening lady, a professional Irish mourner who sat by the coffin and chanted the low, haunting song that reminded every Irishman of some windswept Gaeltacht moor, even if he'd never been to Ireland or heard a word of Gaelic . . . a low, haunting, repetitive song that echoed through the tenement and kept everyone awake, except the corpse.

Around midnight, Eddie whispered, "Who'll help us now?"

"Boss Plunkitt," answered Tim. "Pa always said if we ever got into trouble and had nowhere to turn, we should go to Boss Plunkitt."

"Did Plunkitt say anything tonight about that funny old money?"

"He said I should come and see him on Monday. And that Tammany would pay our rent for six months. So we can stay here."

"Stay here? Who cares about stayin' here?" Eddie sat up. "Let's take some of that funny old money and buy a gun. We'll kill the McGillicuddys and go."

"We don't even know if it *is* money, and we don't even know where Pa hid it, and we don't even know if it was the McGillicuddys who killed him."

"We know. You know. You was there. It was the McGillicuddys. The fuckin' McGillicuddys."

"Don't let Ma hear you swearin'."

"She ain't listenin'. She's keenin' right along with that old Irish banshee. All that moanin' singsongin' is givin' me the willies." Eddie elbowed his brother. "It don't matter if folks at Tammany saw Strong make peace with Pa. It don't matter if folks lied and said the McGillicuddys was someplace else when it happened. It was *them*."

"Okay," answered Tim, "say it was. Where are two kids gonna get a gun?"

"I know places. I know guys. We shoot 'em both and leave New York."

"And go where?"

"Out West. Out where the cowboys are. Out where we can be cowboys."

"You mean . . . ride horses and stuff?"

"Yeah."

"You can't ride a horse. You only got one foot." Tim was sorry that he said that as soon as the words were out of his mouth.

Eddie rolled over and quietly cried himself to sleep.

DICK RILEY HAD been a man with a good reputation, an earned respect, so his friends and neighbors turned out for the funeral.

But in a church that could hold hundreds of people, a polished pine box with brass handles could look very lonely unless a crowd surrounded it. And a good ward boss made certain that every loyal constituent got a send-off worthy of a wealthy man. So George Washington Plunkitt put out the call for three hundred mourners.

And a hundred more appeared at the back of the church because a neighborhood lawyer named Sunny Jim Maguire was planning to run against Plunkitt in the fifteenth, and a funeral was a fine place to garner a few votes. With his blond hair and pearl-gray suits, Sunny Jim appeared to some as a source of light, but others said that no man who counted McGillicuddy's Saloon as a power base could ever shed light on anything. Sunny Jim had put out the word and handed out black armbands, and his "people" had crowded into the back of the church as if Six-Pound Dick had been one of their best friends.

At the end of the service, Father Higgins led the coffin and the family down the aisle, through the fog of sandalwood incense, while the voices of the Tammany Choir filled the church with "Faith of Our Fathers," a grand old Catholic recessional. Father Higgins waited for the hymn to end, then he performed the final blessing. Then he said to the dearly beloved, "There's a song Dick Riley loved. We did not sing it at the Benediction, and so I've asked a young lady of the parish to sing it for us now."

And from the choir loft came a voice as clear and clean as a Donegal stream. That's how people who had actually seen such a stream described it.

Panis Angelicus fit panis hominum

As she began to sing of the heavenly bread that becomes the bread of all mankind, Tim Riley lowered his head and cried.

Dat panis coelicus figures terminum

He cried for his mother and his brother.

O res mirabilis! Manducat dominum

It might have been a miraculous thing, he thought, that the body of Christ nourished the poorest and the most humble. But still Tim cried.

Pauper, Pauper servus et humilis

He cried with the frustration of knowing that the ones who had done the deed were probably somewhere in the church at that very moment.

Pauper, Pauper

He cried for the aching beauty of the song and of the girl who offered it.

Servus, servus et humilis

And he cried because, yes, his father had been one of the Lord's humble servants, but what a man.

He looked up at Doreen, and she gave him a small wave, and something passed between them in that moment, something as permanent as the church. And it made him dry his tears.

It was good that he did, because then he noticed the checkered suit of Strong McGillicuddy and the squashed-in face of Slick. They were standing at the far end of the second-last row, part of Maguire's crew of mourners.

And Tim thought that they were smiling . . . the bastards.

So all in the time it had taken Doreen to sing her song, Tim Riley had passed from despair to comfort and then to resolve.

Someday, maybe tomorrow, maybe years from now, he would do what Eddie wanted: He would kill Strong McGillicuddy . . . and Slick, too.

But not that day, and not in the days immediately thereafter.

THOSE DAYS BEGAN with sadness. It clenched in his chest as soon as he woke and worsened at mealtimes, when the little flat seemed somehow smaller with one less inhabitant. His mother cried when she cooked, then wiped her tears and got on. His brother cried when he sat at the table next to their father's empty chair. But Tim did his best not to cry at all.

It helped to walk after supper. He walked quickly, as if to pound out the sadness. He walked to the west, as if there was more hope toward the water than toward the town. He walked until he found a pier that seemed quiet, where he wouldn't run into longshoremen or local thugs or hootch-stunk bummies cadging coppers to buy more hootch. And he would go to the end of the pier and sit on a piling and watch the sun go down over Jersey.

And with each sunset, the pain grew weaker.

On the fifth evening, he walked onto a pier in the Thirties. It was after seven. The breeze puffed a bit. The water lapped against the pilings. The sky over Newark layered into colors that deepened by the minute. And out in the river, a black-hulled boat with a stack and two raked masts rode at anchor, a sleek silhouette in the setting sun. It was the *Corsair*, the yacht of J. P. Morgan himself.

The paper said that Morgan was living aboard for the summer. Tim had reread the last paragraph of the story many times: "He commutes each morning to Wall Street and each evening returns to sit on the fantail, smoke a cigar, and survey the city now lit by the Edison lights that, in his wisdom, J. P. Morgan financed. He tells friends that the evening breeze has a most salubrious effect whenever he suffers from the blues."

The blues. The richest man in New York suffered from the blues.

The yacht was turned upstream, into the current, so Tim could not see the fantail. He wondered if Morgan was sitting there now, puffing on his cigar, feeling sorry for himself. Morgan could not have felt worse than a boy from Hell's Kitchen whose father was dead, and that fine floating house would go far toward soothing the pain of a poor family.

So Tim Riley resolved something else: some day, after he had killed the McGillicuddys—or maybe before—he would find a way to get rich. As his father had told him, respect was nice, but money was the thing.

On Sunday, Uncle Billy came for dinner.

He sent Tim out to get a scuttle of suds at Deegan's Saloon, and after a few drinks, he told his sister how sorry he was.

Mary Riley took a sip of beer and said, " 'T'ain't your fault."

Tim noticed Uncle Billy's face redden, as if, perhaps, it *was*.

Then Uncle Billy offered to go up to Daggett Tavern and bring back the wagon. "I can take off the tools and sell 'em, I think."

"Sell the tools?" said Mary Riley. "And what will we do if we sell the tools?"

"I don't know, sis." Billy sniffled and dragged the back of his hand across his face. "I don't think I got the brains to run a business."

"Well, I *do*, by God," she said. "So go uptown and bring the wagon back and put it in the stall. We'll get two more horses and get back to business."

Tim had expected that his mother would fight. Her spirit made him proud.

And her bravery gave Uncle Billy some backbone, too. He took another swallow and said, "By God, you're right, Mary. I'm lucky to have a big sister like you."

"Lucky I don't hit you with a fryin' pan for comin' in here half drunk and weepy. We're done weepin'. Have a cry, then have a laugh, then get on. That's what Dick would say if he could."

THE NEXT MORNING, Tim and Uncle Billy went back to Daggett Tavern and found the wagon stripped. Every tool—including Dick Riley's six-pound hammer—was gone. So were the wagon wheels, the seat, the tongue, the hubs, even an old oilskin tarp. And the glue man had dragged off the horses.

Billy kicked at the stripped axle. "I hate to say it, but I ain't surprised."

"The city of dreams." Tim sat down under the oldest tree on the Upper West Side and buried his head in his hands. "More like the city of nightmares."

"It ain't all nightmares, Timmy boy. It'll be all right. Wait and see."

"I heard that stuff from half the people at the wake." Tim pressed the heels of his hands against his eyes and reminded himself what his mother had said, that they were done weepin'. "You gotta tell me somethin' better."

Billy looked out at the carriages and delivery wagons passing on Broadway, then he looked down at his big hands. " 'Tis the best I got. What about Boss Plunkitt? What did he tell you about them pieces of paper?"

"He told me to come and see him."

"A boy sittin' down with George Washington Plunkitt?" Uncle Billy shook his head. "Like Daniel sittin' down with the lion. When's the meet?"

Tim knew that he should have lied, but he was not a good liar, at least not yet. "He told me to come see him at Washington Hall this afternoon."

"Done then." Uncle Billy put an arm around the boy's shoulder. "You and me, we'll meet him together. And there'll be no outsmartin' us."

Tim smelled beer on Billy's breath, saw bloodshot in Billy's eyes, and wanted to pull away. But there was muscle in Billy's emotion, so pulling away wasn't easy.

"I know what your da used to say about me, Timmy . . . that I was worthless, that I drink too much and talk too much and was never man enough to get a family of me own. But now, me sister's family needs me. And like she said, we're done weepin'. You'll see who's worthless and who ain't."

"I know you ain't worthless, Uncle Billy."

"That's the sentiment I was hopin' for." Billy released his grip, then pulled out a hip flask and had a drink. "I'm glad we understand each other."

"We do, but for one thing."

"What's that?"

Tim stood, walked over to the great gray trunk, and looked up into the leaves. "When I was hidin' on the roof, when they was beatin' Pa, I heard 'em askin' about the little papers we found. Only two men outside our flat knew about them. Plunkitt and you."

Billy Donovan's mouth dropped open, then he closed it, then he tightened it until his face turned as red as his handkerchief. Like a lot of drinkers, he could play offended anger as well as an actor in a Bowery theater. He stood and stalked over to Tim and said, "You listen to me, you little squint, I ain't a man who blabs, no matter what your da ever said. And if *you* say that I am, I'll take my fist to ye, God help me."

Tim knew he had pushed far enough, so he said, "Yeah, sure, Uncle Billy, whatever you say."

"All right, then." The red faded from Billy's face. He gave a nod, as if he had proved his point. "I'll meet you at Washington Hall on Eighth Avenue at three o'clock. We'll go see the sachem together."

Yeah, sure, Uncle Billy, whatever you say.

There was no way that Tim Riley would talk to Boss Plunkitt with Uncle Billy along, acting like the new man in the Riley house.

So, after they left the tavern, Tim took the El all the way downtown.

He got off at Chambers Street and walked a few blocks east to the New York County Courthouse.

The majestic pillars and grand staircase announced that this was a place where men did important business. Inside, the rotunda rose to skylights that poured sunshine into every gilded, marbled, painted corner and announced that the men who did that important business would never fear the bright light of day. But even a boy—if he read the papers—knew that this building was a monument to the most vaulting corruption in American history.

There had been a man named Tweed. He had been an alderman, a county supervisor, and the boss of Tammany. He had invented a thousand ways to make himself and his cronies rich through kickbacks, bribes, extortions, payoffs, and twist-arm contributions to the Tammany cause. The courthouse should have cost a quarter of a million dollars, but New Yorkers had ended up paying out fourteen million for it, and most of the money had gone straight into the pockets of Tweed and his Tammany pals.

Boss Tweed died in jail in 1878, but his name echoed through the halls of corruption like Tim's heels echoing across the marble floor of the rotunda.

Plunkitt had come on the scene near the end of Tweed's reign, but he had made himself rich, too, mostly buying land and reselling it to the city when he learned of some new public project. He called it "honest graft," and if he was challenged, he defended himself in the papers with honest bluntness: "I seen my opportunities and I took 'em."

Tim followed the echoing *pop-plop-pop-plop* of a buffing rag down the stairs to the lower level.

His heart was pounding, because he was about to learn the future. If the bonds were good, he would move out of Hell's Kitchen, buy his mother a new Singer, and see that his brother had the best fake foot that money could buy. If not, he would soon have to leave school and go to work to support what was left of his family.

He rounded a bend in the corridor and came to a pair of chairs on a little platform. On the wall above the chairs were two small American flags, and a sign: *GRAZIANO'S BOOTBLACK. BOOTS, 5¢, SHOES 3¢.*

On the left, a small dark man with a bent back was polishing a customer's boot. *Pop-plop-pop-plop-pop-plop.*

On the right, a man sat with one foot propped on the shining brace, the other on his knee, and the *New York Sun* open in front of him.

Tim stood close enough to read the *Sun* headline but not the fine print.

A voice rose from behind the paper. "I thought we was meetin' later."

"I couldn't wait."

Plunkitt lowered the paper. "You got your whole life ahead of you, son. Learn to wait."

"It's just that—" The boy shot a glance at Graziano.

"This here's my confessional," said Plunkitt.

"No kneelin'. No prayin'. But if there's secrets to be kept, we keep 'em. Even with a kid. Ain't that right, fellers?"

Graziano said, "Kid? What kid? I don't see a kid." He looked at his customer. "You see a kid?"

"Ain't no place for a kid." The customer climbed down, dropped a few coins into Graziano's hand, and walked away

Tim climbed up and sat next to Plunkitt, who pulled out a cigar and bit the end while Graziano struck a match.

As Plunkitt puffed the flame into the cigar, he asked Tim, "So what is it that can't wait till this afternoon?"

"My pa's wagon been stripped. And his tools was stolen. And my uncle isn't too smart. And my ma isn't up to takin' in more sewin'. And while we appreciate six months' rent from Tammany, I'm wonderin', did you find out about—"

"You're askin' about the bond?"

"Yes, sir."

Plunkitt winked at Graziano, who went whistling down the corridor. Then he said to Tim, "Worthless."

Tim looked down at his hands and the scuffed tops of his boots. "Worthless?"

"Ever heard the old sayin' 'worthless as a Continental'?"

"I heard my pa use it."

"Well, that bond was printed on the same kind of paper, by the same bankrupt government." Plunkitt took out an envelope and put it on the boy's lap. "It's in there."

"Who said it was worthless?" asked Tim.

Plunkitt could not have been used to questioning, especially from a boy, but a ward boss seldom showed emotion unless it served a purpose. So he chewed a bit on his cigar, then said, "There's all kinds of people in the fifteenth, son. Some work with their hands, like your pa. Others wear white collars and ride desks, like a feller named Daniel Daly. He works at Drexel, Morgan and Company on Wall Street, and—"

"And *he* said it was worthless?"

Plunkitt bit down on his cigar, gave it a good chew, then took it out and said in a voice as calm as that quiet corridor, "Mr. Daly asked a feller in the U. S. Treasury, who said they've seen a few of these over the years but never honored one, for a lot of reasons, startin' with what I just said—they're too old."

"I thought old things got more valuable."

"Some things don't. Old men, old clothes, old bonds from an old government." Plunkitt flicked his ash. "The Treasury man said a few people had tried suin', but the government decides who can sue them and who can't. You have to fight that fight first."

Tim Riley slumped back in the chair.

"Best thing, son, sell them to a collector. Try Daly's boss, J. P. Morgan. He collects old autographs, old government documents, and such. He might be interested. But quit thinkin' that these are worth real money." Plunkitt picked up the paper, as if to say that the meeting was over.

Then Graziano came whistling back.

Tim climbed down from the chair. "Thank you, sir."

And Plunkitt lowered the paper again, "How old are you, boy?"

"Almost fourteen."

"When I was fourteen, I went to work drivin' a cart for the contractor cuttin' in the paths and the pretty bowers of what we now call Central Park. Then I went down to Washington Market and worked as a butcher's boy. Learned knife-sharpenin' and meat-cuttin', learned how to tell the difference 'tween the tenderloin and the chuck—"

"Eh . . . you learn you like the tenderloin," said Graziano. "That's what you learn."

Plunkitt smiled. Sitting on his wooden throne, beneath those little flags, he looked like the benevolent ruler of a small and quiet kingdom, so secure in his power that he took no umbrage when one of his subjects made a joke at his expense.

"What about you?" he asked Tim. "You like the tenderloin?"

"I guess."

"The tenderloin is meat, son, good red meat, not pie in the sky, not like a box of old bonds you found when you was tearin' down a house."

"How did you know there was a box of them?" asked Tim.

"I didn't, till just now. But it don't matter whether you got a box full of 'em or just one. A hundred times zero and one times zero is both zero. That's mathematics."

"That's what my pa said I should study."

"Because he was practical. He didn't want you crammin' your skull with all kinds of college rot like that Shakespeare, who might know about English kings and airy fairies runnin' around English forests, but who don't know nothin' about New York City."

The boy shoved his hands into his pockets and looked at the floor, "I guess I like Shakespeare's stories. I like his speeches."

"I like stories, too," said Plunkitt. "I tell enough of 'em. As for speeches . . . well, it don't matter that I only had three years of schoolin'. I can sling the English with any silk stockin' in the district. But smart men keep their tongues still and their brains active."

"Yes, sir."

"So remember"—Plunkitt pulled out a match and relit his cigar—"education is good, but common sense is better, and when it's yoked to hard work . . . *that's* the best."

"Yes, sir."

"After I learned I liked the tenderloin, I asked myself how to get it. I went into contractin', usin' what I learned drivin' that cart. Then I had to ask myself how to get the best contracts. That's when I decided to go into politics. So I started an association."

For a man who believed in keeping his tongue still, thought Tim, Plunkitt sure could make it move.

"I asked a few fellers in my tenement to back me, and they did. Then I asked a few more on my block, and they did. Pretty soon, I had a gang of fellers who'd stick by me in a political fight or any other kind. That's when I started gettin' attention at the hall. And it all come from common sense and hard work, and rememberin' the first rule."

"What's that?"

"Every man wants somethin'. Figure out what it is, find a way to give it to him, and you'll make a friend for life. . . . Now let me see your hands."

Tim pulled them out of his pockets and offered them, palm up.

"No callus, so I don't guess you've done much drivin', so we won't put you on a team." Plunkitt peered into the boy's eyes. "And you don't look tough enough to handle yourself in the Washington Market just yet—"

Tim resented that. He *was* tough. But he knew he would have to get tougher.

Plunkitt kept talking. "Go home and think what it is you really *want.* Then come back and see me. Bring your brother, too. And Tim—"

"Yes, sir?"

"This is a grand and imperial city you live in. It will reward you, if you make the right choice."

ii.

Tim walked all the way home, so that he could save the nickel carfare and stop off at the New York Society Library on Twelfth Street. He stayed for two hours in the upstairs reading room, surrounded by the railed balcony, the walnut shelves, and the warm wood, all bathed in the gentle glow of the skylight.

By the time he got back to Hell's Kitchen, it was near three o'clock. So he went up Eighth Avenue, on the side opposite Washington Hall, but Uncle Billy wasn't waiting. No surprise. Probably drunk. So Tim turned for home.

As he passed under the El, he saw a gang of kids clustered in front of his tenement, as if there was a fight. He began to run.

"YOU AIN'T PUSHIN' me around," Eddie was leaning on his crutch and trying to stand up to a kid who was a head taller and muscled like a man.

"Things are changin'." That was Dinny Boyle. He was seventeen and already chewed tobacco and drank and ran a crap game at the corner. His father was a conductor on the New York Central. His mother was a drunk, often seen around the corner at McGillicuddy's.

"Things are changin'?" repeated Eddie. "Says who and so what?"

"Says me, and so what *you* got to do, if you want to sit on this stoop and play your harmonica . . . is pay."

"Pay who?" said Eddie.

"Pay me." Boyle said it loudly so that all the kids could hear, and any grown-ups looking out the windows could, too. "I'm the new street captain."

"Street captain?" said Eddie. "What's that?"

"A job I just got," said Boyle.

"My old man needs a job," said one of the other kids. "Who give *you* a job?"

"Yeah," said another. "With this panic thing, everybody's old man needs a job."

What Dinny Boyle said next caused Tim to stop in his tracks: "The Irish Niners give me the job."

"The Irish Niners?" said one of the younger kids. "Who are they?"

"They used to be a gang," said Eddie. "But my pa beat 'em down single-handed."

"Well, they're back," said Dinny Boyle. "And they ain't a gang no more. They're a political organization. They made me captain on this street and told me I could start an association. So"—he spit a wad of tobacco—"join up or pay."

Tim pushed through the crowd to get to his brother.

But Eddie had always been quick on his crutch and quick with his tongue, and he said to Dinny Boyle, "Fuck you and the horse you rode in on."

"Fuck me? No, you crip. Fuck you."

Tim grabbed his brother.

"Yeah," said Boyle. "Get him out of my sight. And tell your ma you can join the Dinny Boyle Association or pay to sit on the stoop."

"THAT DIDN'T TAKE long," said Mary Riley. "Your father not dead a week and the troublemakers already stirrin'."

"You mean Dinny Boyle?" asked Tim.

"She means the fuckin' McGillicuddys," said Eddie.

Mary Riley slapped the boy across the face. "There'll be none of that talk in my house. There never was when your da was alive, and there won't be now."

Eddie brought his hand to his cheek and looked down at the floor, as if trying to control his anger. "No back talk" had been one of Six-Pound's favorite phrases.

Mary Riley raised her apron to her eyes and

wiped them, then she said, "But Eddie's right. The McGillicuddys is the troublemakers."

They were standing in the little windowless kitchen. Their mother had gotten back to baking. She said that a soda bread with a few bits of raisin and carroway seed would cheer them all, but to bake she had to raise the fire, which raised the heat. So she kept the door open to the hallway, but it did little to cool a top-floor flat in July.

Tim wiped the sweat from his forehead and stepped into the front room, where the open windows gave a bit of air. "What do we do?"

"You know what we do." Eddie followed. *Clump-thump-clump-thump*. Good foot-crutch-fake foot-crutch. "I told you what we do the other night."

"What we do," said their mother, "is put up with what we must."

"Tim! Hello, Timmy Riley!" Uncle Billy stomped into the flat, looking angry but sounding hurt. "I waited till four o'clock, Timmy. It was you and me together. That was the plan. But you never showed, so I went up and talked to Plunkitt meself. He said you come down to see him at the courthouse instead."

"I couldn't wait," answered Tim.

"Made me look like a fool," said Uncle Billy.

"At least it was somethin' you're used to," said Mary.

"Now, sis, I stood in front of the sachem himself and didn't know a thing to ask."

"I did," said Tim. "And he said the bonds are worthless."

"Worthless, is it?" Mary Riley seemed to sag, right where she stood.

"They was bonds?" said Billy. "The funny money is bonds?"

"Worthless," repeated Tim.

"So you mean this is it?" Eddie looked around the flat. "This is all we got to look forward to? Just this?"

Their mother stalked across the room and slapped Eddie again, and before he could react, she threw her arms around him and said how sorry she was. "But this is what the Lord give us, son, what your da earned for us, a roof over your head and a family that loves you in a parish that cares. It's better than what most folks have."

"Right," said Billy. "Sayin' less is a black mark on your da's blessed memory."

Eddie pulled away and headed for the hallway.

"Where are you goin'?" asked their mother.

"Downstairs. It's too hot in here, and I want to play my harmonica, and I like to play it on the stoop, where I ain't payin' because somebody wants to start an ass . . . assoshi . . . What did he call it?"

"Association," said Tim. "It's how a man gets power in politics. He starts with his building, then his block—"

"Well, I ain't lettin' that Dinny Boyle get power over me," said Eddie.

The crutch *clump-thumped* down the hallway, then Mary Riley said, "I don't like it that the McGillicuddys is backin' Dinny Boyle . . . or Sunny Jim. Imagine Strong and Slick bossin' a boss. Imagine them bossin' a *district*."

"That Strong ain't so bad," said Uncle Billy. "He come to the funeral. He stood me to a drink this afternoon at his ma's place."

"I wish you wouldn't go in there," said Mary Riley.

"Ah"—Uncle Billy made a wave of his hand—"I go where I want when I want."

Mary Riley wiped her hands on her apron. "If Plunkitt loses his seat to the McGillicuddy man, where do we go for help?"

"Why do you think I drink with them?" asked Billy. "It's so they give me a job. Strong said I could work behind the bar."

"You'd work for the McGillicuddys?" said Tim.

"'Twould put us in good, no matter how the election comes out," said Billy. "Any port in a storm."

"I'd rather see the ship sink," said Mary.

TIM NEEDED A walk after that.

He avoided eye contact with a bunch of kids hanging at the corner of Tenth Avenue. Eye contact could be a challenge in any neighborhood. But he could not avoid the smell of a dead horse on the corner of Eleventh. The flies had gotten there ahead of the glue wagon.

A freight train chugged slowly down the center of the avenue, filling the street with the bulk and stink of cattle cars bound for the slaughterhouse. A man in a scally cap rode a horse a block ahead of the engine and rang a bell to warn people out of the way.

Every kid in Hell's Kitchen dreamed of being the Eleventh Avenue cowboy, except for Tim. He usually avoided this stretch, because this was where his brother had lost his foot.

Eddie had seen a big chunk of coal on the tracks. A kid on the other side of the street had seen it, too. And there was a train coming. But picking up coal that the trains dropped on Eleventh was like picking up pennies that the swells dropped on Broadway. Eddie was a lot faster than the other kid, but only a little faster than the train. And when he stopped to pick up the coal, the train won and crushed his foot.

Tim tried not to think about all that had followed: the horror of seeing that mangled foot, the sad homecoming after a stay in the hospital, the nights of whimpering pain, the unhappiness that could come over Eddie like a cloud on a clear day, the anger that could come even more quickly.

So Tim kept walking. He found his way to that pier in the Thirties. He wandered out to the end, sat on a piling, listened to the lap of the water, and heard a soft voice whisper from behind him, "I'm sorry for your troubles."

He turned to a vision in gray shift and ankle socks: Doreen Walsh. Her strawberry-blond hair shimmered, and the light made her eyes more green than hazel.

"How did"—his mouth went dry—"how did you—"

"I followed you. I felt sad for you, seein' you walkin' down here alone. So I snuck out and followed you."

He looked behind her. "Does your pa know?"

She shook her head. "And I told my ma I was goin' for a singin' lesson."

"You sang real nice at the funeral."

"Thanks." She came over and sat down beside him. It was a big piling. "Someday, I plan to sing in a show."

Her soft thigh pressed against his, and a jolt of life shot through him. It was the best feeling he had known in days . . . or ever.

"That's a . . . a nice dream," he said. "To sing in a show."

"I got the voice." She swung her foot, so that her leg peeked out from beneath the shapeless shift. "You got any dreams?"

He looked at her leg. He did not tell her that touching it was one of his nightly dreams. Instead, he looked off toward the sunset. "I got a dream to get rich."

"My pa says the only way any of us would get rich is to find a box of money."

Tim looked at her, to see if there was something in her eye to suggest she had heard about his box of funny money. All he saw was that fine-colored hair and those sweet features. And he could not help himself. He leaned over and kissed her cheek.

She popped off the piling as if a wharf rat had tugged at her sock. "Tim Riley! Just because I talk to you, it don't mean you can kiss me."

"Sorry."

"My pa would kill me if he knew I was sittin' with a boy. He'd kill me and cut me up into little pieces and dump me in the river if he thought I was lettin' a boy *kiss* me."

"I said I'm sorry. I . . . you just look so pretty."

She studied him a moment more, like someone trying to decide if she should trust a snappish dog, then she sat again. "So . . . what was you starin' at out there?"

He pointed down the river to the *Corsair*. "The papers say J. P. Morgan is spendin' his summer on his boat. Sure would be nice . . . sittin' out there catchin' the breeze after work."

"Sure would be nice to get rich. If you got rich, you could back my show."

And for a while, the two kids sat there thinking about the future and about the rich man on his boat. Then they walked home together, but when they reached the block, they split up and walked down opposite sides of the street.

"We don't want your pa cuttin' you up and feedin' you to the fish."

And Tim Riley went to bed thinking of two things: J. P. Morgan's money and the softness of Doreen Walsh's cheek.

iii.

It was quiet in the neighborhood for the next week or so.

There was a shooting at the corner of Forty-second and Tenth.

A Negro couple stumbled into a gang on Eighth Avenue, and when the husband took offense at remarks passed about his wife, they beat him almost to death.

A dray horse dropped in his traces on Forty-sixth, and before they could drag the carcass out of the way, the driver of a carriage stuck behind the dray started cussing, so the drayman took an ax handle to the driver's face.

Uncle Billy disappeared on Thursday, and by Saturday morning, they still hadn't heard from him. "Another toot," their mother said.

And a new heat wave boiled into town, bringing humidity so dense that the city air seemed cloudy, even though there were no clouds, and the tenement air took on a taste to go with the smell. Every breath was like sipping a foul soup of oatmeal and cabbage and greasy boiled meat.

So Tim was happy to take his mother's grocery list and head for the Paddy Market on Saturday night.

That was when all the peddlers on the West Side gathered between Thirty-eighth and Forty-second, under the Ninth Avenue El. They parked their carts. They lit lanterns and torches. And they hawked and haggled and shouted and sold, and whether you were buying carrots or beef shins or big rounds of upstate cheddar, the bargains got better and better as the night wore on, and the shouting and the selling grew more frantic, until not even the passing of the trains could drown out the din.

Tim loved it.

Eddie usually avoided it. But that night, for some reason, he *clump-thumped* along with his brother. They had almost reached Forty-first when someone called to them.

It was Doreen. "My ma sent me down to get a

dozen eggs for Sunday breakfast. Can I walk with you?"

"Sure," said Tim.

"So long as she don't sing," said Eddie. *Clump-thump-clump-thump.*

"Your brother isn't very nice," said Doreen to Tim as she followed.

"I ain't," said Eddie. "But I hear you got nice bubbies, so you can walk with us."

Doreen stopped and put her hands on her hips. "Who said I got nice bubbies?"

"My brother."

She shifted her eyes. "How do you know what I got that's nice, Tim Riley?"

"He can see, can't he?" said Eddie.

Tim smacked the back of his brother's head and pulled his own hat down over his eyes in embarrassment.

"I think they're nice, too." Eddie pulled the harmonica from his pocket. "So I'll play them a song."

"A song?" She almost laughed. "Tim, your brother is strange."

Tim peeked from under the brim of his hat.

Eddie started in on "McNally's Row of Flats." It came from one of the big Harrigan and Hart downtown shows. Everybody knew it.

And as if she couldn't help herself, Doreen started singing:

Down in Bottle Alley, lived Timothy McNally
A decent politician and a gentleman at that

The girl sure loved to sing, thought Tim.

Beloved by all the ladies, the gossoons and the babies,
That occupy the building called McNally's Row of Flats

She loved an audience, too. Her eyes flashed around at the faces now turning toward them, and she whispered, "C'mon, boys, the chorus. You know it."

Tim decided that if it would put him back into her good graces, he would sing:

And it's Ireland and Italy, Jerusalem and Germany,
Chinese and Africans and a paradise for rats,

More heads turned. Passersby slowed to listen. A few even joined in the chorus.

All jumbled up together in the snow and rainy weather,
They constitute the tenants in McNally's Row of Flats.

Then Eddie launched into an instrumental bridge, a jaunty Irish reel that he played as fast and furious on the harmonica as if it were a tin whistle.

And when the song was done, a dozen people had gathered around, and it looked as if they came from all the places celebrated in the song. And they were all applauding.

Tim was so surprised that he just laughed. But

Eddie was smart enough to take off his hat and make a big show of how hard it was to bow on a crutch. And Doreen was even smarter. She snatched Tim's hat off his head and held it out.

The kids sang two more songs and passed the hat twice more and came away with seventy-five cents in nickels and pennies.

As another train roared overhead, they divided the money.

"We make a good team," said Doreen.

"Yeah," said Eddie. "You're singin' better."

"And you're pretty good on that thing," she answered. "Even if you *are* fresh."

Eddie grinned.

"Hey, mutts!" Dinny Boyle and two pals were hanging by a delivery cart on the corner. "It's good you're singin' down here. You sing on my street, you'll have to pay."

"Says who?" Eddie's mood changed in an instant.

"Says Mr. Strong McGillicuddy. He made a rule. Nobody sings on Forty-eighth without they pay the street captain, which, as I already told you, is me."

"I never heard that rule before," said Doreen.

"You never sang with these nancy-boys before." Dinny stepped up onto the curb and kicked away Eddie's crutch, sending Eddie sprawling onto the sidewalk.

"Hey, there!" shouted a woman trundling along with her shopping bags. "Don't be doin' that to a cripple, especially one who can play the harmonica so nice."

"Oooh, jeez, I'm sorry there, lady," said Dinny Boyle. Then he leaned down to Eddie, who was struggling to pick himself up from the litter of newspapers and cabbage leaves and tobacco spit on cobblestones, and he shouted, "Oopsie-daisy!" Then he spun about, knocked Tim's hat off, and he and his friends went laughing up Ninth Avenue.

By the time another train thundered overhead, Eddie had gotten up and was thumping down the street.

"Hey!" shouted Tim. "Where are you goin'?"

"I got somethin' to do," answered Eddie. "Get the stuff for Ma. I'll see you at home."

"Ain't you gonna go with him?" asked Doreen.

"He gets like that some time. It's the foot. He gets mad at the foot. Then he gets mad at everybody. You can't talk to him. You just let him alone."

Doreen watched him for a moment, then said, "Is it true what Dinny said?"

"About what?"

"About how you're nancy-boys?"

Tim's answer was to kiss Doreen right on the mouth. And when he felt her mouth against his, he opened his mouth and touched her tongue with his. He had never known any experience to equal it. His whole being seemed to expand.

"And what do you think you're doin'?" A police officer came twirling his nightstick. "Get along with you before I find your parents."

WHEN TIM CAME home with the bundles from the Paddy Market, he knew that something was wrong. Eddie was sitting in the front room in the dark. Their mother was slumped in her windowless bedroom, staring at the flickering oil lamp.

"Ma?" Tim put down the bundles.

She gestured to the piggy bank on her dresser. "There was forty-seven dollars in there. I give you two dollars for to buy groceries, so there should be forty-five dollars left. But there's only thirty-five. Did you take it?"

"Me? No!" Tim walked into the front room. "Eddie?"

Eddie just shrugged.

After an hour of interrogation, their mother gave up. She blew out the lamps and told the boys to go to bed. She said she'd expect an explanation in the morning. "And remember, it's a sin to receive Communion if you been tellin' lies."

The boys pissed into the chamber pot. Then they pulled the rolling bed out from under the sofa in the front room. Eddie slept on the inside, facing the wall. Tim slept on the outside, facing the other direction. But it was hot and the street was noisy and Tim's mind was working, so he could not sleep. He rolled over and lay on his back and stared at the shadows of the street lamps, then he rolled over again, and then again, and that was when he felt it.

He jumped up and reached under the mattress and pulled out a pistol. It had a short barrel, a wooden handle.

"It ain't loaded," said Eddie. "I hid the bullets. I took the ten bucks from Ma's piggy bank and bought the gun from a guy on Fortieth."

"Ma will kill you."

"Better her than the McGillicuddys or that prick Dinny Boyle."

Tim did not grip the gun by the handle. He held it in the palms of his hands, like a living thing. The metal flashed blue in the half-light rising from the street.

"I got it planned." Eddie swung around in bed and sat up. "We do it late at night, when they're sweepin' up, right when a train is passin', so no one hears the shots."

"We?"

"*I'll* do it. They won't expect a crip with a wooden foot to walk in and start shootin'."

Across the way, somebody threw something out a window and it splashed on the sidewalk. A full chamber pot.

Eddie said, "It'll be like in the cowboy books. I'll shoot Strong first, then Slick. Then I'll shoot the mother if she's there."

"And then you'll run away?"

"I *can't* run, asshole." Usually when Eddie said something like that he sulked for ten minutes. To-night, he kept talking. "But I got it figured."

Downstairs, a man yelled. A woman yelled back, then she screamed. The Fighting Flahertys were at it again.

Eddie said, "I'll use the fire escape. You drop the ladder as soon as you hear the shots. And I'll climb up. Like Pa used to say, my arms are strong from liftin' my own weight all the time. Then we'll pull up the ladder and—"

"This is stupid."

"The McGillicuddys ain't done, Timmy. You know that. They was lookin' for that funny money when they come after Pa. They heard about it from Uncle Billy, I bet."

"But the bonds are worthless. They must've heard that from Uncle Billy, too."

"What if they don't believe him? They smell money, they'll never let us rest. And they know you was in the house when they killed Pa, so—"

There was movement in the other room.

"Shit." Eddie grabbed the gun and shoved it under the mattress.

Their mother shuffled in. "What are you boys doin' still awake?"

"Can't sleep," said Tim. "Mr. Flaherty's beatin' his wife again."

She listened for a moment to the sounds echoing through the tenement, then she looked around, found the chamber pot, and disappeared into the hot darkness.

The boys lay back. They heard their mother adding to the pot in the other room. They heard Mrs. Flaherty crying.

"If you don't help me," said Eddie, "I'll do it myself."

"What if I could find a way to buy us out of here? What if I had a plan? Would you wait?"

"You promise not to tell Ma about the gun?"

"So long as you promise not to use it."

THE NEXT DAY, their mother gave them the "good conscience" treatment. During breakfast, on the walk to Mass, and all through a stifling afternoon of humid rain, she said nothing about the money. Finally, over a dinner of baked beans, she allowed as how it was possible she had miscounted. Maybe she had been light a ten spot all along.

That, they knew, was another part of the "good conscience" treatment. But the boys held fast and kept quiet.

It was still raining the next morning.

Tim rose early and walked down to the pier at the base of Thirty-fifth Street. On the north side, a freighter was unloading coffee. Teamsters were driving wagons. Longshoremen were shouting. Small ferries were puttering over from New Jersey.

Tim leaned against a tarp-covered pallet and waited.

Around eight o'clock, a black box cab clattered onto the dock and stopped at the head of a gangway. At the same time, a steam launch pushed away from the *Corsair*.

The driver of the cab popped a black umbrella and went down the gangway to the slip dock at water level. About ten minutes later, the umbrella rose above the head of the richest man in New York.

Even if Tim had not known J. P. Morgan by his photograph, he would have picked him out by his imperious gaze, his potent bulk, his Olympian solitude. No entourage of lackeys followed him. No secretary whispered in his ear. Though the dock was busy with comings and goings, no one was audacious enough to approach him. And he offered eye contact to no one. Instead, he kept his gaze fixed on some middle distance, where maybe there was a pile of money that only he could see.

The driver held the right-side door, Morgan stepped aboard, the springs creaked, and the black cab sped off toward Wall Street.

Then Tim Riley went home to refine his plan.

By Tuesday morning, the rain had turned to summer drizzle. The dank overcast lay so low that it was hard to tell where the clouds ended and the river began.

Again the cab arrived at eight o'clock, the launch puttered in, the great man rose beneath his umbrella and stepped onto the cab.

And Tim Riley swallowed his fear. Then he willed his knees to stop shaking and his legs to start moving, and as the cab rolled away, he ran.

He grabbed the left-side door, pulled it open, and threw himself inside.

Later, he would remember the horse's hooves clopping on the cobblestones, the rocking motion, the smell of tobacco and leather. But at that moment, all he heard, felt, smelled, or saw was the presence of J. P. Morgan.

A huge white face—from which erupted a massive, bulbous, red nose—loomed above him. All else around the face—Morgan's black hat and morning coat, the shadowed interior of the cab, the gray world outside—existed to frame that face and the angry black eyes aimed now at Tim Riley.

"Stop!" cried Morgan. "Smythe! Stop! Instantly!"

"Please, sir," said Tim.

Morgan kicked him. "Get out. Get out or I'll flay you."

All in an instant, the cab stopped, the driver

pulled open the door and grabbed Tim by the belt. "Get out, you little bastard."

Tim did not have time to reflect on how badly this was going. As the driver pulled him out, he snatched the envelope from his pocket and threw it on the seat next to Morgan. A moment later, he landed in a puddle of water and horse piss.

"I ought to have you arrested," cried the driver.

"Not today," growled Morgan. "I'm in a hurry."

As the cab clattered away, Tim saw Morgan pick up the envelope.

It was addressed to Mr. J. P. Morgan, Esq. Tim had added the esquire because he thought it sounded important. Inside was a 1780 bond and a letter:

Mr. Morgan,

I am in possession of several of these. They may be of interest to yourself as a collector of historical treasures. If so, please contact me at 436 West Forty-eighth Street.

Yours, Timothy Riley

TIM RILEY DID not hear from J. P. Morgan that day or the day after. He thought about going back and jumping into the carriage again, but he expected that the left-side door would now be locked.

So he read. And he listened to his brother play the harmonica. And he went for his evening walks in the hopes that Doreen would join him again. But her father had heard about that sidewalk kiss, and he had informed Tim's mother that any further liberties with his daughter would result in a busted head for her son.

Then Uncle Billy showed up again.

He had been to the barber, so his face shone like a polished apple. His hair was slick, and he didn't smell of beer but of bay rum hair tonic.

After Billy had been on a toot for a while, he always awoke one morning and decided that he had been drunk long enough. He would clean himself up and get back to work—whatever it was—and then, about a month later, he would have a beer, and the next day he would have two beers, then three, and so on, until the cycle started again.

It had been easy for Billy to go on his toots when his brother-in-law held a job for him. But when he came to the door that afternoon, bearing a bunch of daisies, Tim wondered who had hired him now.

Billy grinned and handed the daisies to his sister.

She took them like a woman receiving a rent notice. "Where'd you get five cents to buy these? Didn't you drink up all your money?"

"I drank most of it." Billy smiled sheepishly. "But I got a job, too."

"A job? Where? Jobs is hard to come by."

"Now, sis, I know you won't be too happy, but—"

"Mother of God . . . you didn't take the job at McGillicuddy's?"

"I went to two or three other places and they all said that with this panic thing, they got no work for a simple drinkin' Irishman who don't have no skills beyond brute strength and ignorance. So I took what I could get, all so's I could give you this." Billy offered her an envelope. "Call it a little advance."

Mary looked at the envelope but did not take it.

Tim looked at Eddie, who had stopped playing his harmonica.

"If you're workin' for the McGillicuddys," she said, "you ain't welcome here."

"What?" Uncle Billy ran through his series of expressions. "Not welcome? But I been tryin' to tell you, they ain't such bad fellers. Even Slick said it's all bygones now."

"Bygones my bottom." Mary Riley grabbed a glass jar from the shelf. "I better go get some water for these flowers." And she stomped out.

Tim asked his uncle, "So what do they want from you?"

"*Want* from me?"

"Every man always wants something. Figure out what it is and give it to him and he'll be your friend for life. That's what Boss Plunkitt says."

"As a matter of fact"—Billy glanced over his shoulder to see if his sister was out of earshot—"Strong asked me again about the bonds. I told him what Plunkitt said. Strong said Plunkitt lies about everything, so he probably lied about that, and if we give him and Sunny Jim a look, they might be able to help us."

A FEW NIGHTS later, Tim went out for his walk. But instead of heading for the river, he went over to Ninth Avenue and half a block south under the El until he came to the words MCGILLICUDDY'S SALOON painted across a plate glass window in gilded block letters. He peered in. The place was deep, but no wider than the flats directly above it. The long bar on the right faced the tables on the left. Sawdust covered the floor. Gaslights burned bright and yellow, but the shadows were dark in the corners. A sign hung above the bar: *THE IRISH NINERS POLITICAL CLUB SUPPORTS SUNNY JIM MAGUIRE.*

It was a quiet night. Two drinkers stood at the bar. Two or three more sat at a table in the back. Strong played solitaire at a side table, a coffee mug next to the cards, a leather blackjack next to the coffee.

Mother Mag worked behind the bar, in the place where Tim had expected to see Uncle Billy.

But Billy had other duties. He came staggering out of the shadows and set an armload of beer mugs on the bar. Then he picked up a rag, got down on his knees, and began polishing the brass foot rail.

Mother Mag leaned over and watched him for a moment. Then she snatched the rag and shook it in his face. Then she grabbed a broom and put it into his hands and gestured for him to sweep.

Tim felt something rise in his throat, a strange mix of embarrassment and pity. Billy wasn't a bartender. He was just a janitor who cleaned the puke from the corners when the drunks threw up and emptied the spittoons in the street when the tobacco-spitters filled them.

Billy began to sweep the sawdust, and Strong leaned back in his chair to watch, like a man enjoying a show.

So Uncle Billy was right, thought Tim. Those fellers had long memories. Kill the husband, then humiliate the brother. Victory for the McGillicuddys, even if it was six years coming.

As Billy carefully pushed the sawdust toward the front door, Tim turned to leave. He didn't want Billy to see him, because it would be an embarrassment for them both. But he bumped right into Slick, who was striding along the sidewalk.

"Watch it, you little snot, or I'll—" Slick's eyes brightened. His breath was foul, and he sounded as if he had a bad cold, which came from the crushed sinuses beneath the mashed-in face, which had come courtesy of a six-pound hammer.

"Spyin' in the windows, are you?" Slick slapped Tim across the face, grabbed him by the collar, pulled him inside. "Lookie here, boys. Look what the cat dragged in."

All the faces turned. Uncle Billy's turned red.

"You ain't a cat." Strong stood. "You're a rat who been out sniffin' whores."

Strong was bigger than Slick, smiled more, meant it less. That's what Tim was thinking as he looked up into those small eyes.

"You need a job, kid?" Strong walked over and smiled down at Tim. "Like your uncle here?"

"No."

"No, *sir*," Strong snapped a hand and knocked Tim's hat off. "Hey, Billy, tell him how good we been to you."

"Oh, yeah, Strong, you been real nice. Real nice."

"See that?" said Strong. "Real nice. We help them less fortunate than ourselves. Ain't that right, Ma?"

"Shit, yeah," said Mother Mag.

"Or maybe," Strong looked into Timothy Riley's eyes, "you *ain't* less fortunate. Maybe you got some spring of money bubblin' somewheres, even if you're out of business and your old man's swingin' his six-pound hammer in the heavenly chorus."

Billy stepped closer. "Now, Strong—"

"Shut the fuck up. If I want anything out of you, I'll give you a spittoon to drink, just to see you puke."

And Billy slipped back into the shadows.

"Now remember, kid"—Strong put an arm around Tim's shoulder, as gentle as a father—"if we think there's someone in our neighborhood who got their snout in somethin' they ain't sharin', we might have to pay them a visit. So you watch what you're spendin', 'cause we're watchin' you."

WHEN TIM GOT home, Dinny Boyle and a couple of his pals were passing a pint on the stoop.

Tim thought about going in by the back door, but they had seen him, so he put his head down and tried to walk past.

"Hey!" Dinny popped up in front of him. "You wonderin' how come your brother ain't down here, tootlin' that fuckin' harmonica?"

"No," said Tim.

Dinny pulled the harmonica from his pocket. "Because I *took* it, that's how come."

Tim looked at the shining metal in Dinny's hands. Tim's father had given the harmonica to Eddie for his birthday.

"You want to know why I took it?" said Dinny.

"No." Tim tried to step past.

"Because I think the Rileys is holdin' out on the Dinny Boyle Association, which means they're holdin' out on Mr. Strong McGillicuddy, which means they're holdin' out on the folks who'll elect Sunny Jim Maguire before long and take the fifteenth away from that limp old prick on the shoeshine throne."

"How can we be holdin' out," asked Tim, "when we got nothin' worth holdin'?"

"That ain't what *I* hear, shitstain." Dinny Boyle slapped Tim across the face.

Tim clenched his fists to fight back. He had taken all the slapping he could for one night. But one of the other boys grabbed his arm, and Dinny smashed him again. Tim saw stars and his right ear started to ring.

Then Dinny brought his boney, pimpled face close to Tim's. "What I hear is that a big black box cab pulls up right in front of this buildin' tonight, and a fancy feller steps out and asks, in a real snooty voice"—Dinny struck his nose into the air and talked through it—"'Do you lads know if a Timothy Riley resides in this building?'"

"*Resides,*" said one of the others. "Snooty word for a snooty feller."

"Real snooty," said Dinny. "And when we say yeah, this fancy Dan nancy-boy goes up to your flat, while the driver stays with the box cab so we don't strip it bare."

Tim was beginning to understand.

"Fancy Dans don't come around here unless they're handin' out money to the poor unfortunates of Hell's Kitchen." Dinny trickled some whiskey onto the harmonica, then wiped it on his shirt, then tootled it a few times. "But after these guys leave, does anybody come down from your flat and give me my dues? Hell no."

Tim looked at the harmonica. "So you took that?"

"Well, your brother come thumpin' up the street from somewhere and starts playin' under the song-girl's window, like he's sweet on her or somethin'."

Tim looked up at the third-floor windows across the street. *Sweet on her?*

"That's against my rules. So I took his toy." Dinny shoved the harmonica into his pocket. "You can get it back from Mr. Strong when you pay. I'm goin' to tell him now about the fancy Dan."

And that, thought Tim, would seal the fate of his family. If fancy Dan swells were visiting the Rileys, the McGillicuddys would be visiting soon after.

TIM'S MOTHER AND Eddie were sitting in the front room.

They had heard all the talk on the stoop.

Eddie had a black eye, courtesy of Dinny.

Their mother was wringing her hands, wiping them on her apron, wringing, wiping. When Tim walked into the flat, she pulled an envelope from the apron. "This is for you. A feller in a fine suit and goggle-eye glasses left it."

Inside was a ten-dollar bill and a note:

I appreciate that you have offered an item. I enclose recompense. Should you come into any more of this sort, please contact me at number 23 Wall Street.

J. P. Morgan.

The mother read over her son's shoulder. "J. P. Morgan? Glory be to God! He's more important than Plunkitt himself. And ten dollars? Why?"

"I sold a bond. Morgan collects stuff. So he bought it. We have four more that I know of. But I don't know where Pa hid the box. Do you?"

"No, darlin'. Your da loved to talk, but he sure could keep a secret." She took the letter and the bill and went into the kitchen to hide them.

"A sawbuck," whispered Eddie to Tim. "If that's your plan, it ain't enough to get us out of here. And once the McGillicuddys get wind of this J. P. Morgan stuff, they'll be poundin' on the door."

"I know."

"Only one thing to do." Eddie took a furtive look into the kitchen, then pulled a bullet from his shirt pocket and held it up.

Tim shook his head. This was not a step he was ready to take. "If we can find the rest of the bonds, we can sell them to Morgan. If he give us ten dollars for every one, that would be two hundred dollars."

"It ain't enough."

"It'll have to be. I ain't shootin' anybody."

THE RILEY FAMILY sat for the rest of the evening in their steaming little flat.

Tim tried to read a copy of the *Times* that he had found on the street. His hands were so sweaty that the ink turned his fingertips black.

Eddie twitched about, and every time he heard a noise outside, he got up and looked down, as if he might see his harmonica being passed like a bottle among the Boyle gang.

The mother hunched over her sewing machine and got down to her piecework for the night. Her foot pumped the pedal. The big gears turned. The small gears spun. And she stopped only to wipe away the sweat or push her stringy hair back around her ears.

The sound had always been like music to the boys, as calming as their mother's song. But that night, the steady whir, punctuated by the clicks and clacks and clatters, simply made them more nervous.

Finally, Eddie jerked his head at Tim—let's go downstairs.

"Unh-unh," said Tim. "Let's stay right here."

"Well"—Eddie got up and clomped to the door—"I'm goin' to the outhouse."

"Use the chamber pot, why don't you," said their mother. "Then get into bed."

"I need more than the pot, Ma."

The mother nodded and kept sewing.

Tim wondered if he should go after his brother. Then he went back to the paper.

Then a thought struck him. If his brother had the bullets in his pocket, where was the gun? He slid his hand beneath the sofa cushion, but he felt nothing. He moved to the other side, but . . .

A train was coming. The picture of Jesus was rattling on the wall. The rumble was growing louder. So, as Tim fumbled among the sofa cushions, he did not know if he heard the sound of gunshot or a leftover firecracker.

His mother did not react, so maybe it was a firecracker.

"What are you lookin' for?" she asked.

"Nothin'. I . . . unh . . . I must've et what Eddie did. I need to go to the privy."

He rushed down the stairs to the first floor just as Mr. Flaherty poked his head out.

"Hey, Timmy," he asked. "Did you just hear a firecracker?"

"No, sir," said Tim, and he kept going.

Down in the yard, there were three outhouses to serve the whole building. Tim pulled open one of the doors: empty.

A second door: empty.

Someone shouted out a window, "You kids better not light off any more of them damn things, or I'll come down and give somebody a beatin'!"

A third door: Tim jumped back at a sight so terrifying that he almost ran. A man was sitting with his pants at his ankles and a bullet hole drilled into the middle of his forehead. Then Tim realized it was no man. It was Dinny Boyle.

Tim whispered his name, but Dinny just stared straight ahead.

So Tim slammed the outhouse door and looked up into the fire escapes.

Where was Eddie?

Had he gone up? Or had he headed for McGillicuddy's on the street?

Tim remembered what Eddie had said: no one would expect a crip to walk in and start shooting.

So he ran back through the tenement and out onto Forty-eighth and up to Ninth Avenue.

At the corner, he looked down the block toward McGillicuddy's, but he did not see the silhouette of Eddie on his crutch. Ninth Avenue was quiet, except for a few passing drays. At night, New York lived its bright life along Broadway, or down at Fourteenth Street, or on the Bowery. What night life there was in Hell's Kitchen lurked in the shadows.

Tim ran down to McGillicuddy's, but this time he slowed before stepping in front of the window. He pulled close to the wall, took off his hat, and peered in.

Mother Mag was wiping a spill from the bar. Slick was drinking a beer with a foot on the newly polished brass rail. Strong was still sitting at a side table. Sunny Jim Maguire had joined him for a late-night conversation. The other drinkers had gone home.

And there was Uncle Billy, collecting spittoons and pouring the oily streams of brown and silver spit into a single bucket.

Then Tim heard a voice behind him.

"Timmy! Timmy!" It was Doreen.

"What are you doin' here?" whispered Tim. "Go home."

"I watched all night to see if you'd come out. I had to tell you . . . I heard what Dinny Boyle said about Eddie bein' sweet on me."

Tim made a gesture with his hand—quiet. "Go home. This ain't a place for a girl."

"Why? What's goin' on?" She tried to step around him and look into the saloon.

Tim grabbed her by the arm and pulled her back out of the light. "Go home."

"Why? You don't want me to see your uncle cleanin' spittoons or somethin'? Everybody knows. The kids all call him Billy-spit."

"I don't care what they call him. Just go. Go or I'll smack you."

She stepped back in shock. "I just come to tell you, to tell you—"

"Tell me what?"

"That *I* ain't sweet on Eddie."

"Okay. That's great." Tim peered again into the saloon.

"I'm sweet on *you*."

Tim looked into her eyes and saw tears glistening. "You are? Well . . . I'm sweet on you, too. But if you don't get out of here, I won't ever talk to you again."

"You mean you won't walk me home?"

He wanted to walk her home more than anything. But he said, "Go on. Beat it."

That was when he heard a sound vibrating through the iron fire escape above him. He looked up.

So did Doreen.

Somehow, Eddie had gotten across the rooftops and was now climbing down. He had put his crazy plan into motion.

Tim said to Doreen, "This ain't no place for a girl." And he pushed her up the street.

She went a short distance, stopped, looked, then went a bit farther, stopped, turned, and faded into the darkness. . . .

Tim thought she was going, and his mind was now turning to his brother. He looked around and saw the awning pipe on the next building.

He could shimmy up the pipe, step on the cornice above the window and . . .

When Eddie reached the last level of the fire escape, right in front of the second-story windows and right above the entrance to McGillicuddy's, Tim was waiting for him.

"Timmy! Jesus. You scared the shit out of me."

"Did *you* shoot Dinny?" whispered Tim.

"I opened the door to go in and take a shit and there he was, so—"

"So you shot him?"

"No. He told me to get out of there and called me a nancy-boy."

"So what did you do?"

"I said, 'Oopsie-daisy.' *Then* I shot him. He's dead, hunh?"

"As dead as Lincoln. Give me the gun. We got to get rid of it."

"I ain't done with it."

A train squealed south out of the Fiftieth Street Station. From where the boys lurked, they could look straight into the light that the engine aimed along the tracks.

Tim tried to push his brother up to the next level of the fire escape.

Eddie pushed back and tried to release the bolt that held the ladder that led to the sidewalk.

"Don't do that," said Tim.

"This is our chance. The train's comin'. They can't hear us."

The rumble was growing into a roar. The light was flickering, widening, sending flashes onto the faces of the buildings on both sides of the street.

Eddie got his fingers on the bolt . . . just as Tim got his hands on the pistol in Eddie's belt . . . just as the train thundered past . . . just as Uncle Billy appeared below them with a bucket of spit in his hand.

The bolt came out. The pistol dropped onto the grating. The lights in the passenger cars flashed and flickered. And for a few seconds, the sound of the train felt like a solid thing, heavy enough to crush two boys against the darkened building.

Then Tim grabbed for the pistol. And Eddie grabbed for Tim. Tim fell against the ladder. And the ladder began to slide. Then the pistol fell through the opening and tumbled toward the street.

As Uncle Billy tossed the contents of the bucket into the gutter, the iron ladder dropped behind him. The pistol hit the sidewalk an instant later.

"Fuck!" said Eddie.

Uncle Billy turned, saw the ladder, then the pistol. Then he looked up and dropped the bucket in shock. "Timmy? Eddie? What the—"

Tim climbed halfway down the ladder and held out his hand. "Give me the gun."

Billy picked it up and looked at it, then he looked again at the two desperate boys on the fire escape.

That was when Slick McGillicuddy appeared at the front door. "What the fuck is goin' on out here?" He stepped out onto the sidewalk. He saw Tim on the ladder. He saw the pistol in Billy's hand. And he said it again. "What the *fuck*?"

And something snapped in Billy Donovan, as if he suddenly saw a way to erase all the insults of a lifetime and all the embarrassment of befriending these thugs and all the shame of knowing that his blabbermouth ways had caused the death of Six-Pound Dick and endangered his whole family.

Without another word, he raised the pistol and shot Slick McGillicuddy right in the forehead.

Slick's derby flew off and landed with a rattle on the floor of the saloon.

Slick dropped like a hod of bricks.

Then Billy stepped over Slick and followed the derby into the saloon.

The train was receding quickly now. The city had swallowed the roar, and the last cars sent a *clickety-clack-clickety-clack* echoing through the rails.

Strong and Sunny Jim were standing as Billy strode in. Strong was pulling a pistol from under the table and was stepping forward. Sunny Jim was stepping away.

Billy put a bullet into Strong's chest, stopping him where he stood.

Sunny Jim turned and ran for the rear door, so Billy shot him in the back. The politician took another few steps and fell flat on his face.

By now, Tim and Eddie had both dropped to the sidewalk and were watching wide-eyed as Mother Mag pulled the sawed-off shotgun from behind the bar.

Eddie screamed, "Uncle Billy, look out!"

Billy turned and aimed.

But Mother Mag fired first, blasting a spray of

shot that tore into Billy and struck the staggering body of her own son, too.

Strong hit the floor.

Billy hit the wall . . . then the floor.

And the room fell silent.

For a moment, the only sound was the distant squeal of the train arriving at Forty-second Street.

Mother Mag broke the shotgun and dropped two smoking shells onto the floor. She was muttering to herself, as if this were no more than a spilled beer bucket, a mess to clean up. "Fuckin' Billy Donovan tellin' fuckin' stories about fuckin' funny money. So we give him a fuckin' job and this is the fuckin' thanks we get."

As she reloaded, she came out from behind the bar in her trousers and cowboy boots. She looked at Strong and poked him with her foot. "Son? Son?" But he did not move.

So she turned to Billy. His face and the apron covering his belly were splattered with buckshot holes seeping blood. He was gasping for breath.

She pointed the shotgun. "Fuckin' weasel is what you are."

And with the last life left in him, Billy Donovan raised the pistol and fired twice. The first shot hit her in the chest and staggered her. The second struck her in the face and blew off the top of her head.

Mother Mag fell backward through the settling mist of her own blood and brain and hit the floor, as dead as her sons.

After a moment of shocked silence, Eddie Riley whispered, "Mother of fuckin' Jesus." Then he started into the saloon.

Tim grabbed him. "Come on."

"But Uncle Billy!" cried Eddie.

"Go!" Billy rolled to his side as if trying to get up. "Go now. Leave the gun. And go . . . go . . . go tell your mother, tell her—" He rasped and rattled and stopped breathing.

Police whistles were sounding from both directions on Ninth Avenue. So the boys turned to leave and walked right into Doreen, who was standing wide-eyed in the shaft of light slanting out onto the sidewalk.

"I told you to go home," said Tim.

"But"—she looked into the saloon—"Uncle Billy?"

"He's dead," said Eddie, "and we'll all be in jail if we don't get out of here." He told his brother to take his crutch, then he grabbed a rung of the ladder and lifted himself.

Tim pushed Doreen up the ladder after Eddie. At the landing, Tim pulled up the ladder, replaced the bolt, and they escaped over the roof.

TWO DAYS LATER, Tim and Eddie Riley stood before George Washington Plunkitt at the shoeshine stand in the County Courthouse.

Plunkitt was reading the *Advertiser*. The headline screamed: ***SUNNY JIM MAGUIRE DIES. ONLY SURVIVOR OF MCGILLICUDDY MASSACRE SUCCUMBS WITHOUT REGAINING CONSCIOUSNESS.***

The voice rose from behind the paper. "It says here, 'There is still no motive for the shooting, but one thing is certain, the field in the fifteenth now belongs to Plunkitt and Plunkitt alone.'" He lowered the paper. "I would've beaten Maguire like a mangy dog. But your uncle done me a favor, and I don't forget a man who does me a favor."

Tim and Eddie looked at each other. Eddie seemed more frightened to stand here than he had been on the night of the "massacre."

"I been lookin' into all this," said Plunkitt, "and I told the police that there don't seem to be evidence of anything but revenge. Your uncle thought the McGillicuddys killed your pa. So did I, even if the only witness was too honest or too scared to finger them."

Tim just shrugged.

"So your uncle decided to do the world a favor. And God bless him for that."

Eddie looked at his brother. Tim could think of nothing to say.

After a few moments, Plunkitt said, "Have you boys made up your mind?"

"About what?" asked Tim.

"About what you'd like to do in life. Why do you think I sent for you? Two fatherless boys with an uncle as brave as that . . . you deserve a leg up."

"Well," said Tim, "I'd like to go to school. To college."

"And do what?"

"Go into business."

"Is that why you introduced yourself to J. P. Morgan the other day?"

"How did—"

"Morgan showed the bond to Mr. Daly. I hear he give you ten dollars for it."

"Yes, sir." Tim had given up wondering how Plunkitt knew everything.

"Well," said Plunkitt. "A boy with your brains, he can learn all he needs *and* help his mother, too . . . if he's practical." Plunkitt wrote down the name of Daniel Daly, Drexel, Morgan and Company, 23 Wall Street. "They need an office boy. Go see Daly."

Tim Riley looked at the address and realized that George Washington Plunkitt had just given him the chance of a lifetime, school or not.

But Plunkitt wasn't done. He turned to Eddie. "What about you?"

Eddie looked down at his foot.

"You're not feelin' sorry for yourself, are you? A boy with your talent? I hear you play the harmonica."

"Yes, sir," said Eddie.

"Do you have it with you?"

Eddie reached for his pocket.

Just then, a police detective walked down the corridor, a burly man with a silver badge on his lapel. Was this it? Had they figured out that Eddie killed Dinny Boyle? Were they coming to arrest him here instead of in front of their mother?

"Good morning, Inspector," said Plunkitt. "Meet the Riley brothers."

The inspector gave the squint-eye. "You boys walkin' the straight and narrow?"

"The inspector works the Lower East Side," explained Plunkitt. "Here to testify in the Swartzkopf case."

The inspector tugged at his mustache. "Man took

an axe to his wife, chopped her into little pieces, everything but her legs. He threw the rest of her in the river but he kept her legs. When we asked him why, he said the legs was the only part of her he liked. He'll hang. So walk the straight and narrow lads. Always the straight and narrow." Then he went into the men's room.

Tim felt his brother let out a long gasp of breath.

Plunkitt smiled. "So, Eddie Riley, are you ready to walk the straight and narrow?"

"I only got one foot. How can I walk the straight and narrow on one foot?"

"You got spirit. I'll give you that." Plunkitt chuckled. "I need a boy to help me in Washington Hall. Keep things straight, sweep up, go to rallies. And when I need a bit of music to lighten the mood, I'll order up a ditty. How does that sound?"

"So long's I don't have to dance no jigs."

"I'll take that as a yes." Plunkitt pulled out a cigar, bit the tip. "Now, about that girl who sang at your father's funeral . . ."

The boys looked at each other.

Plunkitt leaned forward. "Which one of you is sweet on her?"

Neither boy spoke.

Plunkitt's dark eyes danced with amusement. "The both of ye's, eh? Two brothers sweet on the same girl . . . not a good combination. But you're young. You'll figure it out. Or she will. Tell her I want her to sing regular at funerals and rallies."

"Yes, sir," they both said.

"Now, that harmonica, Eddie. Have you played it on the stoop the last few days?"

"My brother won't let me."

"Good counsel." Plunkitt held out his hand. "I'll take it."

"You'll take it? But my pa give it to me. How come?"

The men's room door opened and out came the police inspector.

Plunkitt gave him a nod and watched him go off. Then he turned back to the boys: "The only thing missin' from Dinny's pocket was a harmonica he took from you. I persuaded the coppers to leave you alone till you bury your uncle. Told 'em it was inhuman to be questionin' lads whose Pa and uncle died so close. But after the funeral—"

"The coppers'll come?" asked Eddie.

"As sure as Republicans cheatin' in the next election. So we don't want 'em findin' any wind instruments. I'll buy you a new one when you come to work. That way, when somebody asks if it's the one that Dinny Boyle took, you can say it ain't . . . and you won't be lyin'."

Eddie pulled the harmonica out, gave it a final toot, and put it into Plunkitt's hand.

Plunkitt slipped it into his coat pocket and said, "The last bit of business . . . do you boys know where the rest of them bonds are?"

"No, sir," said Tim.

"We sure wish we did," said Eddie.

Plunkitt ruminated on their answer for a moment, then shrugged as if it didn't much matter, one way or the other. "Well, be off with you, but remember what I told you. This is a grand and imperial city, and it will reward you, if you make the right choices."

THE BROTHERS STEPPED out of the courthouse on Chambers Street. The humidity had faded. The north wind had brought in air clear and crisp.

Doreen Walsh came out from behind one of the pillars and said, "Well?"

"We're in the clear," said Tim.

"Yeah," said Eddie. "And we all got jobs. Even you."

"Thanks for not snitchin'," said Tim.

"Well, some day, you boys can pay me back," she said.

"How?" asked Tim.

"You can help make me a headliner." Doreen spun a little pirouette on the steps of the Tweed courthouse, another grand and imperial space in their city of dreams.

ELEVEN

Wednesday Evening

"What we know"—Peter Fallon was talking on the cell phone—"is that this Timothy Riley of Forty-eighth Street somehow got his hands on at least three of these bonds in 1893 and sold one to J. P. Morgan . . . for ten bucks."

"J. P. Morgan? That's cool. What's your evidence?" asked Antoine.

"Old New York state bond ledgers. Receipts from the Morgan Library."

Peter and Evangeline were walking down Broadway, from the Flatiron Building to Delancey's Rarities. Peter had suggested a cab, but the downtown traffic had stopped moving, and Evangeline needed some fresh air anyway. Anyone would after a meeting with Owen T. Magee, which followed a taxi ride with Kathy Flynn, which came after a shooting in the Harvard Club.

Peter didn't argue. He didn't think that anyone would make a move against them on the street. They hadn't seen or heard from Joey Berra since the morning. As for the supposed Russians . . . if they were interested, it wouldn't matter if Peter and Evangeline were walking down Broadway or sitting in a taxi or hiding in her apartment.

The walk to Delancey's led through the heart of the old Ladies' Mile.

Romance had long since fled this stretch of furniture outlets, delis, and storefronts-to-let, but a few Gilded Age jewels still glimmered, those seven- and eight-story buildings that gave a street a human scale and a bit of fancy with their expanses of plate glass, their cast-iron pillars and trimwork, their turrets and mansard roofs.

So Evangeline walked with her head up.

Peter walked with his head on a swivel. Best be vigilant, whether he expected trouble or not.

Antoine was saying, "Does the Morgan Library own the bond now?"

"Yes," answered Peter. "Number 2510, which was the first number in the series bought by a woman named Loretta Rogers."

"There's your L. R.," said Antoine. "Do you think the Morgan Library has the rest?"

"Three for certain, all from Riley," said Peter. "Morgan liked collecting early American material, autographs, documents, papers relating to Alexander Hamilton and the beginnings of American finance. And these bonds are like the birth certificates."

"I'll check Corsair. That's their online catalogue," said Antoine. "They named it after ol' J. P.'s yacht. Of course, if they held a lot of these bonds, you'd think that some lawyer would have filed an amicus brief in support of the Avid position."

"If I had one of those bonds, I'd be filing, fool. A win on all counts means a hundred-dollar bond from 1780 is worth seven-point-four million today."

"Which means a big bonus for the research assistant who helps find them."

"Big enough that you can get your doctorate and your father will brag on you all day long," said Peter. "But not only does Arsenault need to win the main point, he needs to win the compound interest argument, too."

"So what do we follow?"

"Timothy Riley. If he had three bonds, he probably had a lot of them. Riley Wrecking must have found them when they tore the house down . . . in a wall or under the floor or someplace."

"Either that or they blew off the top of somebody else's pile and he picked them up."

"In that case—"

"We *fucked*, as they say in the 'hood."

Peter noticed Evangeline stopping. He put Antoine on hold and said, "What?"

She was looking up at a beige-colored fantasy castle that wrapped the corner of Twentieth and Broadway. A lot of buildings around it looked old and city-grimed, but this one had been painted and polished and restored with fiberglass patches on the facade, so it was worth a stop.

She said, "This was once the home of Lord and Taylor. Imagine what it must have been like to shop here back in the day."

"What I remember," he said, "is the strip joint on the first floor back in the nineties."

"A strip joint? Here?"

"Time marches on . . . and sometimes it stumbles."

"At least they replaced the strip joint with a storefront. And why do you know so much about strip joints?"

Peter got back to Antoine. He said that if they didn't find the bonds by the time the court handed down its decision on Friday, he doubted that they ever would, because everybody in America who had an attic and a box of old family papers would be searching for New Emission Bonds. On the other hand, if the court denied the claim, the bonds would be worth no more than their value as collector's items.

"So . . . Timothy Riley?" said Antoine.

"Track him through whatever sources you can find. Do it fast."

Peter and Evangeline were approaching Union

Square. Someone was shouting into a bullhorn about genocide or fratricide or fries on the side. They couldn't tell because at another corner, another group was holding a rally for immigration reform, and another bullhorn was echoing off the buildings: "For or against?" "Put up a fence?" "Send 'em all back." "Let 'em all in."

Peter and Evangeline hurried through the crowd, with Peter still on the phone. "Another thing," he said to Antoine, "you once introduced me to a cousin from Harlem."

"Cousin Jonas? Scarborough Security of Harlem?"

"Can you put in a call to him, tell him I might contact him?"

"Sure." And Antoine chuckled.

"What?"

"Sometimes, you call and say 'go and find out this and this and this,' and I find it and everything's cool and we all make money. Then, once in a while, you add, 'oh and find me a guy who can kick some ass.' Sounds to me like you need a New York ass-kicker. You want me to come down, too?"

"No. You have classes. Stay in school."

"Yeah. A mind is a terrible thing to waste."

At the south edge of Union Square, they crossed Fourteenth Street, then they got back onto Broadway.

Two blocks south, they passed the Strand Bookstore, promising "eighteen miles of new, used, rare, and out of print books." Peter had never measured the shelves, but he had spent hundreds of hours and thousands of dollars along those eighteen miles. He loved just walking past the store and looking at the famous red façade wrapping the corner. It reminded him that some things lasted, even when time stumbled ahead.

At Tenth Street, in front of Grace Church, they turned toward Fourth Avenue and the stretch known as Book Row, once the heart of the New York used book trade. Few of the stores had survived. Not even Delancey could have made the rent from what he sold out of Rarities, except that he owned the building on the east side of Fourth between Tenth and Eleventh.

It was a new law tenement from the early 1900s, three windows wide, with a big rusty fire escape above the entrance. Rarities occupied the first two floors. Delancey lived on the second two. And he rented the upper flats. The building to the right was a 1920's apartment house. The building to the left was a 1960's one-story box with a sign outside: *WONG'S DRY CLEANING. SAME DAY SERVICE.*

The east side of the street was in transition. The west side had arrived in the twenty-first century. So the east side had storefronts, awnings, activity. The west side had . . . high-rises. Peter and Evangeline stopped under the twenty-foot trees in front of a twenty-story apartment house and looked across at Delancey's Rarities. Not much foot traffic on this side of the street, even at dinnertime. Plenty of uptown auto traffic, though.

A sign hanging on Delancey's door said, CLOSED, but Peter could see two shadows near the desk inside. Was Delancey one of them?

"Go ahead," said Evangeline. "Call him."

Peter did, listened to the recording, and said, "Come on, Delancey, pick up. I'll be pissed if you dragged us down here for nothing." Then he peered across the street.

"Should we go over and knock?" said Evangeline.

"There's something dicey about this," said Peter. Then he felt the cell phone again, buzzing a text message from Delancey.

I'm here. Come on over.

Evangeline said, "Okay. Let's go."

Peter texted back:

Not till I see you or hear your voice.

"I guess it's good to be suspicious," said Evangeline, "but he must be in there."

"So I'll call him and tell him to show himself." Peter opened the phone again.

Then he felt something poke into his back. "Save dime."

"Save dime? What the—"

"Do not turn." The accent was Russian. "It is cattle prod. Power mite model. Small but forty-five hundred volt. Hurt like motherfucker."

Evangeline did not recognize this one, but she did notice a tattoo on his neck. And stars tattooed on his knuckles. She'd seen *Eastern Promises*. She knew the tattoos all meant something. And stars were bad. Stars meant this guy knew exactly what to do with a cattle prod.

"Eyes front, lady," he said to her. His hair was slicked back. He looked so gaunt that his cheekbones were like little edges routed onto his face. He wore a gold neck chain and a leather jacket, and he was sweating essence of onion. "I got Taser for you, lady, so just cross street nice and slow.

"Cross the street?" said Peter. "You mean jaywalk?"

"Don't be smart-ass. I don't like smart-ass. My boss only want to talk to you."

Peter looked to his right at the traffic coming up from the Bowery and Lafayette Street, which merged above Cooper Square to form Fourth Avenue.

The Russian said, "You ever take cattle prod up the ass? It make balls explode."

Peter put his hands up. "All right. *All right*. I'm waiting for a break in the traffic."

"You don't want him to get hit by a car, do you?" said Evangeline.

"Shut up, lady, or I Tase tits."

Evangeline pulled her purse around to the front of her body.

When the light at Tenth Street stopped the traffic, the Russian said, "Go, now."

Peter stepped off the curb. He could see someone moving inside the store.

Then another stranger—another Russian—pulled open Delancey's door. From a distance, this one looked like a series of cubes, almost a drawing exercise: sketch three cubes and make a human being out of them. Large cube for the body and shoulders, smaller cube for the head, tiny cube for the nose.

Peter did the math: two Russian thugs, a cattle

prod, a Taser . . . *them*. This would not end well. So he decided he wasn't going into that bookstore.

He thought about flopping right in the middle of the street and forcing the Russian to cattle prod him in front of all the idling traffic.

He could take the pain, and it would be better than whatever was waiting. And while he was down, twitching in agony, Evangeline could run. And when the light changed, the cars would come, and . . . suddenly he sensed movement to his right.

A black Ford Taurus shot out of a parking spot at the corner of Tenth, sped halfway across the street, halfway up the block, and screeched to stop right behind the Russian, who said, "What the fuck?"

Then, Peter heard the beeping of the pedestrian light counting down the seconds before the light changed and the traffic roared toward them.

And the beeping became like a metronome for the quick dance that unfolded in the middle of the street.

Ten. Nine. Beep. Beep.

The driver's door opened and Joey Berra popped out.

Eight. Seven. Beep. Beep.

"Get the fuck scrammed," said the Russian to Joey.

Six. Five. Beep. Beep.

Joey raised a Glock 9 mm and fired a round into the Russian's head.

Four. Three. Beep. Beep.

"Jesus Christ!" cried Evangeline as the blood splattered.

"Get in!" said Joey.

Two. One. Beep. Beep.

"Get in?" Evangeline screamed. "No. You're crazy." She turned and ran.

The light changed. But the lead drivers didn't move. Who would after what they'd just seen? So horns began to blare farther down the traffic column.

In New York, if you hesitated at a crosswalk when a light turned green, the city would grind to a halt. That was how it seemed. And it didn't matter if the cops ticketed every horn-blower in the city. The basic rules of life applied in New York, like "He who hesitates is lost" and "Use it or lose it," especially when he who hesitates is slowing you down and you have a horn to use on him.

Peter didn't hesitate. When Evangeline began to run, he ran after her.

"Fallon!" shouted Joey Berra.

Peter turned, "Another one, in the bookstore. And answer your phone."

"Shit!" Joey gave the store a glance, then shouted at Peter. "Where's Delancey?"

"You mean you don't know?"

"I lost him."

"Then who's using his phone?"

"Whoever has him."

A little Chevy got around the cars at the light, blaring its horn as it sped toward the Taurus in the middle of Fourth Ave. Then a panel truck shot up from Lafayette and swerved around the Taurus and the dead man in the street.

Joey Berra took a few steps after Peter Fallon.

But a police car in the traffic turned on its blues and gave three or four *whoop-whoops* on the siren.

Joey Berra jumped into the Taurus and sped away.

Evangeline was running for the subway, the fancy one at Astor Place, the one with the Beaux Arts flair that made it look almost Parisian.

The police car sped past them in pursuit of the Taurus that had just turned down Twelfth. And the traffic began to move, because an empty avenue and a green light formed a vacuum, and nature decreed that cars should rush in to fill it, even if there was a body lying across the lane lines.

"Evangeline," shouted Peter, "we should follow Joey!"

"We should get the hell out of New York. This is just—"

All in an instant, they heard a low thumping sound and a tremendous blast that blew out all the windows in Delancey's Rarities.

Glass shot in shards and sheets and shining pellets out into Fourth Avenue. Flames blew out right after the glass. People on the sidewalk went down in fear or were cut down by the explosion. Alarms went off in parked cars and screamed in buildings all around. Cars swerving to avoid the body of the Russian in the street swerved again and slammed into each other.

Peter pushed Evangeline down into the subway.

THEY CAME UP in Grand Central and moved quickly across the main concourse.

Evangeline had stopped shaking.

And it was good that she was wearing a black suit, because the bloodstains dried quickly and dried black.

She had simply followed Peter's lead since he pushed her down into the subway, pulled the MetroCard out of her purse, and swiped it twice as two transit cops ran upstairs toward the sound of the explosion.

Plenty of police were patrolling in Grand Central, as always, along with National Guards carrying automatic weapons. It had been like that since 9/11. It only made sense in the most famous train terminal in America.

And Peter always felt a bit of awe when he crossed the concourse. With all that marble and the soaring height and the constellations dancing across the blue sky-ceiling, Grand Central proclaimed the majesty of the city itself. Even as it reminded you of your own insignificant anonymity, it said that if this was how they welcomed you to New York, you must be pretty important, too, and if you weren't, you could be.

At the moment, Peter preferred insignificant anonymity.

None of the police seemed to pay attention to a well-dressed man and woman heading toward the west stairway. There was no Roger Thornhill moment, no Russians, and no sketchy Americans who might be working for them. A few bums and bag ladies, but none that caught Evangeline's eye.

Peter had already called Joey Berra twice with no luck. He wasn't sure of what his next move should be, but he suddenly realized that he was running out of energy. He stopped and took Evangeline's arm and turned her in the other direction.

"Where are we going now?"

"The Oyster Bar."

"The Oyster Bar? Why?"

"I'm hungry."

"At a time like this? No." She pulled away from him and started walking again. "Besides, it's too expensive."

"Too expensive? You can take the girl out of New England, but you can't take New England out of the girl."

"Peter"—she turned—"I just want to get in a cab and go home. I'll pack a bag and we'll be on the New England Thruway in an hour."

"Honey, you dragged me down to New York. So humor me." He slipped his arm into hers. "Whole sand dabs sautéed in a ginger-scallion sauce. One of my favorites. And we'll both think better on a full stomach. Besides, my leg is killing me."

"You mean from where you were shot?"

"Yeah, the last time I tried to save America."

He put a little weight on her arm for support. She knew he was acting, but she went along. She always went along. And he was right. She had started this one.

EVANGELINE WASHED HER hands in the ladies' room, then she washed them again. She washed her face and combed her hair and washed her hands a third time. But no matter how many times she washed, she couldn't wash away the images of that afternoon, or the splatter of blood that now stained the sleeve and the front of her suit, so she took off the jacket and carried it over her arm.

When she came back, Peter was studying his iPhone at a table as far from the entrance as possible.

"I hope you didn't order some expensive bottle of wine," she said. "This is not a celebration."

"It's a chance to sit and make sense of things, so I ordered wine." He put down the phone. "But you don't get much on a New York wine list for under forty dollars—"

The place was big and crowded, and even if it wasn't a celebration for Peter and Evangeline, the lights trimming the arches in the tiled ceiling made it feel festive. But the ceiling vaults that gave it the look of some deep Roman grotto also concentrated the conversation all around them. It was noisy.

The waiter arrived with the wine. "Brancott New Zealand sauvignon blanc."

Peter told him to pour. It was screw-capped like most New Zealand wines, and since it didn't have a cork, it couldn't *be* corked, so no need for a big tasting show.

"And we know what we want," he said. "I'll have the sand dabs. And—"

"Broiled red snapper," said Evangeline.

Peter also asked if they had any Island Creek Duxbury oysters.

The waiter apologized that they didn't.

"You should get them. They taste of the waters that welcomed the Pilgrims, the fresh clean estuaries on the fresh green breast of the New World." He ordered a half-dozen Wellfleets instead.

The waiter gave him an annoyed look and went off.

Evangeline took a sip of the wine and said. "If I was the sort who outlined the reasons why I loved someone—"

"And you're not." He raised his glass in a small toast.

"I would include your love of how things look, taste, smell—"

"And feel. Don't forget feel."

"Your well-documented enthusiasm for life. So let's get back to living it. Let's just call the police and tell them everything and that will be the end of it."

"That could mean the end of Delancey, too. If these Russians have him—"

"Why should we care about Delancey? He stiffed me in Fraunces Tavern. He got us into this because he wouldn't be straight with me."

"Maybe he *couldn't* be straight with you." Peter broke a breadstick, ate half, and gave the other half to her. "Maybe there were things he had to keep hidden."

"He certainly wasn't trying to protect me when he stiffed me," she said.

The oysters came.

Peter squirted lemon and a bit of hot sauce onto one and offered it to her.

She said no. Too much on an empty stomach.

So he tipped his head back and let it slither down. "Delancey told you to leave."

She took another swallow of wine. "I wish I'd listened."

"I'm glad you didn't. Otherwise, we'd have no shot at making—how many millions was it?"

"I don't care about the money." As she said it, she wondered if she believed it. She would have meant it half an hour earlier, but she had to admit it, a bit of food and drink was giving her a better perspective . . . or maybe worse.

"Evangeline"—Peter leaned across the table—"I do this work for a lot of reasons, and money is one of them."

"I know." She decided to have an oyster after all.

"I live well. I invest in good things. I give to charities. I help my son pay his law school tuition. I have season tickets to the Red Sox."

She swallowed down the oyster and dabbed at the corner of her mouth.

"I put money into companies like that Duxbury oyster business because they're making life better in some small way. I make money to spread it around."

She had another oyster and a bit more wine. "What happened to the business about saving America?"

"We save America by doing what we do, and doing it as well as we can." He drained the last of the oysters as the main course arrived.

She sat back and stared at him. "So what do you want me to say?"

"That we're still in. We play it smart. We keep trying to connect with Joey Berra. We find the bag lady. And—"

"What about the police? The NYPD could be helpful."

"They could be helpful. And"—he picked up his iPhone—"an e-mail from the Harvard Club tells me the police would like to talk with me about the shooting we witnessed today. So we can go to them at any time."

"Probably better to go to them rather than have them come to us."

"Probably. But we haven't done anything."

She poured more wine into each glass. "Do you think they had surveillance cameras at Tenth and Fourth Ave?"

"No, but they must have had them in the Astor Place subway. They'll find us, once they get through the layers of police bureaucracy, the transit cops, the NYPD detectives . . . By tomorrow, we'll be persons of interest. But all we need is thirty-six hours."

They continued talking as they ate. They tried to lay out the next day and a half and how they would proceed. They read an e-mail that Antoine sent:

> Still tracking Riley Wrecking through *Times* archive, adding names as I find interesting links. This one is good:

Peter angled the iPhone for Evangeline, then clicked the link that took him to the actual story, headline and all, just as it had looked on October 30, 1907:

HELL'S KITCHEN BIDS FAREWELL TO
BELOVED CITIZEN
MOTHER OF THE RILEY BOYS PASSES
MAYOR MCCLELLAN, THE MCMANUS, AND
G. W. PLUNKITT ATTEND RITES

Mary Riley, fifty-three, was laid to rest yesterday at Calvary Cemetery in Queens, after a funeral mass at Sacred Heart on Fifty-first Street.

She arrived from Kilkenney at the age of twelve and lived in Hell's Kitchen all of her life, the last twenty spent on a fourth-floor flat on Forty-eighth Street. More than once, said neighbors, her sons had tried to move her, but she preferred to stay in the old parish, in the old neighborhood.

After her husband, Richard, was murdered in 1893, she took in extra sewing to support her sons. Neighbors said that her Singer could always be heard, rumbling through the night. However, her sons soon took jobs and found success, one in business and the other in politics, and they eased their mother's burdens.

Timothy, twenty-eight, began as an office boy for J. P. Morgan and Co. At the age of twenty, he became a loan officer at West Side Workingman's Bank on Eighth Avenue and Forty-second Street. At the age of twenty-five, he became the youngest bank president in New York.

Edward, twenty-seven, began as an errand boy in Washington Hall, Tammany's Fifteenth District headquarters, and rose in service to his political patron, George Washington Plunkitt. But in the 1904 election, Plunkitt lost his State Senate seat to

Republican Martin Sax, which led to his defeat for Tammany district leadership at the hands of Assemblyman Thomas "The" McManus in 1905. Like his mentor, Edward is now out of politics but planning his return.

After the funeral, Plunkitt said, "Mary Riley was a fine example of New York womanhood. No matter what life threw at her, she faced it with bravery and gave the city two strong sons."

There was no public unpleasantness between Plunkitt and The McManus, as there has been on other occasions when their paths cross in public.

The McManus said, "Mary Riley and her sons are the real backbone of the Fifteenth District."

Plunkitt was heard to say to another mourner, "Half the folks here come to give a good send-off to a good woman. The other half come hopin' that they'd see a corpse in the box and another one standin' upright. Well, I might have lost my seat, but I'm far from dead, and they'll be hearin' from me again."

"What does Antoine see in this?" asked Evangeline.

"I'm thinking he must have cross-referenced Timothy Riley and J. P. Morgan. This shows that they were still connected, long after Riley sold him the first bond."

"Which means . . . what?"

"I'm not sure." Peter read the rest of Antoine's e-mail: "Checking obits now, cross-referencing *Times* archive stories on West Side Workingman's, et cetera. Will deliver as I discover. Have also informed Cousin Scarborough that you might call for security."

"Cousin Scarborough?" asked Evangeline.

"A little backup. If things get hotter."

IT WAS AFTER ten o'clock when they left the Oyster Bar.

As they crossed the marble floor in the grand concourse, Peter called the front desk at Evangeline's apartment.

Jackie Knuckles answered. He was working a double shift.

"Any calls or any visits from anyone that made you suspicious?" asked Peter.

"Nope. Nothin' . . . Buck."

That told Peter that people had been watching, or asking for them . . . the police? The Russians? Joey Berra? It would be best to stay away from the apartment, he thought, so where would they spend the night?

They went up the stairs at the west side of the station and headed for the cabs on Vanderbilt Avenue. At the top, Peter turned to admire the grand space and the half-acre American flag that had been floating above the crowd since 9/11.

Just then, two big guys—both drunk—lurched out of Michael Jordan Steak House on the upper level and bumped into Peter. Then one of them slipped and went stumbling down the steps.

This drew the attention of two police officers down on the concourse. They started up the stairs, which Peter took as a signal to stop admiring Grand

Central and hit the street. He grabbed Evangeline by the elbow and led her outside.

A cab had just pulled away. There was another in line. The driver started to pull up. But suddenly a different cab shot into the space ahead of it.

A black guy was driving. He reached into the backseat and pushed open the door. "At your service, folks."

That sounded a bit strange, and the cabbie he'd cut off leaned on his horn.

"But the other guy was in line," said Peter.

"You snooze, you lose," said the driver. "C'mon, man. Jump in."

And suddenly, Peter heard another voice behind him and felt something jamming into his back. "Get in. This is not cattle prod. It is pistol." Another Russian accent. "And I will use it. I don't give any fucks."

"And he ain't shittin'," said the driver.

Peter looked over his shoulder and had a thought for the second time that night: Draw three cubes. One for the body, one for the face, one for the nose.

"But you were in the bookstore," said Evangeline.

"Bookstore have back door. And leaky gas pipe. Big pity. Get in."

A moment later, they were speeding across Forty-second Street in an old yellow cab. The meter was running, but in this cab, the driver could lock the back doors.

The Russian was sitting on the left, Peter on the right, and Evangeline in the middle.

"You armed?" asked the Russian.

"No," said Peter.

"I don't like searching man. Don't like touching crotch. You pull weapon, I pull off your nose and make girlfriend eat it."

"We're not armed," said Evangeline. "And I don't like nose."

The Russian said to her, "My boss only want to talk. No need to kill anybody on Fourth Avenue. No need to run. No need to be smart-ass."

Peter's iPhone buzzed in his pocket. He pulled it out and asked the Russian, "Can I read this?"

"Yeah. But no sending."

It was a text from Joey Berra:

> Can't talk. Been running. Will meet you midnight. By bleachers in Times Square. If not then, same place, high noon tomorrow. But don't call. Don't text. Throw away phone and buy another. Phones are being tracked.

Evangeline read the message over Peter's shoulder and said, "Now he tells us."

Peter hit the Delete button.

The cab sped along Forty-second Street past the theaters and their spectacular marquees, past the massive McDonald's and Madame Tussaud's and the ice cream shops and B. B. King's. Then it came to a red light on Eighth Avenue.

Peter wondered which corner had been the site of West Side Workingman's.

Then the light changed, the cab accelerated through, and he wondered where they were going to end the night.

TWELVE

October 1907

It was the day after the Rileys buried their mother. It was also the end of the month, and Tim Riley did not think that his family, or the country, or the country's financial markets, would ever see a worse October.

The first tremors had reached New York eighteen months earlier, when an earthquake flattened San Francisco.

Soon, money began to flow out of the nation's financial brain, out along the arteries, out to rebuild a ruined city that soaked up cash like stressed muscle soaking up oxygen. The cost of money rose. Credit tightened. The stock market slid. Most investors grew nervous, but a few saw opportunity. Some felt the first cold-sweat trickle of fear, while others experienced the warm tingle of greed.

Fear and greed, mother and father of financial markets. The first lesson that Tim Riley had learned as an office boy at J. P. Morgan was about fear and greed and the intercourse between them. He had learned to substitute the words *prudence* and *opportunism,* which sounded more gentlemanly, but when prudence worked on opportunism, or fear on greed, the result could be as rewarding as a happy marriage or as destructive as an ugly divorce.

That fall, an opportunist named Heinze had

tried to take advantage of growing prudence to corner the copper market. He failed, with quick and disastrous results for his own balance sheet and for the stock of United Copper.

The problem was that Heinze also headed the Mercantile Bank.

And the directors of the Bank Clearinghouse, a consortium of fifty-three New York banks, suggested that Heinze step down. That news erased gentlemanly *prudence* and replaced it with abject *fear.* And fear's messenger was rumor. And rumor was that the Mercantile would be forced to close. So, on the second Wednesday in October, Mercantile depositors staged a run on the bank.

The Panic of 1907 had begun.

Then depositors turned to the Knickerbocker Trust. When the stately doors opened on Fifth Avenue on October 22, a crowd was beginning to build. By noon, the line twisted three times through the lobby, and people were carrying out cash in sacks. By one o'clock, eight million dollars had gone through those stately doors, and they closed three hours early.

Two days later, the newspapers ran a photograph of Wall Street. Thousands of men (and a few women) were lining up to withdraw their cash from the Trust Company of America, or they were milling about, or standing on the steps of the subtreasury, or leaning against George Washington's statue, watching, waiting, and wondering what was happening to the money they had entrusted to all the august institutions around them.

And while New York banks tried to satisfy depositors, regional banks were pulling money out of New York by the trainload, because people all over the country were catching the panic. And panic fed upon itself, fulfilling its own prophesies.

On Friday, the twenty-fifth, the financial pages listed the failed banks like casualties from a Civil War battlefront: the Twelfth Ward Bank, Empire City Savings Bank, the Hamilton Bank of New York, the International Trust of New York, and four Brooklyn banks, too.

Through it all, things had remained calm at West Side Workingman's on Forty-second Street at Eighth Avenue. Depositors trusted the smart young president who was, after all, one of their own. That, Tim feared, would change when news spread of a default on the worst loan he had ever made.

And the one person who could always give him a bit of confidence or a dose of common sense, the one who could bake him a soda bread and brew him some tea and listen calmly while he talked, was gone.

Tim stood in his mother's flat and listened to the familiar far-off sounds—the rumble of the El, the clop of hooves on cobblestones, the chatter of a young mother and her toddler on a stoop—sounds to make the immediate silence seem all the more permanent.

But when living voices faded, they quickly became part of the music of the past. And in the silence, Tim could hear a hundred conversations, a thousand expressions of joy and sorrow . . . his parents murmuring in the night after the telltale thumping had stopped . . . his father leading the family in grace . . . his brother snickering when Uncle Billy farted . . . his mother keening . . . his parents discussing their dreams, especially one about a box of old bonds. . . .

For the first time in years, Tim wondered where his father had hidden that box.

Then he heard footfalls . . . on the stairs, in the hallway, through the door.

Eddie Riley could not help but announce himself. That's what Plunkitt always said. If you didn't know him by the high-pitched voice and wide-ranging opinions, the sound of that wooden foot and cane always proclaimed that Eddie was coming.

"Bad times." Tim kept his eyes on the windows. "Getting worse."

"Ma always said bad times don't last," answered Eddie. "But they do get worse."

"Worse?"

"Plunkitt can't keep me on the payroll. No matter what he says in the papers, after losin' two straight elections, he don't see the chance of winnin' again."

"Then we need to find you some banking work."

Eddie laughed. "I'm bankin' every night."

"Bankin'?"

"Out of business as a Plunkitt coat holder, now a place holder."

"What's that?"

"A place holder figures out where the next bank run's comin'. He goes there the night before, when the line starts to build, and offers to hold any man's place for ten bucks. Most men'll pay for a good night's sleep. And nothin' guarantees one like knowin' you'll be at the head of the line when the bank opens in the mornin'."

"We need to find you something more dignified."

"A man with two babies and no job can't be worried about dignity."

"Pa kept his dignity, even when we had nothin'."

"Could he keep it with the whole world fallin' apart?" asked Eddie.

Always more serious, Tim had traveled farther along that path in fourteen years. Always angrier, Eddie had lost much of his anger. People liked Eddie. They trusted Tim. Eddie dressed like a dandy, walked into every room as if it were a party, and always left with a joke. Tim favored dark suits and winged collars, parted his hair and his mustache in the middle, and proceeded into a conversation like a man walking down a dark alley.

People said there was a simple explanation. Eddie had grown up in a political hall where the gladhand was one of the tools of the trade. Tim had come of age in the presence of brokers and bankers who measured their words as carefully as their inseams.

But there was more to understanding the Riley brothers than that.

It may have begun with their mentors, Plunkitt of Tammany Hall and Daly of J. P. Morgan. But it ended with the women who had shaped them, the mother they would never see again, the wives they had married, and the song-girl who had kept their secret since that bloody night at McGillicuddy's. . . .

ii.

Tim was the older brother, but Eddie found a wife first.

He met her at Tammany's Fifteenth District Cotillion of 1901.

Tim looked across the hall that night and saw Eddie talking to a pudgy girl with an infectious laugh named Polly Sadowski. After a visit to the punch bowl, Tim looked again, and Eddie was still talking to her. Half an hour later . . . still talking.

That was when Plunkitt sidled up to Tim. "Your brother and a Litvak. Not many Lithuanians in the district, so it won't help if he runs for office. But that's the most I ever seen him talk to a girl. If he starts playin' the harmonica for her, get to work on your wedding toast."

And sure enough, as people emptied out of Washington Hall that cold February night, Tim heard the harmonica. The song was "McNally's Row of Flats," followed by the happy laughter of Polly Sadowski.

Her family had come from Lithuania in search of a better life in 1897. The father, a boot maker, had opened a storefront on Tenth Avenue. Two of the sons were also bootmakers. The third, named Theodore, was an anarchist. They did not speak so much of him.

When Mary Riley learned that her son was in love, she worried that the girl wasn't Irish. She was also suspicious of the Lithuanian brand of Catholicism: "Do these Lith-who-neenians bless themselves top to bottom and left to right, or do they go with that Orthodox business of top to bottom, then *right* to *left*?"

"Ask Father Higgins, why don't you?" said Tim. "The whole Sadowski family sits down front at the ten o'clock every Sunday."

That softened Mary Riley some. Then one day, Polly herself came by and offered to help the missus with her sewing. When Polly proved that she could do a running stitch and take a Singer sewing machine apart and put it back together again blindfolded, Mary Riley made the girl her own.

Eddie and Polly were married at Sacred Heart that summer.

Then everyone processed to Washington Hall for the reception.

Tim gave what everyone said was a grand toast. Later he gave what everyone said was a grand warning, when the anarchist brother drank too much and started grumbling about the oppressive institution of marriage. Tim told him, very quietly, to shut up or leave. "Or I will personally throw you out a window."

TWO YEARS LATER, Tim met the dark-haired and slender Helen Murphy at a church social at Annunciation, on Broadway and 131st Street.

And he was captivated . . . by her wit, by her education (courtesy of the good sisters of the Sacred Heart), and by the blue eyes that watched him so seriously from beneath those dark brows.

Three nights a week, month after month, Tim took the El uptown to the neighborhood called

Manhattanville, and he sat in the front room and listened while Helen's Donegal mother played the piano. Tim had no musical talent, but he could have learned "Galway Bay," "Greensleeves," and "Jeannie with the Light Brown Hair," just from watching Mrs. Murphy's fingers work the keyboard . . . again . . . and again . . . and again . . . because those were the only songs she knew.

Finally, the Murphys allowed Tim to take their daughter to the theater. It was the fall of 1904, and a new show was playing at the Broadway Liberty: *Little Johnny Jones,* by an up-and-comer named Cohan. Tim came out humming "Yankee Doodle Boy." But Helen loved "Give My Regards to Broadway."

Soon they were spending all their free time exploring New York, and for young people in love, it truly was the grand and imperial city that Plunkitt had promised.

They climbed the Statue of Liberty and looked out from the crown. They walked across the Brooklyn Bridge just to feel the majesty of it. They strolled the Ladies' Mile. They stood on Twenty-third Street and felt the wind currents that the new Flatiron Building created, and they laughed when the coppers shouted "Twenty-three skidoo" at the gawking johnny-boys waiting for a gust to blow a lady's skirt up around her waist. They went to the nickelodeon to watch pictures that actually moved. They counted the number of stories on the *Times* building rising at Broadway and Forty-second Street, then they traced the northward progress of the subway trench slicing through Longacre Square. And for her birthday, Tim took Helen to Delmonico's, where they had steaks and an amazing dessert called Baked Alaska, which was both cold and hot at the same time.

Tim was completely in love with Helen, but he scanned the vaudeville notices every week for a company that included Doreen Walsh, or as she was known when her name made it onto the bill, Doreen the Chorine.

Doreen never played New York, but if she was in town to visit her widowed mother, she and Tim would have lunch. She had followed her dream out to what the vaudevillians called the "medium time," out to cities like Providence and Cincinnati, out where she played theaters that were clean but seldom crowded, where a good week ended with fifty dollars in the pay envelope and clean towels in the hotel.

Doreen always told Tim that someday, she would make it back. She had an idea for a show with beautiful girls, fresh songs, dancing, and funny skits about high mucky-mucks like J. P. Morgan, with herself as the headliner.

Tim always assured her that it would happen.

And the meal would end with Doreen saying how nice it would have been if she could have had her dream and *their* dream, too. "We would've made a good team."

Tim would politely agree, but until he saw her again, he would not trouble himself over might-have-beens, because his life was advancing with purpose and promise, and he married Helen at Annunciation in June of 1905.

After Niagara Falls, the couple moved to Forty-seventh Street, to a row of town houses built by William Astor. A full brownstone should have been beyond the reach of a twenty-five-year-old loan officer. But by then, Tim Riley had become the prodigy of New York banking. It had happened the winter before . . .

CHARLES SHAUGHNESSY, FIRST president of Workingman's, had died during a Christmas celebration at Keen's Steakhouse. No one was certain if it was a heart attack that killed him or an exploded stomach, because he had just eaten not one but *two* of their twenty-six-ounce mutton chops. He sat back, patted his enormous belly, turned to say something to Tim, and pitched forward . . . right into the creamed spinach.

So, on the day after New Year's, the directors of the Twelfth Ward Bank tendered an offer to West Side Workingman's stockholders. They were following the simplest rule of business and life: when your competitor is weak, take advantage.

Workingman's had been founded in 1899. The directors—including Daniel Daly, Harold "Squints" O'Day, and saloon-keeper Jimmy Deegan—believed that a man with a Hell's Kitchen address ought to be able to get a loan in his own neighborhood. "A Local Bank for the Local Interest" was their slogan. And once the bank was capitalized, the customers lined up with coins and bills, with dreams and debts, and the little bank thrived. Even Mary Riley traded in her piggy bank for an account paying 3 percent.

But Twelfth Ward offered five dollars a share

above the stated price of the preferred stock. And the board split on the question: capitulate or fight?

Daniel Daly requested a week to mount a defense. Then he proclaimed loan officer Tim Riley the smartest, most mathematically skilled young man he knew and asked him to lead the fight.

A lifelong bachelor, Daly had taken a fatherly interest in Tim on the day that the frightened boy first appeared at the offices of J. P. Morgan. He had made it his business to teach Tim about accounting and bookkeeping. But he had not taught Tim how to handle himself in a room full of gentlemen or how to do complex calculations in his head or how to pick the borrowers who would always repay their loans. Some skills, he said, were simply innate.

So Tim Riley set out to save Workingman's.

For starters, he did what anyone in the Fifteenth District always did, if he knew what was good for him. He went to see Plunkitt.

As Tim came down the courthouse corridor, he heard Plunkitt delivering a disquisition to a young man with a notebook: "There's only one way to hold a district: you must study human nature and act accordin'. And you can't study it in books. Books is a hindrance and—why hello, Tim."

Plunkitt introduced newspaperman Billy Riordan. "He's been puttin' everything I say in the papers. Now he's makin' a book of my wisdom."

"All that free advice," said Tim, "and folks'll be payin' for it?"

Plunkitt took out a cigar. "And ain't that the grandest?"

Riordan begged a deadline and hurried off, so Tim climbed up next to Plunkitt, lit the sachem's cigar, and presented the case for Workingman's.

It did not take long.

"I've made myself a millionaire by not bein' sentimental," said Plunkitt, "unless sentiment had a purpose. When The McManus runs against me come fall, I'll be able to tell voters that I helped saved the neighborhood bank. So you can have my proxy, and I'll lend you fifteen thousand dollars, too."

In the following week, Tim visited every major stockholder and every businessman who had ever benefited because of Workingman's.

On the night before the proxy vote, he called a meeting of the board in the office of the late president. The kettle on top of the coal stove hissed steam that moistened the air but turned to frost on the windows. And he announced that they still needed twenty-five thousand dollars to hold off Twelfth Ward.

Daniel Daly, who had never expressed himself above a whisper in the back rooms of J. P. Morgan or the front rooms of Workingman's, removed his pince-nez and said, "Then it's finished. There's no way we come up with twenty-five thousand to buy out the last stockholders by tomorrow afternoon."

Tim Riley said, "What about J. P. Morgan?"

Daly's face reddened, as if he had just taken a shot of Jameson's, though he was that rarity among the Irish of New York: a teetotaler. "J. P. Morgan? You would ask *him* for money?"

"No," said Tim. "*You* would."

Daly shook his head. "I couldn't. Morgan may have spoken to me a dozen times in all the years I worked for him, unless I made a mistake. Then he yelled at me."

"He never spoke to me, either. But"—Tim tugged at his cuffs—"we're fighting for our lives. And I'm not quitting. If you won't speak to Morgan, I will."

Squints O'Day grinned. "My God, boy, but you are your father's son."

Daly put his glasses on, let them drop again, and said, "I don't know how you'll even get close to Morgan. He sits in his glassed-in office at number twenty-three and lets everyone see him, but he's as unapproachable as the Pope."

"*More,*" said Tim. "More unapproachable."

"Then how?" asked Squints.

"I have a plan."

THE NEXT MORNING, Timothy Riley dressed in his best blue suit and red cravat, put on his wool chesterfield, his kid gloves, his derby. He left his flat on Fiftieth and stepped out into the January wind, hurried across Forty-second Street to Madison, then headed south along a street crowded with morning commuters and box cabs and those noisy new autocars.

He stopped across from number 219. Morgan's brownstone faced Madison. Behind it rose his new library, a marble palace that housed the treasures he had been collecting through a lifetime. At eight thirty, the front door of the town house opened and out came an enormous Cuban cigar attached to the face of . . . himself.

J. Pierpont Morgan was sixty-eight, but he had aged little in the years since Tim Riley had first hopped his cab. It was as if Morgan had arrived at a certain place on a certain day when his hair had stopped graying and his body had grown into a force of gravity rather than simple weight, and there he had stayed. He still went alone, without secretary or factotum, his eyes fixed on the middle distance, out beyond the world of mere men, out where the money was, out in the future that was rushing toward every man every day . . . but few men could say with such certainty that they would be richer tomorrow then they were yesterday.

The cabbie opened the door, the springs creaked, Morgan dropped onto the seat. And Tim Riley made his move. He dodged two horse carts and a pile of horse shit, opened the opposite door, and levered himself in.

Once more, J. P. Morgan filled the proscenium of Tim's vision. Those small, dark eyes seemed even more ferocious when peering over a nose that now resembled an autumn gourd, all red and bulbous and covered with bumps.

"What's the meaning of this?" boomed Morgan as he pounded his walking stick on the roof. "Smythe! Smythe!"

But this time, Tim was unruffled. He pulled off his gloves, took out an envelope, and put it into Morgan's hands: "I've brought you another bond."

"Bond?"

"Another 1780 bond. Number 2511."

Morgan glanced at the envelope and said, "The

office boy. The one who learned basic accounting in my back room. Riley, isn't it?"

"And that is my calling card, sir."

Morgan puffed two or three times on his cigar and told the cabbie to get on to Wall Street. Then he said to Tim, "You preferred to be a small fish in a tiny pool, when you could have been a tiny fish in a mighty school."

"I've always been most appreciative of what I learned at the countinghouse, sir. But Workingman's was a good opportunity, and my father would have been disappointed if I hadn't struck out on my own."

Morgan grunted. He was not known for the display of any emotion except anger. He held the bond up to the window and studied the watermark. "How much?"

"It's a gift."

"Gift?" Morgan looked Tim Riley in the eye. "What do you want?"

"Want?"

"A man always has two reasons for doing a thing," said Morgan, "a good reason and the real reason."

"But—"

"Every man wants something. Find out what it is and you may do business with him. I want items like this bond, for what they say about where we've been and where we're going. So . . . what do *you* want?"

Tim almost laughed. Powerful men thought alike, whether they were pontificating from shoeshine thrones or riding cabs to Wall Street. But Tim did not laugh. He pulled at his cuffs and made his case. By the time that they arrived at number twenty-three, Tim had the loan that would save West Side Workingman's.

A week later, in a move that the banking community both hailed and condemned, the directors made twenty-five-year-old Tim Riley the president of their bank.

And come June, Tim bought Helen that town house, two rooms deep, four floors high, an easy walk to the main branch of the bank.

BUT NEW YORK was still a dangerous place. There were a thousand perils to kill a person in an instant, a thousand more to wear him down over a decade.

On a bright afternoon in March of 1906, Helen Riley stepped into Eighth Avenue just as a horse team was startled by the sound of a horn blasting on one of those newfangled autocars. City horses were supposed to be used to everything from trolley bells to gunshots, but these two bolted.

Helen was seven months' pregnant and just a step too slow . . .

If any pain could have been worse than that of a boy listening as his father was beaten to death, it was the pain that Tim Riley felt for months. Losing a parent seemed somehow in the natural order of things, no matter how violently it happened. Losing a pregnant wife after nine months of marriage was all but unbearable.

So Tim resumed his habit of walking.

When his banking day was done, he would go back to his empty town house and change into work clothes. He would put a blackjack into his pocket because it was still Hell's Kitchen, and everyone knew Tim Riley on the good streets and the bad corners, in the parish halls and the clip joints. And any thug would love to see what a young bank president carried in his pockets after dark. But Tim only met with trouble once. He met it with the blackjack on two thick skulls and kept walking.

His evening routine grew as regular as his banking day. He walked down to Deegan's Saloon, where he drank two beers. Then he walked past Sadowski's Boot Shop and waved to the men of the family, who always worked late, except for the anarchist. Then he walked on toward the water, always toward the water. He was still walking in October, when the nights grew cool and the shadows came early. He feared the approach of winter, because he knew that it would be harder to face his despair in the dark.

One evening, he sat on a piling on the Thirty-fifth Street Pier and stared across the river. The sky over New Jersey was layering into colors sliding down the scale from gold to red to purple. Morgan's new yacht, the *Corsair III,* rode at the old anchorage.

Seeing it reminded Tim of two promises he had made to himself so long ago: that he would kill the McGillicuddys and make himself rich. The McGillicuddys were gone, and he was riding the rails from salaried to well paid to wealthy. And . . . what did it matter?

He looked into the oily water lapping against

the pier and heard a voice, like an echo across the years: "I'm sorry for your troubles."

He turned. "Doreen?"

"I'm sorry I wasn't here to sing your wife to her rest."

"I didn't know you were in town."

"I'm comin' home." She was wearing a blue skirt and matching jacket. Her hat was black. She could have been a schoolmistress.

"Coming home?" he said. "Quitting the circuit?"

"Comin' home to do that play. One way or the other."

He said, "I'll be first in line to see it."

"I'll give you tickets. No standin' in line for Tim Riley."

And a thought echoed back from his boyhood: she was the most beautiful thing he had ever seen. And the thought robbed him for a moment of speech.

Then she smiled. "Say, are you hungry? I've been back to New York half a dozen times since they opened that new Flatiron Building, and I never ate yet in their café."

"The one on the roof?"

"Whaddya say?" Her eyes brightened.

"I . . . I don't know." Tim's mother had said that a man should be in mourning for a year after his wife died. "I haven't had much appetite for a while."

"You have to eat," said Doreen. "We could walk it in twenty minutes. Get there in time to watch the electric lights go on. German food . . . wiener schnitzel . . . bratwurst . . ."

He protested that he wasn't dressed for it.

She slipped her arm into his and said that a café should serve men in work clothes and business suits, too. "Besides, you're with me. And you might be the handsomest bank president in New York, but no one'll be lookin' at you if *I'm* on your arm."

That made him laugh. She was brash and confident and as in love with herself as she ever could be with anyone else. She announced herself. She barged ahead. And while she might not be the most ladylike lady he had ever met, she was the most fun.

So they ate dinner on the top of the Flatiron Building. Then they rode the horsecar back up Broadway, then walked across Forty-eighth to her mother's place.

On the stoop, she kissed his cheek and said she had one more tour, then she would be back for good. "And we'll look to raise money for the show. We're callin' it *The Big Cavalcade of 1907.*" Then she kissed him again, a little sisterly peck on the lips.

He stepped back and instinctively looked up at the windows of his mother's flat.

She said, "So . . . you want to come up?"

"Come up?"

"You can come up. We're old friends."

"But I—"

"It's all right." She gave him another peck on the cheek. "Maybe another time."

TWO NIGHTS LATER, just as Tim slipped the blackjack into his pocket to head out for his walk, Doreen came to the front door with a covered pot.

"I brought you a nice roast chicken with gravy."

He stood there, looking at her in her prim shawl and blouse and skirt, and thought it again: the most beautiful thing he had ever seen.

"So you gonna ask me in," she said, "or do I take this bird down to the old actor's home and feed it to all the second bananas still dreamin' of top billin'?"

They ate in the dining room, at the mahogany table that Tim had ordered the week before the accident. He opened a bottle of white French wine that someone had given him. She lit the candles she had brought and put the pot on a trivet.

"I'm not much for cookin'," she admitted.

He said it looked better than anything cooked in that house in a long time.

As they ate, Doreen told stories of her life in vaudeville, and she made Tim laugh, which he admitted was something he had done very little of late.

"So, *you* got any funny stories?" she said. "If I make you laugh, you gotta make me laugh. It's an old vaudeville law."

"I'm a banker." He pretended to scowl. "We're never funny."

And they both laughed.

Then there was silence between them.

Then she slid her hand across the table, touched his, and said, "Sugar and salt."

"Sugar and salt?"

"That's what you sprinkle on two peas in a pod. Sugar and salt." She leaned closer. "I'm sugar, and you're salt." And she kissed him, but not like a sister.

Tim's whole being rose in an instant, rose out of the darkness of grief, out of the pain of walking alone.

Then she was standing beside him and he was undoing her blouse and pushing up her chemise and pressing his face to her breasts. They tasted of salt, not sugar, and they rose to the touch of his lips just as he rose to her.

And then the two of them were twined on the carpet beside the table and his trousers were at his ankles and her bloomers were on the floor and . . .

They were done quickly. But they weren't done . . .

They went upstairs to the guest bedroom and left their clothes on the floor and slipped between sheets that had not been mussed in months.

And soon they were done . . . again.

And they lay on their backs and stared up at the ceiling.

He licked his lips and tasted salt, tasted her.

She said, "Do you remember that night at McGillicuddy's?"

"Like it was last night."

"I remember thinkin'—when the pistol fell and the ladder come crashin' after it—everything the Riley boys ever hoped for, everything they ever dreamed, was all crashin', too."

Tim did not say that one of their dreams had been fulfilled a few moments later, when they saw the McGillicuddys dead on the floor.

She said, "I've kept you boys' secret all these years since."

"We know."

"So you got to live your New York dreams."

Then she rolled away from him and lay on her stomach. "And that's all I ever hoped for."

He slid his hand down the smooth white skin of her back and along the sweet ridge of her bottom. "Are your New York dreams different?"

"No." She turned toward him. "They just cost more."

He knew where this was headed. But he could not invest in a play. A play had no collateral. It was all future value, all pie in the sky. That's what he told her.

"But a *theater* is real property," she said. "And a theater company can raise the money for costumes and props and talent, so long as the house ain't takin' too much off the top."

"So, the bank invests in the theater, not the show, and the theater gives a sweetheart deal to a new company?"

"Somethin' like that." She propped herself on her elbows. "My friend, Charley Gibbs, he's an old-time vaudevillian from old-time money. Family disowned him when he went on the circuit. Wanted him to go to Harvard or something. But an uncle left him a chunk of land up at Coogan's Bluff. He'd put it up as collateral. He'd buy the theater. We'd produce. You'd lend. Whaddya say?"

Tim knew it was a bad idea. But everyone deserved a chance at their New York dream. So he said, "Let me think about it."

"Think hard." And she lifted her bottom against his hand.

And the sight of it lifted him. And he lifted her hips off the bed and got onto his knees behind her.

He had never done it like this with Helen. He plunged deep. Doreen let out a long, low moan. . . .

iii.

So a year later, the Riley brothers stood in that flat, with their mother dead, and the banks in panic, and a flop called *The Big Cavalcade of 1907* hidden on the books of West Side Workingman's.

Tim said, "Pa would tell us that keeping our dignity matters most when things are falling apart. If you can keep your dignity, you can keep a cool head, and then you can put things back together."

"Maybe that's why J. P. Morgan's so dignified," said Eddie.

The papers were full of the stories: For almost two weeks, Morgan had been plugging gaps. If there was a run on an important bank, Morgan saw that it received the funds to stay open. If the stock market threatened to close early because the banks couldn't provide call money, Morgan got them the cash to keep trading. And when men were seen carrying boxes of money from bank to bank, Morgan was sending them.

"He even saved the city from bankruptcy," said Tim, "with an issue of short-term bonds, covered by the Clearinghouse."

"Savin' big cities, savin' big banks. I hear he saved a small bank in Harlem, too."

"The big and the small," said Tim. "Scrambling at the top and the bottom."

"But the ones at the top of the pyramid scramble to keep things smooth. Down at the bottom, folks scramble to keep alive. At least the ones at the top know that keepin' things smooth at the bottom keeps 'em smooth at the top, too."

"You need to go into banking with a philosophy like that."

"Either banking or anarchy." Eddie grinned. "Bring the whole thing down. Let new forms rise. Human forms. That's what Teddy says."

"Teddy? Teddy Sadowski, the anarchist brother-in-law?"

Eddie pulled a paper from his pocket and gave it to Tim. "He has an article in *Mother Earth,* Emma Goldman's paper."

Tim flipped through the pages. "Have you lost your mind, readin' this stuff?"

"No. Just my job." Eddie laughed and gave his brother a gentle punch on the shoulder. "Don't worry. Readin' this tells me how the enemy thinks."

Tim pulled out his watch and checked the time. "Want to go to the theater?"

"No, thanks." Eddie turned for the door. "That's where you go when you're thinkin' with your other head."

Tim said nothing. Only his brother could talk to him like that.

"You know," Eddie added, "Ma would say that receivin' Communion after spendin' time with a chorus girl is a mortal sin. You been to confession lately?"

Tim gave his brother a long look. "She's not a chorus girl. She's a headliner."

THE BIG CAVALCADE of 1907 . . . there was something sad, almost naked, thought Tim, about a theater marquee in the midday sun. Marquees were meant to be seen at night. But a poster slapped across a marquee—CLOSES WEDNESDAY—was more than sad. It was a punch in the face, especially for the headliner.

No sparkling reviews festooned the message boards. No one would post a notice like this: "Last night on Fourteenth Street, a show opened that may be the most witless, tuneless, worthless piece of foolishness spilled onto the New York stage this season. . . . As for Doreen Walsh, she has the voice of one of the lesser angels, which is a small blessing, but many of the lesser angels chose to sing in Hades, which is where you'll think you've been after a visit to the old Variety Theater."

The house was empty and smelled of bleach. In the pit, a few musicians were warming up. In the outer dressing room, the chorus girls were chattering, swapping makeup tips and stories.

Doreen was sitting before the mirror in the headliner's dressing room. Her costume—a Dutch-style dress with a ruffled collar—hung on a rack. A dry vase of opening-night roses moldered in a corner. She was doing her eyes, which she flicked at Tim. "You hear that?"

"Not even a hello?" Tim pulled over a stool and sat.

"The orchestra. You hear that? They're warmin' up on somebody else's music."

Tim recognized "School Days." Everyone was singing it. "Dear old Golden Rule days." He listened a moment. "I still say you were great."

"You and the thirty-five people who paid." She

shifted her eyes to his reflection. "You could still keep us afloat, you know."

He said nothing. They had been through this.

She dabbed the brush into the black makeup. "Goddamn Ziegfeld."

"Ziegfeld?"

"A month before we open a show about Peter Stuyvesant and his wife, spoofin' New York history and all the bigwigs, Ziegfeld opens a show about John Smith and Pochohantas, spoofin' New York history and all the bigwigs. He stole our idea."

Tim was not so sure about that, but they were past arguing.

"The goddamn *Ziegfeld Follies of 1907.*" She threw her mascara brush down.

"He even stole your year," said Tim.

She glared at his reflection to let him know that she was in no mood for sarcasm. "He killed us. With the same kind of material."

"His was better." Tim offered more honesty than usual. "He also opened on Broadway, in a rooftop theater with a low nut and lots of foot traffic."

"The Jardin-de-Paris? At Hammerstein's Olympia?" She picked up the rouge. "That's not even a real theater."

"It's right in Times Square."

"*Longacre* Square. That's what we called it when we were kids. And it'll never amount to nothin'. Neither will this Ziegfeld." She painted some rouge onto her cheek. "Did you count the house?"

He shook his head. He knew she was heartbroken. He wanted to reach out to her, but whatever had existed between them had begun to fade when rehearsals began. Doreen Walsh had become Doreen the Chorine, then Doreen the Top-Billed Chorine, and finally, when the notices appeared, Doreen the Furious Flop.

She turned to him. "If we keep the doors open another month, we might—"

"Charley Gibbs is in default," said Tim. "And the collateral he put up, that land at Coogan's Bluff . . . it has more encumbrances than a horse pullin' a trolley down Broadway. Even the New York Giants claim it."

"Come on, Timmy. You've got plenty of money in that bank."

"It's not my money. The people of Hell's Kitchen entrusted it to me. I'm supposed to invest it wisely. My books now show a twenty-five-thousand-dollar hole. And you haven't paid me back a nickel."

"And we never will if we're out of business," said Doreen. "Just one more advance, Timmy." And her eyes brimmed with tears. "Otherwise, I'm finished."

"I may be finished, too."

She said, "You would be if I told the true story of the McGillicuddy massacre."

"No more money." He kissed her on the cheek. This time, he tasted her tears.

She slapped powder onto the place he had kissed.

TIM STOPPED THAT afternoon in the New York Society Library. He had never lost the reading habit or felt more at home anywhere else in New York. He took out a new book by Upton Sinclair—*The Jungle*.

Then he went home. He had read all the muckrakers, as Teddy Roosevelt called them. Jacob Riis, Ida Tarbell, Lincoln Steffens. But none of their books had affected him like *The Jungle*, the story of a Lithuanian family that moved to Chicago to become meat cutters and met nothing but exploitation and tragedy.

Around five thirty, he poured himself a glass of Jameson's Irish whiskey. He had been drinking more of late. It helped him to relax. It helped him to think.

And he thought it was a wonder that there had not been a revolution in America, that the anarchists or the socialists or some other bunch of -ists hadn't ignited half the population, because so many Americans lived like the Lithuanians in that book. They labored six days a week, dawn to dusk, in the cold, wet, blood-soaked slaughterhouse of capitalism. They earned five hundred dollars a year, while J. P. Morgan spent millions on rare books, fine arts, and his own spectacular museum.

But some men flourished and some men merely survived.

It was not just the American story. It was the human story, except that men had a better chance to flourish in America than anywhere else. Tim believed that as certainly as he believed that Jameson's tasted of Irish peat. It was the reason that his grandfather had crossed the ocean. It was what his father had told him that day in the cupola of Woodward Manor. And it was why he had left Morgan for West Side Workingman's. A bank might be capitalism's clubhouse, but it existed for the communal good, too.

Tim had seen most of the ways that men made "bad" money in Hell's Kitchen. And he believed in the old saying, "Good money drives out bad." Bringing down the Morgans of the world could do nothing to raise the lot of the meat cutters, the demolition men, the barkeeps. But by carefully lending money that had been carefully banked—good money—Tim could. That made *him* the revolutionary.

He had another drink and perused his brother's anarchist rag.

The anarchists planted bombs. They shot businessmen. And six years earlier, an anarchist had assassinated President McKinley. And what had it accomplished?

The anarchists might say that Theodore Roosevelt replaced McKinley and began breaking up the business trusts that were the governing structures of capitalism. He had also called Morgan and his ilk "malefactors of great wealth." The anarchists would call that a good start. But . . . a pounding on the door interrupted his thoughts.

Daniel Daly, in black suit, winged collar, and flat-topped derby, was peering through the sidelight. He had a sheaf of papers under his arm. "Let me in. Now."

Daly had never come to the door unannounced or impolite, but he stalked into the parlor and threw the papers onto the sofa. "This is how you repay me?"

Tim swallowed his shock and said, "I'm working to rectify the mistake."

"You loaned twenty-five thousand to a vaudevillian to buy a theater? He's in default after six months, his collateral is in litigation, and you covered up the loan. Once we institute foreclosure proceedings—"

"I'm working to rectify the mistake."

Daly walked over to the sideboard and picked up the Jameson's. "May I?"

Tim gave a nod—of course. It was the least he could do, considering that he had just driven the man to drink.

Daly fumbled with the bottle, filled a glass, turned. "When wealthy men are mobbing banks on Fifth Avenue, what hope can we have if something like this gets out?"

"I am working to rectify the mistake." Tim didn't like saying it any more than Daly liked hearing it.

"It was not a mistake," said Daly. "It was malfeasance."

"Misfeasance," corrected Tim.

"And how do you propose to erase it? By redeeming those old bonds?"

"If I knew where they were, I might try," said Tim.

"They're as worthless as your faith in *The Big Cavalcade of 1907*." Daly stepped close to Tim and looked into his eyes. "I trained you, Timmy. I taught you. And you betrayed me so that you could wet your prick in a chorus girl."

That stung. "I'm sorry, Daniel."

"You have one week to . . . *rectify the situation*. Then I want you out." With that, Daniel Daly threw down the shot of Jameson's and left.

Tim sat for a long time, alone, sipping his Jameson's, thinking.

Somehow, he would make this right. Or he would sacrifice himself for his sins.

He went upstairs to his rolltop desk, a wedding gift from his dead wife. He unlocked a drawer. Inside were three more 1780 bonds, the last of the five that his father had saved from the mahogany box.

Tim had heard that J. P. Morgan was traveling to Wall Street each day with his son-in-law, so there would be no chance for another raid on his cab.

But Saturday brought his chance.

At five that afternoon, Tim received a phone call from the Bank Clearinghouse, ordering him to appear at the Morgan Library at eight P.M. His stomach dropped, because at first, he thought they had found him out. But the voice on the other end of the line explained that it was an emergency meeting and that he should bring a secretary.

Tim was summoned not because he was a prodigy or his bank was powerful, but because Workingman's was one of ten small banks that formed a consortium that month by month rotated a different representative to the Clearinghouse meetings.

AT SEVEN FORTY-FIVE, Tim and his secretary for the night, his brother, Eddie, pushed through the crowd of reporters on Madison and Thirty-sixth.

The paperboys, as Eddie called them, had been watching Morgan's every move for days, and as the financial leaders of the city gathered at the Morgan Library on a Saturday night, when most of them would have had dinner plans or theater tickets or wives to appease or mistresses to entertain, even the greenest stringer could see that something was up.

A few of the reporters asked Tim questions, starting with, "Hey, kid, how come they're lettin' you in there?"

But Eddie waved his cane and said, "No answers, fellers. So no questions. So save your breath."

Then the brothers presented their credentials and stepped into a universe of marble. Tim looked up in awe. Eddie whistled softy.

The design was magnificently simple. A rotunda and three rooms surrounding it: Morgan's study to the left, the actual library to the right, and directly ahead, the librarian's office.

Men with winged collars and well-trimmed beards were hurrying across the rotunda from one room to another or collecting into knots of conversation that sent a nervous murmur vibrating off the marble walls and the frescoes on the vaulted ceiling.

Tim nodded to a few of them. Fewer nodded back.

"Glad I wore my new suit," whispered Eddie.

Tim noticed several gentlemen pacing in the librarian's office: Morgan's partner, G. W. Perkins, and Judge Elbert Gary and Henry Clay Frick, both of United States Steel.

Eddie elbowed Tim. "You see Frick? If you get

close, look for the missing earlobe and the scar on his neck. An anarchist shot him twice and still couldn't kill him."

"The anarchists should take that as a sign."

Then Tim took a few steps closer to the office and saw the burly figure of Morgan himself, leaning over a desk, focused on something that must have been very serious, because he was paying no attention to anyone around him.

"Talk about your malefactors of great wealth," whispered Eddie. "If Teddy Sadowski knew about this, he'd be here in ten minutes with a wagonload of dynamite."

Then, a young man approached them. "Trusts or Clearinghouse?"

"Clearinghouse," said Tim.

The young man directed the Rileys into the library.

Two stories of illuminated cases greeted them, along with the curious or disinterested faces of many of the most important men in New York.

Tim nodded to a few who nodded back. But their expressions said, "That's Tim Riley. He's nobody." Tim did not disagree. In comparison to most of them, he was Nobody from Nothing Bank.

The most powerful of them were sitting around the library table. The rest were standing or sitting in chairs in front of bookcases that contained a Gutenburg Bible, a Shakespeare folio, Dante's *Inferno*, and much of the rest of humanity's highest hopes and deepest dreams in their earliest forms.

It seemed that two trust companies and a major brokerage were in danger of collapse because of withdrawals, bad investments, and a panic-driven drop in the value of their securities. If they went down, they would bring the whole economy with them. So Morgan had called these men together to fund a communal pool that would improve liquidity, lower short-term interest rates, and end the panic once and for all.

Tim took little part in the talk. No matter how much he knew, he was a neophyte to these men. He listened and observed from near the library door, and from time to time peered across the rotunda and into the librarian's office.

And the men talked and talked . . . and talked. Midnight, one A.M. two . . . Tim felt his eyes droop more than once and had to elbow his brother for snoring.

Around two thirty, Eddie went outside for some air, but he came right back. "We're locked in," he whispered. "Morgan has the only key and isn't lettin' anyone out."

Tim laughed. "That sounds like something old Plunkitt would do."

Around quarter to three, Tim noticed Henry Clay Frick walking out of the librarian's office, carrying papers into the study. And Morgan was alone.

Tim had been bold before. He would be bold now. He strode across the rotunda, tugged at his cuffs, knocked on the open office door, and stepped in.

Morgan looked up, and Tim saw the cards. All night, with the economic life of a nation in the balance, J. P. Morgan had been playing solitaire.

"Riley? Tim Riley? What are you doing here?"

Tim explained his role on the rotating seat.

"Well, keep your eyes and ears open." Morgan put a black eight on a red nine.

"Men will be writing about this night a hundred years from now, sir."

"Let's hope they've learned something by then."

Tim put a 1780 bond on Morgan's desk.

Morgan shifted his eyes. "Save it. If we fail here tonight, a Continental bond with historical significance may be worth more than a gold bond from the Morgan Bank."

Tim knew that was an exaggeration. But this wasn't: "If I fail here tonight, the passbooks of a lot of hardworking people will be worthless, too."

Morgan put a red ten on a black jack. "What's your shortfall?"

"We've had a default on a $25,000 loan."

"And you can't absorb it? What kind of reserve do you have?"

"It's not the reserve, sir. It's the confidence. You yourself told the newspapers that we would be all right if people just kept their money in the banks, but fear is running things now. I fear what happens Monday if news spreads that we've had a major default."

"What are you foreclosing?"

"A theater on Fourteenth Street."

Morgan sat back, the deck in his left hand, a single card in his right. "I am trying to arrange financing of some twenty-five million dollars to shore up our economy, and you are bothering me about a twenty-five-thousand-dollar loan to a *theater*?"

"To the depositors at West Side, it's just as

important." Tim took a deep breath, and pressed on. "If the bottom of the pyramid collapses, the top must crash down."

Morgan gave Tim Riley a long look and opened his mouth to speak.

And Frick pushed past Tim. "We're ready in the study, Pierpont."

Morgan put his cards on the table and stood.

But Tim held his ground in the doorway. "May I count on your help, sir?"

"Sign the theater over to me. You'll have the cash to cover it on Monday."

Tim wanted to embrace the old man. Instead, he said to Morgan's broad back as it receded across the hallway, "We repaid you once, sir. We'll repay you again. And the depositors of West Side will thank you, sir."

"I always wanted to own a theater. Oh, and"—Morgan turned—"leave the bond."

Tim Riley would have gone straight away to wake up Daniel Daly, but he knew that he was witnessing history. So he stayed. Besides, they were locked in.

At three in the morning, a hundred and twenty men crowded into the study with the roaring fire and the red damask walls. At four thirty, they had an agreement: they would form a pool to rescue the trusts, the brokerage, and in the process, the national economy. But parts of the plan would need the approval of President Roosevelt, who didn't trust any of them. And all of them would need the approval of their boards.

Even the most powerful of men were answerable, thought Tim.

Still, Morgan wanted signatures that night. He said, "Your directors will be perfectly supportive, when they learn the alternative." Then he waved his hand invitingly toward the document.

No one stepped forward, so Morgan went over to Edward King of the Union Trust and pointed to his desk. "There's the place, King, and here's the pen." Morgan put a gold pen into King's hand, and King became the John Hancock of the night.

At five o'clock, the library doors were unlocked, and the Riley brothers stepped out into the cold.

"Still dark." Eddie looked up into the sky.

"Brighter than it was," said Tim. "At the top of the pyramid and the bottom, too."

EDDIE WENT HOME to bed.

Tim decided to go to the six o'clock Mass.

Though Sacred Heart parishioners were meant to keep holy the Sabbath, some had to work on Sundays or their families would starve. For them it was an early Mass or no Mass at all.

Tim sat in the half-full church, surrounded by familiar faces, by depositors, by friends, and he felt that for all his transgressions, he had done them a great service.

Then, as the Mass ended, he heard a pure, clear voice, singing the "Ave Maria" in the choir loft. He looked up and there was Doreen.

She caught up to him outside church. Her face was scrubbed clean of makeup. Her hair was loose and flowing to her shoulders. She said, "You're up awful early."

"I never went to bed."

"Anyone I know?'

"J. P. Morgan."

"That's a relief. I thought maybe you'd found somebody else." She slipped a hand into the crook of his elbow.

He hadn't expected that. He almost pulled away, but instead, he turned west and walked to the corner. New York at seven o'clock on a Sunday morning in November was as quiet as it ever got. Ninth Avenue was deserted and still dark under the El.

"I know you usually go to the ten o'clock," she said, "but I wasn't takin' a chance. How about some some bacon and eggs?"

"Whenever you start feeding me, I wonder what you're after."

She stopped in the street and turned toward him.

An uptown train was rumbling from Forty-second Street.

She glanced toward it, then she said, "I missed my monthlies."

"Missed them?" After a sleepless night, Tim's mind was not working as quickly as usual. "Missed—"

"My ma always said, 'Where God closes a door, he opens a window.' I guess you could say, 'Where God closes a show, he opens a family.' "

"Family?" The word penetrated the sleepy fog in Tim's head. Then dozens of questions and emotions surged through him. *When is it due? What happens to your career?* Even the unthinkable . . . *Am I the father? Are you planning to have the baby*?

But from the way she looked at him, with a mixture of hope, trepidation, and fresh seductiveness, getting rid of the baby was not something she had even considered.

The train roared over them, but her lips were moving.

When it passed he asked her, "What did you just say?"

"Sugar and salt. Sugar and salt and another pea in the pod."

TIM WAS SO exhausted that once he fell asleep, he slept until five in the afternoon. When he awoke, the idea of Doreen Walsh as his wife seemed perfectly natural. So he spent the evening at the Walsh flat on Forty-eighth. Her mother made pot roast. They talked of the banns, of the wedding, and of the birth that they all knew was coming.

Tim left around midnight.

He wasn't sleepy. So he decided to walk past the bank he had saved the night before. As he came down Ninth, he expected that all would be quiet. It was raining lightly. It was late. It was Sunday. All good reasons for quiet. But as he turned onto Forty-second Street, he saw dozens of men in the shadows beneath the gaslights, forming a line that began at the door to West Side Workingman's.

Tim hurried ahead and looked for familiar faces and saw, "Eddie?"

"Evenin', Tim," said Eddie. Then he asked the man in front of him to hold his place.

"I do not like lines," said the man, "but I will hold for you."

Tim recognized Sadowski the anarchist, of all people. He gave Sadowski a look, then led Eddie away from the line. "What the hell is going on?"

"Word is out. Everybody knows your girlfriend's show flopped. And the papers had us goin' into Morgan's library. So there's talk you're on the ropes."

"You know we're not, but . . . who are you holdin' a place for?"

"Myself."

"Jesus, Eddie. You were there last night. You saw what I saw. You should be tellin' these people that it's all right instead of joinin' them."

"What I saw last night," said Eddie, "is nothin' compared to what they fear tonight. And come mornin', I fear that you'll see a real run on your bank."

Tim knew he had to stop this, or it didn't matter what Morgan had promised. He jumped onto a wagon parked beneath a gaslight and shouted, "Listen to me, all of you! Your money's safe! Go home!"

"Ahhh, you go home," shouted someone in the line.

"Your money is safe!" cried Tim.

"That ain't what we hear!" shouted someone else.

"You are a banker," said Sadowski. "Why should men who labor believe you?"

"Because I am one of you. I'm—"

"Don't say you're our brother!" shouted Sadowski. "You're a tool of rich men."

"Don't you say *you're* our brother, either," shouted someone who liked anarchists even less than bankers.

"Some day you will listen to the truth," said Sadowski, "but for now, protect what little you have from these money-grubbers."

"Ignore him!" shouted Tim. "We went into the Morgan Library because Morgan is going to guarantee our loans and cover our losses."

"We'll believe that when we read it in the papers," said someone else.

So Tim snatched a late edition *New York Post* from someone in the line. He flipped from front to back, but found no mention of his bank and scarcely a mention of the plan that had emerged from the Morgan Library. Then he ran to Times Square, bought several more papers, but could find nothing in them that would persuade that ever-lengthening line that J. P. Morgan was backing West Side Workingman's.

Tim Riley stayed all night. He told everyone who arrived to go home, that there was no cause for worry, that the assets of the bank were sound.

But the line kept growing longer, and the rain fell harder, and those who had umbrellas put them up, and those who didn't made friends with those who did.

At eight o'clock, Daniel Daly came around the corner of Eighth Avenue, with his newspaper under his arm and his umbrella over his head, and he stopped at the sight of three hundred people lining

Forty-second Street. His lips formed the words, "Sweet Jesus."

Theodore Sadowski said, "Sweet Jesus was an anarchist."

Tim pulled out his watch and looked at his brother. "I need you to do an errand."

"An errand," said Sadowski. "Every society has its hierarchy. And every family is a small society. There are order givers and errand boys. "

Eddie said, "I'm nobody's errand boy."

"But your brother is a banker," said Sadowski. "That makes him your superior, in his own mind."

"That makes me responsible for the future of everyone in this line and half the people between Eighth Avenue and the river," said Tim.

"That makes you an oppressor of the working-man," said Sadowski.

Tim felt the blackjack in his pocket. He had put it there the night before, anticipating that he'd be going for a walk. He pulled it out now, snapped it up, then snapped it down. And Theodore Sadowski hit the sidewalk.

Eddie looked down at his brother-in-law. "An anarchist with a bank account. Like a dray horse with a college degree."

Tim took Eddie by the arm and led him to the door of the bank.

As the guard let them in, someone shouted, "You better not be givin' him special treatment! No seein' to your brother's deposit before you take care of ours!"

"We'll see to all of your deposits," said Tim.

It took ten minutes to collect the papers on the Variety Theater. Tim told his brother to go down to J. P. Morgan and Company, and exchange them for cash.

"The lawyers will go over it all later," said Tim. "But now, it's in your hands." Then he gave Eddie the blackjack for protection and the money to hire a cab.

The doors of the West Side Workingmen's opened at nine A.M. The bank run began in the time it took George Delahunt, a lawyer from Fifty-ninth Street, to grab a withdrawal slip, cross the floor, and place himself in front of a teller's window.

By nine thirty, the cash reserves were down by fifteen percent.

The armed guard allowed one person into the bank at a time. Daniel Daly worked behind the counter and kept track of the dwindling cash. Tim Riley greeted each customer with Morgan's quote to the papers: "If everyone would just keep their money in the banks, everything will be all right."

Some people listened. Others laughed in his face.

And the rain fell as if it meant to rain all month.

By ten o'clock the reserve was falling as fast as the rain.

Tim Riley was beginning to wonder if there would be a riot. He had already arrived at the conclusion that he would have to leave his old neighborhood if the bank failed. He had damaged his reputation. Now it would be destroyed.

But at ten fifteen, an auto taxi skidded to a stop in front of the bank and Eddie Riley climbed out with two bags of cash containing twelve thousand five hundred dollars each. The words J. P. MORGAN & CO. were stenciled on the sides of each bag.

Eddie held them up, and Tim shouted, "If Pierpont Morgan believes in this bank, maybe you should, too."

A few people cheered, about half of them went home, and that was just enough.

The run, and the rain, petered out around eleven. Later someone actually made a deposit. When the doors closed at three o'clock, the tellers cheered.

Tim Riley went into his office and put his head in his hands.

Daniel Daly stood over him and smiled, the avuncular mentor yet again. "It's the sign of a brave man that he learns, adapts, and rectifies his *mis*feasance."

Tim raised his head. "I'm resigning."

"Resigning?"

"You said banking is about confidence, not gossip. I'm marrying Doreen Walsh. She's having my child. That will damage confidence and engender gossip."

"You're marrying Doreen the Chorine?" Daly dropped into the chair, looked out the window, then said, "I suppose resigning is a good idea."

The full dark of November fell by four thirty. A few sporadic showers were still splattering down. The wet macadam of Forty-second Street reflected the street lamps and the headlights and the lanterns on the box cabs.

Tim walked west, wondering what he would do

next. Then he remembered something his father had told him: a man who worked with his hands would never go hungry. So he would work with his hands if he had to.

At the corner of Ninth, he heard someone shouting. A small group had gathered around a man on a soapbox.

It was Theodore Sadowski: "Come to Union Square tonight. Hear Emma Goldman open your eyes to all that you saw on this street today . . . the lies of little bankers . . . the paternalism of big bankers . . . the indifference of a system that oppresses you. All will be laid bare."

A few people were listening. A few were heckling. And one was standing in a doorway in a peacoat with the collar turned up: It was Eddie.

"What are you listening to him for?" asked Tim.

Eddie shrugged. "Sometimes he makes sense, especially on a day when we have to ask the malefactors of great wealth to save our asses."

"At least our asses were saved."

Sadowski was shouting, "Once you have heard her, you will want to attack the nearest police station! You will join the cause of direct action."

"Oh," said Eddie. "Congratulations. I knew you'd marry Doreen sooner or later."

"Thanks," said Tim, and he walked home through the rain.

Doreen was waiting for him when he got there. He smelled beef stew.

"I cooked it myself," she said.

And he was glad to be home.

iv.

So dreams ended. But life went on. And years passed . . . thirteen to be exact.

On a cool September night in 1920, Tim Riley sat in the parlor of the Forty-seventh Street brownstone that he had converted to a two-family. A fire crackled on the grate. His son Richie sat at the big rolltop desk in the corner and did his homework.

Above the desk was a photograph of Doreen in a military-style cape with a doughboy's overseas cap perched jauntily on her head. It was not a costume. She had lasted as a wife and mother for ten years. Then came the war, and the cry for soldiers, and the cry to entertain them. When old Charley Gibbs tracked her down and told her he was forming a vaudeville troupe that was heading to Europe, Tim told her to go. He said it would be good for her and good for the soldiers, too.

Now she lay in a small cemetery near a place called Chateau Thierry, the victim of a slick road and a Model T speeding to the next show.

It had only been in the last few months that the boy had begun to talk about his mother and ask about his parents' youth.

So one morning, as he rode the subway to Wall Street, Tim had decided to leave a written record of his days for the auburn-haired boy who had inherited his father's mathematical skills and his mother's singing voice. Besides, anyone who had lived forty-one years in New York had seen changes worth writing about. Skyscrapers, subways, Broadway. No place seemed to change more quickly, and yet somehow it always stayed the same.

So Tim had filled four notebooks for his son. He wrote about his mother and her sewing. He wrote of his father, who could have been "the best tank-bottom man in New York," but preferred to start his own demolition business. He described his meetings with J. P. Morgan, including the famous night at the library. He tiptoed around the McGillicuddy massacre. He told the story of *The Big Cavalcade of 1907* so that the outcome—a happy marriage and a son named Richard Daniel Riley—made the disappointments of his parents worthwhile.

Tim still had much to write about, like the day he went back to work as an accountant for Morgan and Company, or the 1918 afternoon when he looked out the windows of 23 Wall Street at thousands of people packed from Broadway to Water Street, all to hear movie star Douglas Fairbanks shouting through a megaphone, urging them to buy bonds. That was democracy in action, thought Tim, the money of a democratic nation put to work to win the Great War.

He also had to write about the anarchists, the enemies of democracy in action.

They had been conducting a war of terror in America for thirty years, a war with governments, capitalists, and the social order itself. They had plotted to set off a bomb under a magistrate's bench in the Tombs prison. They had tried to blow up St. Patrick's Cathedral, because church hierarchy was as abhorrent as any other. They had sent thirty bombs through the mail to kill politicians and industrialists, including John D. Rockefeller.

They would have included J. P. Morgan, too, except that nature had already done the job. The bombs were discovered, but for one that blew off the hands of a Negro housemaid. So much for social justice.

Eddie's brother-in-law, the anarchist Theodore Sadowski, had been in and out of the country, in and out jail, and had lately shown up again in Hell's Kitchen, railing against the treatment of two Italian immigrants from Massachusetts named Sacco and Vanzetti. But the family did not speak so much of him. The Sadowskis could not understand his hatred of a country that had given them such opportunity.

So, on that September night, Tim was writing and his son was doing his geometry proofs. Tim heard the snap of a pencil and glanced up as the boy rummaged for another.

"Check the middle drawer." Tim flipped him the key.

The boy opened it, pulled out a few pencils, and said, "Hey, Pa, what are these?"

The last two bonds. Another story for a father to tell his son. So Tim told it. "Somewhere your grandfather hid a mahogany box containing another nineteen thousand five hundred dollars worth of them."

"And he didn't tell you where?"

"He gave me clues." Tim described his father's talk about clouds, rain, water, and money. But he could not talk about the death of his father, even then. So that night, he wrote about it. He wrote about his father lying on the steps, the white X drawn on the tread, and his father's last word, "eyes," and about that last moment, when his father seemed to be squinting into the future.

Before bed, Tim took a bit of air up on the roof. He liked it up there, looking across Hell's Kitchen at the jumble of chimneys and fire escapes and the water tanks on the newer, taller buildings in the distance. It wasn't a world of perfection. But it worked. And he had helped, in his small way, to make it work.

Knowing that was almost as profound as a prayer before bed.

Like a lot of people who wrote, Tim slept with his notebook beside him. An hour or so after he had fallen asleep, he woke, fumbled for a pencil, and scrawled something he thought was eloquent: *Rainwater O'Day. X marks the . . . spiffle.*

THE DAY DAWNED clear and bright, crisp and blue. In a city where clouds of industry and commerce always seemed to darken the sky, this was what Tim called September perfection.

He cooked bacon and eggs for himself and the boy. Then they walked out together. He gave Richard a pat on the back and told him to study hard. He never sent his boy off without a pat on the back. Then Richard turned toward Sacred Heart School, taught by an order called the Irish Christian Brothers, mostly tough New Yorkers who had answered a call.

Tim headed for the subway. He read the paper on the way downtown. There was more about Sacco and Vanzetti, but he didn't really care about them.

When he thought about Massachusetts, he thought about a gift from the Boston Red Sox named Babe Ruth. Fifty-one homers and still counting. What a hitter.

At eight thirty, Tim arrived at the canopied entrance to J. P. Morgan & Co. It was a new building, but it still sat at the most prominent financial intersection in the world, the corner of Wall and Broad, across from the subtreasury and Washington's statue. It was September 16. The quarterly reports were due in two weeks, and Tim was the assistant chief accountant. So he worked hard all morning and had lunch at his desk. But while he ate his cheese sandwich, he opened his notebook.

And he saw the cryptic notes he had written in the night. *Rainwater O'Day. X marks the* . . . he couldn't read the last word. It looked like *spiffle.*

He was puzzling over that when the telephone rang.

"Accounting."

"Timmy, is that you?" It was Eddie, who worked now for the McManus machine.

"What's wrong?"

"Something funny goin' on. Polly just called me, said that her brother Teddy borrowed some money from her today."

"So what else is new?"

"He told her he wanted all that she had in the cookie jar and under the rug, and if she gave it up, she'd never see him again."

"If that's a promise," said Tim, "I'll give him a few bucks myself."

Eddie didn't laugh. "Then, a little while ago, she

was cleaning up his room and she found a tourist map of New York."

"He's no tourist."

"He'd drawn a route from Hell's Kitchen to Little Italy, where he made an X, then down to Wall Street, where he made another X, right across the street from you."

Tim could hear the noon bell chiming at Trinity Church. He glanced at his watch, as he always did when he heard the bells. Right on time.

Eddie said, "Polly saw him ride off in a wagon pulled by a dark bay horse. I think that stupid Litvak is in business with the dago anarchists. I think—"

"What do you want me to do?"

"Just look out the window. If you see the son of a bitch, tell him to go home. His father's scared to death that he'll do something stupid and get them all deported."

Tim said, "Hold the line."

As he stood in that sea of desks in the middle of that enormous open banking floor, Tim glanced down at his notebook. And he saw his father's eyes, squinting. And in the strange way that a distraction can lead roundabout to an insight, he knew. In an instant, he knew where his father had hidden the bonds. But from the corner of his own eye, he saw motion outside the window.

A wagon was pulling up, directly across Wall Street. Now the driver was jumping down and walking quickly east.

Tim hurried over to the big window and tried to see if it was Sadowski.

And his mind froze everything that he saw:

The dark bay horse nodding its head . . . a messenger boy hurrying along the sidewalk . . . two women angling across the street and one of them glancing up at him . . . a man opening a newspaper in a shaft of sunlight . . . a chocolate peddler looking east . . . a dozen people taking the sun on the steps of the subtreasury . . . a Model T clattering along . . . a horse-drawn carriage coming right behind it. . . .

The chiming at Trinity Church stopped.

A horn honked.

William Joyce, the head trader, called to Tim.

As he turned, Tim felt a sudden, inexplicable pressure. He felt it outside him and inside his head and deep in his chest, too.

An instant later, everything was consumed in a flash of orange flame.

The window in front of Tim exploded inward. His eardrums burst. He was struck with the force of air that slammed him against a desk and shook the whole building. Then six-inch lead missiles—sash weights—were flying like bullets in every direction.

And it seemed to go on and on and on, a sound feeding off its own fury.

His ears were screaming in a cloud of smoke and flying debris.

Then he saw William Joyce through the smoke . . . standing . . . lurching . . . reaching to the hole in his forehead . . . collapsing.

And Tim realized that his trouser leg was soaking wet. He saw his own blood pouring onto the floor. A long shard of glass had dug deep into his groin.

He pulled it out, and a fountain of dark arterial blood spurted.

One . . . two . . . three . . . spurts, each lower, each under less pressure. He rolled over on the blood-soaked, glass-covered, marble floor of the J. P. Morgan Bank.

His ears kept screaming, but he tried to stand, tried to find his phone to call his brother, to tell him that he knew where the bonds were. But his mind was fading. He was leaving great puddles of blood on the floor. And he simply could . . . not . . . stand . . .

His face pressed against the shards of shattered glass. He made an X on the marble with his own blood. He hoped that his son would understand.

He prayed for the boy. He began to say the Act of Contrition. He made it to "for having offended Thee . . ."

THIRTEEN

Wednesday Night

The boss only wants to talk . . . only wants to talk . . . only wants to talk.

Evangeline kept reminding herself as the cab reached the West Side Highway.

Peter was reading an article on his iPhone. The headline: *WALL STREET BOMBING!*

The Russian—he said his name was Vitaly—leaned across Evangeline to look at the small screen in Peter's hand.

She could feel his muscle through his boxy suit, and she could have smelled his cologne through a hazmat suit. Aramis: big in the seventies but not unpleasant.

"Fancy phone," he said to Peter. "What you reading?"

"An article from *The New York Times*." Peter held it up.

The Russian's eyes widened. "Bomb? On Wall Street? Arab son of bitches." He looked at Evangeline. "I waste so much time chasing you, I don't hear news all day."

"This is an old newspaper," said Peter. "It was an anarchist bombing."

"Anarchists? Like terrorists?"

Peter nodded. "Striking at the heart of capitalism. The bomb went off in front of the Morgan Bank. A hundred pounds of dynamite, five hundred pounds of sash weights."

"Sash weights?" Vitaly nodded. He approved of sash weights.

"It wrecked cars and wagons, killed forty people, injured four hundred, shattered windows for six blocks, including the wall of glass at the stock exchange."

"Why did Antoine want you to see this?" asked Evangeline.

"Because the bomb destroyed the interior of the

Morgan Bank and killed three people inside, including assistant chief accountant Timothy Riley."

"Oh, no," said Evangeline.

"He friend of yours?" asked Vitaly.

"This was ninety years ago," said Evangeline.

"But he was kind of a friend," said Peter. "They all become friends in a way."

The cab was heading south on the West Side Highway. Evangeline kept waiting at every light for the left turn that would take them back to . . . wherever they were going.

"These anarchists . . . executed?" asked Vitaly.

"They never found them," said Peter. "Wall Street insisted on opening the next day, so they brought in floodlights, cleaned up, got rid of all the blood, all the bodies—"

"All the evidence?" said Evangeline.

"Exactly," said Peter. "The street got right back to work, bandaged but not beaten."

"That why America greatest country," said Vitaly. "Think how fast they clean up World Trade mess. Most country, destroy thirteen acres of big city, mess still there ten years later. Not in America. But Americans fight ten years over what to build next."

Peter looked at him. "If you weren't holding us against our will, I might like you."

"I like America." Vitaly smiled, revealing a stainless-steel incisor, hallmark of Soviet dentistry.

The cab was turning, thumping over cobblestones someplace in SoHo. Parked cars hulked on either side of the street, except where Dumpsters and panel trucks took up spaces. Street lamps did little more than sharpen the shadows, and few lights burned in the windows above. The cab pulled up at the end of a block, at a doorway beneath a sign edged in red lights spelling out the words, *MAY DAY.*

They called the place May Day.

The only white light shone on a poster: "The Rats," in letters that resembled a rat. The muffled pounding of a bass guitar made the windows rattle up and down the street.

A few kids stood outside smoking. One had green hair. Another had silver-studded eyebrows. The third had a tattoo that covered her whole face with *another* face, a giant fly's face . . . except that her eyes were the fly's eyes.

"A bad thing in America"—Vitaly pointed to Ms. Fly—"no law against that."

The girl buzzed at him.

"Be quiet or I swat you," said Vitaly.

Two big guys in black leather jackets were working the door.

Vitaly gave them a look, and the door opened.

Sound shot onto the street like light. Driving guitars, pounding beat, a powerful voice singing, "Let's keep it superficial."

Vitaly gestured for Peter and Evangeline to go inside.

The floor of the club was a lake of waving arms and bobbing heads, all turned toward a raised platform: a lead singer, a girl bassist, a drummer. "The long legs and the pretty mouth, but you open up your lips and the shit falls out."

"I was hoping it might be karaoke night," said Evangeline

"Too bad," said Peter. "This crowd would have loved your Joni Mitchell."

A guy in black T-shirt and black jeans was taking the cover charge, cash money hand over fist. The Rats were hot.

Vitaly gave the guy a look—he was good at looks—then he pointed down a stairwell. At the bottom, tattooed shadows drank at another bar or sought out darker corners to sniff things. Sewage pipes and steam lines crossed overhead, each vibrating at a different pitch with the pounding of The Rats' bass.

Vitaly pointed Peter and Evangeline down a passage behind the bar, past two guards built a lot like him, then he pulled back a dirty curtain to reveal a desk, a few chairs, and a leather sofa against a damp wall.

A man sat in the bubble of light from a desk lamp. He had turned to the wall. His hands were moving furiously back and forth, up and down, up and down, and then . . . they dropped to his sides, as if in exhaustion.

Vitality tapped him on the shoulder.

The man spun around, pulled off a pair of headphones, smoothed his hair, stood. He was taller than Vitaly, more slender, and while his features were not so square and Slavic, they had a distinctive Russian cast—lidded eyes, slack mouth, an expression that seemed morose until something lit it up, a face born of a climate that could make anyone morose, thought

Evangeline. But he was dressed like a businessman: expensive blue suit, starched white shirt, and—Peter looked a bit closer—yes, a Harvard tie.

He said, "Forgive me. I am Yuri Antonov. Tchaikovsky drowns out the—"

"Your personal history is shrouded mystery" was the lyric.

"The Rats?" said Evangeline. "Why would you want to drown out The Rats?"

"Because their bass is giving us lung cancer." Antonov glanced at a trickle of asbestos powder floating down from some pipe insulation.

"Then we shouldn't spend any more time here than we have to," said Peter. "What do you want with us?"

"Sit." Antonov gestured to the sofa. "It is leather, cleaned every week with saddle soap . . . no blood, no bodily fluids."

"That's reassuring," said Evangeline.

"New York basements can be scary places," said Antonov without a hint of scary and not much of an accent. "Roaches, rats—with claws, not guitars—and many bad people who must be punished. Not you, of course."

"That's reassuring, too," said Peter.

"So sit." Antonov dropped behind his desk, and Vitaly placed himself on the other side of the curtain.

Peter and Evangeline both perched on the sofa.

And the music continued to pound above them. "Let's keep it superficial. Let's keep it superficial, yeah!"

Antonov cast his eyes to the floor above. "Tchaikovsky never said that. He went to the deep places . . .

where humanity abides." Antonov pulled the headphone plug from his laptop to fill the room with beautiful anguish. "'The Pathetique.' Saddest fourth movement in music. Deep. Very deep."

"Very deep," said Peter. "Very nice. What do you want from us?"

Antonov turned down the music. "Do you know, Mr. Fallon, that just a few greedy people nearly destroyed the American economy in the great crash of 2008?"

"I've heard it said," answered Peter.

"Those people who brokered the subprime mortgages," Antonov went on, "loans to borrowers who could never repay under terms they never understood, teaser loans that reset at rates certain to force foreclosure. These American patriots, these sultans of capitalism, these masters of the universe, they bundled these loans and sold them for big dollars and were gone when the buyers defaulted."

"Thieves selling garbage to morons." Evangeline repeated something the bag lady had said two nights before on the Bowling Green.

"Very good," said Antonov. "First little thieves sold garbage to poor morons, then big thieves put it all in plastic bags called mortgage-backed securities and sold it to . . . all of us, through pension funds and banks and other brokerages."

"High-class loan sharks," said Peter.

"Loan sharks have more class," said Antonov. "I know loan sharks."

"I'll bet you do," said Peter.

"Do you have a credit card, Mr. Fallon?"

"Why? Am I paying for the drinks?"

"They said you were a smart-ass." Antonov smiled. "If you have a credit card, you do business with loan sharks. Banks borrow money for one half percent from Federal Reserve, then charge fifteen . . . twenty . . . even thirty on credit cards. Legal loan sharks."

"Enough to make a Russian heart bleed," said Peter.

"No." Antonov tightened his Harvard tie. "I am a capitalist. I own bank stocks. Let them charge forty percent, enslave the American people in the yoke of debt."

"So long as the American people can make the vig," said Peter.

Antonov nodded. "That is the dream of every loan shark."

"So you *are* a loan shark?" said Evangeline.

"I am an import-export agent who loves pretty women and music, from Tchaikovsky to The Rats . . . but I forget myself. Coffee? Vodka? A nice glass of Russian tea, maybe?"

"No, thanks," said Peter. "It might keep me awake."

"Keeping awake would be good"—Antonov looked at his watch—"since you have now thirty-four hours to find what rightfully belongs to me."

There was a moment of silence in the little basement office.

"Let's keep it superficial, yeah."

Then Vitaly stuck his head in the door. "Mister Spic is here."

"You must forgive my security chief," Antonov said to Peter and Evangeline. "He can be crude."

Antonov flicked his eyes back to Vitaly. "I will see Mr. Beltron in one minute. We are almost done."

Three dark men stood outside, and none of them looked too happy.

Antonov said to Peter, "Business. My feeder funds."

Peter heard one of the men in the hallway say something, low and growling. Then he heard a yowl of pain, and the man fell through the curtain, right into Antonov's office.

Peter and Evangeline jumped up.

Antonov did not even look at the man twitching on his floor. He merely shifted his eyes and raised his voice. "Vitaly, those men are guests. Do not Tase them." He looked again at Peter and Evangeline. "Vitaly grows too fond of his toys."

"Sorry, boss." Vitaly dragged the twitching man out of the office.

"Vitaly's got a gun, too, I hear," said Evangeline.

"Many people have guns in this country. I came here as a young boy, expecting a civilized place. But here is like anywhere else. You must fight to get and fight to hold or someone will take. Someone like Austin Arsenault."

Peter and Evangeline glanced at each other, then Peter said, "He's your broker?"

"The word should be *breaker*."

"Did Arsenault break you?" asked Peter.

"Do I look broken?" Antonov let those morose Russian features harden.

"No." Evangeline spoke before Peter provoked him further. "You look like a man who breaks others. And likes good music."

"And pretty women." Antonov's expression slackened again. "I am the Russian soul, the hard and the soft, the fighter and the poet."

"Americans often forget the poetry," said Evangeline.

"That is true. So"—Antonov smacked the table—"we see eye to eye."

Peter and Evangeline turned to each other and both said, "We do?"

"You work for me now." Antonov stood. "One Harvard man to another."

"Wait a minute," said Peter.

"Yes, Harvard. My father was very proud."

"So was mine," said Peter. "But he wouldn't be if I broke a contract."

"With Magee?" Antonov made a wave. "A thief, like his boss. They steal from me, so I will steal from them. A simple equation. What you find, you bring to me."

"What have they stolen from you?" asked Peter.

"Do not trouble yourself. He who works for me knows what he needs to know."

"I'm not working for you," said Peter.

Evangeline tugged on Peter's elbow. She'd gotten the message. It didn't matter that Antonov liked nice music and had a good wardrobe. Men who met you in dungeons beneath rock clubs were making a point. She said, "You must forgive us. It's been a long night. We saw someone killed in the Harvard Club. We had a bookstore blown up in our face. So we're just about dead ourselves."

Antonov stepped around the desk. "The big city can be dangerous. People get shot. Accidents happen. Gas leaks come, even in famous old bookstores, especially famous old bookstores owned by men who betray me."

Peter caught Antonov's meaning. "Is that why Oscar Delancey has disappeared?"

"I do not know where Delancey is, but he is not to be trusted. I have found that out." Antonov turned to Evangeline. "So have you."

"I have?" said Evangeline.

"Did he not use you as bait on Monday night?"

"Bait?" said Evangeline. "Me?"

Antonov shrugged. "The details are . . . sketchy."

Peter said to him, "Delancey's deal with Avid is for twenty percent. Mine, too."

"I will give you thirty."

"Is that the deal you made with Delancey?" asked Peter.

"I made no deal with Delancey."

Evangeline tugged again on Peter's elbow.

"So how did you get his phone?" asked Peter.

"Who says we did? We are resourceful. We know electronic tricks."

"So Joey B. is right about the phones," said Peter.

"Berranova? Another dangerous man," said Antonov. "There was no need to kill Sergei on Fourth Avenue this afternoon."

"Or your man in Central Park?" said Peter.

"He was not our man," said Antonov.

"Not your man?" said Peter. "Then who was he?"

Antonov shrugged again. "A competitor. A traitor. An enemy of my late father. My father had many enemies. I am a businessman."

Outside the door, Vitaly growled something at

someone, then delivered another Taser shock to a man who screamed and fell to the floor.

"Vitaly! Put that thing away!" cried Antonov. Then he said to Peter and Evangeline, "As for the shooting in the Harvard Club, we wanted to talk to the accountant. Why would we kill him?"

"Then who did?" asked Peter.

"I am not sure. So trust no one. Not Joey Berra. Not the police who should arrest him for murder. And remember, if you trust the police, you may find that you get a gas leak of your own."

Upstairs, The Rats were playing a new song.

Evangeline tugged Peter's elbow again. They went through the curtain.

Vitaly put an arm out to move Mr. Beltron aside, then he gave Peter a small bow of the head and Evangeline a little smile, just enough to show a bit of stainless steel.

Then Evangeline heard Antonov's voice. "Miss. Miss, you've forgotten your purse."

He thrust his hand through the curtain.

She took the purse. "Thanks."

"Fendi. Nice. But heavy. What you got in there? Rocks?"

"A gentleman shouldn't ask," said Evangeline.

THE BLACK CABBIE drove them back to Times Square. They got off at the corner of Seventh Avenue and Forty-second Street.

And Evangeline told Peter, "That cabbie was the guy watching us on the Bowling Green the other morning."

"Maybe Joey Berra will know who he is. We'll wait fifteen minutes."

"It's after midnight. We're too late," said Evangeline. "Besides, Antonov told us not to trust him."

"So you trust Antonov? Because he says he went to Harvard?"

"Well . . . no. But he has good taste in music, and he liked my purse."

"Yeah, and he has lots of poetry in his soul."

Somewhere above them, the sky was dark. Somewhere around the edges of the square, the shadows reached out. Somewhere below the street lay the memory of the farm that sat there in 1776. But this was the land of the midnight LED, the crossroads of the Big Apple, the place where American commerce, money, and entertainment collided in a giant pinball machine of light and noise.

It didn't surprise Peter that New York had written ordinances requiring Times Square office buildings to display neon. Neon was as natural here as snow on the Tetons or sugar maples in Vermont.

He looked up at the wall of red lights extolling Coke, at the ribbon of words wrapping the Times Building, at an illuminated sign for—of all things—an accounting firm. He took in the giant billboard images of anorexics modeling underwear and athletes eating hamburgers and the huge television screens, too. It was night transformed into neon noon. He said to Evangeline, "Somewhere, a glacier is melting—"

"Glaciers? Peter, we have a missing bookstore

owner, a dead accountant, a bag lady, a Vinnie-Boom-Bah named Berra who plays catcher in the rye whenever we get into trouble, a Russian in a rock-club dungeon, a stock market slut named Kathy, a phony businessman and his phony lawyer—"

"You think they're phonies?" He led her north through the perpetual Times Square crowd.

"Or thieves, as Antonov said—"

"Not exactly an unimpeachable source—"

"Who may blow up Fallon Antiquaria if he doesn't get what he wants, so let's just agree with him, find him the bonds, and forget the goddamn glaciers."

"If America can't make good on its bond obligations, starting with the unretired debt of the Revolution, we'll have all we can do to keep the lights on, never mind trying to save the glaciers while we do it. So there *is* a connection."

They hurried toward the bleachers on Duffy Square, the triangular traffic island between Forty-sixth and Forty-seventh. Father Duffy had been chaplain of the Fighting Sixty-ninth in World War I. His statue stood in the middle of the triangle, backed by a Celtic cross better suited to some Galway graveyard, and a hundred feet in front of him, at the tip of the triangle, stood the statue of another Irishman, George M. Cohan.

Evangeline said, "You should feel right at home with all these micks."

"We're not looking for bronzed Irishmen. We're looking for an Italian named Berra. So let's sit down and wait."

The bleachers: eighteen steps of architectural glass rising to cover the new Broadway TKTS Booth, room for a thousand tourists' asses. Even after midnight, people were climbing all over the steps, looking, laughing, posing for flash pictures that would illuminate their faces but wash out the brilliant backgrounds and leave them disappointed when they got back to Indiana or Indonesia.

Peter and Evangeline sat about halfway up, next to a pair of old ladies.

One was chattering away about how exciting it was to be up so late.

The other was tapping her cane on the glass that formed the seats, the steps, the risers, and complaining about the waste of electricity. "You wouldn't see this in Bangor. They even have lights underneath this thing, so people can see up our skirts."

"Who'd want to see up your skirt?" said her friend.

Evangeline whispered, "This is surreal."

"What's surreal?" Peter asked. "Old ladies sitting on bleachers in Times Square? Or us sitting with them, reading about ourselves?"

"Reading?" she said. "About ourselves?"

He pointed to the news ticker crawling around the Times Building. There wasn't much left of the architecture that once made it one of the most iconic buildings in the city. But it was one of the most icon-covered: Samsung, Prudential, NBC, Nissin's Cup of Noodles.

Letter by letter, Evangeline read the words going by on the northern edge of the building. "NYPD

Investigates Harvard Club Killing. Suspect Loose. Witnesses Sought."

"'Witnesses sought,'" said Peter. "That would be us." He pointed to two officers doing sidewalk duty near the statue of George M. Cohan. "And there's cops everywhere."

"I don't think they're looking for us," said Evangeline. "But he is." She pointed to the west side of Times Square. It was his stillness that caught her eye. In a fast-moving stream of late-night strollers, gawkers, and drunks, one man stood motionless on the corner of Broadway and Forty-sixth: Oscar Delancey.

"The son of a bitch." Peter stood and peered across fifty yards of people on the new pedestrian-mall section of Broadway.

Delancey was holding his cell phone to his ear.

Peter felt his phone vibrate. He answered.

"Hello, Pete."

"Hello, Pete? All you can say is 'Hello, Pete'?"

"I'm sorry."

"Apology accepted. And don't call me Pete. Now how did you find me?"

"I didn't. My partners did. They been on that fuckin' Vitaly's trail since he blew up my store this afternoon. This is a war we're in, Pete, and you gotta choose sides. Fast."

"How fast?"

"I'd say you got one minute."

"A minute? What are you talking about?" Peter looked around for some new threat . . . at the crowd on Broadway . . . into the traffic on Seventh Avenue.

But halfway up the bleachers, ten feet off the street, he saw only motion. . . .

Meanwhile, the old women from Maine asked Evangeline to take their picture with Times Square behind them.

"This is so exciting," said the cheery one. "The girls back in Penobscot County will never believe we were up past midnight."

"They don't call it the city that never sleeps for nothing," said the grouchy one. "Might as well stay up late. Can't sleep. Noisiest goddamn hotel I've ever been in."

Evangeline took the camera and looked through the digital viewfinder, but instead of hitting the shutter button, she hit the zoom. The screen image grew. She saw a man step around the statue of Father Duffy and start climbing the bleachers right behind the old ladies.

He looked familiar. Receding hairline, but solid . . . a little like Vladimir Putin.

Evangeline pressed the button again, to make his image grow even larger. And she remembered: the shooter on the balcony of the Harvard Club.

Delancey was saying to Peter, "Looks like your minute is up. Sorry. It's just business. I told them you'd be holding a cell phone."

Peter shoved the phone into his pocket.

Evangeline cried, "Peter!" just as he saw another man fix his gaze on them and start to climb from the Broadway side.

Peter took it all in: two guys closing from two sides. The quickest way to escape was to make a scene. So he shouted, "Gun! Gun! He's got a gun!"

At the same moment, one of the old ladies turned to Putin. He had a hand in his pocket and maybe a gun in his hand. And he was standing way too close to a grouchy old lady from Maine, because she shouted, "Get back, you perv!" and swung her purse right into his face.

The other old lady smashed her cane off his head, so that his hand flew out of his pocket and the gun flew into the air, and he fell back onto a gang of kids sitting three steps below.

"Gun!" cried the grouchy one. "He's got a gun."

One of the kids pushed him down two or three more steps, while dozens of people were turning, stumbling, running, and practically falling to get off the bleachers.

Peter was dragging Evangeline straight for the other guy, who was smaller, more compact, and had flaming red hair. If he'd been planning to use a weapon on Peter, he was thinking better of it with all those witnesses, and if he'd been planning to use the strong-arm, he'd have to do it himself because his partner had just taken another smack off the skull.

Peter pulled out his cell phone and aimed it at him and fired a picture as the redhead disappeared into the crowd. Then Peter pointed the phone toward the other guy, who was on his knees, looking for his gun. Click. Click. The animated iris on the iPhone closed twice, catching the gunman, the fleeing people, and the golden arches of the Times Square McDonald's in the background.

Then Peter and Evangeline sprinted for the corner where they had seen Delancey, but Delancey had vanished again.

"Do you think Joey B. set us up?" said Evangeline.

"If he's in cahoots with Delancey, but"—Peter grabbed the back door of a cab idling at the light and they hopped in—"I'm not trusting any of them. I'm getting my own security."

THURSDAY MORNING WAS another warm, sunny May day.

They had used Evangeline's credit card to spend the night in the Grand Hyatt. They had also used it to do what could only be done in Manhattan: purchase a new laptop and cell phones and set up accounts, all at one o'clock in the morning.

At six, Peter called his partner, Orson Lunt, and told him to meet Antoine at Fallon Antiquaria and remove three cases of books, including the Shakespeare Second Folio, and put them into safety deposit bins. If Antonov decided to do to Fallon Antiquaria what he had done to Delancey's Rarities, at least the most valuable items would be safe.

Then Antoine called with bad news. Cousin Jonas, of Scarborough Security in Harlem, didn't want to handle their case. He said they were too "hot." He said a legit businessman couldn't be annoying the NYPD by helping a guy whose Facebook picture was now in the *Daily News,* right next to a sketch of a guy in a Yankees hat, a person of interest in a Central Park drug death. The caption: "Resemblance?"

"Cousin Jonas is smart," Peter said, "but I need to stay on the loose at least another twenty-six hours. I need the Russians to think I've done all I can to find those bonds."

"Jonas suggests you call Henry Baxter," said Antoine. "He was half brother to our dads. Special ops in Vietnam, did long-haul truckin' for a lot of years. Works for Scarborough sometimes, for himself the rest of the time. Lives on Fifty-first Street."

"That's the Rileys' old neighborhood," Peter said. "Hell's Kitchen."

HENRY BAXTER SAT at his desk and looked at his notes. He was so big that he blocked the sunlight bouncing off the trees outside the window. He wore a blue T-shirt, jeans, and a smile. "Cousin Jonas say you got cops lookin' for you and Russians after you, and you're makin' big scenes in Times Square, and all you tryin' to do is save America by findin' a itty-bitty little box."

Peter laughed. "By tomorrow."

"By tomorrow. I like a man with a plan." Henry laughed too, and the residue of a thousand truck stop hamburgers made little waves over his muscle.

While they talked, Evangeline was taking in the office. A big rottweiler named Ripper was snoozing in the corner. The furniture was spare. The only decoration a few certificates and some photographs on the walls: a skinny Henry with his unit in Vietnam, Henry and Willie Mays, Henry and Derek Jeter, Henry and Lady Ella herself standing in front of Sylvia's in Harlem. Henry got around.

"But tomorrow comin' fast, and Antoine say you runnin' out of people to trust."

"Starting with a guy named Joey Berra," said Peter. "We were supposed to meet him last night in Times Square. But if he didn't show up, he said we should meet him there at noon today."

"And he didn't show up last night?" Henry stroked his goatee.

"We were late," said Evangeline.

"But you ain't trustin' him?"

"Would you?" asked Peter.

"Well, don't know 'bout this Berra cat, but you can trust old Henry. My little brother spoke nothin' but good about your daddy. He said that when Big Jim Fallon went to work, so did he."

"First hired and last fired on every Fallon job," said Peter.

"It didn't roll that way for too many of the brothers back in the day. That's why I go into business for myself." Henry grinned. "So I got your back. This your safe house as long as you need. Bedroom down the hall. My wife and me and Ripper, we live upstairs."

"You rent *two* places?" said Evangeline.

"Honey, I own the buildin'. If you get scared, just holler. If it's something we can't handle, we run across the street and say a prayer."

"If I hire security," said Peter, "I don't want prayer. I want a license to carry."

"I'm licensed to carry and licensed to snoop. You got a wanderin' wife you want watched? You got a brother-in-law who owes you big and been outta sight for a while? You wonderin' if the woman workin' your cash register dippin' in the petty? I'm your man. I know my way around this town better 'n anybody, and I know who to meet and how to talk wherever I go. And if I really need to, I can make myself invisible."

"I'll bet you can," said Evangeline.

"Learned a lot, survivin' two tours in Nam and twenty-five years on the long-haul highway. But it wasn't till I met my Sonia that I learned prayin'. Never went Catholic like her, but"—he jerked his thumb to the church diagonally across the street—"every day I look out at ol' Sacred Heart and say thank you Jesus for a happy life."

Peter looked out the window. "That's where the Rileys worshiped."

"Who are they?" asked Henry.

"You wouldn't know them," said Evangeline.

"I know just about everyone in the neighborhood. Gettin' as gentrified as the Upper West Side. We got yuppies and their puppies everywhere. I liked it better when we had Sharks and Jets—"

"Like *West Side Story*?" said Peter.

"This was the neighborhood," said Henry. "And before that, we had all them crazy Irishmen. Gangsters, priests, politicians . . . ol' Mr. Tammany hisself, George Washington Plunkitt . . . buried out of that church back in the twenties."

"They buried a lot of people." Peter was thinking of all the Riley funerals.

"That's why I like it here," said Henry. "The roots go deep. But not just black roots, or Rican roots, or Irish roots. New York roots. Now, make yourself at home."

"Do you have wireless Internet?" asked Evangeline.

"Yes'm, and water pressure good enough to beat the oil off a grease monkey. For a old soldier or a long-haul trucker, a hot hard shower's as good as the company of a lady."

And Evangeline just began to laugh. She had not admitted it yet to Peter, but she didn't know how much more she could take. She was wishing she hadn't been in that bookstore when the bag lady wandered in, because she'd been running ever since. Being in the presence of this big man, who had seen so much and seemed so comfortable, comforted her, too. And she kept laughing, just put her head in her hands and laughed.

Until Peter decided to calm her a bit. "It's not that funny."

"I know," she said, "but if I don't keep laughing I'm going to start crying, because this is starting to wear me out." She said it, and saying it made her feel better, too.

"Crazy shit like this, it wear anybody out," said Henry. Then he stood. "Y'all just relax while I go upstairs and vacuum. Little Sonia work as a nurse and she like for me to do the housework. Nothin' make me happier than makin' the missus happy."

Evangeline wiped her eyes and looked at Peter. "A license to carry, *and* he does the vacuuming."

"Out on the road," said Henry, "my handle was

Big Mama's Baby. Now they should call me Little Sonia's Daddy. You two got any nicknames?"

Evangeline said, "Someone has been calling himself Buck, like the knife."

Peter just shook his head.

Henry looked at him. "You ain't no Buck. Let me think on somethin' better. I be back at quarter to twelve. Then we see about this Joey Berra cat. But we do it my way."

"Good," said Peter.

"Oh, Antoine say you took pictures in Times Square last night. You got 'em?"

EVANGELINE MADE SOME coffee, then went into the bedroom to change.

Peter went online, to MarketSpin.com. First he checked the stocks: Dow Jones down another 175 points. How long would the Chinese let it keep spiraling?

Then, in the little video box on the lower left corner, Kathy Flynn began to talk to the camera: "Good morning. Asian markets responded predictably overnight to the Chinese action. The Nikkei was down two percent, the Hang Seng was down two and a half. European markets are on the same path."

In the bedroom, Evangeline was picking the labels off a pair of blue jeans she had bought on their way across town. Enough with Chanel suits and heels. She had bought running shoes, too.

But when she heard that voice, she came out. "Can't keep your eyes off her?"

"It's happening." Peter pointed to the stocks running across the top of the screen.

"And we can't stop it." Evangeline stood there, in a blouse and underpants, with the jeans still in her hand.

"All the more reason to get those bonds," he said. "If the stock market crashes, nobody'll be buying rare books."

"And at home," Kathy went on. "The assassination of Carl Evers, chief accountant for Avid Investment Strategies, has set off a round of speculations regarding the health of the company headed by anti-deficit crusader Austin Arsenault. We caught up with Arsenault this morning outside of his co-op."

Cut to Arsenault, not a hair out of place, under his awning. "We are deeply saddened. We have every expectation that Mr. Evers's killer will be apprehended."

Kathy said, "There is some speculation about the SEC and accounting practices at your organization. Is that true?" Then she shoved a microphone into his face.

"Kathy, I'm surprised that you'd ask a question like that," said Arsenault. "Simply raising that specter produces rumors, and there is nothing worse for a financial market in the throes of turmoil than rumor."

"So his death has nothing to do with your effort to redeem two ancient bonds?"

"Those bonds are a symbol. We're pursuing that case for America, and Carl Evers would tell you that the deficits we run in this country are unsustainable." Arsenault pointed his finger at her. "I've been fighting the deficit since Reagan."

"So Evers said nothing about the potential of

the bonds to improve your balance sheet?" asked Kathy.

Peter said to Evangeline, "You have to admit it, she's good."

"Don't say that to me when I'm standing in my underwear."

On the screen, Arsenault gave Kathy a scowl. "The bonds in my possession would be worth in the range of fourteen million dollars. Avid is a multibillion dollar fund. One is symbol, the other is reality."

Cut back to Kathy, sitting again in the studio: "There you have it. Symbol and reality. But what, we are beginning to wonder, is the reality with Avid?"

Peter clicked off the little TV screen.

Evangeline pulled on the jeans, then the sneakers, then she paced around to test the fit of both.

Peter went through the e-mails: there were a few from Owen T. Magee, all on the same theme:

> Where are you? What have you discovered? Please respond. Our hope is to make the announcement at the annual meeting of the Foundation. We have rented the Museum of American Finance for Friday morning.

"I don't trust him," said Evangeline.

"You were the one who told me to sign a contract with him."

"But I never said I trusted him." She sprang up and down in the sneakers. Then she looked over his shoulder. "What else is there?"

"A few more things from Antoine."

She read with him. And both of them thought it was strange to be reading the obituaries of Timothy Riley and his brother, Eddie, who had lived until 1965, right across the street from the church where they had been baptized and elegized.

They found little to glean from the obits, but Peter always said that Antoine had an instinct for the extra bit of information and a willingness to dig more deeply than most. Antoine had also sent the obituary of the son of Tim and Doreen, August 12, 2008:

> Brother Richard Daniel Riley, CFC, the oldest living Irish Christian Brother, died in New York after a short illness at the age of 101. A 1929 graduate of Fordham, he taught in Boston and New York. He leaves a host of nephews descended from his uncle, Edward Riley, longtime political operative. His mother, Doreen, died overseas in World War I. His father, Timothy, an accountant for J. P. Morgan, died in the 1920 anarchist bombing. Taking the vow of poverty, Brother Riley had no estate, but for a collection of his father's papers, including a set of journal notebooks. Brother Riley donated his father's papers some years back to the New York Society Library.

"New York Society Library?" said Peter.

"One of the first public libraries in America," said Evangeline. "Opened in 1754 in City Hall. Even Washington and Hamilton borrowed books."

"So after we meet Joey Berra, we go to the library."

And then the telephone rang on Henry's desk. They let it ring through until they heard Antoine's voice: "Uncle Henry said to call you on his landline. Just checkin' to see if you two are in tight with Big Mama's Baby."

Peter grabbed the phone. "We like Henry. He likes to laugh, but he's got some danger in him I think."

"More than a little. But he keeps it hidden . . . I got one more thing for you: I called a college friend of mine. She works at Treasury. I asked her to see if she could find out the names of people who've brought suit to get these bonds redeemed."

"And?"

"Before Arsenault, Treasury had issued only two opinions on these bonds in twenty-three years. They rejected a claim by the Massachusetts Historical Society in the early nineties and another by the law firm of Magee and Magee in 1987."

That brought Peter halfway out of the chair. "Magee and Magee? In 1987?"

"Yeah," said Antoine, and he shuffled some papers on the other end of the line. "The attorney on the case was named Jennifer Wilson."

FOURTEEN

October 1987

Jennifer Wilson came out of the heartland in 1983 and took New York by storm.

That was how she imagined her autobiography would someday begin.

But for now, she'd have to settle for the first clause.

She grew up in Youngstown, graduated from Ohio State, and a week later took a bus that dropped her at the Port Authority Terminal on Forty-second Street. After stepping over two drunks and avoiding eight panhandlers, she walked thirty blocks south to Greenwich Village. Three years later, she graduated from NYU Law School.

That was not by storm.

At least, she told herself, she got to live in the Village, where a girl could embrace the favorite cliché of every small-towner who ever moved to New York: She could find egg foo yong or pastrami on rye at any hour of the day or night. She could make the scene at all the cool places. She could hear jazz at the Blue Note on a Tuesday night. She could cab it down to Odeon at one o'clock on a Sunday morning and end up partying with the cast of *Saturday Night Live*. And she could always find *somebody* to party with . . . someplace.

And since the life of a junior associate at a New

York law firm meant ferocious spells of eighteen-hour days, finding a party and finding it fast mattered to Jennifer Wilson. So did having a nice place to walk her little terrier named Bits.

Every morning, she led Bits twice around Washington Square, patted him good-bye, double-locked her apartment door, and walked uptown to the Flatiron Building.

That October morning was warm and humid, and Jennifer was perspiring politely when she got to work. So she was glad that the elevator was empty. With its mirrors and trim work and little vaulted ceiling, it always made her feel like a character in a Joan Crawford movie, riding to meet her destiny, even though her destiny was no more than a day of reviewing agreements, digesting changes to the tax code, and drafting a simple will for a woman leaving her assets to her only child. She straightened her hair in the mirror, buttoned the top button of her brown Donna Karan suit, dabbed a touch of wetness from her hairline, and got off on the eighteenth floor.

She could have turned to the left to go through the blank door that led directly to her office. But she turned right, because she liked to go in by the front, through the glass doors with the gold lettering: MAGEE & MAGEE, ESTATES, TRUSTS, AND TAXES. It made her feel like a full-fledged lawyer when she greeted the secretary at the reception desk, and she could show her flag to any of the partners who came in early.

Magee & Magee was busier than usual that

morning. As she headed down the hall, she passed a dozen lawyers already working the phones.

At the corner office overlooking Fifth Avenue and Twenty-third, she glanced in at Owen T. Magee, second Magee on the masthead, second-best office.

He had the phone to his mouth: "I know that the overseas markets are down and—yes, the Dow futures, too—but my advice is not to panic. We were down ten percent last week and the foreign markets are simply following our correction, and—"

Jennifer kept walking. Shouldn't eavesdrop at the door of a partner.

In her little office, she opened a drawer and pulled out a pair of Versace knockoffs. She didn't always wear them at work. Sometimes she went for flats, but when she was feeling a little low, or a little hungover, or a little depressed because another weekend had passed and she still hadn't found the love of her life, the heels lifted her spirits and lifted her to near six feet.

She went to the ladies' room, then got a cup of coffee, and by the time she got back to her desk, she knew that this would not be just another blue Monday.

At eleven o'clock, Owen T. Magee called a meeting in his father's office in the apex of the Flatiron triangle. The elder Magee, semiretired, was out of town. So Owen T. took the chair, framed by the window with the view of the Empire State Building. He wiped a bead of perspiration from his upper lip and told the ten lawyers and ten associates that the

Dow was down a hundred and fifty points. "And there's no support. It seems that we are crashing."

"Clients are terrified," said one of the lawyers.

"It's not our job to dispense investment advice, but we must take a position," said Owen T. Magee. "Remind our clients that our job is to help them build for the future while protecting the past. Counsel them to calm down and think long term."

"Hard to do when so many of them live off their trusts," said another lawyer.

"No matter how far and fast it goes down," answered Magee, "our position is that it will come back. We don't want anyone trying to get into the corpus of a trust just because of a bad day in the market. Remind them that this firm represents stability."

So all day, the lawyers of Magee & Magee told their clients to stay the course.

It took courage, because the Dow Jones dropped . . . and dropped . . . and dropped some more. It never blipped up for an instant. At the closing bell, it had dropped more than on any single day in history, both in raw numbers and as a percentage: five hundred points, twenty-two percent, and not a sector spared.

No one spoke on the elevator that night. Too many people had lost too much. Too many had seen retirement accounts gutted, plans deferred, dreams destroyed.

And Jennifer knew what most of them were thinking: they had just lived through a turning point in their own lives and in the life of the country, too.

She hadn't lost much because a first-year associate didn't make much to lose. But she realized that she should not let a day like this go by without calling her mother. So she rode the elevator to the bottom, then rode it right back up. Better to call Ohio on the firm's dime.

Owen T. Magee was still on the phone: "Sit tight. See what the market does tomorrow before you go out and get a job. Unless, of course, you're bored." When he saw Jennifer, he waved her in and pointed to a chair.

In the fourteen months since she had come to work at Magee & Magee, this was the first time that he had asked her to sit in his office after hours. He hung up the phone and ran his hands over the widow's peak that was already receding, even though he wasn't yet forty and hadn't been married so he couldn't be a widower. "That client has lived for twenty years on the trust that his father established. He has no worries."

"You gave him good advice, sir." She perched on a chair and remembered what her mother had told her: always say something positive to start a conversation. "I was impressed with your words this morning, too."

"It's been such a day, I don't remember what I said this morning."

"About how this firm represents stability."

Owen T. Magee smiled. "Well, it does. People wonder why we stay in the Flatiron, why we aren't uptown someplace like the Chrysler Building, or downtown in the World Trade Center. And behind our back, they always say it's because we're cheap and this is a low-rent neighborhood. But we've always been here. It's a . . . a—"

"—tradition?"

"It's more than tradition. It's an identity."

"I can see what you mean."

He studied her a moment and said, "Are you free this evening, Miss Wilson?"

And the questions shot through her mind: Is my boss hitting on me? Is this a test? How should I play it? Coy? Disinterested? Direct and blunt because he looks like Nixon, which I would list as my biggest turnoff if I ever filled out a *Playboy* questionnaire?

"It's business, Miss Wilson. Drinks at '21' with a client and his broker."

Drinks at "21." She had been waiting ever since she got to New York for someone—anyone—to say those words to her.

Her mind filled with names and images, real and fictional, and all alive to anyone who loved New York . . . Nick and Nora downing martinis at the bar . . . Roger Thornhill—Cary Grant—planning to meet his mother for dinner . . . Walter Winchell getting the latest from J. Edgar Hoover . . . Joe DiMaggio and Marilyn Monroe avoiding the cameras . . . Jennifer Wilson and . . . Owen T. Magee? It was not how she would write it in her future autobiography, but it would have to do. She went into her office and put on her heels.

THE CAB PULLED up in front of the brownstone at 21 West Fifty-second Street. Two dozen lawn jockeys offered their hands from the wrought-iron railings around the entrance. A few were as black as the lawn jockeys of Ohio, but most were white. . . . New York lawn jockeys, she thought, so some of them would be Irish and Italian and Jewish, a whole United Nations of lawn jockeys.

She was so taken by the sight of them that she did not notice how completely, ineffably, almost frighteningly quiet the street was on the night of the day that the networks were already calling Black Monday.

Owen T. led her through the empty cocktail lounge, into the famous Bar Room.

Jennifer had expected that the place would be jumping. It was "21", after all. But it felt as if America had a lost a war. The few people dining at the checkered tablecloths and the five people drinking at the bar all seemed to be spending their last pennies on pleasure before the enemy came to overturn the tables and smash the liquor bottles.

One of the men at the bar popped up when he saw Magee.

Jennifer's first thought was that he was the handsomest man she had ever seen. Dark hair combed straight back and curling at the collar, a double-breasted blue suit, yellow tie, Rolex flashing: Austin Arsenault.

Magee had filled her in on the cab ride. Arsenault had left an old-line brokerage in 1980 to begin his own firm, specializing in start-ups and technology. Since his family had long done business with Magee & Magee, he had come to them for legal advice and clients, and now, one hand washed the other.

The man sitting with Arsenault, an overweight

ophthalmologist named Gary Smith, looked a generation older and acted a generation more depressed, as if he understood how bad this crash really was. Magee had explained that after eyeballs, Dr. Smith's passion was cannonballs. He was chairman of the New York Museum of Revolutionary War Weapons in Westchester. Since he was a good client of Avid Investment Strategies *and* Magee & Magee, Austin and Owen both met him for drinks on the third Monday of every other month, no matter what kind of Monday it was.

As Magee approached with his assistant, Arsenault extended his hand. "Owen T., come to put a brave face on I see?"

Magee looked around at the empty room. "Unlike the rest of New York."

"So we're either the bravest men in town, or the biggest fools."

Jennifer liked this talk. She felt that she was sitting right at the center of the New York action with two men who knew enough to laugh at the darkness.

So she laughed, too. And as she shook hands with Arsenault, she checked for a wedding band: *single*. But a bit of tan line around his finger. So maybe he was lying.

She ordered a Chablis and watched two masters work. Arsenault and Magee first calmed Dr. Smith about his investments, then about the assets of his little museum.

Smith said, "I'm also worried about the clients I've sent you, Austin."

"Don't worry about them," said Arsenault.

"They know that I'm all about the new technology. Technology will lead us out of this mess. Now"—Arsenault drained his drink and called for another—"I'd like you to show Owen T. that bond you've brought."

Dr. Smith pulled an envelope from his pocket and removed a piece of paper, about half the size of a dollar bill. "In addition to weapons at the museum, we have primary source materials relating to the Revolution. This"—he placed it on the table—"is a New Emission Bond."

"And this"—Owen T. Magee nodded to Jennifer—"is my expert in such bonds."

She was? Jennifer looked at Magee and saw the wink. So . . . yes, *she was*. She raised her glass to Dr. Smith and took a sip of her Chablis.

Dr. Smith looked her over. "Very pretty, but she seems too young to be an expert in anything—"

"Sometimes, the youngest and prettiest are the smartest," said Arsenault.

There was a line to make a girl cringe. But it didn't. She hoped she wasn't blushing. She said, "I'm sure Dr. Smith is interested in 'the smartest.'" Be professional. Stay smooth. That's what her mother always told her.

Dr. Smith must have agreed because he pressed ahead. "I hate to sell something out of our collection, but our endowment took a terrible hit today. Terrible. And it wasn't much of an endowment to begin with."

"Don't panic," said Owen T. Magee. "That's been our counsel to all our clients."

"Ours, too," said Arsenault.

"I'm not panicking," answered Smith. "But we have two of these bonds. And I'm wondering about them. What does this smart young lady think?"

Owen T. Magee laughed. "You wouldn't want to force her to give an opinion until she had worked with the material."

The old doctor put a hand on her arm. "If these bonds were valid, my museum would be safe from any crash. They'd give us all the operating capital we'd ever need."

"There you go." Owen T. Magee patted Dr. Smith on the back. "Money doing what it's supposed to, generating more money to make society a better place."

"Well said," added Arsenault. "And if she can't redeem the bonds, I'll buy them as collectibles . . . assuming that we have any money left in the morning."

No one laughed at the joke.

OWEN T. MAGEE insisted that Jennifer cab it home with him. "Nobody in my firm does after-hours work like that and takes the subway. New York is a dangerous place."

So they sped down Fifth Avenue, through a city that had gone quiet, shocked.

Magee looked out the window and shook his head. "Five hundred points. No wonder the old doctor is worried. I'm worried. So is Arsenault."

Jennifer didn't like that. If they were worried, how should *she* feel? So she changed the subject. "What am I supposed to do with these bonds?"

"Whatever you want. You are now a 'minder.' "

"A 'minder'?"

Owen T. Magee leaned a bit closer.

If she had felt an impulse to distrust him earlier, she did not feel it now. He had been a gentleman all through dinner. And she was feeling more relaxed in his presence. Perhaps it was his manner . . . or the wine. She didn't even think it strange that he had insisted on riding downtown with her though he lived on the Upper East Side.

He said, "Haven't you ever heard the expression, 'Find 'em, mind 'em, and grind 'em'?"

She shook her head.

"What do they teach in law school these days?"

She gave a little shrug. "I—"

"It's what we do in estate law. We find clients through other clients or feeders like Arsenault. We mind 'em by writing wills, drafting trusts to fulfill their wishes, stroking them when they're worried, satisfying them when they're discontent. Then, we grind 'em with fees, adjustments, revisions, and responses to the regular changes in the tax code, a whole range of legitimate expenses that protect their estates and our lifestyles. And tonight"—he flashed that nervous Nixonian smile—"you became a minder."

"You want me to mind Dr. Smith?"

"I want you to make him think that we're fulfilling his every wish. That means taking seriously the silly notion that a bond from 1780 may still have redemption value."

The cab pulled up in front of her apartment on Bethune Street.

He licked his lips and looked at hers.

She had been here before. She had kissed her share of men, often just like this, in the back of a cab, and it almost always began with the "lip looks."

But he was not so bold, or perhaps not so interested. He said, "You know, I've been watching you since your first firm interview. I made sure you had a callback."

"I appreciate that, sir. I love the law, and I love the idea of all that can be done in a practice like this." That was not entirely true. She had taken the job at Magee & Magee because it was the best opening if she wanted to stay in New York.

Another long look from him had her wondering if the kiss was coming. But no.

He said, "Prepare a report on the bonds. Good night, Miss Minder."

MISS MINDER. SHE liked it.

If one good thing came from Black Monday, it would be her new job as a minder.

By noon the next day, she had familiarized herself with the history of the 1780 bonds and the reasons they were sold, redeemed, or denied. She ate lunch at her desk and waded into Hamilton's *Report on Public Credit*.

It was good to be in the eighteenth century, she thought, to be involved in the problems of the impoverished and debt-ridden United States, because it gave her some perspective on a day that the Dow was gyrating like a sixties go-go dancer, opening up two hundred, giving it all back by twelve thirty, then recovering a hundred and fifty points in half an hour.

By three thirty, it had gone down again and up again, but Jennifer Wilson didn't notice, because she and Alexander Hamilton were deep in conversation across the centuries, as only a reader and writer can be. Hamilton was telling her that the words on the back of the bonds, "engage the absolute promise of the United States for the payment of interest indefinitely, for the United States are bound to pay the interest perpetually till the principal is discharged."

And if a girl had Alexander Hamilton on her side, what should she fear?

At five o'clock, she went into Magee's office. Like everyone else in the firm, Owen T. was in a much better mood. The Dow had closed up by a hundred points. The world was not coming to an end. No meteor was streaking toward Wall Street, about to wipe out life as they all knew it.

She told him her plan to test the United States Treasury. If she succeeded, the two bonds held by the New York Museum of the American Revolution were worth, at five percent per annum, over two million each.

He rubbed his hands together and said, "A wild-goose chase. Nothing I love more than a client's wild-goose chase, because even if we don't catch the goose, the client pays. And if we do . . . the client still pays."

BY FRIDAY'S OPENING, the Dow had recovered half of Monday's losses. Whatever had happened was beginning to look like a blip in the trend since 1982, when Reagan's policies and the business cycle took hold and the Dow began its rise from the 700s to near 2,400.

Jennifer Wilson traveled downtown for her first big on-her-own meeting.

To get in the mood, she ate breakfast in Fraunces Tavern and imagined the ghost of Hamilton in one of the upper rooms, churning out his enormous work in five months. Then she walked a few blocks north to the Federal Reserve Bank. It had been built to resemble a Florentine palace, a monument to the solidity of American finance. And as proof to the doubtful, the bank offered daily tours into the New York bedrock itself, where the vault held the largest store of monetary gold on earth. But Jennifer had an appointment on an upper floor, with a vice president in the Financial Services Group.

His name was Edgar Meadows. He wore a bow tie. He looked annoyed.

"Thank you for seeing me," she said.

Meadows glanced at his watch. "I have fifteen minutes. I don't know what could be so important that you couldn't simply speak to one of our clerks."

Jennifer Wilson withdrew a copy of one of the bonds from her briefcase and placed it on the desk. "My client has two of these, all properly signed and executed."

"Really?" Meadows inclined his eyes but not his head. "And what would you like us to do with them?"

"Why . . . redeem them, of course."

Meadows flicked his eyes back to Jennifer. "Is your client crazy, or are you?"

Jennifer Wilson offered the slightest smile. She had rehearsed all of her facial expressions and thought she delivered that one perfectly. "We believe that the bonds are legal tender."

"These bonds matured in 1785."

"But they continue to accrue," she said. "That's Alexander Hamilton's opinion."

Meadows picked up the copy, studied it front and back, dropped it onto the desk. "You'll need more of an argument than that to collect what amounts to"—he tapped a few figures into the electronic calculator on his desk—"two million, four hundred thirty-three thousand, two hundred thirty-nine dollars."

"And seventy-eight cents," added Jennifer. "Times two."

"Two times zero is still zero."

Maybe she was just twenty-six, on a legal wild-goose chase, but at that moment, she was backed not only by Magee & Magee and Alexander Hamilton, but by the full faith and credit of the United States government. So she maintained her calm, raised her chin, and said, "Perhaps we should call in one of your superiors."

"They're all in a meeting."

"But of course they are." She stood. "Discuss the matter with them. Talk to Treasury. Talk to Justice. But it would be better if we did not have to go to litigation."

Meadows said, "My superiors will want to know on what basis your claim rests."

Obviously, thought Jennifer, Mr. Meadows had no legal training. Otherwise he would have known that you didn't ask a question unless you already knew the answer.

She, on the other hand, had an answer all planned. She pulled out a booklet copy of the United States Constitution. "Article Six: 'All Debts contracted and Engagements entered into, before the Adoption of this Constitution, shall be valid against the United States under this Constitution, as under the Confederation.'" She returned the booklet to her pocket and said, "The government backing that bond was organized under the Articles of Confederation, which were—"

"I *know* what they were," said the government's man.

ii.

The Dow had fallen, but Jennifer's stock was rising rapidly.

Owen T. Magee took her twice to dinner to discuss "minding" Dr. Smith, and he gave her three more clients. He told her he liked her touch . . . with them.

She expected that at some point, he would try to touch her, but it never happened. She wondered if he was gay. She didn't think so.

When Dr. Gary Smith came to town to visit his money again on the third Monday of December, he asked that they invite that "smart young Miss Wilson."

Owen T. Magee informed Jennifer that he had to go out of town. "So you'll get to deliver the bad news alone. See it as part of the learning experience."

The market was headed to a positive finish for the year, despite the October crash, so Dr. Smith and Austin Arsenault were waiting upstairs at "21", where the tablecloths were white, the silverware silver, the service discreet, and the prices astronomical . . . at least to Jennifer.

They began with chitchat . . . about Christmas in New York . . . about the Giants, slumping badly after their Super Bowl . . . about the prospects for the '88 election.

And Jennifer had something to say on each topic, even the football. Part of being a good "minder," Magee had told her, was to know what a client liked to talk about and learn to talk about it. Dr. Smith had season tickets.

He seemed nowhere near as depressed as two months earlier. Amazing what some holiday cheer and a healthier portfolio could do for a man's spirits. As he ordered his third Manhattan, the portly doctor looked like he could party all night. Then he asked Jennifer, "What news do you have of the bonds?"

Arsenault leaned forward. "Yes. I'd love to manage a few million dollars for the Museum of the American Revolution. Conservatively, of course."

At that moment, the waiters brought the first course, a mussel soup called billi-bi, Arsenault's recommendation. "Craig Claiborne calls it the most elegant and delicious soup ever created."

Jennifer hadn't wanted to appear ignorant by admitting she didn't know who Craig Claiborne was, so she had allowed Arsenault to order without protest.

Now the dishes were placed steaming before them. She picked up her spoon, tasted the subtle seafood flavor, said how delicious it was . . . stalling for time.

But the doctor ignored his soup. "The *bonds*, Miss Wilson. The New Emission Money. Has the Treasury responded?"

Her mother always told her never to bring up bad news early in the meal, but both men were waiting over their soup, so she took the envelope of bonds out of her purse and placed it on the table.

Dr. Smith did not even look at it. "The news is not good?"

She shook her head.

Arsenault dipped into his soup.

Dr. Smith kept his eyes on Jennifer. "What did they say?"

"They countered all our arguments regarding the Constitution, the validity of the bonds, Hamilton's opinions, the redemption practices of the states that bundled them when the national debt was first securitized—"

"Well, the billi-bi is wonderful, at least." Arsenault took another spoonful. "Did the Treasury finally fall back on sovereign immunity?"

"That was the last part of the letter," said Jennifer. "The government determines who can sue them. And they said we can't."

"Doesn't seem fair." Arsenault took a sip of wine.

"Mr. Magee thinks that unless we got lucky with a strict constructionist court prepared to rule that Article Six validates the bonds, it could take ten lawyers ten years to get this case advanced," she said. "And it's not something to win on the angles."

"If that goddamn Ted Kennedy hadn't torpedoed Judge Bork," said Arsenault, "we'd have a strict constructionist on the Supreme Court right now."

Jennifer said nothing to that. She had grown up in a house where all three Kennedy brothers had been idolized.

Dr. Gary Smith took the envelope and put it into his pocket. "At least you tried. And I liked the job you did. So, I'm telling Owen that I want you in on the redrafting."

Arsenault's soup spoon stopped in midair. "Redrafting?"

"My estate. I have a grandson. He needs money. He has a dream, a dream of being in computers."

"Like Bill Gates?" asked Arsenault.

"Who's he?" said Dr. Gary Smith.

"YOU MENTION BILL Gates and he asks, 'Who's he?'" Arsenault laughed. "It makes me wonder if this high-tech business has a future."

"Dr. Smith comes from another generation," said Jennifer. "And thank you for the ride home, only—"

"Only what?"

"We're headed uptown."

They were in a black limo sleeking north on Madison Avenue. She had often imagined herself in the back of a black limo with a man like Austin Arsenault. But in some things she was still a small-town girl . . . or a grown-up cynic. She had looked at his ring finger during dinner, but the tan line had faded, so she was still wondering about his marital status. Owen T. Magee had been notably silent on the subject. She was also wondering what she would do if he made a move. She did not have long to find out.

He leaned back and unbuttoned his overcoat. "I thought you'd like to see how we live uptown. Along the way, we can admire the Christmas lights. New York's magical at Christmas, don't you think?"

She looked out at the light snowfall. "Yes. Magical. But—"

"What are you doing over the holidays?"

"My mother's coming to town. She has a sister in L.A. But—"

Arsenault reached into his pocket and pulled out a small blue box. "My gift to a young attorney. I handle the investments for the Smith trust, as you know, so your 'minding' has been a boon to me, too."

A blue box. Tiffany's. Whatever was happening was happening way too fast.

He said, "Go ahead, open it."

So she did. Inside was a pair of white gold earrings with blue stones.

"Sapphires," he said. "Your birth month."

"I . . . I don't know what to say."

"Don't say anything." As the limo turned on Fifty-ninth Street, he slid across the seat and kissed her, just like that, just gently enough to show that he knew what he was doing.

When she did not respond, he pulled back, but only a bit.

Her eyes flicked toward the front seat.

He reached up and closed the Plexiglas window, sealing them in. Then he brought out a flask. He took a sip and handed it to her. The silver flashed in the moonlight. "Cognac. Courvoisier."

She took a sip. It burned but it warmed. Part of her wanted to go along for this ride. But another part of her said that she was supposed to be on business. And a young businesswoman shouldn't be taking gifts like this . . . or rides like this.

He kissed her again, another gentle touch, but this time, he parted his lips.

She kept hers closed.

He pulled back and said, "I like your boots."

In the winter, she wore boots, calf-high, leather. She liked how men looked at her when she wore them into the office . . . or into "21".

The limo was heading north now, along snowy Central Park West.

Arsenault placed a gentle hand on her cheek and kissed her again.

She couldn't deny it. He was good at this. She had always heard that older men knew what they were doing, and he was about forty, so . . . what the hell?

She brought her hands to his face and tasted the cognac on his lips.

After the kiss, he pulled away and said, "That's more like it."

He took another swallow from the flask and handed it to her. After she sipped, he placed it in a convenient little mesh holder on the door.

Then he kissed her again and unbuttoned her coat and slipped a hand in around her waist. "Let's get more comfortable."

Too fast, she thought. She twitched subtly and leaned herself against the door, so that the hand couldn't slide up to her bra.

Another kiss and the hand withdrew. He said, "Hard to get. That's good."

Her response was to kiss him again. Now that the game had begun, she did not want to seem *that* hard to get, but she was not giving it up in the backseat.

He had other ideas. And the hand dropped now to the boots. "I like the leather," he said. "I like the way it feels." And he lowered his face toward her thighs. "I even like the way it smells." He inhaled deeply, then he kissed her thigh through the nylon.

At least he didn't kiss the boots, she thought.

But he brought his lips to hers again, this time with less delicacy. Then she felt his hand on her boot, heading upstream, over her knees, over her thigh—

She brought her legs together.

But that didn't stop his hand. He pushed it all the way up and pressed against her crotch. And he said, "Panty hose. I hate panty hose."

She pulled away from his kiss and from his hand.

First the dinner, then the gift, then the flask, and the old close-the-slider signal: it's a go, so drive slow. Arsenault and his driver had done this all many times before.

And she was realizing that she didn't like being

the Monday-night conquest, the little piece of knockoff before he went home to listen to Howard Cosell and Dandy Don.

But Austin Arsenault had other ideas. "Take them off." Something new crept into his voice, something deep and elemental . . . and a bit scary.

"Take what off?"

"The panty hose. I told you, I don't like panty hose. Take them off. But leave the boots on. I like the boots."

"Now wait a minute—"

"Why do you think Owen T. stayed home?" he growled.

"Stayed home?"

"All right. Leave the fuckin' panty hose on."

"I will, and—" She was so shocked at his next move that the words caught in her throat.

He opened his overcoat and unzipped his fly. "Come here."

"What the hell are you doing?"

It was standing up from the folds of fabric like a white stalagmite in a cashmere cave. And he pulled her toward it.

"Mr. Arsenault, no." She tried to resist. So he pulled harder. And he was stronger. It struck her chin and pointed toward her mouth, but she turned her head so it struck her cheek, then her other cheek, and finally he let her go.

She fell backward against the front seat and turned and slammed her hand on the Plexiglas, "Stop! Stop the car!"

But the driver kept his eyes and the limo heading straight into the snow.

"Jennifer"—Arsenault leaned toward her—"this is supposed to be fun. I am *not* having fun."

She looked again at that white prick, now a little less certain of itself. Then she looked at the face, now contorted with anger and lust and painted strangely with the remnants of her lipstick. And she said, "Let me out right now."

"We're almost to 110th Street. You want to get mugged?"

"I've *been* mugged," she said. "Let me out."

He cursed and pulled up his fly and called to his driver.

The limo screeched to a halt. The locks popped. She jumped out.

Austin Arsenault pulled a fifty from his pocket and threw it at her. "Cab fare. I could have made you rich. And you blew it. . . . Or didn't."

The big Lincoln growled on through the snow. And for a moment, Jennifer Wilson felt completely alone. She hadn't been raped. But it felt like it.

What would she do? Think on it. And walk the dog. Little Bits loved the snow.

She looked around for a cab, then she cursed. She had left her briefcase in the limo.

THE NEXT MORNING, the briefcase was on her desk, along with a bouquet of red carnations, poinsettias, and evergreens. *A Christmas bouquet.*

She almost threw the flowers in the wastebasket. But now that they had been delivered, tossing them would prompt more gossip among the paralegals than if she kept them on the windowsill.

She opened her briefcase and inside was the blue

box with a note: "You forgot these. Thanks for your good counsel last evening. Your well-considered responses remind me of the things that are always more valuable."

Like what? His marriage? She still hadn't figured that one out.

"I look forward to further conversation about estates, markets, or anything else."

So, it was going to be like that, was it?

She had spent the night considering her options vis-à-vis Austin Arsenault. And she didn't think she had any. She had done a turn with the DA's office. She had seen how a good defense attorney, representing a well-heeled gentleman of a certain age, could shred the testimony of any young woman: "And after he bought dinner, he gave you a Tiffany's box in the back of a limo, and so you kissed him, and then . . ."

There was no real evidence of sexual assault. And as for the only witness? The driver? On the Arsenault payroll.

So, she would put that experience in a dark corner, as other young women probably had. And she would never leave herself alone with Arsenault again. And if she could ever find a way to hurt him, she would.

But what about Owen T. Magee? Could she trust him any longer?

He came into the office at nine o'clock that morning, so whatever had called him away had not called him far. And he seemed—what?—cool to her for the rest of the week. But she did get a good Christmas bonus.

iii.

So she told herself she had to trust Owen T. Magee, because he put such trust in her. But she never really liked him after that.

She became "the minder" of certain male clients who were happy to know that Owen T. was looking over her shoulder while *they* got to look at her. The pay was good, but when he introduced her to yet another old guy whose eyes lingered a little too long on her high heels and shapely legs, she felt that her boss was just pimping her.

And there were plenty of old guys becoming new clients in the next few years because Owen T. Magee set out to make Magee & Magee the estate lawyer to the stars.

Not all the New York stars were on Broadway, however. There were stars on Wall Street, and in the publishing houses and agencies from Midtown to Madison Square, and at law firms all over the island. And some people were stars simply because they lived in some of the richest real estate on earth. In fact, there were more stars, making more star money, in New York City than anywhere *else* on earth. And by using every legal strategy to protect the star money, Magee and his partners got to make star money of their own.

So he was soon living in a co-op overlooking Central Park, renting a corner of the basement for his collection of '82 Bordeaux, and as Jennifer discovered late one night, indulging a very expensive habit.

She had to return to the office to pick up some papers. She came down the dark hallway and heard sounds from his office. And there were two long, leggy women, one white and blond, the other almost cobalt black. The white girl was sitting in Owen's desk chair, completely naked, with her legs hooked up on the armrests. The black girl was on her knees in front of the chair, and Owen T. Magee, of the widow's peak and pallid skin and obviously bony ass, was kneeling behind the black girl and . . .

Jennifer turned and hurried out, certain that Owen T. Magee could not command such an event without the application of thick poultices of cash.

So . . . they all had their foibles.

But what the hell? It was the eighties . . . in New York.

So Jennifer went to parties. She fell in and out of love. She had affairs with men her own age and twenty years older. She drank. She even tried a few toots of the white powder, but it didn't do much for her. She was glad of that, because a taste for cocaine would never benefit an officer of the court.

DR. SMITH CONTINUED his association with Magee & Magee, and annually extolled the superb service that Jennifer Wilson delivered to him and his museum. She had even educated herself about the differences between the British Brown Bess and the French Charleville musket, just to impress him on her trips to Westchester.

All of this led to annual raises, so she moved from old Bethune Street to a high-rent building on Abingdon Square. At the age of twenty-eight, she had a sunken living room and a balcony with a fabulous view of the World Trade Center.

And then, over lunch on a January day in 1991, Dr. Smith returned to a subject he had not spoken of since that pre-Christmas dinner three years earlier: his grandson.

Jennifer said, "You mean the ne'er-do-well who wanted to get into computers? You never brought him up again. So I never did."

"Because he decided to take a few years and sail around the Caribbean."

They were eating in the greenhouse room of the Italian Pavilion on Fifty-fifth. She'd never been here before. Dr. Smith liked it because it was a favorite of the William Morris agents who worked in the building at the corner, and he once had seen James Michener lunching here with his agent. He counted that among the great thrills of his life.

"Don't look now," she said, "but I think Gore Vidal just walked in."

Dr. Smith sniffed. "I'm not interested in him. Did you ever read what he said about George Washington in *Burr*?"

She leaned across the table. "Back to your grandson sailing the Caribbean."

"Everybody thought it was another ne'er-do-well thing to do. His father, his mother. . . . But you know"—Dr. Smith looked around at all the plants growing happily on a gray winter day—"maybe he was right to do it. I wish I had traveled more, seen more exotic plants in bloom instead of in a restaurant."

"I'll take Manhattan," she said.

"Now the boy has an idea. It has something to

do with computers. There's this thing called the Internet that's"—the doctor looked through windows—"up there someplace. And he has this company that has these platforms and programs and, well . . . I don't understand any of it, but it's the new technology."

"Have you discussed it with Arsenault?"

"He says he's ready to offer capital. He says this company is called a start-up, basically a few smart guys with an idea. The boy estimates that he'll need four million to leverage ten more in loans. So I want to redraft my will, open the corpus of the family trust. My grandson says his partner, Dmitri Donovan, has what they call an angel, too."

"Dmitri Donovan?"

The doctor chuckled. "Yes. American father, Russian mother. It's the mother's family connections. I want you to meet my grandson and talk with him. Call it your due diligence before we sit down with Mr. Magee."

SO JENNIFER MET John Smith for lunch a few days later. They went to a little favorite of hers called Novita, near the Flatiron.

She took one look at this young guy, who seemed so wide-eyed and yet so savvy, and she decided that she did not want to go back to work that afternoon. She wanted to go to bed with him.

Not professional? Sure.

But he was six feet tall and built like a surfer. He wore tight jeans and a leather jacket over a turtleneck. And he knew this Internet stuff backwards and forwards, but he acted as if he didn't quite know it all because there was just so much yet to discover.

And maybe, she thought, he might need somebody to discover it with him.

The first course came. Caesar salad. *Be cool.*

The second course came. Veal piccata. *Stay cool.*

Dessert. He suggested tiramisu with two forks.

Oh, shit, she thought. *Two forks.*

And she heard herself saying, "How about a little limoncello to go with it?"

They ended the afternoon in her bed. She called in sick. She was anything but.

THAT SATURDAY, HE introduced her to his partner, Dmitri Donovan.

Dmitri was the research brain but nobody's idea of a front man. Skinny, pallid, sarcastic, and smarter than Einstein, especially when he started talking about bits and bytes and the many ways to achieve personal nirvana while playing something called Final Fantasy.

"He knows it all," said John, whom Jennifer had taken to calling "Smitty."

"You're damn right," said Dmitri. "And the best of both worlds . . . Irish last name and relatives in Brighton Beach. And they all love me. My mother's uncle, Andrei Antonov, will put up half the money."

"So," said Smitty, "I need two million from my grandfather's trust. Then Dmitri and I start off fifty-fifty . . . as equals. We each bring an angel."

THE FOLLOWING WEEK: the big meeting, on one of those brilliant, bitter January days when the

Empire State Building sparkled like a giant crystal rising into the sky.

Owen T. Magee now occupied his late father's office, the one with the view.

Austin Arsenault came because his firm continued to handle investments from the trust. It was plain that he did not want the Smith portfolio emptied. He also had a proposal, and he had brought his accountant, Carl Evers.

The three of them had their heads together when Jennifer brought Dr. Smith and his grandson into the office. Owen was whispering to the other two.

Jennifer knew what he was saying, because he had already said it to her: "There's a way into the trust. But we aren't telling Dr. Smith because if we break into it to fund a start-up, we lose control of it and Dr. Smith probably loses his money."

She expected that they were more concerned about the control. "Isn't that unethical?" she had asked.

"Not at all," Magee had responded. "We are simply protecting a client and his money from himself and his family."

Now there were greetings all around, everyone took a seat, and before John Smith had a chance to make a case, Owen T. Magee said, "Mr. Evers has something to say."

"Yes," said Evers. "I've been doing an analysis of operating expenses in a high-tech start-up like this and I've come to the conclusion that the best way to operate is not to invade the trust, but to borrow the money. Mr. Arsenault has brought together several investors who can offer venture capital."

"Venture capital?" said Dr. Smith. "Isn't that what I'm providing?"

Owen T. Magee said, "Your trust is your security, Doctor, now and in the future. You don't mortgage future certainties for present possibilities."

"Where would we be," asked Dr. Smith, "if George Washington and Alexander Hamilton thought that way? What if the Continental Congress had not done all that it could, even backing those New Emission Bonds in 1780, in order to gamble future certainties for present possibilities?"

That was the first time that Jennifer had heard mention of the bonds in more than three years. And nicely used, she thought. Good for something at last.

"A revolution is not the same as a business venture," said Arsenault. "Don't you agree, Miss Wilson?"

She flicked her eyes toward him. He always pretended to defer to her in any meeting, as if he was still trying to get into her panty hose, the son of a bitch.

She said, "Perhaps a business venture like this is the modern equivalent of a revolution."

John Smith, the subject of this debate, leaned back and laughed. "You have to admit it, she's good, Mr. Magee. She's very good."

Dr. Smith said, "So I'd like to know what she thinks about redrafting."

Owen T. Magee had already prepared her: "Keep your mouth shut. Don't offer any opinion contrary to ours." Now he was hunched down in his chair, his brow furrowed, his eyes shifting. *Tricky Dick?* Tricky Owen.

"Go on," said John Smith to his new lover. "Say what you think."

"Yes," said Doctor Smith.

Jennifer Wilson knew that she was about to close a chapter, but she would be opening another. "Mr. Magee and I both know a way into the corpus of the trust, entirely legal and easily done. And John Smith may be the smartest man in this room. So I say do it."

Owen T. Magee almost spit.

Dr. Smith said, "There's my smart girl."

Austin Arsenault gave a disgusted laugh, like a man putting his unused prick back into his pants.

Accountant Carl Evers wrote a series of notes about how quick she was on her feet. He showed them to her later when they became friends and, for a brief time, lovers.

THE TRUST WAS reopened so that Dr. Gary Smith could invest in the future.

The mission statement of Intermetro proclaimed that it would "provide new platforms for Internet connection in urban environments."

John Smith took one seat in the board as president. Two seats went to the Smith family, one to Doctor Gary and one to Owen T. Magee, as trust representative. Dmitri Donovan's family received two seats, one for Dmitri and one for his cousin, businessman Yuri Antonov, whose father had been the Russian "angel." Two other seats went to thought leaders in the field, an NYU math professor and an expert in router hardware, the "gateway" technology of the moment.

Jennifer Wilson joined as in-house counsel and compliance officer. She was also living with the company president.

They would all get rich . . . on air, and they would end up floating.

FIFTEEN

Thursday Morning

Around eleven forty, Henry knocked on the door.

"You look like a lawyer," said Evangeline.

He was wearing a three-piece brown suit. He tugged at the tie. "The party of the first part shall hereby be known as the party of the first part. So let's party in Times Square. Smoke this Berra boy out, 'cause if he's as good with a gun as you say, we may need him on our side."

"Why?"

"Those pictures from last night." Henry stepped into the apartment, went over to his computer and called up the photos that Peter had taken with his cell. "Those are very bad boys in those pictures. How'd your friend Delancey get hooked up with them?"

"Delancey's not our friend," said Peter.

"Well, he's friends with a Russian who call himself the Redhead."

"Oh, great," said Evangeline. "More redheads."

"Say what?"

Peter rolled his eyes. "Keep talking."

"The Redhead is a bona fide bad dude. Name of Ivankov. And he runs with a feller called KGB, 'cause he look like Putin."

"The Harvard Club shooter," said Evangeline.

"You found all this out in the last hour?" asked Peter.

"Like I say, I know the places to ask the questions."

"What's their game?"

"Oldest game in town. Power. They want to knock over your friend in the cellar."

"Yuri Antonov? The Russian boss?" said Peter.

"Say, boys"—Evangeline glanced at her watch—"shouldn't we be going?"

Henry raised a finger. "Let's do our talkin' indoors. I don't want us bunched up on the street, even comin' out of the safe house." Then he turned back to Peter. "Yuri Antonov is what they call a oligarch. His papa was a boss. The Russians around Brighton Beach, they called him Andrei the Avenger. Come here in the seventies."

"Back when they started letting in Russian Jews?" said Peter.

"Yeah. And some of the troublemakers is bona fide, circumcised members of the tribe. But a lot of bad actors got in on forged papers, sayin' they was Jews, just to get their black bread in the good ol' American borscht pot." Henry clicked off the computer. "The Avenger had one badass temper. He'd kill his mama to make a score. Extortion, gamblin', credit cards, drugs, girls, money."

"Money?" asked Peter.

"To launder. All these wiseguys—Russkies, dagoes, spics, micks—"

"Mr. Baxter," said Evangeline. "That's not very nice talk for a—"

"A man of color?" Henry hooked a finger into his vest and struck a pose. "A man of the world, of whatever color, must also know the argot of the street. Now all these wiseguys—of whatever their ancestral origins—"

"That's better," said Evangeline.

"Take their dirty money and put it into somethin' clean. Pretty soon, they payin' taxes and Social Security and lookin' like they all legit. Sometime they have to wait for a son to come along to give them a touch of class—"

"Like Yuri Antonov?"

"When his avengin' daddy died of cancer about five years ago, the son took over. Likes classical music, claims he went to Harvard, works with a big-time broker."

"What would happen if that broker lost a lot of Antonov's money?"

"He be way pissed off at shit like dat." Henry talked a little street for emphasis.

"I think that Antonov laundered money through a broker who may not be all that he seems," said Peter. "Now Antonov wants the bonds that the broker hopes will save him. And then there's Delancey, and—"

"The Redhead," said Henry. "The thing about these crime organizations, one of the leg breakers is always tryin' to take over. Happened to the first big Russkie, back in '85, a guy named Egron. His own boys whacked him . . . or so they say."

"Antonov's got a leg-breaker named Vitaly," said Evangeline.

"I'd say he's loyal to the Antonovs, not like the Redhead." Henry opened the door and kept talking as he led them down the narrow stairs. "Most of your Russians who settled in Brooklyn, they's like the Irish in Hell's Kitchen a hundred years ago. They come with big dreams and good hearts, ready to do the hard work.

"But there was Irish gangs then, and there's Russian gangs now. And the smart Russkies do business with the Five Families. Pay the dons their tribute, and the dons side with you when you need sidin' with. But remember, when it come to bein' nasty, these Russkies make the dagoes look like the Little Rascals."

"Do you think Joey Berra is some kind of mafia go-between?" asked Peter.

"Whether he is or not"—they reached the bottom of the stairs, and Henry put up a hand—"we go meet him now like we was in Vietnam. I walk point. I stop, you stop. I drop in a doorway, you drop in doorway. But not together. Miss, you come twenty yards behind me on the other side of the street. And Pete—why you makin' a face?"

"Don't call him Pete," said Evangeline. "He hates to be called Pete."

"Okay, we call him No-Pete."

"Anything's better than Pete," said Peter.

"It's No-Pete and"—Henry looked Evangeline up and down—"you need a nickname, too. Your name one big mouthful. But since it start with a E, we call you the E Ticket. 'Cause you a fine-lookin' woman and the E Ticket the finest ride at Disneyland. E Ticket mean the best."

Henry pulled open the door, looked up the street and down. "Coast look clear. So, we stay in touch with cell phones—"

"But can't the Russians track them?" asked Evangeline.

"They'd need more hardware than NASA to do that . . . or permission from *you.* You didn't give 'em permission, did you?"

Peter shook his head.

"So how did they find us when we left the Oyster Bar?" asked Evangeline.

"Beats the hell out of me," said Henry. "You go in a big restaurant, they's usually somebody workin' a side street. Could've been a busboy who does a little drug-dealin', a waiter sellin' credit card numbers. Fellers like that, they do anything to stay on the good side of the bad guys. You didn't do nothin' to draw attention, did you?"

"Oh, no," said Evangeline. "He just gave the waiter a speech about Boston oysters."

"Oysters?" Henry shook his head. "No-Pete, maybe we start callin' you No-Brains. Word goes out to all Vitaly's peeps that he's lookin' for a guy from Boston, and you start talkin' about Boston oysters?"

"Duxbury," said Peter.

"Say what?"

"Duxbury oysters, not Boston."

"So put on a Red Sox hat. Get the job done

faster. Even if your waiter ain't in with V. and his boys, he goes into the kitchen, starts bitchin' about some guy from Boston talkin' about Duxbury motherfuckin' oysters, and—"

A little Hispanic woman trundled up the walk and up the steps and into the foyer.

Henry put on a big smile and gave her a bow. "Hello, Mrs. Sanchez."

"Hello, Mr. Baxter. I said a prayer for you at Mass this morning."

"Thank you, ma'am. All prayers most welcome. Most welcome indeed." He waited as she let herself into her first-floor apartment, then he opened the front door and told the others, "Watch me now. If I cross before I get to the corner, don't come out. Otherwise, follow like I told you. No-Pete, you come twenty yards behind the E Ticket."

After Henry went out, Evangeline said, "No-Pete and the E Ticket—"

"Up to their eyeballs again."

"I wish I bought you those golf clubs after all."

Peter kissed her on the forehead. "Go."

TEN MINUTES LATER, they were approaching the bleachers and the TKTS Booth again. The neon and the LEDs flashed and flickered in defiance of the sun.

Henry strode toward the statue of Father Duffy, just as the clocks all passed noon. He positioned himself right by the Celtic cross.

Peter took a seat in one of the patio chairs on the pedestrian mall that they had made of Broadway, and he pretended to watch the world go by.

Evangeline got into the line that stretched around the corner of the TKTS booth.

And they waited.

Evangeline wished she was as excited as the people around her. Going to a musical. That would be fun.

Peter was watching a giant LCD TV on the side of a building. It was the screen for Market-Spin.com. And there was Kathy Flynn again, doing another report for all of the Times Square passersby to see.

Evangeline saw it, too. She couldn't tell what the story was about, but there was—good God!—she grabbed her phone and called Peter and told him to look at what Kathy Flynn was showing on the big TV.

"I'm looking," he said.

"That's the bag lady from the Bowling Green." It was a split screen. On one side: a security photo of the bag lady and her scruffy little dog. Beneath it: ERICA CALLOW? On the other side: a photo of an attractive woman, blond, forties, smiling with all her teeth, holding a pretty little dog. Beneath it: ERICA CALLOW?

Then Peter's call waiting line beeped.

It was Henry: "I think I just seen your boy, but he took one look at that big screen y'all been watchin' and he turned right round. Go get the E Ticket, then grab a cab uptown. Meet where we said."

"Right."

"Looks like this thing is goin' viral."

* * *

WHERE THEY SAID was the top of the escalator in the Time Warner Center, overlooking Columbus Circle.

"So the Dollar Diva decides to out the bag lady," said Henry Baxter. "Puttin' up the picture of a toothless old hag and a scruffy little dog, then a picture of a pretty blond lady with a pretty little dog."

"But why?" said Evangeline.

"That's the big question," said Peter. "And why did Joey Berra disappear again?"

"I was watchin' that dude. He was comin'. So I was comin', but when he saw that screen, he hit the hotfoot, like there was somethin' he had to do."

"Get to the bag lady, maybe?" said Evangeline.

"I'm going to find out," said Peter. "Kathy's right here in the building."

"Say, that's convenient," said Henry.

"Yeah," said Evangeline, "as convenient as a condom in your wallet."

"Whoa," said Henry. "Did I pick the wrong meetin' place? I figured I'd see anybody followin' you from the top of this escalator. Up here, you got a view all the way down Fifty-ninth Street. But . . . No-Pete and the Dollar Diva?"

"A long time ago," said Peter.

"You want us to go with you?" asked Henry. "Protect you from yourself?"

Peter typed a text message. "Kathy: The Bag Lady? WTF? Must talk. Now." He showed it to Evangeline, "Can I send this?"

She just shrugged.

"Look like somebody pissed," said Henry. "Y'all ain't got time for bein' pissed."

"Right," said Peter. "So you two go to the New York Society Library and see what you can find in those Riley notebooks. I'll see what Kathy has to offer."

"She has a lot to offer," said Evangeline. "Just see what she has to *say*."

Peter's phone vibrated. It was Kathy: "Come up."

He showed the message to Evangeline.

Henry Baxter said, "What you think, Miss E Ticket?"

She looked at her watch. "We'll trust No-Pete."

"Meet back at my place," said Henry. "Two hours. And keep your head on a swivel."

"But keep your eyes to yourself," said Evangeline.

KATHY FLYNN WAS waiting in her office. She told Peter to close the door. She was watching the Dow Jones on her computer.

He looked over her shoulder. "Still falling?"

Her red hair shone. She smelled of soap. Something simple, maybe Ivory, but nice. "Down another two hundred." She kept her eyes on the ticker. "Is *she* with you?"

Peter said, "She's following another lead."

Kathy leaned back and drummed her fingers on her desk. "Are you close?"

"To what?"

"Don't play games, Peter. Arsenault told me *what*. A whole box of these bonds."

"When did he tell you that?"

"This morning, off camera. He said he had you chasing it, so the annual meeting of the Paul Revere Foundation tomorrow might be truly spectacular."

Peter went to the window and looked out at Lincoln Center. "What chance do you think we have of finding a single mahogany box in all of that?"

"You might have more after this." She tossed him a photograph. It was a little fuzzy, with numbers at the bottom for date and time—a security shot.

"That's the woman who stole the finial from the New-York Historical Society. It was in a box with all those letters, and—"

"I know the story," he said. "I was there Tuesday. But no one showed me this."

"That's because you didn't charm the boys in the security booth." She leaned back and put her feet on her desk.

He looked at her legs. "My charms aren't of the same . . . caliber . . . as yours."

That brought a smile. "Last night in the cab, Evangeline said the bag lady had gotten you into this, and that she had seen the accountant on the Bowling Green—"

"The bag lady was bringing Delancey to the Bowling Green. Evangeline just got caught in it."

"Whatever." Kathy twirled her hair in her finger. "I got to thinking about the story of the stolen finial from the Bowling Green, and I compared the pictures—"

Peter said, "The bag lady had the finial that night."

"No shit?" Kathy sat up, swung her legs off the desk. "I was right. I compared the pictures and said, these two look a lot alike. They even remind me of somebody else I used to know, but . . . that was a long time ago."

"Why did you decide to put her on your Webcast, so that her face was blasted all over Times Square?"

"Sunshine is the best disinfectant. Right?"

"So they say."

"I'm trying to put a lot together, Peter, in a very short time. Whatever was that bag lady chasing? What brought her to me? What brought her and Evangeline together on the Bowling Green . . . with the accountant? What got the accountant killed, which was supposed to happen in front of me? I think this damn bag lady is engineering the whole show. Did Evangeline see the finial?"

"She has it."

"She has it? Too much." Kathy jumped up. "Come on."

"Where?"

"A restaurant called Eleven Madison Park. Austin Arsenault has lunch there every Thursday with Magee. My spies tell me they're having Will Wedge today . . . to eat."

Peter looked at his watch. He was running out of time. The Russians might already have the gas company piping schematic of the streets around Fallon Antiquaria in Boston. He was beginning to worry that they'd light off the store on general principle if they didn't get what they wanted.

So he should have been trying to digest whatever clues they were finding at the New York Society Library. But he was following Kathy down the hallway. Instead of looking at her ass, he opened his cell phone and texted Evangeline. "Any luck?"

THE NEW YORK Society Library: The mansion on Seventy-ninth Street, a block east of Central Park, had been built by J. P. Morgan's architects as a private home in 1917.

Evangeline had been a member since she moved to New York. For a hundred and seventy-five dollars, you had access to gracious reading rooms, research materials, writing rooms, and an enormous range of fiction and nonfiction. It was the best deal in town.

Henry looked up at the five stories of limestone, at the pear trees blooming out front, and gave a low whistle. "You say anyone can join? 'Society' don't mean 'High Society'?"

"No. Just decent society. You want to join?"

"I'll stay outside. I'm your eyes on the street."

"I may need a secretary," she said. "They don't let you Xerox the rare material."

"Okay. Do we know what we're looking for?"

She hitched her purse on her shoulder and started up the stairs. "We'll know it when we see it."

"That ain't where you want to be with twenty hours to go," said Henry.

"When Timothy Riley says, 'My father hid the box of bonds in the chandelier of the famous old City Hall subway station,' you sing out."

"Gotcha."

She opened the door and said, "Now, be cool."

"I always cool, baby."

At the desk, Evangeline showed her pass while Henry scoped out the stone walls, the beamed ceiling, the magnificent grandfather clock at the entrance to the catalogue room. They took the staircase to the second story. She showed him the Members' Room and the rare British Army field map of Manhattan hanging by the elevator.

Henry studied the map. "It don't look like there's nothing but a few houses north of Chambers Street back then."

"New York wasn't the city of dreams . . . yet."

"City of dreams?" Henry chuckled. "You do my line of work for a while, you be callin' it the city of *schemes*."

"It's that, too." Evangeline pointed him up the stairs. "Come on."

Miss Casey Nolan, the pleasant young librarian of rare books and special collections, took their order and told them to have a seat at the research table in the Marshall Room.

Henry looked around at the Governor Winthrop desk, the big table, the historical prints on the wall, and he said, "Mama would be proud."

Miss Nolan returned quickly with the Timothy Riley notebooks. "This is quite an interesting box. It came to us from an Irish Christian Brother. When he took his vow of poverty, he donated us a portion of his family's estate and these notebooks. You'll see that the edges of the last of them were scorched in the famous 1920 anarchist bombing. But it survived and was returned to the family with Mr. Riley's effects."

"Has anyone else looked at them?" asked Henry.

"Not in the last month. That's as far back as we keep borrower's records. May I ask what you're researching?"

"Well, now"—Henry sat back and stroked his chin—"we're exploring the interrelationship between the intellectualization of the historiographical experience of twentieth-century New York with the primary source recollections to be found in the materials left by the practictioners of Monafisterian analysis and deconstructive theory. You know what that is, don't you, Miss Nolan?"

"Oh, yes," she said as she scurried away. "Good luck."

Henry winked at Evangeline, "See . . . I told you I could talk about anything."

PETER FALLON AND Kathy Flynn were now in the back of a cab heading downtown.

She said, "You tell what you know, and I tell what I know. Okay?"

If Evangeline had been in the cab, she would have told Peter to keep his mouth shut. But she wasn't, so he talked Kathy through the events of the last twenty-four hours.

Kathy pulled out a notebook.

Peter said, "Come on, Kathy. This is all off the record."

"I'm publishing an article about Avid Austin and his antideficit crusade tomorrow. I'm doing whatever I can to smoke people out."

"Why?"

"It's my job, Peter." She leaned closer to him.

"And I'm ambitious. Otherwise, I might have married you. We could be living in Boston, enjoying life."

"Why do I always have the feeling that you're coming onto me?"

"Because you'd like me to. You're a dreamer. Like me. Evangeline is all nuts and bolts. And people may try to tell you that opposites attract. But a pair of dreamers, imagining themselves discovering artifacts lost for centuries or exposing financial frauds in New York, they can be attracted to each other, too."

He was listening, remembering, but remaining motionless.

She was good, and she was seductive, especially when she whispered, "It's what makes power couples, Peter. This town is full of them. Big dreamers on both sides of the bed."

It would have been easy to lean over and kiss those lips or whisper something back to her. He was glad that he was on the run, in the midst of way too much trouble as it was. It made it easier to keep his arms folded and his lips to himself.

"So"—she clicked her pen—"how about letting me take just a few little notes?"

"About what?"

"About Antonov going to Harvard," she said.

"Why?"

"Why do you think we're going to see Will Wedge from Boston?"

The cab had arrived.

"Because he's Harvard, too?"

"It's called affinity fraud," she said. "Madoff did

it with rich Jews. I think Arsenault is doing it with rich Harvard guys who think they're too smart to get Madoffed. Pay the fare."

By the time Peter got his change and gave a look around, Kathy was already parading into the restaurant. That was how she walked, long legs loping, ass swaying, always like she owned the place.

Peter liked 11 Madison Park for its high ceilings, its twenty-foot windows looking out onto the square, and its two-course prix-fixe lunch for twenty-eight bucks. A bargain by New York standards. Just so long as no one was tailing you, spying on you, shooting at you, or otherwise trying to keep you from enjoying your meal.

But as he went in, he asked himself again, why the hell was he here when he should have been uptown, poring over those Riley notebooks? Most of the time, when he went after something, the clues accumulated logically: a line of quotes from *Paradise Lost* led to a lost Paul Revere tea set. A single line, repeated through history, echoed across New England until it drew him to the hiding place of a lost U.S. Constitution. But where was the logic in this? He hoped that Evangeline was doing better.

Kathy was telling the hostess that they were meeting the Arsenault party.

The hostess glanced at her book, "So there'll be five of you rather than three?"

Peter noticed the eyes turning, but they were turning toward Kathy. Some were recognizing her, brightening, following.

It was a good lesson. If you were trying not to be noticed in a half-full restaurant, walk in with a well-known woman who also looked fabulous.

Will Wedge had arrived first. He was sitting on the banquette in the corner, so that he could see the whole room. He must have been spooked from the night before in the Harvard Club. He was sipping something amber, neat.

A little early, thought Peter, but under the circumstances . . .

Wedge looked shocked to see them, then he put on his old hail-fellow face, stood, and offered a big handshake. "Well, the MarketSpin lady and the treasure hunter. What a surprise. I didn't know that you were joining us."

Kathy put a finger to her lips and gave him a little wink. She could play anything, from hard-nosed to coquettish, from moment to moment. "It's a surprise."

Wedge turned to Peter. "Did the police ever interview you?"

"Not yet." Peter sat with his back to the room. He was brazening through at the moment. A man wanted for questioning by the police would never be strolling into a fancy restaurant as the lunch crowd arrived, so he couldn't be the guy whose picture had been in the papers.

And no one paid particular attention, except for the waitstaff. They slid another table into place. They brought Perrier, breadsticks, menus.

Wedge recovered nicely. He even glanced at the wine list and told the waiter, "Bring us the Jacques-

Frédéric Mugnier, Clos de la Maréchale, Premier Cru 2006."

"Nice bottle," said Peter.

"Nice pronunciation," said Kathy.

"Nice price," said Wedge. "But what the hell? Arsenault is paying."

"Is he?" asked Kathy.

"What do you mean?"

"Isn't Wedge, Fleming, and Royce a feeder for Avid?" asked Kathy.

Wedge sat back. "A long and positive relationship. You could call it stellar."

"In the good years and in '08, too?"

"Well, yes. And if they were good in '08, you know that they are rock solid."

"Have you ever had a problem withdrawing funds for your clients?" asked Kathy.

Wedge leaned forward. "What are you getting at?"

Peter asked, "Who else from Harvard has come for the meeting of the Paul Revere Foundation? Anybody I'd know?"

Wedge said, "A dozen or more, all committed to fighting the deficit."

"Glad to hear it," said Kathy.

The wine arrived. Wedge told Peter to taste it. Peter approved.

Wedge took the time to recover. "As Arsenault has told this country for years, unless we get control of our deficit, we will turn our economy into a big Ponzi scheme."

"Interesting term," said Kathy.

Wedge kept talking: "But the people at the top of the pyramid won't be stealing from the ones at the bottom. They'll be stealing from their grandchildren."

"And all the other Harvard men on the board agree with you?" asked Peter.

"They're not all Harvard men," said Wedge.

"We can look at the 501(c)(3) filing," said Peter. "I'll bet that most of them are."

Kathy gave Peter a playful punch on the shoulder, "Very good. I wish I'd thought of that. Looking at the 501(c)(3). You should be a reporter."

Wedge looked from one face to the other. "What is this all about?"

"A lot of Harvard brokers pouring money into the operation of a bigger Harvard broker. Getting nice annualized profits, never looking at the books, never questioning," said Kathy.

"Sounds familiar," said Peter.

"Now wait a minute," said Will Wedge. "There has never been a moment when we haven't been able to withdraw as much money as we've needed from Avid. I don't think that—" Will Wedge shut up, because Austin Arsenault and Owen T. Magee were striding across the room.

And neither of them looked happy to see two extra guests.

"Please tell me that you have good news for us," said Owen T. Magee to Peter Fallon. "Otherwise, this is a private lunch."

But as if he understood that it was never cool to make a scene, Austin Arsenault sat and said, "On the other hand, we can make it a friendly lunch, if the both of you promise not to talk about business."

EVANGELINE AND HENRY were still working away in the Marshall Room on the fourth floor of the New York Society Library.

The four notebooks were a hundred leaves long, lined paper, bound in marble boards, like ledgers. Since they were written over about a year, there were no drastic changes in handwriting. Sometimes Tim Riley wrote in pencil, sometimes in ink with smudges and splotches.

And the notebooks told the story of a man and his city, from the day he first rode uptown in the Riley Wrecking wagon, to the meetings with G. W. Plunkitt, to the encounters with J. P. Morgan, including the night when Morgan locked the bankers in his library. Then there was the run on West Side Workingman's Bank, stopped by bags of Morgan money.

Henry loved this line from Tim's father, who looked out from the cupola of an old house, at the smoky, steaming air of the city, and called it, "the great cloud of commerce that rains money like water on the city of New York."

Evangeline was touched by this: "In the turmoil of the '07 panic, your mother and I both suffered great disappointments. All people do in life. But out of it grew an understanding of what is most important. And out of our understanding came a fine son."

She gave that sentence a lot of thought and wrote it down and read on.

The final passage was dated September 15, 1920:

"I must write of my father's death. But I cannot write much. I only heard it happen. His bravery saved my life. He stood up to thugs. I found him on the steps of the old house that, if we could go back, would sit at the corner of Broadway and Eightieth. He had drawn a white X on the steps. This meant we should take up the board and save to sell to Squints O'Day, the cooper who made water tanks. My father sometimes worked for Squints, who called him 'the best tank-bottom man in New York.' I have always puzzled about my father's last word, 'eyes.' When he said it, he seemed to be peering into the future. We all peer ahead and hope for our children. We all have big dreams. But what matters is what my father gave to Uncle Eddie and me: 'A roof over your head and food on your table and a family that loves you in a parish that cares.' "

Evangeline showed that to Henry.

"Man was a philosopher," said Henry.

Then she read ahead: "Tonight, after you were in bed, I took my evening walk to the roof. I counted several new water tanks. When I was a boy, there were few, and now there are many. The sons of Squints O'Day still make the tanks. And as my father once said, they hold the water that washes like life into the city."

Evangeline puzzled over that, then turned the page and saw a final entry, in pencil, in a handwriting that was scrawling, almost impossible to read, "*Rainwater O'Day. X marks the . . . spiffle.*"

Henry read that and said, "What the hell is a *spiffle?*"

IT WAS NOT a pleasant lunch.

Will Wedge was silent for most of the first course.

Peter guessed that Austin and Owen were planning to pump him, maybe to urge him to raise his stake in Avid Investment Strategies. That was how Ponzi schemes worked. They had to get more in because others were taking out, or would be soon.

Once the main course was placed in front of everyone, Will looked at Arsenault and said, "These two are suggesting that you're another Madoff."

"Print that," Owen T. Magee said to Kathy Flynn, "and I will sue you, your Web site, your network, and the people who make the computer you write on."

But Owen T. was the bad cop.

Arsenault was the good cop. He swirled his wine and said, "Kathy, you can look at our fund performance over a decade and you'll see solid results, well-managed portfolios. And you'll see the years when we took a beating just like everyone else. Go back to 2001, for example. We can show you the books. It's all public record."

"So why is your accountant dead?" asked Kathy.

Owen T. Magee said, "You'd have to ask the people who killed him. But remember this, Carl Evers wasn't some nonentity from Long Island, like Madoff's rubber stamper. He audited all our financial reports before he signed off."

"But something had him scared to death." Kathy

turned to Will Wedge. "Why was the accountant walking toward you when he was shot? And why would someone shoot him in the middle of the Harvard Club?"

Will Wedge shook his head. "I don't know. I honestly don't know."

Peter asked, "What's your annual fee to feed Avid, Will?"

Arsenault said to Peter, "I don't like that line of questioning. Will Wedge is an important broker. So am I. We do not hide like Madoff. We are part of the community. We support charities. We have big ideas. And we will make a national statement tomorrow, whether the court supports us or not . . . whether you find anything or not."

"Got it?" said Owen T. Magee, as if to put a punctuation on the speech.

"Got it," said Peter.

EVANGELINE AND HENRY were finished.

Henry walked over to the window and looked down. Then he laughed. But something wasn't funny. "How in the hell did they know we were here?"

"What are you talking about?" Evangeline came over.

"See the black car up at the corner? Two shadows sittin' in the front seat? They weren't there when we came in. But they been there a while." Henry called to Miss Nolan. "Did you tell anyone we were here?"

"Why would I do that?"

Henry grinned. "If I go through the rare book

catalogue, I won't see any items that say, 'Gift of Oscar Delancey,' will I, Miss Casey Nolan?"

The young woman shook her head. But her face reddened like a Courtland apple.

"Is there a back way out of this place?" Henry asked.

PETER AND KATHY came out of the restaurant.

Peter looked around. No Russian redheads. No Putin look-alikes. No police. A man sitting in Madison Square Park, over by the dog run, taking pictures. But there were people taking pictures in New York all the time.

Arsenault and the others came out, too. Magee and Wedge got into the limo.

Arsenault stopped on the sidewalk beside Peter and Kathy. He was still in "big man" mode. No harshness, no threats, just lots of visionary conversation, grandiose schmooze:

"It's an amazing city. So much endures, like the old Flatiron over there. Yet so much fades." He gestured up to Twenty-sixth Street, the site of the first Madison Square Garden. The building at the corner replicated the archways that once led into the Garden, like a shadow of an echo.

"Think of all that has disappeared," said Arsenault. "The old city hall where Washington took the oath, gone. The Croton Reservoir, gone. The mansions of Fifth Avenue, gone. Even the World Trade Center—"

"Things change," said Peter.

"Do they ever," said Arsenault. "Go to Boston

or Philadelphia and see the past. Come to New York and watch time fly. The wonders of the age are not wonders until they are proclaimed here, Fallon, and I have been part of it for thirty years."

Kathy shook her head. "What a fucking windbag."

Arsenault just laughed and got into his limo, then rolled down the window. "I intend to be around a whole lot longer. There are still wonders to see. So long as we can control the deficit." And he sped off.

Peter looked at Kathy, "Now what?"

She shrugged. "I guess I go look at his books. He offered to show them."

Her cell phone rang. She answered. She knit her brow. Then her eyes widened. When she clicked off, she looked shocked.

"What is it?' said Peter.

"An old friend."

"And?"

"She's been dead for almost ten years."

SIXTEEN

September 2001

At least she hadn't married him.

Jennifer Wilson finished her second cup of coffee and thought about her autobiography for the first time in years.

What would this chapter say?

She had not taken New York by storm, but she sure had taken it. She only hoped that she wouldn't have to give it all back, because like every bubble before it, like every big thing that had driven the American economy for a day or a decade, from tobacco to trains to Florida swampland sold as top-shelf real estate, the dot-com bubble had burst.

So thank God she hadn't married John Smith, because they might have had children, and who would raise them if both parents went to jail?

She stood on her balcony above Abingdon Square and took another sip of coffee.

God, but she loved that neighborhood. She loved New York, period. And she told herself that no matter what happened that day, coming to New York had been the best thing she ever could have done.

She had to admit that she liked the cleaner, brighter, safer city that New York had become. She thanked the booming economy and gave Rudy Giuliani his due. But she still missed the New York she had first seen on that day she dragged a suitcase from the Port Authority Terminal all the way down to the Village.

The rest of America had made *that* New York a symbol of all that was wrong with urban life—the crime, the drugs, the homeless bums, the graffiti, the rats, the roaches, the derelicts in the derelict buildings, the squalor in the alleys, the soaring deficits, and the astronomical prices of everything from apples to apartments.

But the rest of America missed the point. All those people sitting out there in mom-and-pop land saw only what they wanted to see in the big scary city. Jennifer had found real excitement in the New York of the eighties, a kind of dark magic, even in a black limousine a week before Christmas. Thinking about it now almost felt like nostalgia. Now she could go up to the Meatpacking District—where butchers in bloody aprons used to slice ribs by day and gays in black leather cruised by night—and order Chablis in a fern bar.

The air was late-summer warm, September clear. So she lingered outside to feel the sun on her face and enjoy the view a few minutes more. The Twin Towers no longer seemed like a symbol of the sad seventies, when they had been built to revive Lower Manhattan. Back then, people used to say that they looked like the boxes that the Empire State and the Chrysler buildings came in. No . . . on that September morning, they shimmered silver, like the new century that lay ahead.

Still, she hated going down there.

Since the March afternoon in 2000 when Lucent earnings missed Wall Street estimates, a shitstorm had been blowing through the high-tech world. And it had finally found her in that fancy office on the ninety-first floor of the South Tower.

So . . . what to wear for a shitstorm? A raincoat?

She thought about putting on a skirt. A skirt with no stockings would be cool and keep her from sweating. She still had a summer tan. And even though she had passed the big 4-0, she still had nice legs. Nice everything else for that matter, because she worked out three times a week. She even went down to the World Trade Center on Saturdays, showed her ID, and *ran* the whole ninety-one flights to her office. And her legs were even nicer when she slipped on the Ferragamos that she kept in a drawer in her desk.

But why give the FBI anything to look at when they were coming to grill her?

So she put on slacks and a pair of black cross-trainers. She preferred slacks because she'd been purse-snatched back in those good old eighties, and now she liked to carry her wallet in her pocket, like a man.

She stuck her coffee cup in the dishwasher and patted Georgie, her little terrier. He wanted to play. He always wanted to play. He was less than a year old and still chewing things. So she put up the baby gate to keep him in the kitchen. He whimpered a bit, then he began to chew the gate.

In the bedroom, Joshua was still sleeping with the sheet half over him, one long leg and one muscled butt cheek exposed.

After Smitty, Jennifer had been with lovers who got up and made coffee for her and lovers who got up and left before she was awake.

But Joshua was an artist. So he slept late because he painted late . . . and loved later . . . but longer. However happy she was that she hadn't married Smitty, she was even happier that she didn't love Joshua, because once they were done in bed, there wasn't much to say. But if having Joshua was what they meant by "unlucky in love," she'd live with it. She gave that handsome ass a little pat and let him sleep.

She dabbed a bit of Chanel no. 5 behind the

ears. Then she grabbed her purse and her laptop. Then she decided to grab one more thing. She went to the top drawer of her dresser, to the compartment where she kept her Hermès scarves, under which she had hidden the false ID she had used to open one of her safety deposit boxes.

Maybe the meeting with the FBI would be so terrible that she would decide to disappear that day. Or maybe she was just being a little crazy, because there were plenty of steps to take and plenty of angles to play before she finally went to jail. When the feds took down an inside trader like Ivan Boesky, they always did some trading themselves. So maybe she could give up Smitty, or Dmitri, or Brink Leekman, their chief financial officer. Or maybe she could talk them all out of it. That's what she was hoping.

Still, she took the fake ID, and as an afterthought, she grabbed one of the scarves. It was yellow. It would bring a bit of color to her navy blue pantsuit.

She went by cab that morning. And even though it cost a bit more, she told the driver to go down Broadway, the street of dreams in the city of the same name. Who didn't come to New York and dream of seeing her own name in lights on her own professional Broadway? At least it had happened for Jennifer.

Within three years of its start-up, Intermetro had become a bellweather for the expansion of the Internet. The company had ten employees, then twenty, then thirty. So they left their R & D in factory space on the Brooklyn docks and moved their business operations to the World Trade Center. They grew. They grew some more. And they began to talk about the dream of every start-up, the initial public offering.

They knew all the stories of overnight IPO wealth. Come up with a better way to distribute information, so that it moved even a nanosecond faster . . . find an easier way to assure that every time someone clicked on your Web site, someone else had to pay you some money . . . dream up a catchy name for a new way to sell anything from books to mutual funds to pet supplies online . . . do any of that, and it didn't matter if your business plan was light on specifics and your balance sheet had never shown a profit. Traders saw future value. In the nineties, anyone who put a dot-com at the end of their name or an e-dash in front of it could go from blue jeans in the garage office to beating the blue chips on the big board overnight.

The Intermetro IPO had come on June 15, 1998. The stock opened at twelve. By the afternoon, buyers had bid it up to forty-two. And it kept rolling. For two years, Intemetro appeared to hit every earnings estimate, and they were promising a new software sensation called Skylink, "an enhanced application for platforming on existing Internet systems to produce optimum search capacity in the new information environment."

Intermetro stock spiked on the release of Skylink, but Skylink turned out to be as worthless as all the words they'd wasted trying to describe it, a marginal improvement on a lot of other search engines. And by 2000, marginal was no longer enough in the world of dot-coms. Intermetro had hit the innovation wall at just about the time that all those smart traders realized that companies selling nothing but air, equations, and dancing electrons might not be the best investments after all.

So here they were . . .

Jennifer told the cabbie to stop at St. Paul's. She liked to walk to work past the old church. She liked to imagine it all as it looked in 1776, when the brothels stretched along Vesey Street, and Vesey Street ended at the wharves just beyond Greenwich Street. Now the landfill from the Trade Center foundation had pushed the city another quarter mile west, while the towers had pushed it a quarter mile into the sky.

She cut through the graveyard, under the sycamores. It comforted her to pass among all those people who had lived their quiet lives and grand crises in New York and now lay peacefully in the ancient earth, especially on a morning when her own crisis was coming to a head.

She hurried across the Grand Plaza. If it was hot, the plaza was hotter, if it was cold, the plaza was colder, and the wind always blew a little harder, because the towers were so big that they created their own climate. She gave a glance to *The Sphere* in the middle of the fountain. It was meant to symbolize a world united in peace through trade. More irony than inspiration, she thought, because trade was about business, and business was about struggle. All that Adam Smith stuff—the invisible hand leading businesspeople to do what benefited others, because in the process they would benefit themselves—all of that might have worked in the eighteenth century, but not now.

She pulled out her ID, swiped it at one of the turnstiles, and headed for an express elevator. After the '93 bombing, the Port Authority had secured the World Trade Center. Now you needed ID everywhere, and you never knew where Big Brother was—or wasn't—because every floor, every hallway, every elevator had a security camera. And they had closed the garages to the public, too.

The terrorists would have to find other ways.

ii.

The offices of Intermetro were in a suite on the ninety-first floor of the South Tower with a view west toward New Jersey. It was quiet at eight thirty.

Nancy Torrez, at the reception desk, gave Jennifer a nod.

In the office beyond, Dmitri Donovan was looking out. He turned. His face was pale. He was plainly terrified about the upcoming meeting.

"We'll set up in the conference room," Jennifer said. Then she went down the hall. She looked in on Brink Leekman, who was going over papers in his office. He glanced up, his long face even longer than usual. He said he'd be with her in a minute.

She headed straight for Smith's office. He was facing the window, but he wasn't enjoying the view. He was bouncing a racquetball off the glass, leaving little smudges.

Typical, she thought. He never put the toilet seat down, either.

Bounce. Bounce.

Without turning, he said, "Somebody dimed us out. I'm convinced of it."

"Good morning to you, too," she said.

He spun in his chair. Ten years since they met, and he still had the chiseled features, the surfer's body, the casual Friday wardrobe on a Tuesday. She had told him to wear a tie for this meeting, but he never listened to her about that, either.

Bounce. Bounce. This time off the wall. "I'd love to figure out who it was."

"What does it matter? The SEC watched what you've done in the last year—"

"You were doing it, too."

"I haven't done anything that could be construed as illegal," she said, maintaining the professional calm of a good lawyer.

"You sold stock with inside information." *Bounce. Bounce.* "So . . . where's your stash? Numbered Swiss account? Safety deposit box? Mattress?"

"Some reinvested," she said. "Some in cash."

He gave her a grin. "Safety deposit box. Hope you didn't use your real name." *Bounce. Bounce.* "And I hope you're right about not needing outside counsel."

"Haven't you ever seen *Law & Order*?" she said. "The cop just wants to chat and the suspect says, 'Should I have a lawyer?' What does the cop say?"

Bounce. Bounce. " 'Do you *need* a lawyer?' "

"Exactly. So . . . no red flags. Not yet."

Bounce. Bounce . . . bounce. Bounce.

She knew he didn't believe her. So she took the letter off his desk and said, "This is very soft, just the opening gambit." And she read, " 'In reference to your Intermetro stock options, the SEC has noted irregularities in your personal trading patterns over the last fourteen months. These may be easily explained. Therefore, our FBI representatives will be visiting your office on September 11, 2001, at nine A.M. Please have your compliance officer and chief financial officer in attendance, and all your company papers in order.' "

"I'm worried," he said.

"Try not to show it. If we handle this right, we can make them go away."

"Not likely." Smith got up and started pacing and bouncing. "I didn't want this to happen, you know." *Bounce. Bounce.* "I just wanted to do something good." *Bounce. Bounce.* "I just wanted to leave a mark."

"You *are* leaving a mark . . . on the wall."

Bounce. Bounce.

She watched him for a moment, then said, "Just let me do the talking. And put the fucking"—she snatched it—"*ball* away." She stuffed it into her purse.

He walked over to the desk and picked up another racquetball. "The SEC never would have noticed that we were dumping stock if somebody hadn't tipped them off. I think it was Arsenault. He's always been mad that we cut him out, since that day with my grandfather." *Bounce. Bounce.* "Once Magee went off the board, he could have been feeding Arsenault."

She didn't say what she was thinking.

So he said it, with a lowered voice. "Or it could be Dmitri's relatives. And I don't mean the Irish side of the family. I told Dmitri to warn them, but he waited because he still thought we'd turn things around. He didn't start to sell until the stock was dropping like the express elevator out there. His family must've lost a shitload."

"Off the peak. But they made a shitload off their original investment."

"Do you know what they call Dmitri's uncle? Avenging Antonov."

She looked at him a long time, then she blinked and hoped that she didn't look too frightened. "But Yuri was on the board. Yuri's reasonable." She looked at her watch. "What you need to focus on right now is this: the FBI is coming to interview us in a little more than fifteen minutes."

The telephone buzzed, and he picked it up.

Jennifer watched his expression change:

Neutral: "What is it?" Puzzled: "Two men? One has red hair, the other has a stainless-steel tooth?" Shocked: "Nancy!" Then frantic, turning to Jennifer: "Get under the desk."

"What?"

"Just *do* it!"

Then they heard two *pops* and someone falling. *Dmitri?*

Then came Brink Leekman's voice. "What the hell is going on out—"

Pop. Pop.

Brink appeared in the doorway to Smitty's office. He was holding his pile of papers. He looked at them as they turned red with his blood. Then *pop.* A bullet struck the left side of his head and blew most of his brains out the right.

Smitty turned and gestured frantically—under the desk. Get under the desk.

Now she did what he told her. And she listened.

Smitty's voice: "What the hell is this?"

A deeper voice: "Business."

"Business?"

"Where is lady lawyer?" Another voice, a Russian accent.

Smitty tried to cover for Jennifer: "She's late . . . no!"

Pop. Pop.

She heard Smitty fall back, bounce off the edge of the desk, hit the floor.

If she had moved, she would have seen his eyes peering under the desk. Lifeless.

Instead, she was wedged into the leg hole, her head twisted toward the window, her breathing as shallow as she could make it, her hand to her mouth.

"Where the fuck is girl?" said one of them.

"Hello?" called the other. "Miss Wilson?" The voice went down the hallway, calling, "Hello! Hello!" Then it was back. "Not in office. Not in ladies' room. Maybe she's late?"

Jennifer could almost hear them thinking, see them scanning Smitty's office. Then footfalls came closer.

Her purse. She had left her purse on the desk. Right in front of them.

One of them said, "What's this?"

What's *what*? The purse? She held her breath . . . and her bladder.

"That's a racquetball," said the other one.

"Look like handball. I handball champ of Brighton Beach." *Bounce. Bounce.*

If they'd found a raquetball, they would find the purse, then they would find her.

Then one of them sniffed. "You smell perfume?"

She almost whimpered.

"Aramis," grunted the other one. "On me."

"Vitaly, I know you are a fucking Russian pussy, but I smell lady perfume."

She stared into space and waited and—

Suddenly, inexplicably, horribly, the fabric of blue sky beyond the window was ripped by flame.

Jennifer gasped, but the sound was lost in the low, muffled thud of an explosion.

The flame inflated into an obscene red-orange balloon right outside the window.

She could not tell where it was coming from because the windows were only twenty-two inches wide. There were no panoramas from the World Trade Center, no hundred-and-eighty-degree views, unless you were in Windows on the World or you had your nose pressed against the glass.

One Russian said, "What the fuck?"

The balloon of flame lifted as debris came flying past the window—shards, slivers, chunks, pieces . . . plastic, metal, glass, paper, people. *People?* And now smoke came billowing, deep and deathly black, darkening the office.

Jennifer stayed absolutely still as one of the Russians went to the window and craned his neck. She could see him now. He looked like a cube in a blue windbreaker. He was wearing a blue ball cap and sunglasses, to shield him from the security cameras.

He said, "Holy fuck my mother."

"How many times I tell you, Vitaly, swearing in

America is like poetry. 'Holy fuck my mother' . . . this is doggerel." The other Russian was leaner. He wore a hooded sweatshirt that did not entirely cover his flaming red hair. "You got to be—holy shit!"

"Holy fuck my mother," said Vitaly. "Bomb go off over there. Big bomb."

"Let's get out of here."

"What about lady lawyer?"

"Worry about her later. We know where she live."

"But boss—"

"Fuck him," said the redhead. "Stupid to lose money on stock, then shoot company bosses. Good way to lose more money. We should shoot him and his son, then we take over, eh?"

Vitaly said, "You shoot boss, I shoot you. Antonov get me into America."

"Yeah. Yeah. Loyal Vitaly. In America, you don't be loyal. You look out for number one." The voice was echoing down the hallway now. "Is business, Vitaly, and in America, in business, you grow or die. So fuck everybody . . ."

Jennifer heard the words but was listening for the sound of their footsteps. She could not tell if the killers were going, or if they had decided to make one more sweep through the office, because the phones were ringing on Smitty's desk and in every office up and down the hallway. And people were leaving voice mails on all the telephones. Smitty's mother was saying that she hoped everything was all right. Then his latest girlfriend called . . . then . . .

Jennifer stayed there, curled up in a ball under

the desk, watching the world end outside the window. She did not move for two minutes . . . three . . . five.

The phones kept ringing. The messages kept coming.

From her own office, she heard Joshua's voice. She couldn't tell what he was saying because she couldn't leave that little wooden box, because she knew what she would see when she emerged. A body, another body . . . and down the hall . . .

She stayed there, trembling, watching the black smoke boil past. And for some reason she remembered falling from a tree when she was a little girl. She remembered hearing a pop, knowing that something terrible had happened to her wrist . . . but she never looked at that wrist until it was in a cast.

Get up. Stop thinking about your girlhood. Get up and get out. The shooters are gone. You have to get help. Smitty might still be alive, or Brink, or Dmitri, or Nancy. Poor Nancy, just doing her job. Get up.

But she just kept trembling in that wooden cocoon while the blackness boiled outside the window.

Then another terrifying sound caused her spine to snap and slam her head against the top of the desk. It was a high-pitched, electrical wail: *Whoop-whoop! Whoooop! Whoop-whoop! Whoooop!* The building alarm.

Then a voice came over the PA: "Your attention, please, ladies and gentlemen. Building Two is secure. There is no need to evacuate Building Two. If you are in the midst of evacuation, you may use the reentry doors and the elevators to return to your offices. Repeat, Building Two is secure."

Secure from what? She still didn't know. But she stretched a leg and crawled out from under the desk. She went to the window and craned her neck. Something had happened in the other tower. But what?

The phone was ringing in her office again.

Go to it. Don't look at anything else. Don't look at Smitty. But—oh, my God. Two shots. Right in the forehead. Step over him. And poor Brink. Oh, God.

She wished her mother were calling, but her mother had passed away. Her only relatives were in California. They weren't even awake and wouldn't know where she worked anyway.

She grabbed the telephone in her office. The caller ID: her own number. "Hello."

"Oh, Christ, Jen, get out of there." It was Joshua again.

"What happened?"

"A plane hit Tower One! Get out of there."

"But they just made an announcement. They said Tower Two is safe."

"Look out your window, for chrissakes!"

"Okay. Okay. I'm going. And Josh, get out of my apartment now. Take the dog."

"What are you talking about?"

"Just *do* it. Do it now. Go to your loft. I'll meet you there." She almost said, "I love you." But she didn't, because she didn't.

He was right. She couldn't stay with the dead

bodies and the blackness blowing past the windows, no matter what the PA told her. But what if the killers were in the hallway? What if they were coming back in? Then her phone rang again. She read the caller ID: COOK MEDICAL CENTER.

She knew who it was, and she couldn't bring herself to talk to him, because she would have to tell him what had just happened. But she listened to his message.

The voice was older, out of gas, or maybe just out of bourbon and vermouth. "Hello, Jen. Ol' Doc Gary here. I just wanted to see if you kids are all right. I'm watching on television and . . . I'm hoping you've left. . . . Take it from an old pilot . . . this was no accident. It's terrorists. We're at war, honey. And if Bush is smart, he'll call for war bonds to pay for what's ahead. Just like they did in the Revolution, only this time, they'll pay off"—he chuckled—"not like our 1780 bonds, eh?"

She hadn't thought of them in fourteen years. Suddenly, she had to talk to him. She reached for the receiver, but he was signing off:

"I guess I've said enough. . . . Sorry things went bad with Intermetro . . . but it was worth it. . . . You kids reached for the sky. . . . And take it from me, that's what life's all about. That and . . . and . . . dying before you finally break your hip." He clicked off.

She hung up, looked again out the window, and decided that the best thing she could do would be to go up to that nursing home and say something good to that old man about his grandson. That's what would drive her now, to take the hand and ease the pain of a man who had become the father she never had.

She pointed her eyes front and headed down the hallway. She didn't look at Brink Leekman. She gave just the briefest glance at Nancy, who lay back in the chair with her eyes pointed at the ceiling. Dmitri was in the doorway of his office. Only his feet showed.

The core of the building around the stairwell and the elevator shafts smelled of smoke and fear. The smoke was real. It was seeping into the ventilation system and sucked down the miles of elevator shafts. The panic was real, too. She smelled it on the others who were stepping onto the elevator, two accountants from the firm next door. One of them said that they really shouldn't be riding the elevator in an emergency. The other said he just wished that building security could get their stories straight:

"Evacuate. Go back. The building is safe. Get out. What the hell do they want?"

"I got my PalmPilot and my papers," said the other. "So I can work from home till they put that fire out over there."

Jennifer thought they were right. They should have taken the stairs. But today she was gambling.

They popped out on the seventy-eighth floor, the Sky Lobby where riders changed from local elevators to big express cars that could carry fifty-five people to the ground in sixty seconds. She came around the corner from the bank of locals, and stepped in the crowd bunching up around the expresses.

Two men in gray suits were heading for the locals. They stopped and looked at her, then looked again, as if they recognized her.

She hardly noticed them. She was scanning the mob—a hundred, maybe two hundred, frustrated, angry, frightened people. *Go up. Go down. Stay put. Stay calm.* They had heard it all in the fifteen minutes since the plane struck the other tower. Now they were all looking for direction, looking to one another, and looking up and down the marble-lined concourse that ran the length of the sky lobby.

Jennifer watched the lights flashing above a bank of elevators and gauged which one would arrive first.

Then she heard another PA anouncement: "If the conditions warrant on your floor, you may wish to start an orderly evacuation."

A great groan of frustration rose on the concourse, and a deeper groan of fear played beneath it.

Then the doors of one of the express elevators opened, causing the movement of the whole crowd. There was nothing panicked about it, just a slow, quietly frightened push of people.

And then, the two men who had noticed Jennifer were on either side of her.

One was tall, serious, silent.

The other, who did the talking, was shorter, stockier, and all attitude. He flashed a badge. "I'm Agent Berranova. FBI. This is Agent Johnson. Are you Jennifer Wilson?"

"Yes."

"We are supposed to be interviewing you and

your associates." Berranova started to lead her north on the concourse to the elevator that would take her back upstairs.

She pulled away. "Are you nuts? Look around you. Look what's happening."

Agent Berranova said, "We understand. We'd just like you to—"

"I just want to get out of here. I just—"

At that moment, she thought she saw something moving toward the south windows.

Toward the windows? The windows!

And then she died. . . .

BECAUSE WHEN SHE woke, she was in hell, paying for her sins.

Hell choked and burned and crushed. Black smoke boiled and flames roared and a heavy piece of Sheetrock lay across her. Walls had collapsed everywhere, the ceiling had turned to fire, bodies lay in bunches and in pieces and in hopeless tangles of debris. Some were still, some were moving, and some cried out for help, but she couldn't hear them because of the roaring inside her head.

She saw one of the FBI agents. He had been sliced in two by a piece of aluminum. It looked like part of an airplane.

But the other guy was gone. Blown apart? Buried?

She still did not know what had happened, but she knew that in hell there were stairways. Some led to more misery and some led to escape. She could have stayed to help those who were still alive. She should have stayed. She told herself that, even then.

If she knew a way out of hell, Jennifer should be an angel of the light and show others. If someone was uninjured—and she had been protected by the Sheetrock—she should help others. But she could not hear for the ringing in her ears. She could barely breathe for the acrid smoke. So she staggered toward stairway B, the one she had always run on.

And a young Hispanic man came stumbling through the smoke. He wore a name tag: Gomez. He worked in the World Trade Center. He shouted to her, "No. Stairway A. It's the only way out."

She couldn't hear him, so she kept walking, so he turned her, pushed her, helped her stumble over the debris and the people till they reached the stairway door and pushed it open, and she stepped out of hell. She looked for the glow-in-the-dark strip at the edge of each tread, and . . .

Down. . . . Down. . . . Turn. . . . Down. . . . Down. . . . Turn. . . . Turn. . . . Down. . . . Don't look. Don't count. Don't talk. Can't hear yourself anyway. Don't cough because you'll stop and slow and cough your guts out and vomit and die.

She looked over her shoulder, but the Hispanic guy had never followed. He had gone back.

Down. . . . Down. . . . Turn. . . . Down. . . . Down. . . . Turn. . . . Turn. . . . Down. . . .

She did not know how long it was before she realized that the fluorescent lights were on and shining now through the gloom. She did not know how long it was before she began to pass firemen climbing the stairs in their heavy helmets and heavy turnout coats and hundred-pound equipment packs. And she did not know how long it was before she began to hear her feet hitting the steps, because her ears were clearing. . . .

Down. . . . Down. . . . Turn. . . . Down. . . . Down. . . . Turn. . . . Turn. . . . Down. . . . Down. . . .

And as she got lower, she realized that her feet were wet. Water lines had broken and the stairs grew slick. But the air was clearer. So . . .

Down. . . . Down. . . . Turn. . . . Down. . . . Down. . . . Turn. . . . Turn. . . . Down. . . .

Five minutes . . . ten minutes . . . twenty minutes . . . And more people joined her on every floor.

Just down. . . . Down. . . . Turn. . . . Down. . . . Down. . . . Turn. . . . Turn.

And then, finally, sunlight. She had reached the plaza level, the upper part of the huge two-story lobby. But—

"Don't look out. Keep moving. Don't look out." A Port Authority policeman was shouting, directing, doing his best to keep everyone going. But Jennifer glanced back at the plaza and *The Sphere* outside, and she saw why she shouldn't be looking. The plaza had become a battlefield. Then something hit the ground and burst red, like a . . . like a . . . like . . .

Don't look out. . . . Down. . . . Down. . . . Down. . . . Down. . . .

Down . . . to the underground shopping mall and the PATH plaza where the trains from Jersey came into Manhattan. And now there were more Trade Center workers, and firemen, and police, and ordinary people, who had taken up the task of encouraging the rest, shouting, directing, doing their best to keep the crowd moving to safety. Hundreds of people were splashing though the ankle-deep water gushing from broken mains and sprinklers, past the blown-out windows of the stores that sold clothing and books and breath fresheners.

She felt as if she were watching herself run, through a world half real and half Hollywood, a world that she remembered but had never seen, the kind of world she would inhabit in a dream.

Keep moving . . . Keep moving . . . Keep moving.

Toward the light. Toward the escalator. Toward Bugs Bunny, six feet tall, standing there in front of the Warner Brothers store. Bugs . . . fucking . . . Bunny.

She came up into the bright sunlight of Church Street and saw a line of ambulances along the back of the St. Paul's fence. The air itself seemed to be screaming. A dozen sirens . . . two dozen . . . a hundred . . . she couldn't tell. What did it matter?

She tried not to look down. There were puddles of blood on the street, and papers, some of them burning, and airplane parts, and shoes. Empty? Most . . . but not all.

An EMT came up to her and said, "Lady, you need help?"

She just shook her head and kept going. She just had to keep going.

The paramedic grabbed her by the arm. "But, lady, your face. You need help."

She brought her hand to her mouth and realized that she was missing two teeth. Something had hit her a blow of such surgical perfection that it had knocked out her two front teeth. Nothing else.

"Come on," he said. "Let's clean you up, anyway."

She shook her head again. She didn't know what she should do or who she should see—her lawyer, a cop, the FBI, but she couldn't give herself up yet, and if the Russians were watching . . .

The young EMT pushed her toward the ambulance.

She said, "Listen, I don't need help. I saw people up there who were burned, broken arms, broken legs. Help them."

That was when a woman screamed, "Oh, my God!" But not just one "Oh, my God!" A rising crescendo of "Oh, my-God-oh-my-God-oh-my-God-oh-my God!"

And at the same time a man screamed, "Holy shit!" But not just one "Holy shit!" A rising crescendo of "Holy-shit-holy-shit-holy-shit-holy-shit!"

And the screaming air filled now from every direction with human screams, male and female, and something far worse, a thundering roaring, as if the sky were splitting open.

And it was.

She saw it and screamed, too. "Oh, my God!"

The paramedic said, "Holy shit!" and he tried to push her into the ambulance, but she was already running for a place that always protected her. She was running through the gate and into St. Paul's graveyard.

She tripped and fell next to one of the crypts. Then she looked up again.

The building was falling and falling and falling from so far above her that steel was floating and glass was fluttering and aluminum was taking wing, almost as if it were all being blown into the air by the force of the downfalling storm.

The tower truly did create its own climate.

And it sent out a cloud that pulsed down and pulsed out and—

It all happened in ten seconds. No time to run from the little graveyard. Just time to roll over and put her face against the grass and press herself against the little six-inch shelf of crypt that rose from the soil . . .

And the cloud was upon her, bringing a splattering rain of concrete pebbles and tiny shards of glass.

She pulled that Hermès scarf from her neck and wrapped it over her face and hoped that she could keep breathing.

And while the screaming of people and the wailing of sirens went muffled in the cloud, she could hear all around her the sounds of steel splitting, glass breaking, metal smashing, great solid masses of concrete shattering, and huge splinters of debris tearing through the trees, while the roaring, thundering, rumbling went on and on and on, while the compressing mass of hundreds of thousands of tons of poured concrete, welded steel, mortared blocks, bolted aluminum, skim-coated Sheetrock and ramset doorbucks, all collided with the escaping energy of all the people who had done all the work to put them all in place, like two columns of air colliding in the atmosphere to create a great storm.

The cloud billowed around her and blinded her and almost choked her, and the concrete snow fell and fell. And she coughed and prayed and coughed some more.

She did not know how long she lay there, with her face pressed against the side of the raised crypt and a small patch of green grass below her. It might have been five minutes, maybe ten.

By then, the noise of sirens and car horns had sharpened again, and she could see shafts of sunlight and patches of blue sky.

She coughed again and knew that she was still alive. Then she stood and looked around.

First she looked at the ground in the little graveyard, now covered in three or four inches of pulverized building and larger debris and paper.

Then she widened her gaze and looked up. St. Paul's still stood, its roof covered in the same concrete snow. And its spire still pierced the noxious sky.

Then she turned and looked back across Church Street, at the row of ambulances covered in dust, at a shattered car, at the shattered building beyond it, then up at the tower still standing and gushing flame and pouring smoke, then over at the space where the other tower had been, where now there was nothing but a column of dust.

And she looked into the air itself, into the cloud hanging low and spreading ever farther, uptown and down and out over the rivers, carrying with it the souls of thousands of people who were now like those in the ancient earth around her, people who had lived their quiet lives and their terrible crises and had gone to God. But they were not sleeping in a small graveyard. They were rising into the air and mixing their elemental selves with the essence of the city itself.

As she turned, she stumbled on the crypt that had been her only protection. She bent down, brushed the surface, and read the names of the Lawrence family—John, Harriet, and their daughter Sally.

Then she read the inscription: The Lord seeth all and loveth all.

Maybe He did, she thought. Maybe He still did.

And she started walking across the graveyard and out to Broadway.

She noticed that street lamps had gone on in the concrete gloom and police cars had put on their headlights.

She started walking north with scores of others, north through a cloud as thick as Long Island fog, north away from this hell.

Soon her cross-trainers, soaked when she ran over the flooding concourse, were caked with concrete mud from the snowfall of pulverized building that was now accumulating on Lower Manhattan.

At the corner of Chambers Street, she stopped to scrape it from her soles.

A man stood at a big stainless-steel lunch cart. He and the cart were covered in dust. He could have been made of plaster, except for his eyes. He said, "Water, lady? You need water." And he held out a bottle.

She took it, rinsed her mouth, spat. Then she took a long drink. It revived her. It didn't make her feel better. What could? But it refreshed dehydrated cells that were part of the simple physical system that knew nothing but its own chemistry. So the water gave her the strength to keep walking. She reached into her pocket for a few coins.

He put up his hand. "No. No paying today."

"Thanks," she said.

"Just do me favor," he said.

"What?"

"Never forget and never forgive."

She began walking, then turned. "You sound Russian. Are you Russian?"

"No more. American now. And this"—he brushed the dust off the roof of his cart—"this is nothing. And that"—he pointed at the remaining tower—"that is a wound. It will become a scar. But this is America, lady. This is New York. No quitting in us."

"Right." And she walked on through the gray landscape, with all the other gray people. She did not know where she was going.

She had reached Canal Street by the time the second building fell.

People screamed and cried again, to the sacred and the profane, to holy God and holy shit, to the highest aspiration and to the lowest leavings.

Jennifer Wilson did not turn around.

iii.

A week later, the woman who now called herself Sally Lawrence looked at a picture of Jennifer Wilson.

It was attached to the fence outside St. Paul's Chapel, along with thousands of other pictures of people who had not come home, thousands of souls who had given their lives for no other reason but that they went to work and did their jobs. That alone made them American heroes. And so it was right that candles burned like votaries before those images, so lovingly printed on posters and taped to the fence of the chapel that had seen so much of the New York parade.

The wound was raw. The city seemed stunned, still in shock. The mountain of rubble now known as Ground Zero sent smoldering metal smoking into the sky and the stink of it settled everywhere downwind. But that coffee man was right. The wound would heal. It would scar. New Yorkers would rebuild. They would never quit.

Sally Lawrence had already decided that she would never quit. But she would change. She *had* changed. She had been reborn in that little graveyard.

She pulled a Mets hat low and looked closer at Jennifer Wilson.

Jennifer's picture showed her smiling on the Battery on a bright March day with her brown hair blowing in the wind.

Sally had short hair. But she remembered that day, her first Sunday afternoon with Joshua, the day when she began to think that he might be "the one."

Jennifer had a toothy smile.

Sally did not, but the space was healing. The gums were no longer tender. Some things healed more quickly than others.

Beneath the picture were the words: "If you see this woman, call Attorney Janet Sharp. . . ."

Her attorney. So she had been right about Joshua after all. He wasn't "the one." He hadn't even bothered to use his own phone number on the poster. Maybe he knew the truth, that once Jennifer Wilson was officially declared dead, Joshua would not get a cent.

And Jennifer Wilson *was* dead. She had been consumed in the collapse of the South Tower. She would not go to jail for insider trading and see her life's work wiped out by legal fees, restitution, and fines. She would not be shot down by the henchmen of an avenging Russian investor. But she would never be seen again.

A good forensic accountant would figure out what portion of her Intermetro holdings she had dumped with inside information. Her executor, accountant Carl Evers, would insist that her lawyer make a quick deal with the government because Evers would not allow the estate to burn thousands of dollars in a losing battle. That was one reason that she was better off dead.

Evers would then liquidate everything. He would sell the condos on Abingdon Square, in Stowe, Vermont, and on Useppa Island in Florida. He would empty the stock portfolio and pay the debts.

And what remained would do some good. She had left a quarter of her estate to the Episcopal Charities of New York. She had been raised Episcopal, had been a congregant at St. George's, and had been reborn in the graveyard of an Episcopal church. She had left a quarter to legal aid of New York. She had left 20 percent to her New York friends, four women—a lawyer, a housewife, a parishioner at St.George's, and a financial reporter named Kathy Flynn, whom she had met one day in a shoe store. She would miss them. They would mourn her. But it was better this way.

She had left 10 percent to her cousins in California. She had not seen them in twenty years, but blood was blood.

And she had left 20 percent to the New York Animal Rescue League.

She had performed an animal rescue of her own that morning. It had been her first foray out of the flat that she had rented on Grand Street in the Lower East Side, a lonely brick tenement surrounded by parking lots a block from the Williamsburg Bridge. Rent in cash. No questions asked.

In a Salvation Army shelter, she had gotten clean clothes, including a single-breasted London Fog raincoat and the Mets hat. She had found a shopping cart parked against a chain-link fence just up the block. So she had put on the raincoat and hat and thrown a few paper bags into the cart, and she had started uptown. And she had realized as she went, that she was becoming a character, and to the people who passed, that character was invisible.

She had reached Madison Square Park at around quarter to eleven . . .

Fifteen minutes later, right on schedule, along came Marie MacCallan with three leashes in each hand, the big dogs on the right, the little dogs on the left.

Jennifer had paid Marie two months in advance, so she was still walking Georgie the terrier. But for some people, dog-sitting was a passion. For others, it was just a day job. Miss MacCallan told anyone who would listen that she was really an actress. So she put the dogs into the pen with a few others, sat on the park bench near the gate, and took out a copy of *Happy Days* by Samuel Beckett.

A little young to be playing Winnie, thought Sally.

But the girl's inattention made it much easier for Sally to step inside the gate, pretend to be enjoying all the frisking dogs, crouch slowly, and whisper, "Georgie."

The little dog looked up from inspecting the urine of a bigger dog.

Sally glanced at Marie—still reading—and said it again. "Georgie."

She was sure that the little guy smiled, because dogs could smile. She believed that. Then he ran to her and jumped onto her lap.

The other two people inside the pen, a man and a woman, were conducting the oldest ritual of the urban doggy park: they were hitting on each other. So they were paying Sally even less attention than the dog-sitter was.

The raincoat had a huge inside pocket. She grabbed the dog, dropped him into it, and walked right past her twenty-something dog-sitter.

A block south, Georgie the terrier was riding in the shopping cart.

JENNIFER WILSON HAD also created another persona.

Her name was Erica Callow. She had a taste for

nice clothes, Chanel no. 5, and expensive shoes. Her hair was a blond wig. Her New Jersey driver's license was forged (thanks to the friend of a friend, who owed a friend a favor). Over a period of eighteen months, from the bursting of the high-tech bubble to 9/11, Erica had filled a safety deposit box at an East Side Chase Bank with stacks of hundreds, totaling a quarter million dollars.

The day after Sally rescued Georgie, Erica Callow visited the bank and took out $10,000 in a large purse. She figured that would get her through her first winter as another person . . . or people. Then she walked up Fifth Avenue to the Terence Cardinal Cook Health Care Center at 106th Street.

She chose midday visiting hours because it was likely to be quiet. With a bouquet in hand, she found her way to the room of Dr. Gary Smith. He had no other visitors, and the second bed was empty, so she didn't have to pretend that she had stumbled into the wrong room.

She set the flowers on the window sill. Her movement blocked the sun pouring in the west-facing windows. The old man's eyes fluttered open and he frowned, as if the warmth of the sun was his only comfort and she had taken it from him.

She was shocked at the sight of him. He had lost twenty pounds since she'd last seen him.

"Who . . . who are you?" he asked.

"I'm a friend. I had to come and tell you that your grandson . . . he was a wonderful man. And he died bravely." As she said it, she realized it was the truth.

"My grandson?"

"I worked with him." She spoke carefully and smiled with her mouth closed, so as not to reveal the missing teeth.

"Oh . . ." The old man rolled his head on the pillow and his eyes rolled, too. He was drugged, perhaps. Or just dying. Broken hip or maybe, like a lot of New Yorkers, broken heart. His eyes drifted into the distance, out over the trees in Central Park.

She reached down and took his hand.

He rolled his head toward her again. His eyebrows rose, then furrowed down. Was it morphine dancing in his brain, or did he feel something in her touch, or did he see something that she could not?

She held his hand in both of hers. The need to hold that hand a final time had gotten her moving on that terrible day. Dr. Gary, in a way, had saved her life.

She said, "Smitty wanted me to tell you that he loved you. And Jennifer Wilson wanted me to tell you that you were like a father to her."

"Jennifer." He said the word with no sense of recognition. Then he said it again. "Jennifer."

Then his eyes fluttered and closed. She stood there for a few minutes more, holding the hand, glancing occasionally at the hallway so that she was not discovered. Then she slipped her hand from his, leaned forward, kissed his forehead.

And from the bed she heard her name: "Jennifer."

Did he know? Or was it simply another reflex in a sequence firing for the last time?

He rolled his head again and said with sudden clarity, "Read the ledger."

"What?"

"The bond ledger. Two hundred bonds in one batch. J. P Morgan owned three of them. Where are the rest?"

She swallowed. She ran her tongue between the space in her teeth. She said, "I'm not sure what you're talking about, Dr. Smith." It pained her to stay in character, but she felt it was the best way.

He nodded as if to say, "Yes, you do." And his eyes fluttered. Then they popped open, and he looked straight at her. "Do something good for America." Then his eyes fluttered again as if he had used up the last energy in him.

She kissed him again, walked out, and walked south on Fifth Avenue.

SEVENTEEN

Thursday Afternoon

"I love this Google Earth," said Henry Baxter.

He and Evangeline hunched over the computer in the Marshall Room of the New York Society Library.

Evangeline ran her finger across the image, tracing a route: "We can go out the back and then into the little alley that leads to Madison Avenue, then over to Fifth."

The phone rang, and Miss Nolan looked at the caller ID. "It's the front desk."

Henry went to the phone and inclined his head to listen with her.

Miss Nolan said, "No, Miss Carrington left some time ago."

Henry gave Miss Nolan thumbs-up.

The person on the other end said something, and Henry shook his head again.

"No. There never was a black man up here," said Miss Nolan.

Henry gave her a big nod and another thumbs-up.

"He says that he wants to come up?" Miss Nolan looked at Henry.

Henry nodded again.

Evangeline looked at him and shrugged—what the . . . ?

Henry made a little calming gesture, like this was something good. Then he looked at Miss Nolan and gave a rotating motion with his hand—keep talking.

Miss Nolan said, "Does he have a subject that he's researching? The history of New York? Well, yes, we have a lot of pertinent information."

Henry walked his fingers along the palm of his hand, then pointed to himself and Evangeline.

Miss Nolan nodded. She was getting good at this. "Do me a favor and tell him to take the elevator on the second floor." Then Miss Nolan hung up.

"That's my girl," said Henry. "We need to give you a nickname after all that."

"Casey is good enough," said Evangeline. "Let's get out of here."

"I'm really sorry." Miss Nolan led them across the floor to the back stairs.

By the time they reached the lobby, the Russian had gone up. Henry told Evangeline to wait by the circulation desk, then he crossed the catalogue room—once the paneled receiving room of the old mansion—and he looked out onto the street.

An East Side lady, deep in her seventies and deeper in concentration over a card tray, looked up and said, "Young man, I don't care if one of your people is the president of the United States, this is a library. Please tread lightly."

Henry said, "Mama, I don't know what more surprisin' . . . that somebody callin' me young, or that one of my homeboys is the prez. But you just keep studyin'. Them equivalency tests is hard."

The woman huffed, and Henry stalked back to circulation. "They still at the corner. We need the back door."

The woman behind the desk didn't hesitate. Whatever was happening, she wanted it outside, and fast. So she led the way.

Out the back, a left turn, down an alley, and they were on Madison Avenue.

Evangeline stuck out a hand to hail a cab.

But Henry gave her a jerk of the head and started walking toward Seventy-ninth. "Let's have a look at the do-bads."

"Oh, Jesus, Henry—"

He raised his finger for quiet. "I told you, I can make myself invisible."

"Henry, you're six foot four, you must weigh two fifty."

"Two fifty-*five*. And when I'm carryin' this"—he opened his coat to reveal a .44 Magnum—"make it two sixty."

"Henry!" said Evangeline. "This is the Upper East Side. People don't flash guns on the Upper East Side."

But Henry was already moving.

The sun was high. The day was warm for May. So the black car was idling, probably running the air conditioner, in front of the Chase Bank on the corner.

"Well, I be damned," said Henry.

"What?"

"The Redhead's in the library. KGB is up the block watchin' the front door. Let's scare the shit out of the dude in the car."

"But Henry!"

In three long strides, he crossed the street and pulled open the door. Then he called to Evangeline to jump in the back.

"What the hell?" The passenger was Oscar Delancey. "Do you know who you're fuckin' with?"

"Do they know who *they* fuckin' with?" said Henry.

Evangeline watched KGB step out from under a tree and look toward them in total shock. His own car was hanging a U-turn in the middle of Seventy-ninth and shooting west toward the park.

Delancey looked back at Evangeline. "And you!

Are you crazy? I told you to get out of this the first night at Fraunces Tavern. What are you doin' with this . . . this . . ."

"You watch what you callin' me," said Henry. "None of them *racialized* epithets."

Delancey looked out the rear window. "They're jumping in a cab, they'll be on you in a minute."

"No, they ain't. The Redhead still upstairs, and KGB, I don't think he have the balls to come chasin' on his own," said Henry. "Now, what you got goin' on with the little gal in the library?"

"I've donated some nice New York material over the years. Good tax write-off, good business. So I asked her to call me if my nosey friend in the backseat came in."

Evangeline leaned over the front seat and got in Delancey's face. "You just figured you and your Russian pals could follow my research trail?"

"They're not my pals. But we're in business," said Delancey.

"I thought you worked for Owen T. Magee," she said.

"So did he. But I made a better deal."

"Magee will sue you," she said.

"Not from jail, he won't, and that may be where he ends up," answered Delancey. "That may be where we all end up, for chrissakes." He was usually cocky and cynical, one of the standard New York combos, like bacon and eggs or oysters and Rockefeller, but Evangeline thought that just then, Oscar Delancey seemed about as frightened as a man could without wetting his trousers. Was it just the effect of Henry Baxter? Or had the Russians already done the frightening?

As the car sped across Central Park, she said, "Why did you set me up on the Bowling Green?"

"I didn't. I was as curious as you were. But I didn't want to let on. Then I saw Joey Berra come into Fraunces Tavern and take a seat. He was watching me. He was following us. I didn't really know *who* he was, but I knew *what* he was, so I disappeared. I didn't even know that KGB was trailin' me, too. Dumb luck that I lost them both. So Joey followed you to the Bowling Green. Lucky thing for you he showed up when he did."

"Even luckier if I never went to your store that day."

"What you mean?" said Henry. "Then you never woulda met me."

"Listen," said Delancey to Evangeline, "I felt so bad about it, I came up to your apartment to warn you off, but that doorman, that ex-pug, he looked at a security cam behind his desk and said, 'Is that guy outside one of yours?' "

"And it was Boris-loves-Mary?" asked Evangeline.

"Yeah. So then the deskman calls Pete and gives him some kind of coded message, and, well, I just ran. Maybe I wasn't thinkin' straight. Maybe I ain't been thinkin' straight for a while—"

"The smell of big money make lots of fellers stop thinkin' straight," said Henry. "Like the smell of pussy. A man just lose all sense of reality when he get around the pussy or the Benjamins."

Traffic was light on the Seventy-ninth Street transverse road. So the limo sped through Central Park.

Delancey looked out toward the trees. "I thought I could lose the Russian. So I headed for the Ramble, and thanks to Pete—"

"You mean No-Pete?" said Henry.

"Whatever. Did he kill the Russian with the tattoo?"

Evangeline said, "Of course not."

"Well, he was chasin' me one minute, and the next he was dead. But his pals got to me that night, told me that I had to play their game or I was a dead man."

"Is that why you set us up last night in Times Square?" asked Evangeline.

"I . . . I . . ." Delancey looked out the window and just started to cry. "I'm sorry."

Evangeline put a hand on his shoulder. "It's all right, Oscar, it's—"

"Oscar, you no fuckin' help at all." Henry turned onto Central Park West and pulled into the first parking spot. Then he pulled the keys out of the ignition. Then he pulled the .44 Magnum out of his holster and pressed it against Delancey's temple.

Delancey squawked like a parrot and shrank from the gun.

Henry said, "I could blow your motherfuckin' brains out right now for settin' my friends up last night in Times Square. And if them Russians get in our way, the Redhead and KGB, I will. You got it? You got it, bookseller?"

Delancey nodded.

"Now, give me your cell phone."

Delancey did as he was told.

Henry opened the door. "Thanks for the ride. Let's go, Miss E Ticket."

As Evangeline got out, she said, "I'm sorry about your store."

"That was Antonov, punishing me and warning you. That's an awful nice store Pete has in Boston."

PETER AND KATHY Flynn got out of the cab at the Battery.

Girls with red hair usually had light complexions. But Kathy had gone pure white when she got the telephone call in front of the restaurant. And she had said little on the ride downtown, except that the caller claimed she was Jennifer Wilson, who had died on 9/11.

"I don't know why she wanted to meet us down here," said Kathy.

"If she is who you say she is, she might take some comfort in looking at that." Peter pointed to *The Sphere*, the bronze globe that now guarded the entrance to Battery Park.

It had once sat on the Grand Plaza of the World Trade Center. Somehow, it had survived the collapse of the towers. It had been dented and gashed through, but now it stood as a symbol of a city's resilience.

People were strolling, lounging, kissing, singing, making speeches, talking to themselves . . . doing all the usual things people did in a New York park. And everywhere, the human Statues of Liberty stood silently, their torches held aloft and the sweat beading on their foreheads. They spray-painted their skin the color of oxidized copper, put on long robes and gloves the same color, perched on home-made pedestals, and waited for the tourists to gawk. Then the statues would talk, "Take your picture with Lady Liberty?"

The New York hustle went on, even in the shadow of that sacred *Sphere*. And that was as it should be, thought Peter.

He and Kathy sat on one of the benches lining the walkways that led toward the ferries and Castle Clinton and the blue harbor beyond.

Peter sat close to her, but he did not feel any of the usual redheaded confidence radiating off of her. She was quiet, nervous.

Meeting a dead friend? Who wouldn't be nervous.

Peter knew that he should have been uptown by now. He had gotten almost nothing from Kathy that he could use to find the bonds, just a bit more dirt on the guys he'd gone into business with. But this Jennifer Wilson might offer answers to some big questions.

So Peter had come along. He also liked Kathy's company.

"Jennifer Wilson was about to become my first big story," said Kathy after a time. "She was house counsel for a high-tech firm. But she and all the corporate leadership were going down for insider trading. They built the thing on hot air and promises, like all the high-tech gang, and when the air got thin, they cooked the books with the oxygen that was left and got out before the shareholders. Osama bin Laden got them before the FBI could."

"Did you write the story?"

"Of course. It made some news because of the 9/11 angle, but nobody was saying, 'Oh, yeah, they got what was coming to them.' The real story was about the FBI guys who went to see them that day. They were in the Sky Lobby when the plane hit. Only one of them made it out. And he was finished. Survivor's guilt because his partner died."

As if on cue, a guy in a Yankees hat sat down next to Peter and said, "Does your girlfriend know you're spendin' time with gorgeous redheads?"

Peter looked at Joey Berra and said, "Why am I not surprised to see you?"

"How's it shakin', Boston?"

Kathy Flynn looked around Peter and said, "Hey, pal, beat it. We're waiting for someone. We don't want to scare her off."

"You already have," said Joey.

Kathy looked at him a bit longer and said, "Do I know you?"

He offered his hand. "Joey Berra. How ya doin'."

She took the hand, looked into the eyes, and said, "I *know* you."

Joey said, "I have a message from Jennifer Wilson. She decided not to blow her cover just yet. But she wants you to know that you were right."

"About what?"

"About the bag lady and Erica Callow. She did not appreciate it that you spewed those pictures all over the Internet—and Times Square—this morning."

Kathy said, "Why would she care about—wait a minute. You mean, Jennifer Wilson is . . ."

Joey Berra stood. "Can't stay, gotta run. Jennifer and I have a lot of angles to work before tomorrow."

"Jennifer and *you*?" said Peter. "The *bag lady* and you?"

"She ain't really a bag lady, Fallon, so don't call her that."

Peter sensed that Joey was getting a bit agitated. Maybe the New York cool-breeze bit was just an act, or a role he had once played very well and was now relearning. So he said, "Joey, I never laid eyes on her. I'm just goin' on what people say."

"Well, *people* don't know. But we got some work to do before tomorrow. I just wish all you jamokes from Boston and Brighton Beach would stay out of our way. We might have found that damn box by now."

Kathy said, "Jennifer Wilson is after Arsenault's bonds, too? The box of bonds?"

Joey gave her a long look, then he sat and said to Peter, "Remember what I told you the other day? When you asked me who I'm working for?"

Peter nodded.

"Tell Miss Dollar Diva, here."

Peter looked at Kathy. "He said he was working for the American people."

"Right," said Joey. "Those bonds don't belong to Arsenault. They belong to the American people."

Kathy shook her head and looked out at the water. "All of you people scrambling to find something you think is worth a fortune, and the Supreme Court may reject the suit altogether. Won't all of you feel pretty damn stupid if that happens?"

Joey jerked a thumb at Peter. "Boston might. He's only in it for the money. I'm bettin' he signed a deal with Arsenault and Magee. And for all his Harvard brains, he don't know that they'll cut him off at the knees, as soon as he finds what they're after."

Peter just listened. Sometimes, the best course was to let a talker talk. And Joey was a talker.

"As for the Russians, you got your dangerous Russians and your *more* dangerous Russians, all descendants of Andrei the Avenger, in one way or the other. So somebody is doin' America—and the FBI—a favor by takin' a few of them off the streets."

"Meaning you?" said Peter.

And Kathy snapped her fingers. "I remember now. You were the FBI man who went to arrest Jennifer Wilson and her boys in the World Trade Center."

"To interview, not to arrest," said Joey. "Me and my partner, Jimmy Johnson. When the first plane hit, Jimmy knew right away that it was Al Qaeda. He says, 'Joey, if they hit one tower, they'll try to hit the other, so we shouldn't go up.' He was right, but I was a hard-ass in those days."

"You had all kinds of troubles after that. Right?"

Joey looked off toward the water. "Divorce, drink, a discharge from the bureau. That's trouble. But the shrinks called it post-traumatic stress disorder, because up inside that building, up on seventy-eight, that was a fuckin' battlefield, a goddamn massacre."

The three of them were silent for a time . . . imagining . . . or remembering.

Then Kathy said, "You disappeared, didn't you?"

"Into a straw-covered Chianti bottle." Joey stood. "But now I have a purpose. Jennifer Wilson says that you should go to the meeting of the Paul Revere Foundation tomorrow. It's going to be a very big story."

"I won't believe her until I see her," said Kathy.

"I've convinced her to stay hidden a while longer." Joey looked down at Peter. "Till we know we can trust you guys."

"Why didn't you tell me all this from the beginning?" said Peter.

Joey looked around, as if to check that no one was watching. "I like the secrecy thing. And me and Jennifer, we're after this for more than money . . . not like you."

Peter stood. He was a head taller than Joey. He stepped close to him, and said, "You got me very wrong, Joey B."

"If you aren't in it for the money, then what?"

Kathy stood. "Peter is an idealist, Mr. Berra. Haven't you noticed?"

So Joey said, "Well, Mr. Boston idealist, let's join forces."

"And if I do?" said Peter.

"We share what we know. You tell us where you are, and I'll bring you an exact replica of what it is we're lookin' for. Tonight. Where are you stayin'?"

"Can't tell you," said Peter. "It's our safe house."

"Wrong answer." Joey turned and started to walk away. "You're safe with *me*. I already proved that on the Bowling Green and in Central Park and in the middle of Fourth Avenue."

Joey was right, thought Peter. "Wait a minute."

Joey waved his hand bye-bye. He had one more quality of the New York street. He could be way too volatile when he had been insulted.

"Hey, Joey Berra"—Kathy followed him along the path—"don't go yet."

Joey stopped and turned.

Kathy said, "Jennifer knows where I live. If she has proof of how far you've come, bring it to my apartment. Tonight."

"We'll see what Jennifer says." Joey took another look around, then headed for the subway. "And no cell phones. They can track the cells."

"The Russians can't track your cell phone calls, Joey," said Peter.

"No," said Joey. "But the FBI can."

They watched him go, then Kathy said to Peter, "I guess I have plenty to write about now. Share a cab back uptown? I'll drop you off wherever you're going."

He did not want to get into a cab with her again. She was way too enticing when the excitement of the chase colored her cheeks and lit her eyes. He said, "I'll take the subway."

"Don't want to reveal your safe house?"

"That's it."

She reached forward and took his hand. "You can tell me where it is."

"Then it wouldn't be a safe house."

"Peter, we're on the same side in this. And I may need a safe house, too."

"You can call if you get into trouble."

"What if it's too dangerous to call?"

She was right. There was a team coalescing here, a group of like-minded people gathering around the idea of finding the truth as well as the bonds, and Kathy was part of it. So her safety was important, too. So he told her. Then he added, "Just don't abuse the privilege."

And she stood a bit closer and kissed him on the lips.

Peter Fallon did not move a muscle.

She pulled away and said, "We would have made a great power couple."

"If you need safety, Evangeline and I are there."

She gave him a little pat on the chest and strode off, long legs swinging.

He did not look at her ass.

EVANGELINE AND HENRY had ridden back to Hell's Kitchen in a cab. Now they were walking south along Ninth Avenue.

"I can't believe it, Henry. We're trying *not* to attract attention, and you steal their goddamn car? What were you thinking?"

"I was thinkin' we might get somethin' out of the little dude in the front seat. I didn't think he'd start cryin'. Can't stand a dude cryin'."

"Now he'll describe you to the Russians, and they'll figure out where you live."

"Him? He's scared shitless. He'll say he saw a big black guy with a big gun. How many big black guys with big guns you figure we got in this town? And unlike myself, most of them have rap sheets. We fine."

"But I thought you said these Russians were—"

"Nastier than athlete's foot?"

"Nastier than nuclear fucking weapons!" she said.

"Now, E Ticket, watch your language. This here is no longer Hell's Kitchen. Folks call it Clinton, and it's gettin' to be a very uppity place."

She wasn't exactly sure why he was leading her down Forty-eighth Street, between Ninth and Tenth. Both sides of the street were lined with brownstones and tenement buildings. As on almost every cross street in Hell's Kitchen, they formed a wall on both sides, broken here and there by an alley or a driveway. But he slowed as they approached a breach.

"This is where the Rileys lived," said Henry. "I just wanted you to see it."

Evangeline read the sign: THE CLINTON COMMUNITY GARDEN.

"Four or five buildings, all came down in the late forties or early fifties. The rubble pile was still there in the seventies. Just a lot of bricks and shit, so the neighborhood turned it into a beautiful garden."

Where once there had been six-story buildings overflowing with people, fruit trees flowered. Where the tenement yards and outhouses had festered a hundred years before, neighborhood people were working garden plots, tending roses, taking the May sun.

"Maybe the box is buried under somebody's pansies," she said.

"Well, they might be old foundations down there under the topsoil. Maybe we could come back with a shovel."

Evangeline imagined the Riley brothers sitting on the stoop on a spring day before their father was beaten to death and their lives changed. Then she looked up higher. Most of the buildings did not rise above six stories, but out on Tenth there was a twelve-story building, and on top of it stood one of those famous New York water tanks.

"I wonder if Tim Riley's father helped to build that," she said.

"Hard to say, but I bet his son helped finance it."

PETER STRODE ALONG Fifty-first with his head down. He had come home—and it felt like home—via foot, taxi, foot, subway, taxi, taxi, foot. If someone had been following him, they would have thought he was drunk . . . or lost.

He had also bought a throwaway cell phone. He made a call, just to warn them he was coming up. And he walked right into a young black man heading in the other direction.

"Hey, watch where you're goin', man." He was wearing a New York Giants hoodie, jeans, and sneakers.

"Sorry."

"You goin' up to see Big Mama's Baby?"

Peter stopped. *Damn it.* He'd been made. Now what?

He turned slowly, right into a big smile. "Antoine? I thought I told you to stay in Boston."

"I had to see you guys in action with Uncle Henry. So I drove down. Parked in a lot on Eleventh Avenue, right across from Midtown Hardware."

"You scared the hell out of me." Peter patted him on the back. "But I'm glad to see you."

"I hear Uncle Henry already gave you nicknames."

"Don't ask."

Antoine said, "Aunt Sonia sent me out to get a few things at the groceria. I'll be right back."

"Do you have anything new?"

"The Morgan Library just has three bonds. But the E Ticket has some good notes."

Peter let himself in with the key that Henry had given him.

Evangeline was waiting, and as he stepped into the flat, he flashed on another life, one that might have been lived there a hundred years before: He had just come from Deegan's Saloon, and his long-suffering wife was waiting with a rolling pin. That was how Evangeline looked at him when he walked in.

"What?" he said.

"Two hours. We said *two* hours. Then we'd meet back here. You've been with her all afternoon. It's six o'clock now."

He shrugged. "Time flies."

She gave him a long look, then she stalked over and sat at Henry's computer.

"What did you find?" he asked.

"'Rainwater. O'Day. X marks the spiffle.'"

"What?"

"I don't know what it means, but—"

She leaned back in the chair and threw up her hands. "This is pointless, Peter. I'm combing through old notebooks, and you're running around with a girl I decided not to trust a long time ago, and—"

He just said, "The bag lady is after the bonds, too." And he told her what he had learned with the help of Kathy Flynn, about Arsenault, Wedge, Joey Berra, and the woman whose real name was Jennifer Wilson.

When he finished, Evangeline chewed her cheek, drummed her fingers, and decided not to be mad after all. "That's good stuff."

Then they went over the notes she had taken from Tim Riley's narrative.

They liked the father's description of the smoke that must have hung over the city—and still did—day and night: "the great cloud of commerce that rains money like water on the city of New York."

Evangeline said that the father had once built water tanks and was known as "the best tank-bottom man in New York." Then he started his own demolition business, selling wood and other materials to a guy named O'Day, who made the tanks.

Then she read Tim's explanation to his son of why he had become a banker: "My father used to tell me that the clouds bring water that rains on the good and the bad alike. And water makes things grow. It washes away dirt and sins, too, in baptism. And he told me that money was like water, except it didn't wash sins away. It made it easier to live on the right path, since you don't always have to be scheming."

Peter looked out at the church. "Good Catholics. Plenty of cleansing water imagery."

"Yeah, but money doesn't cleanse original sin. It *is* original sin."

"Only if you don't have it," said Peter.

Evangeline said, "Tim's father would have agreed."

She flipped a page. "I love this part: 'Without water, there's no life. Without money, there's no America . . . or no New York anyway.' Tim Riley tells his son that he decided right then that he would handle money."

"A Catholic and a capitalist," said Peter, "even though Christ was a socialist."

A REAL FAMILY dinner. That's what Henry called supper that night.

His wife Sonia, a tiny little Filipina woman with a big voice and a mountain of energy, cooked two roast chickens, and they all sat at the dining table, said a grace in which Henry thanked the Lord for his smart nephew, Antoine, and for the Boston Fallons, "who helped my little brother when he moved north to that strange land."

Just as they began to eat, the buzzer sounded.

Henry looked at Sonia. "You expectin' anybody?"

She shook her head.

Henry gestured for Antoine to go over and look down into the street.

"I don't see anything, but the trees are in the way—"

The buzzer snapped again.

Henry went over to the intercom and put on his nastiest voice: "Who is it?"

"It's Joey Berra."

Henry looked at Peter. "Joey Berra?"

"Let me in," said Joey on the speaker. "I got something for you."

Henry said to Peter, "You good with a shotgun?"

"I am," said Evangeline.

Sonia blessed herself.

Henry pointed to the closet.

Peter pulled out the gun and flipped it to Evangeline. It was a pump action. She chambered a round.

"*Madre de Dios,*" said Sonia.

"Don't worry, Aunt Sonia," said Antoine. "It'll be all right."

Sonia said, "I'm not worried. My chicken get cold."

Henry pulled his .44 and stepped into the hallway.

Footfalls down. Footfalls up.

A moment later, Joey Berra stepped into the apartment, looked around, and took off his Yankees hat. His hairline was receding and he had a bald spot on the back of his head. He was clutching a paper bag.

Henry came in right behind him, closed the door, locked it, bolted it, chained it. Then he put the Magnum to Joey's head. "How did you find us?"

"The address was in Kathy Flynn's purse."

Evangeline looked at Peter. "You told her where we were? Are you crazy?"

But before Peter could stumble through an answer, Joey B. said, "She's dead."

"Jesus," said Peter. "Dead? How?"

"Killed in her apartment."

"Russkies?" said Henry.

"Whoever didn't want her writing a big piece about Avid Investment Strategies," said Peter.

"What was you doin' in her apartment?" said Henry.

"Jennifer and me, we went to show her the other box, like she asked us to. But Jennifer got spooked when we found Kathy. So I took her home."

Then Joey opened his paper bag and took out a mahogany box and put in on the table next to the roast chicken. "This is what you're looking for. Another one, just like this. Erica stole this for us, right out of the New-York Historical Society."

EIGHTEEN

September 2008

Sally and Erica had lived so long in the same skin that they really thought they were two people, very different people who supported each other like sisters.

Sally Lawrence always wore the old Mets hat and a dirty raincoat, pushed the little dog around town in a shopping cart, rifled trash bins, ate in food kitchens, read newspapers left on park benches, outfitted herself at the Salvation Army, and went home every night to that lonely tenement.

But once a month, Erica Callow emerged with

her groomed and ribboned little dog, walked up to Delancey Street, and hailed a cab. She usually wore a pantsuit and flats, because she still had good legs and didn't want to attract attention to them.

She would stop at a midtown Starbucks for a grande something-or-other and lounge on a sofa with the dog on her lap and read the *Wall Street Journal*. Then she would walk on to the Chase Bank branch on Seventy-ninth, where she had her safety deposit box, and take out the cash that she needed. Then she would parade down Madison Avenue with her dog on a leash, just like any East Side lady who lunched. And when she sat at the banquette in some little restaurant to enjoy a beef bourguignon and a glass of wine, she might catch a glimpse of herself in a mirror. And she would think, *not bad*.

Sally had gotten free dentures at a dental school, so that Erica could have front teeth. Sally had also stolen a couple of wigs, one with dirty dreads for herself, and for Erica, a bobbed blond wig that made her look like Eva Marie Saint in *North by Northwest*, which made Erica think of train trips, so every few months, she took one.

While Sally never left the city, Erica loved to travel, usually by Amtrak, sometimes by bus, always in cash. She had been as far south as Key West, as far north as Bar Harbor. She never stayed in hotels. At bed-and-breakfasts, they didn't question you if you paid in cash. A lot of them preferred it.

And Sally approved of Erica's wanderings, even though they took a bite out of the budget. Travel was good for the soul and for the perspective, too.

It always helped Erica to see New York through Sally's eyes because Sally knew that living in New York as a bag lady was better than paying cash and wandering anywhere else.

And that was not the only thing that Sally and Erica agreed on. They both believed that they had been allowed to live for a purpose. Sally believed what she had read on the top of that crypt: The Lord seeth all and loveth all. Erica tried to fulfill the charge of an old man on his deathbed the week after 9/11: celebrate your survival by doing something good for America.

So Erica had gone to the New-York Historical Society and tracked down the ancient bond ledger. And sure enough, there was a cache of bonds unaccounted for, numbers 2510 to 2709, sold to a woman named Loretta Rogers in 1780.

And what did it matter? Jennifer Wilson had led the last fight to cash the bonds, and she had failed. Why waste any more energy on that?

So Sally and Erica found other ways to make America and New York better places to live. Sally picked up litter in the street and collected bread bags that she gave to dog walkers who looked as if they might leave their droppings on the sidewalk. Erica volunteered once a month in the soup kitchen where Sally got her meals.

Then, in September of 2008, the shit hit the fan. That's how Sally put it.

Erica thought about a decade of profligacy, from the high-tech bubble to the repeal of Glass-Steagall to the Bush tax cut to low interest rates after 9/11, which inflated the real estate bubble and re-inflated American wallets, to the fourteen-billion-dollar-a-month war that we put on a credit card, to the mess at Fannie Mae and Freddie Mac, to the relentless, reflexive, reactionary greed of big banks and small borrowers and every operator of every size in between, and now we were paying for all of it.

But Erica thought Sally said it better: "The shit hit the fan, and a lot of people got splattered."

Lehman Brothers failed. Credit froze. The stock market plunged. The country went into panic mode. Then came the seven-hundred-billion-dollar stimulus package.

Sally read all about it in papers she picked from trash bins. She read it aloud to Georgie at the wobbly table in her little kitchen overlooking a parking lot with orange lighting. She read about it all winter.

By March, the stock market had lost half of its 2007 value. It had not been like 1987, a precipitous crash and quick recovery. It had been a slow, steady, disastrous withdrawal from everything. Even stockbrokers were calling clients and asking for permission to sell out.

"We're damn near capitulation," Sally told Georgie one cold spring night.

The dog cocked his head.

"That's when the no-balls nervous nellies give up . . . when they decide things'll never be good again. No rebound, no reward, no light at the end of the tunnel. But GE at five dollars a share? I tell you, boy, Jennifer Wilson would back up the truck."

Then she came across an item that caused her to shout, "Holy Christ!"

The dog looked at her again. *What's wrong, Mom?*

She held the paper closer to the bare bulb that lit the kitchen: "'Oscar Delancey, one of the last rare bookmen on Book Row, has sold two 1780 New Emission Bonds to'—you won't believe this—'Austin Arsenault of Avid Investment Strategies, founder of the Paul Revere Foundation.

"'The bonds, which Mr. Delancey bought from a New Jersey fireman named Tom Riley, had been found in an envelope among some old family photographs. Little else is known of their provenance, according to Mr. Delancey, except that the bonds, numbers 2513 and 2514, follow in sequence from three that Timothy Riley, a collateral ancestor, sold to J. P. Morgan. Those three are now at the Morgan Library.

"'Mr. Arsenault, a scripophilist and antideficit crusader, has determined to redeem the bonds. He says, "When our country is confronting the meaning of its economic philosophy, it is well to remember Alexander Hamilton. He said that these bonds, like all our debts, are debts of honor. With compound interest,a hundred dollars in these bonds is now worth over seven million. So redeeming them will demonstrate for one and all the consequences of kicking our financial responsibilities down the road."

"'Attorney Magee added, "We will take this all the way to the Supreme Court, because no matter what happens along the way, this court will hear the case."' "

The dog got bored and curled up into a ball.

Sally skimmed the rest of the piece, which talked about Article Six of the Constitution. Then she leaned down to the dog. "You know what I say, Georgie?"

The dog cocked his head to the change in her voice.

"There's no honor among thieves. This is desperation, tryin' to cash these two bonds. I know, because we tried to cash them over twenty years ago."

The dog stood and wagged his tail.

Sally raised a finger. "Arsenault is in some kind of trouble. These bonds are a smokescreen. Knockin' him over would be good for America and good for gettin' rid of what still sticks in my craw whenever I think of that bastard."

SHE DID NOT sleep well that night, but not because of the groans of the heroin addict upstairs or the scuttlings of the roaches and mice in the kitchen. Jennifer Wilson, the real brains behind Sally and Erica, the one who always asserted herself in the dark, was hatching a plan. She was even thinking that she might have a new chapter for that autobiography she knew now she would never write.

The next morning, Sally made coffee. She always allowed herself that luxury. Then she microwaved her oatmeal. The microwave she had found in a trash barrel. The oatmeal was cheap. Then she and Georgie headed uptown with their shopping cart.

It was one of those March mornings when the sun was high and bright but the north wind cut like a scythe. Sally was glad she had decided to wear the dreadlock wig. And she hung a blanket over the front of the cart to protect the dog.

"Smitty was right, Georgie. Arsenault dimed us out. He was mad that we cut him out on the Intermetro start-up in '92, even though we told him to load up on the stock on IPO day. He made his clients fifteen mil before lunch and got himself a nice brokerage arrangement with the Antonov import-export firm. So he did just fine."

The dog jumped up on the edge of the carriage and barked.

"Why would he blow the whistle on Intermetro if he owned so much stock? Because the stock was tankin'. People won't forgive a stupid broker, but they'll forgive one who buys a stock, then discovers that the company was cookin' the books. And let's face it, Georgie, we were cookin' with gas."

They had rattled up to Houston and were turning onto the Bowery, right into that cold wind. A pair of passing teenagers gave her a sidelong glance. One of them giggled.

"Ah, what are you lookin' at? Ain't you ever seen anyone talk to their dog before?" Then Sally said to the dog, "You gotta stick up for yourself out here, Georgie."

The dog twitched around in the cart, hopped up and looked where they were going, then turned around to look at her again.

"Now, where was I? Oh, the shootings . . . some people drop dimes, and others are do-it-yourselfers.

They didn't call Andrei Antonov 'the Avenger' for nothing."

At the bookstore, she parked the shopping cart where she could see it through the window, then she peered in at Delancey, then she pushed open the door. She smelled coffee. She heard Brahms. A little bell rang.

Oscar Delancey turned from his computer screen and gave her a look.

Sally knew all the looks . . . the right-through-you look she usually got on the sidewalk . . . the sidelong glance-and-giggle those teenagers had given her . . . and the look that came from someone *forced* to look, the kind Delancey gave her: eyes traveling head to foot, a study of the orange Converse All-Stars, an annoyed, "Can I help you?"

Sally smiled toothlessly. She knew the smile fixed in people's minds. Afterward, it was all they remembered of her. "Brrr . . . cold out there. . . . Say, I been readin' about your store, so I thought I'd come by."

"What have you been reading?"

"About the New Emission Bonds. I sure would like to get my hands on a little piece of paper that's gonna be worth a fortune. You got any more?"

"They're pretty rare," said Delancey.

She gave a loony hoot of a laugh, like Walter Brennan in some old Western movie. She had worked on it until it came naturally. "I ought to start lookin', then. If I ever find any, can I bring them to you?"

Delancey showed his stubby little teeth, a fake smile. "Sure. You got any ideas where to look?"

She gave another hoot. "Well, sir, I might. I just might."

She knew that Delancey was rolling that around in his head. The sign above his desk said, FREE APPRAISALS, IN-STORE OR ON-SITE. How many first editions of *For Whom the Bell Tolls* or *The Great Gatsby* had he found in the overstuffed apartments of batty old ladies whose children had moved them to nursing homes? He probably respected batty old ladies more than most.

So he didn't throw her out or talk down to her. He said, "I'd love to see anything you find. Old money, engravings, books. Bring them in, and I'll be square with you."

She was trying to be cynical, but she liked him for that, so she pulled off her fingerless gloves and offered her hand. "Can't find too many these days who's square."

He shook her hand and invited her to have a look around.

As she walked down the American history aisle, she noticed him take a squirt from a bottle of Purell. At least he shook her hand.

AFTER THAT, SHE went to Delancey's Rarities on the second Monday of every month and always brought something . . . a book she pulled from a trash bin, an 1894 newspaper she found under the linoleum in her bathroom, a worn set of the Harvard classics that she wheeled from the Salvation Army. Delancey actually gave her twenty bucks for that one.

Usually, she'd go upstairs to the used book area, sip some of Delancey's free coffee, listen to his classical music, and flip through the old *Life* magazines that he sold for twenty dollars apiece.

And sometimes, when she sat in the chair by the front window, she'd notice a guy standing across the street. He always wore a blue windbreaker and a Yankees cap. Sometimes he'd be there when she left. Sometimes not. But she fixed a little rearview mirror to her cart, so that she could watch behind her to make sure he wasn't following.

ii.

She kept up this routine all summer and fall. She got to know him. She schmoozed him. And she always had a comment or two when a headline appeared about the bonds:

TREASURY REJECTS ARSENAULT BONDS,
CITING SOVEREIGN IMMUNITY.
ARSENAULT ATTORNEYS PRESS STATE
SUPREME COURT
ON SOVEREIGN IMMUNITY ARGUMENT.
STATE SUPREME COURT REJECTS ARGUMENTS IN
BOND CASE.

Meanwhile, Erica was doing the uptown research. If you looked like Eva Marie Saint, people trusted you. If you looked like a bag lady, they didn't let you near the rare books, and they counted the pencils when you left the reading room.

So Erica went to the Morgan Library to inspect their three bonds and glean what she could about

Timothy Riley. Then, she went to the New York Public Library, sat down with the *Times* index, and tracked every reference to Timothy Riley. What she learned, Sally collected to use like bait with Delancey.

On her December visit to Rarities, she was carrying the *Times* story that had run a few weeks earlier: ***UNITED STATES SUPREME COURT HEARS ARGUMENTS IN NEW EMISSON CASE; TO DECIDE IN MAY.***

"This bond business sure is gettin' excitin', Mr. Delancey."

"Yeah, yeah."

"Say, you got any new *Life* magazines?"

"Sally, I want you to quit thumbin' through them. People like to buy them for birthday presents. You know, if you were born in 1960, you get one for your fiftieth birthday . . . it's a nice present. But if there's greasy bag lady fingerprints all over—"

"Understood." Sally started for the stairwell in the corner, then turned. "Say, those bonds you sold to Arsenault . . . did you know they're part of a single purchase of twenty thousand dollars? Sold to someone called Loretta Rogers?"

Delancey, who usually half-ignored her, raised his head slowly.

She had gotten to him. She even worried that she had revealed too much.

He walked over and stood close enough that she could see the thin line of perspiration under his comb-over. "Where did you get that bit of information?"

She heard something in his tone that made her grip the handle of the six-inch carving knife she carried in her pocket. "In the papers, I guess."

"You couldn't have," he said. "I never told any reporters. Do you think I want to start a treasure hunt? What do I look? Stupid?"

"No, Mr. Delancey. If I was drawin' a picture of a smart man, I'd draw you."

"So I'm gonna ask you again, Sally Lawrence from Zero-Zero-Zero Nowhere Street, New York. Where did you hear about the rest of those bonds? Tell me, or I might get mad."

Get mad? She hoped he didn't, because he'd end up with a six-inch blade in his belly, and she would lose her bridge to Arsenault and the bonds.

So she decided to create a half lie. "I done some research." Then she described Erica's journeys to the various libraries, only she made them her own. Then she said, "Why you so interested? Do you think these bonds are all together?"

He just stared at her.

"You do!" And she gave him one of her Walter Brennan hoots. "You think all these bonds are wrapped up in an elastic somewhere, don't you? I guess I'll keep lookin'." She turned and started up the stairs. She wanted to get out of there as fast as she could, because she was afraid he was going to come at her, or call someone who would. But she could not show fear. She had to keep to her routine.

"Sally," he said when she was halfway up the stairs. "You promised to show me anything you found. Remember that promise." He said it like a threat.

She didn't stay long after that. She flipped through a few musty old magazines, then she said it was getting cold and she didn't want to leave her little dog to freeze.

As she stepped outside, she froze herself . . . but not from the cold.

Someone was watching her from across Fourth Avenue. It was not the stocky man in the Yankees hat. She had grown used to seeing him. It was someone she had never forgotten. He wore a hooded sweatshirt and a leather jacket. And the hair peeking out from under the hood was red-orange. He had been there that day, the day she died.

She did not look a second time. She did not need to. She adjusted the rearview mirror on her cart and watched all the way home.

THAT NIGHT, THE weather turned rotten with rain and sleet.

Sally sat with a cup of tea in her little flat, and she shivered, and she remembered.

With the first winter storm, she always remembered the winter after she died. She remembered how hard it had been to see a future when the wind splattered rain and wet snowflakes against the single rattling pane of glass. She remembered looking around the little two-room flat and asking herself if this was all that life would ever hold for her.

Even now, she wondered what would have happened had she not decided to stay dead. Would she have gone to jail? Would she have become a target of the avenging Antonov family? Was she now? The one with red hair worked for them.

She warmed her hands on the cup and thanked

the Lord for Erica. Erica had not been one to sit still or stay down. She had shown Sally how to live again. But in two or three years, they would be out of money. What would they do then? Sally had learned plenty on the street, but she had always been able to retreat to her anonymous little flat. Rent in cash. No questions asked. Real life on the street would kill her. So would life without Erica. Or the redhead might get to her and—

Georgie heard it first. His head popped up and he looked toward the door.

"What, boy?" she whispered.

Then she heard a creak on the little landing, then—good Christ!—a knock.

The dog growled and scratched across the linoleum to the door.

She kicked off her shoes and tiptoed after the dog, picked him up, shushed him. Then she reached into the kitchen and grabbed the carving knife.

If the redhead was out there, come to finish the job he started on 9/11—

Then there was another knock and a low voice: "I mean you no harm." Then a minute of silence, then the rustling of paper and a large manila envelope appeared under her door. The voice said, "Take a look."

Sally put down the dog and opened the envelope. And there was Jennifer Wilson in a series of surveillance photos: walking out of her apartment, talking with John Smith, swiping her security card at a World Trade Center turnstile. And there was Sally Lawrence: going in and out of Delancey's. Finally, a side-by-side of Sally and Jennifer, with computer lines drawn, showing the similarities between the eyes, the noses, the chins.

The voice whispered, "I know who you were."

But who was *he*? He didn't sound Russian, at least.

"I was with you that day. You read my story in the papers. I just want to talk."

"With me? Are you the FBI?"

"Not anymore. Besides, the statute of limitations on insider trading is five years."

Sally looked at the dog. *What do you think?* The dog looked at the door.

So she opened it but kept the chain in place. The dog growled and bared his teeth.

The man in the Yankees hat was standing there. "I'm former federal agent Joseph Berranova." He took off his hat, then he pulled out a dog biscuit and offered it through the space in the door.

The dog looked at her, and she said, "Okay." The dog snapped up the biscuit.

"What do you want?" she said over the chain.

"I think you know, but like I say, I mean you no harm."

"That's good, because I've had plenty of that harm shit. I don't need any more." And she decided to let him in.

That night, for the first time, another person sat with Sally and drank tea at her wobbly table.

He said that after 9/11, he left the agency with a pension as his life unraveled.

Then he had read the story of Arsenault and the bonds, and he remembered the woman named Jennifer Wilson, from the Intermetro case. She had tried to cash a similar set of bonds in 1987. And he started making connections. "So many of the same players as in 2001, back together, Arsenault, Magee, the ghost of Jennifer Wilson, the Antonov family."

"You knew about the Russians?"

"We knew there was dirty money behind Intermetro in '01. We were hoping to flip you and Smith, take down the Antonov syndicate."

"That explains a lot," she said, and she described the murders on that awful morning.

All Joey could say was, "As dangerous as we thought they were."

"But it wasn't me you wanted to flip. It was Jennifer Wilson. I was born on September 11, 2001. Jennifer died that day."

Joey sipped his tea. "I know what you mean."

After a moment, she touched his arm. "No one has said that to me in a long time. No one could."

The wind splattered sleet against the windows.

"You and I saw things. Terrible things." Joey shook his head. "Anyway, I started spiralin' back into how I ended up in that tower, and it led me to Arsenault—"

"He told the SEC about Intermetro, didn't he?"

Joey nodded. "And his name led to the bonds, so I decided to stake out Delancey's, just to see if any of the old principals from the '01 case showed up."

"And along came Frivolous Sal." She smiled her toothless smile and gave a hoot. "You're not here to arrest me, are you?"

"I'm here to see if we can work together."

"Doing what?"

"I don't know." Joey shrugged. "I just feel a pull. Don't you feel a pull?"

"Every day."

"I remember all the brave people, even the ones who were scared . . . even in the Sky Lobby. Nobody panicked, everybody tried to be orderly, movin' to the elevators, takin' directions. . . . People helped people that day, even after the plane hit and we were all in hell. . . . I was blown twenty feet. When I woke up, I thought you'd been vaporized. But I saw Johnson . . . cut in half."

"I remember a guy named Gomez." And she just shook her head. "He worked up there, a janitor or something. He saved me, then he went back."

Joey gave the dog another biscuit, watched him for a moment, then said, "Somebody helped me find stairwell A. And there were people in the lobby and on the concourse, showin' us how to get out. Some of them didn't make it, either."

Another splatter of sleet hit the windows.

"And do you remember the spirit in the city for a while after that?"

"Yeah. People were generous . . . friendly . . . the way people ought to be."

Joey poured more tea. "Then we just got right back to bein' who we are . . . a bunch of what's-in-it-for-me backstabbers. Like all the bankers and brokers and greedy bastards in '08, makin' their thirty and forty million, while the whole economy was goin' up the chimney and the government was scramblin' to stop a depression. Do you think any of *them* would have helped you in that tower? No way. And guys like Arsenault are the worst, hidin' their greed—and maybe their failure—under an umbrella of patriotism. Make you sicker than a dog eatin' rats, seein' him cashin' those two bonds. He'll cash 'em, take the fourteen million, and say he's doin' it all for America."

"It's not fourteen million," she said. "There's a whole stash of bonds. Sold to someone named Loretta Rogers. Worth twenty grand in 1780. Compound the interest, it comes to one-point-four billion."

"Jesus." Joey Berra sat back. "He'd bankrupt the country if he could."

"One-point-four wouldn't bankrupt a county."

"No, but it would *save* a bankrupt company, and still look like good PR." Joey cracked his big knuckles. "Arsenault talks about these bonds bein' a symbol. But he's a symbol of everything that's wrong with us."

And that night, two people whose lives had been shattered on 9/11 joined forces.

Sally slept very well, because at last, she had a friend who could talk back.

iii.

Joey told her to stay away from Delancey's, because he had seen Ivankov the Redhead watching the store.

Instead they agreed to meet a week later in Katz's deli at three o'clock.

Sally got there early. She ordered coffee. She didn't have money for more.

Ten minutes to three: no Joey. Three o'clock: no Joey. Ten past three: no Joey.

She hated herself for getting nervous when it stretched to fourteen past. She hated herself for trusting someone. When the clock on the wall reached three fifteen, she took a last deep breath of all the aromas of the deli, gathered her things, prepared to leave.

That was when Joey hurried in. "Sorry I'm late. I been tracking Avid's accountant."

"Carl Evers?" She didn't say how well she knew him.

"He's scared shitless. Did you order yet?"

She pointed to her cup.

"Coffee? You don't come to Katz's and just have coffee." Then he got it. He put a hand on her arm and gave her a little pat. "It's on me, Sal."

She grinned, revealing the missing teeth, then brought her hand to her mouth in embarrassment. She realized this was the first time she had covered her mouth like that since it happened. "In that case, I'll have the biggest hot pastrami I can get."

He ordered, then leaned across the table. "So . . . this Carl Evers, like I say, he's scared shitless. I came up behind him on the street."

"That would scare the shit out of anyone."

He grinned. "I just came up behind him and said, 'How come your bosses waited till the economic shit hit the fan before they started moving on this bond business?' He didn't have an answer. Didn't want to talk to me. Kept walking."

Joey's eyes lit up when the sandwich plates landed on the table. "Look at that, will ya? As big as your head."

Sally slathered hers with mustard and bit with

her canines. She ate as fast as Joey. Faster. And after she wiped the mustard from her mouth, he pointed to the corner of his, to let her know she'd missed a spot.

Only a friend would do something like that, she thought.

And after they ate, she told him about a trip to the *Times* archive. She didn't tell him that Erica did the work. She hadn't told anyone about Erica yet. She'd need to trust him more. But she told him about Tim's father, murdered at Woodward Manor.

Then she pulled out a tattered picture book she had bought for two dollars at Delancey's: *Lost New York,* a series of images of the city that had grown, flourished, and given way over three centuries, including a photo of the ancient house, as it had looked just before its demolition. An old oak tree extended its branches over the roof.

She said, "Tim Riley's father was a demolition man. He tore out walls and floors. He kept what he found. So I'm trackin' the name Woodward to see where it leads."

"Good. And I'll keep hauntin' that accountant."

BUT BEFORE ALL that, Erica insisted that they take a bus trip at Christmas. Sally didn't tell Joey, but Erica never stayed in New York at Christmas. It depressed her. So she traveled to Washington, then on to Key West for New Year's. But for the first time in almost a decade, she was thinking of someone in New York when the clock struck midnight at the southernmost point in America.

And for the first time in that long, a Christmas present was waiting when she got home, a box of chocolates from Joey.

Sally went down to the pay phone and called him to wish him happy New Year.

"It will be if we take down Arsenault," he said. "Or the Russians."

They agreed to have dinner on Saturday night in Little Italy.

But Sally stayed home. Erica Callow went instead and walked into the restaurant ten minutes late.

Joey glanced up from his Diet Coke, then he looked again when the blonde in the shiny red shoes came over and sat. "Excuse me, miss, but—"

"Sally sent me."

And Joey Berra, former FBI agent, who had lived through hell in the sky and descended into hell on the ground and was now emerging, sat back as if she'd smacked him and said, "Jennifer?"

She grinned like a movie star. "I'm Erica. Order me a glass of a nice Tuscan red."

It took Joey about ten minutes to get over his shock, while Erica explained that without her, Sally would go crazy. "Sally does the dirty work. I do the dress up."

Joey looked her over. "You dress up nice."

She waited until after they had enjoyed the first course of pasta carbonara, then she said, "I think I know where the bonds are."

Joey was lifting his glass to his lips. It stopped in midair.

Then she told him about her trips to the New-York Historical Society. Her search for Woodward had led to Abigail Woodward, mistress of the manor, wife of a loyalist who hanged himself. That led to the mahogany box Mrs. Woodward had donated to the Society.

Then Erica described its contents—the finial, some old clippings, a letter to a Gil Walker. She slipped out a notebook. "And get this, 'Our good deeds will come back to us many times over in the blessings of freedom, stored safe and sound in a mahogany box. I await your return to show you our investment in the future. Love, L. R.' "

He grinned. "You look beautiful."

She leaned across the table. "If Sally was here, she'd smack you in the chops."

"If Sally was here, I wouldn't want to kiss her."

She liked hearing that, but not yet. "This is it, Joey. L. R. Loretta Rogers! The bonds are in the box. They have to be."

"Did you see them?"

"No. I think it has a false bottom. *And* it's mahogany. We have to get it and open it."

He looked at her a long time and said, "Then we have to steal it."

She gave him her best dental school grin. "Right answer."

That night, Erica Callow stood in front of Joey Berra in the semidarkness of his little apartment in the East Village, and as Sinatra sang "Nice and Easy Does It," she raised her skirt, revealing long legs, smooth nylons, garters, and . . . Joey gasped.

* * *

THEY SPENT TWO months planning the theft of the box. Erica returned several times to the Historical Society, pretending she was a scholar writing about Fraunces Tavern. Meanwhile, Joey scoped out the security measures. Then he made a plan. And when the moment came, he made the phone call that distracted the librarian. It could not have gone more smoothly.

They brought the box back to his apartment. It took them fifteen minutes before they figured out that a sliding piece of molding on the outside actually released the false bottom.

"Here goes," said Joey.

They slid the bottom out. And—nothing. Empty.

"Shit," said Joey. "Back to the drawing board."

"At least we have a nice finial." Erica held up the little brass crown.

SPRING CAME, AND the world, or at least that part of it that cared, waited for the Supreme Court decision. Historical institutions filed amicus briefs. Scripophilists started making markets in the bonds again. Some bought on the bet that the court would uphold the Avid argument, some bet the other way and sold.

And Sally, who usually met Joey at Katz's to discuss strategy, told him that they had hit the wall. Erica, who usually appeared only when things were going well, never showed her face, her front teeth, or her blond wig. So there was no romance, because Erica handled that, too. Sally would never even go into Joey's apartment. Still, thought Sally, Joey treated her with a gentleness and respect that she hadn't known even when she was Jennifer. So she never stopped trusting him.

Joey told Sally that he missed Erica, and Sally couldn't blame him. But Erica had tracked the Timothy Riley story to a pile of notebooks in the New York Society Library. And when they could make no sense of what she found, there was less reason for Erica.

By late April, Austin Arsenault began appearing more often on television and on MarketSpin.com, which gave Sally an idea.

She gambled on revealing herself to someone she had known in her previous life. So she pushed her cart uptown to Columbus Circle, chained it to a lamppost, and carried little Georgie into the Time Warner Center, where she waited until Kathy Flynn stepped off the elevator.

Kathy gave her the right-through-you look and kept walking.

So Sally hefted the shopping bag holding Georgie and trundled after her and got behind her on the escalator.

"I got a scoop for ya!" Sally yelled. "I got a big scoop."

Kathy Flynn made a cell phone call and started talking.

When they got to the bottom, Sally came right up behind her and said, "Austin Arsenault is a fraud. What he says he's doin' for America he's doin' for no one but himself. Talk to him. Talk to his accountant."

Kathy looked at Sally as if she recognized something. The voice? The face? Sally and her little dog turned and disappeared into the crowd.

A FEW NIGHTS later, Sally and Joey stopped Carl Evers on his way home.

He lived on a quiet side street in the East Sixties. Trees, brownstones, wealth. Not bad for an accountant. He moved with a long-legged stride that seemed more frightened than confident, as if he were afraid that someone was following him.

When Sally saw him, she started along the sidewalk with her shopping cart.

Carl Evers gave her the sidelong glance, and she rammed the cart right into him.

"Watch it, you old bag."

Joey came up behind him. "Don't be callin' her an old bag, Evers."

"And you!" Evers's eyes widened. "Whoever you are, it's time I called the cops on you. This is harassment."

Sally said, "We hear that Kathy Flynn is investigatin' you and your company. Gettin' ready to do a big piece."

Evers looked from one face to the other. "Where did you hear that?"

"And even worse," said Joey, "there's a member of the Paul Revere Foundation called Antonov, whose father was known as the Avenger."

Evers's eyes widened even more. "What does that have to do with me?"

"We're thinking of telling him that we know a

few things about the guy who's been certifying that he audits Arsenault's financial statements."

Evers started walking. "You know nothing. You're two street bums. Beat it."

"Come on, Carl," said Sally Lawrence.

He stopped at the sound of the voice. "Do I know you?"

"No," said Joey. "But we know Arsenault was paying you twenty Gs a month. More than Madoff paid his know-nothing accountant. And the SEC might be slow, and understaffed, and they got burned when they missed Madoff. But if someone drops a dime on Avid, they'll be all over you like fleas on a rat. And the FBI comes right behind them."

Evers started up the steps to his brownstone.

"But the FBI would be better than Antonov's boys," said Sally.

Evers hesitated at the door.

"Cookin' the books, aren't you?" said Joey. "And Arsenault is bettin' on those bonds to cover some kind of huge shortfall. If he finds them and wins his case, he makes one-point-four bil. Is that enough to cover his losses?"

Evers walked down the stairs and over to Sally. "I *know* you."

And Sally Lawrence made a decision. She had trusted this man once. Maybe she should trust him now. So she said, "Yes, you do. And a friend of mine would like to thank you for seeing that her estate was distributed properly."

"A friend?" Evers knitted his brow.

"What's Arsenault doing, Evers?" said Joey. "Why does he want the bonds?"

"He's trying to save America. That's what he told me."

"And two and two equals five," said Joey.

Evers looked from one face to the other. "What do you want from me?"'

"I want you to show up once, Carl," said Sally. "Where we ask you to, and tell somebody the truth about Arsenault. Somebody you know."

"Why should I do that?"

"If I know you," said Sally, "I think it's what you want to do, because Jennifer Wilson once told me you were an honest man."

"Jennifer Wilson?"

And they stood for a moment in silence, in the shadows beneath the trees on a dark East Side street. Then Sally told him everything.

And it was as if he were thankful for the chance to tell someone the truth. They had been right. He had been helping Arsenault to hide his losses for years. "It didn't start as a Ponzi scheme. He's not a Madoff, but he's been in trouble since 2001, and in desperation since 2008. Without the bonds, he goes to jail. Me, too."

"He'll go to jail anyway," said Joey. "You, too. They'll get you for half a dozen counts like securities fraud, investment adviser fraud, obstructing tax law administration. But if you help us, we won't tell the SEC till Kathy Flynn runs her story. We'll give you time to disappear or make a deal. I can help you. I still know people in the bureau."

Sally said, "Jennifer knew you as an honest man. You can be that again."

Carl Evers agreed, but he said he would only

come to a meeting under his own terms, on turf he chose. He feared that he was being watched already, and he was terrified.

THEIR PLAN WAS to use the truth from Evers to turn Delancey to their side because they believed that Delancey knew more.

So the following Monday, Sally Lawrence finally went back to Delancey's. She doused herself in rum, even though she didn't drink. Then she tried to open the door. Locked.

Delancey buzzed her in and said, "I thought you were dead."

"It's been five months. How ya been?"

"So, so." Delancey wrinkled his nose. "You been drinkin'?"

"Sober for six months, drunk for six." She cocked her head. "The music? Usually you got some long-hairs goin' on. That's 'Lady Be Good.' Benny Goodman, right?"

"What do you have for me?" asked Delancey.

She sidled up to the counter and leaned against it, far more familiar than she had ever been before. "You're an expert in old money, right?"

"Yeah, yeah."

"Me, too. So, how about this, how about we team up, because I think I know where there's a shitload."

Just then, she heard a voice coming from the back of the store. Someone was there, talking on the phone, a woman, good looking, tall, blond, in a skirt. Sally had scoped out the place, watched it for half an hour before she made her move. And this broad had been in the back the whole time. Shit.

But Delancey was leaning across the counter. "What do you mean by 'shitload'?"

Sally shook her head. "Not here, no way. What I have I don't show you here. This is your turf. If we start talkin', we do it on my turf."

"I don't make house calls."

Sally pointed to the sign behind the desk. "Yes, you do." Then she heard that voice from the back.

The blonde was saying, "Peter," in a really cold, calm voice.

The bitch was listening, thought Sally, and telling some guy named Peter what was happening. Well, thought Sally, she could listen, but she couldn't see.

So Sally pulled a picture out of her pocket. "You see this? You know what this is? It's Woodward Manor on the old Bloomingdale Road."

The woman in the back said, "Peter, *screw you*."

Sally looked back there. Then she said to Delancey, "I think this is where your bonds are . . . or where they were a long time ago. But I ain't tellin' you more till you give something up."

"What do I look like? Stupid?" said Delancey. "I hear stuff like this all the time. Old broads are always comin' in, tellin' me about rooms papered in money."

"Well, Mr. Oscar Fuckin' Delancey"—Sally really drunked it up now—"I know things. So we should team up. But I ain't tellin' nothin' unless you come to the Bowling Green. Eleven o'clock tonight. That's my turf. That's where I do my talkin'."

"Yeah, yeah. In your wet-brained dreams."

"I'll show you somethin' to make your greedy old dick go stiff, and I'll introduce you to someone, too."

She could see that Delancey was intrigued now, but he was still playing the cynical New Yorker. She wished they could have made it easier, but the only time that they could get Carl Evers to agree to come out was late at night, in a public park, not too big, with a good view of the streets all around. He was, as Joey said, scared shitless.

"See ya tonight." Sally staggered out and slammed the door.

AT ELEVEN FIFTEEN, on the Bowling Green, Sally was glaring down at the woman from the bookstore. The plan was falling apart. "If I hadn't seen you in the store, I wouldn't be talkin' to you now. I came here to talk to Delancey. Why didn't he come?"

"Something made him nervous," said the blonde in the jacket and jeans.

Something was making Sally nervous, too. She couldn't see Joey. She didn't see Delancey. She wasn't sure if Evers would show up under any circumstance. And the construction overhang at One Broadway could hide all kinds of trouble. But stay in character. "I make a lot of people nervous. Do I make you nervous?"

The blonde chewed her lip. "This whole thing makes me nervous."

"Well, I do business on my turf, or I don't do business at all."

"I . . . I can understand that."

"You can understand? Well, isn't that fuckin' sweet of you." Sally found a Pepsi bottle in the barrel, checked for a bar code, then threw it into the cart and peered toward the south entrance, where she expected that Evers would show himself.

Then she pulled out the rum bottle and took a swallow and almost gagged. She hated rum. But it sure did smell. "We're all nervous these days."

The blonde—her name was Evangeline—turned down a drink.

So Sally gave a laugh, just to show the missing teeth. Then she launched into a diatribe on the economy, to fill time. Then she said, "So, are you Delancey's assistant or something?"

"More like a new partner," said Evangeline.

Sally guessed that was a lie. But she had brought the finial to get Delancey's attention, so she decided to show it to this Evangeline. She pulled it out of her pocket. "I'll bet you don't know about this."

Next thing she knew, she was dropping it into Evangeline's hand. "This is just the preview." And then she saw Carl Evers. So the game was on. No more screwing around. Evers could tell his story to this Evangeline, and she could tell Delancey. So Sally told Evangeline to look toward the south entrance.

Evers wore a gray suit and rimmed glasses. His stride was long but more frightened than confident as he flicked in and out of the pools of light cast by the street lamps.

"Slow down there, cowboy," said Sally. "You're supposed to be bringin' a message to Delancey."

"I don't see Delancey." The man never broke stride. "And I've been made."

"Made?"

"I told you this would happen. Even on the Bowling Green late at night." He was heading for the north entrance. "Two of them, under the canopy over by One Broadway."

Sally looked over her shoulder. "Fuck." Then she looked to her right, because Joey was over there someplace, she knew.

Evers began to run. And Georgie did what dogs do. He jumped out of the carriage and ran after the running man.

And now, two men were appearing from under that plywood and pipe canopy, moving toward the south entrance of the park.

Sally ran after Georgie, who was barking near the north entrance. Then she realized that Evangeline had the finial. The goddamn thing was worth ten grand. So she turned and ran after Evangeline, who had started running herself. "Come back, you silly bitch. Stop, thief!" And Christ, but where the hell was Joey?

Georgie was still barking madly out by the statue of the charging bull.

Sally looked again toward Evers, who was jumping into a cab. Then she looked toward that Evangeline, who was vaulting the fence.

Sally let out a scream and began to wave her hands. She didn't know what those two coming out of the shadows had in mind. But screaming might scare them off.

Evangeline was jumping into a cab and speeding away now.

And for all Sally's screaming and waving, the cars just kept moving on either side of the Bowling Green, because she was just another crazy bag lady making a scene.

Then Sally heard the squealing of brakes. Then Georgie yelped and stopped barking.

At the same moment, Joey was jumping the fence from Whitehall.

"Sorry." He called to her. "I was watchin' another guy. I picked him up in Fraunces, after I lost Delancey. They call him KGB."

Then Joey pulled a sawed-off shotgun from under his jacket and pointed it toward the two shadows who quickly retreated into the darkness.

Then Joey bent to pick something up by the fountain.

A moment later, Sally felt his shoulder against hers.

He said, "Are you all right?"

She heard the wail of a police siren. Someone had called 911.

"We have to go." Joey took her by the arm and turned her toward the north entrance.

And she saw a little rag of fur in the middle of the street. She said, "Oh, my God," and ran to it. When she realized the dog was dead, she let out a wail.

Somehow, Joey got her away before the police arrived. He dragged her to his black Taurus and drove off. He took several turns to make sure that no one was following him. Then he headed for his apartment.

* * *

HE MADE TWO phone calls as he drove. He used the cell phone that the blond woman had dropped to make a call and played the smart-ass with the guy who answered. Then he called Delancey and told him that there had been a problem, but that he would be on the Bowling Green the next morning if Delancey wanted a rerun.

Sally listened and said, "I won't be there. "

"Don't worry. Neither will Delancey. I just want to see if anyone else shows up. See whose side Delancey is really on."

"I don't care," she said. "I won't be there."

"That's okay. You should be reading that Riley notebook again. If we can't enlist Delancey, it's our only chance."

"I don't care. I won't be there." She looked up at his apartment.

"I know, I know," he said. "Sally doesn't come into men's apartments. That's Erica's thing, but just for tonight. I'll sleep on the sofa."

She was getting annoyed. He wasn't hearing what she was saying.

"I don't care," she said, "I won't be there. I don't care. I won't be there. I don't care. I don't fucking *care* anymore . . . so I won't be there."

Joey threw his arms around her. He took off her hat and wig, revealing her real hair, just a brush cut of brown and graying bristles. "Listen, baby. We started something. I'm not sure we know how to finish it, but Georgie would want us to—"

"Georgie was a fucking *dog*, for chrissakes. He didn't want us to do anything but play with him, talk to him. He didn't want anything but his life. Just his little fucking life. And now . . . I don't care anymore. I won't be there. I lost my best friend. My only friend and . . . shit."

And she started to cry. And she swore. And she cried. And she held her hand to her mouth and cried into it. Then she took a breath and said, "I haven't cried in almost ten years." And she cried for another hour.

NINETEEN

Thursday Night and Friday Morning

Just after nine, Joey Berra pushed back from Henry Baxter's dinner table. "So Jennifer hasn't been much help this week, and seein' Kathy Flynn like that, after losin' her little dog, it's really done a job. She doesn't know if she's Erica or Sally or someone else right now."

While they ate the roast chicken, Joey had told his story, from the day that the Intermetro case landed on his desk to the day he met Jennifer in the Sky Lobby to the death of Sally's dog.

Now the stolen mahogany box sat in the middle of the table, flanked by two chicken skeletons.

Peter looked at Evangeline. She wiped a tear. And little Sonia looked like she was sniffling, too.

Joey had explained that he found the Baxter safe house address in Kathy's purse. And the purse had been unopened, so whoever had killed her had wanted it to look like a hit rather than a robbery.

Henry had answered with one of his favorite aphorisms, "Better packin' heat than sorry." Then he had placed the .44 right next to his chair, alarmed the front door, and put his dog, Ripper the rottweiler, out to patrol the rear fire escape.

"I'm sorry that I dragged you down to the Bowling Green that morning," said Joey. "I used you as bait. I called Delancey, just to see who'd show up on the Bowling Green. And sure enough, there were players everywhere. The black guy was on Antonov's payroll, and he was watchin' the other two, who were workin' for the Redhead. That was when I decided Delancey had gone over or was gettin' pressured."

"So we were playing hide-and-seek with a killer on the subway," said Evangeline. She looked pasty. She had eaten very little. News of a second murder in two days had sent her to the bathroom to throw up. Now she was sipping ginger ale.

Joey said, "I don't think they knew what to make of you. So they were just watchin' you. I think Delancey went to your apartment and tried to warn you off. He was doin' you a favor *and* gettin' you out of the way."

"He knew that his competition was in town," said Antoine.

"Don't get cocky," said Uncle Henry.

Peter said, "I thought Delancey worked for Arsenault."

"Worked for him," said Joey, "and fed him business. To get into the Avid Investment Fund, you had to be an Ivy Leaguer or a scripophilist."

"Scripophilist?" said Henry. "That sound like some kind of pervert."

"It's a man who collects money," said Peter.

Henry started to ask, "How . . . ah, never mind. Explainin' that one take all night."

And Joey just kept talking. "Carl Evers admitted to us that Arsenault started gettin' in trouble right around the time the high-tech bubble burst. Then he started using one client to pay another."

"Like Madoff."

"But Arsenault had been a real broker handling, among others, a lot of Antonov money. When he went bad, Antonov must have smelled it and started pulling money out of the Avid Fund. If Arsenault goes down like Madoff, there'll be claw back. A trustee starts looking at how much each client put into the fund, how much he took out . . . Antonov would rather be holding one-point-four billion in bearer bonds and let Arsenault go down. Or maybe he gets the bonds, then props up the great antideficit crusader. Then he owns him. That's even better. An oligarch owning a major player in American finance . . . one more step up the ladder."

Evangeline said, "So, why not just call your friends at the FBI? Or the SEC, or the NYPD? We can step back and be safe."

"Yeah," said Sonia. "I like that idea. No more cold chicken."

Peter said, "Then Antonov blows up my bookstore, taking with it some pretty amazing elements of world literary history."

Joey looked at Peter. "I warned you, Boston. You stick your nose in messy New York business, expect to get it busted."

Peter would have given him a comeback, but this was no time for joking. If not for the threat to his bookstore, he would have been with the NYPD right now, trying to help them figure out who had killed Kathy.

Besides, Joey didn't give Peter a chance for a comeback. He just kept talking. "And this is plenty messy. Not only is it Antonov against Arsenault and Arsenault against the U.S. Treasury. It's Antonov against one of his father's lieutenants, Ivankov the Redhead. In the old days, Ivankov would have just capped Antonov in some steam room. But he's trying to play it like Antonov, like an oligarch, a businessman. So he's co-opted Delancey—"

"Which is why Antonov blew up his store?"

"Shit, yeah," said Joey. "You can bet that Delancey is workin' overtime to make sense of any clues they can get their hands on. If the Redhead gets the bonds and the court rules that they're valid, Arsenault goes down, Antonov gets a fortune clawed out of his pocket, and the Redhead turns out to be the new big man in Brighton Beach."

Evangeline sipped a bit more ginger ale. "So who killed the accountant and Kathy?"

Joey said, "The Redhead hasn't gone all gray suit. He's still an assassin. He killed the accountant in the Harvard Club to make a public statement about Arsenault. The accountant had been so scared before the Bowling Green business that he had gone to the Harvard Club to lay low and get in touch with

Kathy. Then the Redhead killed Kathy because, what's more detrimental to Arsenault? A negative article about him, or the murder of the reporter who's writing it?"

"All's I know," said Henry, "is we stay on this till we get the all clear, so nobody thinkin' about blowin' up No-Pete's store."

Joey picked a last bit of meat off one of the chickens and popped it into his mouth. "Need my strength. When I get back to her flat on Grand and Clinton, I don't know if I'll be talkin' to Sally or Erica. It's hard talkin' to both of them."

"Good luck," said Evangeline.

Joey said, "We're runnin' out of time."

"If it's all true about Arsenault," said Peter, "he'll unwind all by himself, whether they find the bonds or not."

"I'm talking about Jennifer and me," said Joey. "We're running out of time. This is about something more."

After a moment, Henry picked up his gun and said to Joey, "Y'all ready? I'll see you out."

"I'll leave the box." Joey picked it up and showed them the length of side molding that worked the false bottom. "Practice openin' this one. Get it fixed in your mind. It might come in handy. I'll call you in the morning."

THAT NIGHT, WHILE Peter and Evangeline and Antoine brainstormed over the notebook and all the other material, Henry Baxter patrolled the perimeter.

No one was getting in.

Around one in the morning, Evangeline said that she just had to go to sleep. But first, a bit of air.

So she went to the fire escape that opened onto a back window and stepped out.

She heard Ripper huff and snuff somewhere below her.

And from above, came Henry's deep voice. "Nice night. Come on up."

She saw the tip of his cigar flare in the dark. So she climbed the metal ladder to the roof and stepped over the parapet.

Henry was sitting on a chaise lounge, puffing away with the .44 on his lap. "This the only place little Sonia let me smoke."

"I love the smell of a cigar." Evangeline sat on the chaise beside him.

"Very politically incorrect." Henry pulled another from his pocket. "Want one? Cohiba Churchill, finest smoke an American can get till Castro take the dirt nap."

"I just like the *smell,* Henry . . . fresh smoke, floating off into the New York night."

Henry chuckled and took a big puff.

"Of course, that thing could change your carbon footprint."

"Naw." Henry blew the smoke into the air. "This just a wisp from that great cloud of commerce y'all been talkin' about. I buy these babies at Barclay Rex over on Forty-second Street, fourteen dollars apiece and worth every penny. I get all this enjoyment, and a nice shop get some profit, so they can pay their tobacconists, who cash paychecks and pay taxes and buy all the goods and services of the big city, some of which I provide, so"—he took another puff—"we all just part of one big, beautiful system."

"Condensation to evaporation to rain." Evangeline looked across the roofs of Hell's Kitchen. "And the rain fills the reservoirs and flows back to the water tanks."

"But the beauty of the water tank, whether you on the top floor or the bottom, you get the same water pressure. And that's where our economic metaphor get shaky." He arched an eybrow. "*Metaphor*. You surprised I use big words like that?"

"I'm surprised you don't use more."

He took another puff of the cigar. "In the real world, them at the top get the best water pressure, when it's them at the bottom who need it most, but"—Henry shrugged—"they ain't a lot to do about that. We still got the best chance in the world to make somethin' out of nothin', right here in the big city."

She looked out. "I love the roofs of Hell's Kitchen."

"This one of the oldest parts of town. Mostly six-story buildings . . . for a reason. Seven or more, the law say you need a water tank. Pump the water up, and every time somebody draw it down, a float in the tank trip the pump in the cellar and pull more up."

She lay back in the chaise.

Henry said, "One-point-four billion dollars. That sure would rain a lot of water bucks down on a lot of folks."

She gazed up into a skylit New York night that was starless even though it was cloudless, and she thought again of those strange, final words in Tim Riley's notebook. *Rainwater O'Day. X marks the . . . spiffle*. Then she said, "Henry, say that again."

"I said those bonds sure would rain a lot of water bucks down on a lot of folks."

She sat up. "And where did Antoine park his car this afternoon?"

"Say what?" Henry took out his cigar. "In a lot on Eleventh. Why?"

"Across from what?"

"Midtown Hardware. Everybody shop at Midtown Hardware."

"*Whose* Midtown Hardware?"

Henry took another puff of the cigar, and the tip flamed, like light dawning. "*O'Day's* Midtown Hardware, Carpentry, and Cooperage."

AT SEVEN O'CLOCK the next morning. Henry Baxter, wearing a gray three-piece suit, headed west on Fifty-first Street with a Bluetooth in his ear.

A few moments later No-Pete and the E Ticket came out of the apartment and followed. Peter was also wearing an earpiece, and his phone was on.

A few minutes later came Antoine, in a hoodie, with a gym bag over his shoulder.

As Peter passed Sacred Heart, he tipped the brim of the Brooklyn Dodgers replica hat that Henry had given him as a new disguise.

"Interesting tradition," said Evangeline.

"My father taught me to tip my hat when I went past a church, or when a lady passed. So"—Peter tipped his hat to her—"I'll bet that Tim Riley's father gave him the same advice. One is good manners. The other is a good prayer."

"I suppose we can use all the prayers we can get," said Evangeline.

"Yeah. And we should say a few for Kathy Flynn."

Evangeline hitched her purse on her shoulder and slipped a hand into the crook of his elbow. "I'm sorry about that, Peter. I really am. And honestly, I'm scared shitless myself right now."

"Me, too. But not for the first time."

"If I hadn't been in Delancey's on Monday, Kathy might still be alive."

"No. If Joey's right, the Redhead was going to kill her no matter what." Peter had been trying not to think of her death, but he couldn't get it out of his head. "If I had let her come to Henry's safe house, she might still be alive."

Evangeline let go of his elbow. "Now you're making me feel really guilty."

He stopped and put his arm around her shoulders. "No one's to blame but the people who shot her. And the best thing to do for her now is to find what we came for."

"It's the best thing to do for ourselves, too," said Evangeline, "and for two souls lost in the World Trade Center who've been trying to find themselves ever since."

They had heard plenty of news that morning over bacon and eggs at Henry's table.

The police had discovered Kathy Fynn's body, and questions were already being raised about

Austin Arsenault, especially since she was working on a story critical of his investment fund.

The Dow futures had turned positive for the first time in a week, which suggested that the world was not as concerned about the impending Supreme Court bond decision as it was about the announcement of the Chinese that they would not consider selling American Treasuries at the next auction and start buying at the one after that.

And from Boston came word that two members of the Rhode Island mob had been caught on a surveillance camera breaking into the Newbury Street Bistro. They had set off burglar alarms and fled just a few minutes before the police arrived. This news reached Peter from his aunt Bernice, whose son was a BPD detective. It looked as if the New England mob was doing a favor for their Russian friends in New York because the Newbury Street Bistro occupied the first floor of the building that housed Fallon Antiquaria.

So, unless he wanted his store to end up like Delancey's, Peter had to keep up the illusion of chasing this story as far as he could.

With Henry walking point, they went from under the tree-shaded block between Ninth and Tenth to the blank brick block between Tenth and Eleventh, always in telephone connection.

They feared the Redhead and KGB. How many more thugs could they raise with a few phone calls? What if the shooter had gone through Kathy's purse and found the address and simply left it? Maybe the Russians were watching right now, just to see what they were doing.

From the beginning, Hell's Kitchen had been the working side of Midtown, and it still was. The rents were lower than a few blocks away. There was more space. Eleventh Avenue was a two-way street, unlike the avenues to the east. So this was where you went to find a gas station or a tire shop, a car dealer or a car wash, an equipment rental or a FedEx depot, a lumberyard or a hardware store.

And there, in the block between Forty-sixth and Forty-seventh, on the west side of the street, they saw the sign:

O'DAY'S
MIDTOWN HARDWARE,
CARPENTRY, AND COOPERAGE
PLUMBING, LUMBER, PAINT, SUPPLIES
SINCE 1884

It was a big old three-story building made of sandstone blocks that somebody had painted a forest green, with two loading bays in the front, along with a half flight of stairs leading up from the sidewalk into the main store. A big Midtown Hardware delivery truck was parked at one of the bays. Another one was pulling down the block and turning into a driveway in the back, beneath another sign: LUMBER YARD, TRADE ONLY, RETAIL PURCHASES FRONT DESK. And just beyond, another driveway and another sign: VALIDATED PARKING FOR MIDTOWN HARDWARE AND USS *INTREPID.*

The old World War II aircraft carrier sat serenely a block west, waiting for its daily invasion of tourists.

Henry walked past the half a block of storefront and down to the corner, turned, and leaned against a lamppost. Then he whispered into the phone, "All clear. Go ahead in. Put the phone on vibrate and lose the earpiece. Them fellers in there'll think you some kind of businessman asshole with the Bluetooth."

"They wouldn't be the first." Peter pulled out the earpiece. Then he and Evangeline went up the stairs and into the store.

Because Midtown Hardware served the contracting trade as well as the carriage trade, they opened at six in the morning, so the place was bustling with men in overalls and steel-toed shoes, men buying bags of nails and lengths of PVC pipe and faucets and lag bolts and a thousand other items that lined the two-story shelves.

Peter said, "How in the hell has everyone else missed this place?"

"Maybe they haven't missed it. Maybe there's nothing," answered Evangeline. "But it's an easy clue to miss. More like a hunch."

After a few questions at the front of the store, Peter and Evangeline headed back to the bank of offices overlooking the sales floor, to talk to Mr. O'Day.

"You'll know him," said the salesman. "Red face, squinty eye."

O'Day was just coming down a rickety set of stairs from an upper office.

"What can I do for you folks?" He gave them a squint and a smile. He had huge hands and looked as if he preferred a carpenter's apron to the sport-coat he was wearing.

Evangeline introduced herself. "I'm a writer for *Travel & Leisure* magazine. I'm doing a piece on the New York water tanks. I'd say they're one of the most distinctive sights on the New York skyline."

O'Day nodded. "They sure are."

"Peter's my photographer. We're hoping you'll answer a few questions."

O'Day looked at his watch and said, "Okay. Fifteen minutes. Then I gotta get out on the road. You want the tour?"

"Sure," said Peter.

The man offered his hand. "I'm Buddy O'Day. Fifth generation. One of three families in New York that's been buildin' water tanks since the late 1800s. You got the Rosenwachs and the Isseks and us. We been here since the beginning, when this side of Eleventh was mostly riverfront." He led them down a flight of stairs, beneath a sign: *CARPENTRY SHOP. AUTHORIZED PERSONS ONLY.* "We stay in town because we own the real estate and have the retail operation."

"Are you the biggest?"

"We're the smallest. But there's plenty of work for all of us. You got between ten and fifteen thousand water tanks in Manhattan, plus new construction all the time. And while we all say we're the best tank builders, we all work basically the same way."

"How's that?" asked Peter.

"We do most of the work right here, so there's less to do when we send our crews up on the roof of some ten- or twenty-story building."

At the bottom of the stairs, Peter glanced into a little glassed-in office where an old man was working at a draftsman's desk. O'Day gave the old man a wave and led Peter and Evangeline onto the shop floor. Two or three guys were already working. And the three big delivery bays were open to the yard, where a forklift was buzzing around the lumber piles.

A table saw was screaming into a length of wood. A machine planer groaned a bass line for the saw. Then someone turned on a band saw, adding a new pitch.

But the sweet smell of fresh-cut wood almost made up for the noise.

The forklift swung around from the yard and brought in a pallet of long boards and dropped them on the floor. Then it swung back out again.

"The forklift is bringin' in our raw material!" shouted O'Day over the sound of the saws. "We use a nominal six to eight-inch cypress board, three inches thick. We plane it down to two-and-three-eighths, then notch it and cut it to whatever length we're using."

"Did you always use cypress?" shouted Peter.

"Sometimes we use redwood. And back in the old days, they used fir, too. Some people like stainless steel, but wood lasts longer."

"How long?" asked Evangeline.

O'Day squinted harder at her, then made a motion with his hands to the guys on the floor. "Hey! Hey!" And the saws stopped. "What did you say, miss?"

"How long?" asked Evangeline again, and she hoped for the right answer. "How long does a tank last?"

"We like to say twenty-five to thirty-five years with proper maintenance, which we also handle."

She looked at Peter and shook her head.

"Any ever last longer?" asked Peter.

"Redwood will give you forty," said O'Day. "And my father tells me that he came across a few that lasted fifty back in the old days."

Evangeline gave Peter a jerk of the head—let's get out of here. If the tanks only lasted thirty or forty years, her theory was dead. They would have to keep looking.

But Peter made a little gesture—hold on. Let's see this through. Then he asked O'Day, "Did the early tanks use three-inch boards?"

"Well, I can't give you the codes from the old days, but—"

"What about the tank bottoms? Ever use double-thickness tank bottoms?"

"Hunh?" said O'Day, as in what is this amateur talking about?

"You know," said Peter, "two thicknesses of wood on the bottom of the tank?"

O'Day just squinted at them, like that was a pretty stupid question, then he led them toward the back and pointed to the floor. "There's how we do a bottom."

Two men were drawing a twelve-foot diameter circle on a square of cypress boards already fitted together.

"Once they chalk in the circle, they make a cut on each board to the exact curve of the chalk. It's like a set of Lincoln Logs, everything fits, everything is precut, everything is numbered. And like I say, all our wood starts with a thickness of three inches. But in the old days, before the codes were so strict"—he shrugged—"they might have used double thicknesses of one-inch fir. But the problem is that the lower layer wouldn't get wet, so it wouldn't swell, so it would rot . . . or leak."

One of the guys on the floor said, "Hey, Dad, if they want to know about the old days, have them talk to Grandpa." The son had a big belly and a squinty eye, too. A family trait, a family business.

"Good idea. My pa's eighty-four now, but he's still the floor supervisor." Buddy pointed to the glassed-in office at the base of the stairs. "Can't get him to retire."

"Yeah," said one of the other guys, "and he don't miss a trick."

"So stop yappin' and get to work," said Buddy O'Day, then he jerked his head to Peter and Evangeline. "I'll pass you off to Pops."

Evangeline rolled her eyes.

Peter gave her a stay cool gesture. Then the phone buzzed in Peter's pocket. A text from Henry: "How going? All clear here."

Peter texted back: "OK."

Walter O'Day was smaller than his son. But he had the same squint eye and the same barrel belly, the same good nature, too. His office was about six-by-six, a pile of papers here, another there, a pile of architectural drawings, a large stool, a draftsman's slanted desk. The back windows looked out onto the yard. The half-glass partition on the left looked out onto the shop floor, and the half-glass door opened into the base of the stairs. About a two hundred and seventy degree view. *Didn't miss a trick.*

After Buddy excused himself, Walter O'Day took right over, told Peter and Evangeline to sit in the two hard-back chairs in the corner, offered them coffee, then sat on his stool. "So what can I tell you about water tanks that Buddy didn't?"

Evangeline said, "We've learned a lot from your son."

Peter knew she was itchy to leave, but he still saw reason to push ahead. "How far back do you keep records on tank construction?"

Walter O'Day grabbed a big ledger from the shelf and opened it onto the desk. We got one of these for every decade, goin' all the way back to the 1880s. This one we started in 2001. Addresses, costs, materials, the names of the men who worked the jobs, all of it . . . a real New York history."

Evangeline looked at Peter and arched a brow. Maybe he was right after all. She said, "So you could tell us what you were building and who was building, even in July of 1893, if you dug out the ledger."

"Oh, yeah, sure."

"You ever heard of a guy from way back named Dick Riley," asked Peter. "They used to call him 'the best tank-bottom man in New York'?"

"No, but if he worked for us, we'll have a record."

Evangeline said, "This Mr. Riley worked for you in the 1890s. Would any of the tanks you built back then still be in service?"

"Oh, no, but we'd have replaced them all. I bet I worked on some of them myself. They would've been wearin' out right when I was learnin' the business. Learned it from the top down, startin' up there in the sky on a steel frame. So"—he opened a drawer beneath his desk—"let's go upstairs, where we keep the ledgers."

He lifted a box out of the drawer and put it on the desk. "I just need to find the key to the locker."

And Evangeline Carrington said, "Oh, my God."

The old man gave her an even more quizzical O'Day squint.

The box was scratched and dinged, but it had been polished and polished again. It was about ten inches by seven inches by four inches high. Its identical twin sat, at that very moment, on the table in Henry Baxter's apartment.

Peter put a hand on Evangeline's arm. Then he swallowed, took a deep breath, and said, "Where did you get that box, Mr. O'Day?"

"This?" He laughed and held it up. "This is my key box. Always losin' my keys."

"Where . . . where did you get it?" asked Peter again, as politely as he could.

Evangeline wanted to grab it and run.

"I still remember," said Walter O'Day. "We was takin' down a sprung tank over on Tenth. And underneath, right where the upright boards make a little lip that notches under the bottom and connects to the legs, there was a neat little box of fir, mortised right in, with a tiny little carved X on it, something you wouldn't have seen unless you was lookin' for it. This box was inside, wrapped in an oilskin tarp."

"And you kept it all these years?" said Evangeline, trying to sound chatty rather than absolutely shocked.

"Look around you, honey," said O'Day. "I'm a pack rat. Always have been. And that whole store upstairs is a pack rat store."

"Was there anything in it when you found it?" asked Peter.

"Nope. As empty as my grave will be for another twenty years, I hope." He gave a laugh. "Just a nice box for keepin' stuff. So, I brought it back here and used it for my keys. Like I say, always losin' my keys." He shook the box and made the keys rattle. "If I hadn't been losin' them when I was in my twenties, I'd think I had Alzheimer's now."

Peter swallowed and said, "May I hold it?"

"Sure."

As Peter reached for the box, his cell phone vibrated in his pocket.

"I'm sorry, Mr. O'Day." He opened the phone to a text from Antoine: "Henry says get out now."

At the same moment, Evangeline gasped—"Peter"—and gestured toward the windows overlooking the yard.

KGB and two others were coming past the piles of lumber. They moved quickly, with a sleek, predatory grace, as if they knew exactly what they were looking for and had no fear of anyone who might be watching them.

Peter told Evangeline to get down, then he said, "Mr. O'Day, put the box back in that drawer and lock it."

"Hunh?" The old man gave him another squint.

Then Peter looked up the stairs, which ended right outside the office door.

A guy was coming down. He was wearing a tool belt and sunglasses, a Yankees hat and a hooded sweatshirt over the hat. He stopped at the bottom and looked around.

When he turned, Peter saw red hair.

Evangeline had already crouched against the door, and now Peter dropped onto one knee. The windows of the office were at waist height, so there was a bit of hiding space . . .

But not if the old man kept talking, and he said, "What the hell is going on here?"

Peter raised a finger to his lips.

One by one, the machines out on the floor were stopping as the workers noticed the three guys standing in the entry bays, silhouetted by the bright May sunshine.

The O'Day grandson walked over to KGB and said, "Can't you guys read the fuckin' signs? This is the shop. You need somethin' cut, place an order upstairs."

"You in charge?" said KGB.

"No, my—"

"Then shut the fuck up." KGB smashed the handle of his pistol into the kid's face, sending young

O'Day onto the floor with blood spurting from his nose.

"Hey!" cried Walter O'Day.

All in an instant, the Redhead pulled a 9 mm and smashed it through the window in the office door, sending glass flying all over the crouched figures of Peter and Evangeline . . . the old man cried out . . . the Redhead told him to shut up . . . and Peter Fallon, knowing he had half a second before the Redhead saw him, reached up, grabbed the forearm, and pulled it down, knocking the gun out of the hand and jamming the forearm down hard onto the jagged glass.

The Redhead let out a scream and pulled back.

Evangeline jumped up.

Peter started to fumble on the floor for the gun.

Walter O'Day shouted, "Son of a bitch!" and pulled a billy club from under the desk.

KGB fired three shots into the little office. One hit the wall. One ricocheted off the ledger and out the window. One hit Walter O'Day and knocked him sideways.

The other two thugs whipped sawed-off shotguns from under their jackets and held them on the men who a moment before had simply been doing a hard day's work and now had to be wondering, was this going to be some kind of massacre?

KGB smashed the other window in the little office and pointed the gun in at Peter and Evangeline. "Stop moving."

Peter looked up into the lifeless eyes of the assassin from the Harvard Club.

The Redhead was ripping open the office door.

He had pulled another 9mm from somewhere in his tool belt, and he pointed it at Evangeline, "Out."

Then his eyes brightened at something on the floor.

Walter O'Day had knocked the box off his desk.

The Redhead said, "Son of bitch. You found it!"

Walter O'Day had slumped in the corner and was gasping. The bullet had passed through his arm and into his side. "Get the fuck out of here, you—"

The Redhead told Evangeline to pick up the box. Then he grabbed her by the hair. Then he looked down at Peter, who was still on his knees. "Goodbye, Mr. Fallon."

He gave KGB a nod. Then he dragged Evangeline out of the office and pushed her up the stairs.

She cried Peter's name. She wanted her voice to be the last one he heard.

Then she heard the pop of the 9mm.

She turned to see KGB's head fly back.

"Peter!" she cried again.

"Go!" growled the Redhead. And he forced her up the stairs.

KGB staggered.

Peter stood. He had found the pistol on the floor. He had used it.

Evangeline saw him and called his name again.

The two thugs with the shotguns were turning now, one of them toward the office, one toward a new sound, coming from the yard: the roar of an engine.

A forklift loaded with a pallet of cypress boards was speeding straight for them.

A shotgun blast tore into the wood and sent chunks of cypress flying.

But the forklift didn't stop. It smashed into the shooter, then into his partner, then into the staggering body of KGB, and drove the three of them right into the wall of the little office.

The wall collapsed toward Peter. The forks punctured the wall. And KGB came right through the glass. He died hanging in the window, staring at Peter Fallon, while the other two were squirming like worms on a hook.

"Serves those son of a bitches right." Walter O'Day was back on his feet, the billy club in his hand. He reached around Peter and whipped the club twice on the two heads, and the worms stopped squirming.

Peter lurched out of the office and stopped to steady himself.

Henry hopped off the forklift. "The motherfuckers all come in the back, 'cept for the Redhead. But he wore that tool belt. Threw me off. I ain't much for doin' chores with tools, so a feller with a tool belt, he's like a priest to me."

UPSTAIRS, THE REDHEAD was dragging Evangeline toward the big double doors at the front. He had her by the hair with his left hand, while he held the box under his right arm and his gun in his right hand.

She screamed, and two men at the register turned.

The security guard, an old guy with a pot belly, appeared at the head of the aisle.

Even with the box under his arm, the Redhead

was better with a gun, and he shot the poor guard in the pot.

The guard fell back and his gun flew from his hand.

Evangeline grabbed a screwdriver from a display shelf and drove it into the Redhead's back. But he did not let go. He barely flinched.

Peter was coming up the stairs now, running after them, and Henry was right behind him.

A painter buying two gallons of Dutch Boy dropped the cans and crouched to pick up the security guard's gun.

"Don't move!" cried the Redhead, and the painter froze.

The Redhead kicked open the front door and dragged Evangeline down the steps to a blue Nissan Maxima waiting on Eleventh.

Oscar Delancey was sitting in the front passenger seat.

The Redhead yanked open the back door and threw Evangeline across the seat. The he jumped in and said, "Go. Go. Go."

Instead, the driver slowly turned and smiled.

"Why the fuck—you!"

It was Joey Berra. "Say good-bye, Mr. Ivankov."

"Go and fuck your mother." The Redhead tried to raise his pistol, and Joey Berra shot him in the heart.

Evangeline screamed.

"Get out," said Joey calmly. "Right now."

"But—"

"Go!" said Joey. "We got things to do."

"You and Delancey?" cried Evangeline. "You and goddamn Delancey?"

"Delancey? Shit no. He's dead, which is too good for him. Now get out, will ya?"

She opened the street-side door and stepped onto the body of another Russian.

As Joey sped away, Peter and Henry came barreling out of the store.

"Are you all right?" said Peter.

"Just barely." Evangeline looked at Henry. "Way to keep watch."

"Now you know the truth, baby. I ain't perfect."

"How in the hell did they figure this out?" said Peter.

"Delancey figured it out," said Evangeline. "He must have figured it out yesterday."

"I thought he'd be too scared," said Henry.

"However scared he was," she said, "he's dead now. The Redhead, too. Joey Berra did it."

"Joey Berra?" said Peter.

She pointed down the street. "He took the box."

Police and ambulance sirens were blaring from every direction now.

But Antoine's Camry was spinning out of the parking lot across the street, shooting across Eleventh, screeching to a stop. "Come on."

Peter jumped into the front, the other two in the back.

Antoine floored it and said, "They're in a blue Maxima. Just turned on Forty-second, probably headed down the West Side Highway."

"Did you see what happened?"

"I never saw anything like it," said Antoine. "That Joey Berra came right up to the car, popped the driver, popped the one in the passenger seat, and Jesus—"

Henry was looking at his cell messages. "Little Sonia writes that the nice Mr. Berra came by the house to find us this morning, and she sent him down to Midtown Hardware."

"You need to have a talk with her, Uncle Henry," said Antoine.

The car made every light to Forty-second where Antoine hung a right and headed for the river.

But before he reached the next light, Peter told him to pull over.

"Why?"

"Just do it," said Peter.

So the car screeched to the curb.

"We're in enough trouble as it is." Peter opened the door and jumped out.

"You got that right." Henry jumped out, too, and held the door for Evangeline.

"So, instead of taking a left," said Peter, "I want you to go right. Right now, up the Henry Hudson, to the Merritt, to Ninety-one, to Eighty-four, to the Mass Pike. You'll be home in three and a half hours. But don't speed. You don't want any tickets."

"That's right, kid. You don't want any record of bein' in New York, because you was never here. Y'understand?" Henry smacked the roof of the car and said, "Now go."

And Evangeline hailed a cab.

TWENTY

Friday Morning

"Now what?" Evangeline hitched her purse on her shoulder.

They were standing in a ratty little front room in a lonely flat in a lonely building near the corner of Grand and Clinton.

Henry had forced the door.

The flat was empty. Not only was it empty, the dresser in the corner had been pulled apart. Drawers lay on the floor. Old clothes were scattered all about. Somebody had cleared out . . . and fast.

Evangeline noticed a little dog's bed in the corner. She crouched and picked up a chew toy.

"Look at this." Peter found two wigs in the top drawer, one all dreadlocks, the other a silken blond.

Henry picked up a blue hat from under the bed. "Mets fan anyway."

Evangeline looked at Peter, "Do you really think she was orchestrating everything from here?"

He shook his head. "Looks like she was just surviving."

Henry gave a little shiver. "This the kind of place where you kill a rat, the roaches carry him off for you. Let's get on out of here."

"Wait a minute." Evangeline sniffed at the air. "Do you . . . do you notice that?"

"Notice what?" said Peter.

"Chanel."

"Chanel *what*?" said Henry. "Chanel number *Ass*?"

Evangeline ignored him and followed her nose toward the little windowless bathroom off the kitchen. "A lady splashed perfume here."

Henry looked over her shoulder. "I wouldn't take a leak here. Let's go."

Back on the street, Henry looked around at the sea of empty lots. "Like the E Ticket says, now what?"

Peter hailed a cab and told the others to get in.

"This better be good," said Henry, " 'cause I'm thinkin' we do ourselves a favor by sittin' down with my friends on the NYPD and givin' out with a few explanations just about now."

"This show isn't over yet." Peter told the driver, "Forty-eight Wall Street."

"From the fryin' pan into the green money fire," said Henry.

WALL STREET WAS one way heading east. You couldn't access it in a car from Broadway, and since 9/11, there were barriers, posts, pillars, hard solutions, soft solutions, security guards, and security cams just about everywhere. So the driver dropped them at the corner of Pine and William streets.

They walked a block down William and turned west. On the left was the famous Morgan Bank. And at the head of the street, staring down on American commerce like the benevolent eye of God, was Trinity Church. On the right, at the head of Broad

Street, were the steps of the Federal Hall Museum, leading to the statue of George Washington.

Peter stopped for a moment and took it all in.

"Like I asked the E Ticket," said Henry, "y'all still think this is the city of dreams, or the city of schemes?"

"I'd have to say that it's both," answered Peter. "Come on."

At the polished brass doors of 48 Wall, a green banner proclaimed, THE MONEY, THE POWER, THE HISTORY.

Henry read the banner and said, "That's what it's all about, baby."

"They could be talking about us this week," said Evangeline.

Peter pulled open the door. "Welcome to the Museum of American Finance. Former home of the Bank of New York."

A small sign in the vestibule announced, *PRIVATE EVENT. MUSEUM REOPENS AT NOON.*

The ticket booth was to the right, the coatroom to the left, and directly ahead, a half-story entrance rotunda, with marble and bronze staircases curling right and left around a marble and bronze floor medallion. Somewhere above the rotunda, the amplified voice of Austin Arsenault was echoing. The meeting had already begun.

As they entered, a guy in a chauffeur's uniform stepped out of the coatroom: Vitaly, scowling.

Henry flipped open the coat, and whispered, "No matter what you carryin', mine's bigger, baby. So be cool."

The woman at the ticket booth did not notice this little exchange. She was speaking to Peter. "Yes, sir, the Paul Revere Foundation Meeting is up the stairs. Are you members, sir. Sir?"

But Peter and Evangeline were already heading into the little rotunda and taking the staircase to the right. Henry was going up on the other side.

Peter read the medallion as they went. "'On this spot, Alexander Hamilton founded the Bank of New York.'"

"The Plymouth Rock of American financial history," said Evangeline. "And there's nothing we can do here except look at it."

"Look and be seen. Antonov will know we did our due diligence. Then maybe he'll leave us alone. He might even thank us for wiping out his opposition."

"He gonna have some opposition from the FBI, I think," said Henry from the other side.

"And we owe it to ourselves to be with Arsenault when the decision comes down in"—Peter glanced at his watch—"about fifteen minutes."

"He headed for trouble, too," added Henry.

In a short climb, the stairs ended in one of the most magnificent spaces in New York, the grand mezzanine banking hall.

Evangeline said, "I feel like I've died and gone to marble heaven."

After the Bank of New York moved, this columned, coffered space had been protected as a national landmark. Now it was filled with exhibits that Peter thought were among the best that he had ever seen. He had been here before, and as a trustee at a few New England museums, he knew good work when he saw it.

Hard to go wrong when you started with all that marble, and architecture designed to impress well-heeled customers, and the 1928 Hewlett murals depicting commerce and trade in New York. An exhibit under an archway showed the history of money. Others explored the effect of the Civil War on finance, the reasons for the crashes of '29 and '87, the workings of the bond market. And on the right was a time line of the 2008 credit crisis, a marvel of clarity for all its complexity, explaining how we had come close to a financial meltdown long after we thought we had safeguarded such things out of the system.

One of the three video kiosks—dedicated to explaining stocks, bonds, and futures—had been removed so that the main exhibit floor could accommodate two hundred chairs for the annual meeting of the Paul Revere Foundation.

And this was Austin Arsenault's show. Not only was he standing at the podium. He was on every video screen in the place—screens that usually ran interviews with modern entrepreneurs, or old archive film, or clips from *It's a Wonderful Life* that explained in simple terms how money flowed from individuals into the credit and capital system and back again to individuals.

"In some fifteen minutes," Arsenault was saying, "we expect one of the most important Supreme Court decisions in our history, and by 'our' I mean the nation *and* the Paul Revere Foundation and—"

Arsenault saw Peter and Evangeline, and he

hesitated, then he stumbled over a few words, and then he scowled, perhaps at himself because he never stumbled in front of an audience. Then he caught Owen T. Magee's eye and nodded toward the top of the stairs—go talk to them. Then he got back to his speech.

The room was almost full. Lots of gray heads and gray suits. Some younger people, too. No one looked as if they were worried about their next meal or their next trip to Europe. And no one even bothered to look at Magee as he scuttled along the outer rim of chairs and back to the stairwell at the top of the rotunda.

Evangeline whispered to Peter, "You should hand out business cards. Probably some money collectors here."

"Scripophilists, you mean?"

"No. The kind of people who collect the money in banks."

"So?" Magee came right up to them and whispered, "Did you find the bonds?"

"We think so," said Peter.

"You *think* so?" Magee twitched his eyes toward Evangeline. "Where are they?"

"We lost them," said Evangeline.

"You lost them?"

"As you said, there are a lot of dangerous people after them. In fact, one of them is sitting right there." Peter gestured to Antonov, who was watching from his aisle seat.

Antonov gave Peter a look and a small gesture—do you have something for me?

Peter shook his head and opened his palms—afraid not.

"And one of the dangerous people won," said Evangeline. "He killed a man right in front of me."

"Great," said Owen T. Magee. "Just great . . . great fucking news."

"Way to show sympathy for what I've just been through," said Evangeline.

Now heads were turning, because it was a room where voices echoed. And while Arsenault was talking into a microphone, even a whisper rose to the ceiling and reverberated.

Magee wiped a line of perspiration from his upper lip. "This means it's over." He looked back at the podium, then he pulled out his phone and turned for the stairs.

"Where are you going?" asked Peter.

"To save myself."

Peter watched him go down into the little rotunda and heard him say, "Agent Sullivan, please. This is Owen T. Magee returning his call."

Peter whispered to Evangeline, "The little weasel is calling the FBI. He's—"

At that moment, Vitaly appeared from somewhere under the staircase and ripped the phone from Magee's hands, opened the door, and threw it out onto Wall Street.

Owen T. Magee went chasing after it.

Vitaly looked up at Peter and Evangeline and grinned, flashing that tooth.

At the podium, Arsenault was fumbling, distracted by the noise from below. "We . . . ah . . . we believe that we have two bonds that will soon be redeemable. And . . . ah . . . the New Emission Money, ladies and gentlemen, will . . . unh . . ."

Peter led Evangeline over to the back row. Henry positioned himself at the place where the staircases met, where he had a view of the entrance below.

Arsenault gave Henry a long look, then he fumbled on for a few minutes more about the New Emission Money, the role of the Paul Revere Foundation, the importance of membership in the organization.

Then there was a commotion down at the rotunda entrance. It echoed up. Heads turned. And Henry disappeared down the stairs.

Peter heard the sounds of struggle, of voices, of someone hitting the floor.

Then Henry reappeared to the increasingly nervous and distracted audience of big players and Wall Street rollers. He tugged at his tie and grinned at Peter.

Arsenault fumbled again. "As I was . . . unh . . . saying . . ."

Then came a new sound, the distinct *tick-tick-tick* of high heels on marble.

And Evangeline thought that she smelled Chanel no. 5.

Then a woman appeared at the top of the staircase. She was wearing a suit of light brown silk over a tan blouse, accented by a yellow Hermès scarf. Her hair, cut short and spiky, was brown graying fast.

She was also holding a mahogany box . . . *the* mahogany box.

"My God," whispered Evangeline. "That's the bag lady."

A moment later, Joey Berra appeared at the top of the other staircase. He was wearing a blue pin-striped suit and a gray tie that picked up the color of the pinstripe.

Henry leaned over to Joey. "This your show, baby."

Joey said, "It's hers." Then he made a gesture to the woman.

By now, everyone was watching. The woman hesitated a moment, then she started down the aisle between the two hundred members of the Paul Revere Foundation.

Her heels *tick-tick-ticked* over the black-and-white marble floor.

And once she started moving, Joey stepped in behind her.

Arsenault went to say a few more words, but the smooth had completely deserted him. He fumbled and fell silent.

The woman carried the box in front of her as though it contained jewels, and depending on the court decision, its contents might be worth more than the Hope diamond.

Peter whispered to Evangeline, "This is going to be good."

Evangeline said, "What do you mean 'going to be'? It's good already."

Her shoes—Jimmy Choo? Versace?—*tick-tick-ticked* past all those rich men and women of finance, so many of them running feeder funds for Avid Investments, past Will Wedge and a dozen other Harvard-educated brokers who did business with Arsenault because he was a Harvard man and had to be trustworthy, past the empty seat of Owen T. Magee, and up to the podium where Arsenault stood, watching this high-heeled advance.

Tick-tick-tick.

Finally, Arsenault said, "What is this about, miss? What is in that box?"

Joey Berra moved his bulk close to Arsenault, put his hand over the microphone, and said, "Please sit down, sir."

"Sit down?" said Arsenault. "At my own meeting? I don't think so."

Joey whispered through clenched teeth, though everyone could hear, "Sit down. Now."

Several of the ladies and gentlemen in the audience, who weren't used to such scenes and certainly weren't used to seeing one of their own talked to like that, murmured, grumbled, stood. A few of the males made moves to the podium.

But from the back of the room came Henry Baxter's big, deep voice. "The man said sit down and listen. He meant y'all. So sit the fuck *down.*"

After another moment of snapping heads, reddened faces, confusion, Henry Baxter said to the podium, "Proceed, ma'am, if you please."

The woman put the box in front of her.

"My name"—she cleared her throat—"my name is Jennifer Wilson."

"What?" Austin Arsenault, who had not gone far, stepped forward again. "That's a damned lie. Jennifer Wilson is dead."

That brought a murmur in the room. A few of

them probably remembered the Magee & Magee associate who had gone on to fame and ignominy with Intermetro.

Joey put a finger to his lips.

Arsenault said, "I won't have you besmirching—"

And from the back came Henry's voice. "Don't make me come up there, Mr. Avid Austin. I ain't as polite as Joey B."

Arsenault gave Henry another look, then stepped back.

Peter had to chuckle. He knew that Henry was having a helluva time.

Evangeline wasn't chuckling. She was watching wide-eyed with a lump in her throat. From the moment she met her on the Bowling Green, she knew that the bag lady was more than she appeared. Most people were.

Jennifer Wilson's face seemed drawn from age and stress, but a bit of eye shadow and blush gave her a brightness she never had as Sally, a naturalness she never had as Erica.

"Mr. Arsenault was half right," she said. "I died, with so many other Americans, on 9/11. But I escaped death and was reborn." She looked at Antonov, who looked over his shoulder as if looking for Vitaly.

"Don't you worry about your boy, Mr. Antonov," said Henry. "He be all right when he wake up. Them handcuffs ain't too tight."

Jennifer gave a nod to Henry and went on. "I used to dream of writing my autobiography, but in an autobiography, you're supposed to tell the truth about yourself. I could not admit that I disappeared because I was guilty of insider trading. But I admit it now."

Joey Berra leaned into the microphone and in his best FBI official voice said, "Just to inform you all, the statute of limitations on that crime has expired."

Jennifer nodded to Joey, licked her lips, shifted her eyes around the crowd. "I was guilty. And I ran. A man I'd never seen before—a janitor—pointed me to life that day and probably died himself. And there were so many others who helped, who saved lives, and sometimes sacrificed themselves. And then Americans came to work at Ground Zero, to volunteer, to give money, to play the role of citizen in the best sense." Her voice wavered. She paused and looked back at Joey.

He whispered something in her ear that seemed to give her strength.

She turned again to the audience. "I may have my guilt. But I've never stopped being proud of the way New Yorkers reacted on that awful day. And I've never stopped dreaming of doing something good for the country and the city that endured so much yet gives us so much."

And Joey stepped in again. "That's why she's here, and why I'm here, to pay our debt to New York."

Then Jennifer continued. "I've lived on the street. I've dug in trash bins for food. I've climbed to the pinnacle of wealth. And"—a smile fled across her face and was gone—"like the man says, I've been rich and I've been poor, and I'd rather be rich."

Henry chuckled and said, "You got that right, babe."

"But where does wealth end and greed begin?" she went on. "Does the glutton ever say he has had enough? Or is there always room for another big bonus while your company is laying off workers and you're calling it creative destruction? Can you always justify strapping on the golden parachute when your company's stock tanks and you say, 'It would have been worse if not for me?' And when stockholders who hoped to educate their kids with that tanking stock go into debt to pay tuitions, do you go home to your East Side co-op and count your money? When it's bailout time, do you take your big slice, while the people who sweep the floors and wash the windows lose their jobs and wonder who's bailing them out? And will you credit card titans ever admit that your twenty-nine-point-nine percent interest is not just wrong, it's evil? Christ condemned usury in the Bible. Maybe you should listen to him."

Evangeline wiped a tear from her eye. "She's getting stronger."

Peter said, "But where is she going?"

"When we talk about the economy, it's always somebody else's fault. The Democrats blamed Bush for the recession from 2000 to 2002, even though Clinton was president for half of it. The Republicans blamed Obama for the recession from 2007 to 2009, even though Bush was president for most of it. And they're both wrong. We are all part of one big system. As the late Kathy Flynn used to say—"

That brought murmurs, turning heads. Most

everyone in the crowd knew Kathy Flynn of MarketSpin.com, but apparently not everyone knew of her murder.

"—it's like the cycle of condensation to evaporation to rain. And cycles turn, as they always have. But sometimes, there's a money drought. That's the nature of capitalism." Jennifer looked at Austin Arsenault, who was still standing at her shoulder. "And the Paul Revere Foundation is right. If we don't act responsibly, the cycles may stop. The drought may last until we are a desert, a twelve-trillion-dollar deficit desert."

"That's the smartest thing you've said yet." Arsenault folded his arms and struck a pose.

She said, "We cannot inflate the deficit away, though we may be forced to try. We cannot tax it away, though all of us in this room may face tax increases. We cannot cut it away, though we must cut, too."

"That pretty much covers it all," whispered Evangeline.

"And we cannot surrender our national sovereignty to those who buy our debt. So"—she looked them over—"what to do?"

"You had your chance and you threw it away," said Arsenault.

"My chance in the backseat of a limo?" she answered.

But he didn't back down. "You had your chance in the greatest country in the world."

She looked at him for a moment and said, "If I ever need to be reminded of that, I think of what a hardworking Russian immigrant told me after the first tower fell. He said the wound would heal and scar, and we would go on, because Americans don't quit. New Yorkers don't quit."

"You got that right, too," said Henry Baxter.

Jennifer gave him a nod. "But in a generation, we have gone from the largest creditor nation in the world to the largest debtor nation. So . . . do we quit on our future and just let the deficit grow? Or can we in this room—men and women who have enjoyed the sweetest fruits of the financial system that Alexander Hamilton gave us—can we make a difference? Can we give something back?"

"That's why we're here," said Will Wedge in his best honking accent.

She looked at him and smiled. "And this is why I am here."

She opened the box and held it up so that the cameras feeding the meeting to sites around the country, and to CNN and FOX News, could pick it up. Then she slid a piece of molding from the side of the box. Then she slid a false bottom out through the space left by the molding. Then she held up the box again.

And there, on television screens around the room and around the country, were one hundred and ninety-five tiny, crudely printed pieces of paper in two neat stacks, compressed down to almost nothing.

Peter leaned closer to Evangeline and whispered, "This is *your* moment."

"My moment?"

"Without you, those bonds would still be in Walter O'Day's desk."

Jennifer Wilson said, "If you believe Hamilton, you are now looking at the unretired debt of the American Revolution, almost twenty thousand dollars worth of bonds purchased in 1780 by a woman named Loretta Rogers. And this debt, like all our debts, is still growing, still throbbing like a carbuncle on the bottom of the body politic."

Arsenault stepped closer and leaned over her shoulder. "This is what I have been saying all along."

Jennifer held up a thin bond and showed it to Arsenault.

He reached for the box, but Joey grabbed his arm. "Look. Don't touch."

Jennifer glanced up at the video screens. "If the Supreme Court rules the right way, I will be rich again, because these are bearer bonds, and I am the bearer. Not Mr. Arsenault"—she jerked her head in his direction—"nor Mr. Antonov"—she glared at him. "But like Loretta Rogers, I am a patriot. So what should I do with her bequest?"

"I think you should give them to our foundation," said Arsenault, "we can—"

She just laughed. *Not on your life.* "Anyone else?"

Evangeline whispered, "She used to be a lawyer. She must have been good."

"Give the money to charity," cried someone.

Jennifer nodded. "I like that. But our whole country is a charity. Anyone else?"

"I say wait until the court decision, then decide!" shouted Will Wedge.

"Mr. Wedge, Harvard genius, cutting things close and neat as always." She no longer seemed nervous. Her voice was strong, her eye contact was good. And people were leaning forward, listening, waiting, wondering where she was headed. "You're telling me that if Arsenault's argument is rejected, I can forgive this debt and pretend that I'm a patriot. If it's upheld, I can cash the bonds and proclaim that I'm doing it for the national good, for the"—she looked at Arsenault—"what do you always call it? Symbolism. But you'd take the money anyway, as you've always planned to."

"That's a damn lie," said Arsenault.

She gave a little cock of her head. "You wanted Will Wedge and all the other smart people in this room to think that you were a patriot. But you just wanted the bonds because you've been losing money for years, and half the people in this room have been burned, only they don't know it yet."

"What?" shouted someone in the back.

"That's a damn lie," said Arsenault.

"Don't know *what* yet?" cried someone else.

Antonov looked again toward the back, as if he might make a run for it.

And Henry's voice boomed out, "This show ain't over yet, folks. So y'all keep your seats and quiet down."

Jennifer waited a moment and looked again at Arsenault, "If what I've said about your financial straits is a lie, if you really started this treasure hunt because you wanted Americans to see the hazards of a deficit and what it means, then you'll appreciate my solution for these bonds." She positioned the box in the middle of the podium. The she pulled from her pocket a small can of lighter fluid.

"Oh, no," gasped someone.

Arsenault moved toward her.

Joey said, "Another step and I will shoot you. And you will not be the first man I've shot today."

Arsenault looked toward the left side of Joey's jacket, saw the bulge of the holster, and stepped back.

Jennifer said, "No matter what the Supreme Court says, the best that a true patriot could do today, on this street, where Washington took the oath of office, where brokers made the Buttonwood Agreement that started a stock exchange, where J. P. Morgan did his business, is to forgive this debt . . . as thanks for all that America has done for us and for all that it will do in the future."

She doused the bonds in fluid and pulled a cigarette lighter from her pocket, and another gasp rose.

Arsenault cried, "No!"

Peter Fallon began to laugh. There was nothing else to do. Just laugh at the audacity of what these two had probably been planning all along.

Jennifer snapped the lighter and the flame popped.

Two men in the back stood. Someone cried, "Stop her!"

Henry growled, "Y'all remember what I said. Let the lady make her point."

And she touched the lighter to the bonds.

In an instant, a small funeral pyre sprang to life on the podium of the Museum of American Finance. A flame jumped and a curl of smoke twirled up toward the ceiling. Then she held out her hand and Joey Berra gave her a metal pen, with which she dug into the box, turning over the bonds to keep the flame going.

Arsenault let out a cry of pain, of true anguish, and buried his head in his hands.

Antonov stood to leave.

Henry raised a finger and said, "Don't you be thinkin' about goin' nowhere. They's folks comin' to talk to you."

Jennifer turned the box over and shook it to empty the smoldering bonds. Then she handed the box to Arsenault. "You should have this. It's an antique."

And, as cool and practiced now as if she had spent the last decade in the courtroom, she said to the audience, "That is what I have done for my country. What will all of you, the richest and most blessed among us, do now?"

She didn't wait for an answer. She turned and took Joey Berra's arm and gave a jerk of the head. And together, they started to walk down the aisle, Joey in his gray suit, Jennifer in her high heels, heads up, eyes front. *Tick-tick-tick*.

People started to stand. Someone stepped in front of Joey. Will Wedge began to climb over people in order to—what?

"Y'all stay seated," said Henry to the crowd, and he removed the huge .44 Magnum from under his arm. "No need to follow 'em and throw rice. This ain't no motherfuckin' weddin'."

But it was, thought Evangeline. Oh, but it was.

As Joey and Jennifer reached the back of the crowd, they turned to Peter and Evangeline.

Jennifer took an envelope out of her pocket and gave it to Evangeline. "That's for the O'Days. Four bonds. It'll be a good payday, if things work out."

"And this is for you." Evangeline took the crown finial from her purse and put it into Jennifer's hand.

Peter laughed. "So that's what you've been carrying around in that thing."

"Thanks, but"—Jennifer gave it back—"this belongs to New York."

And Joey said, "Thanks, Boston."

Peter said, "Go Yankees . . . but just for today."

Then Joey and Jennifer went down the left stairwell to the street level while Henry dropped down on the right.

After a moment, Evangeline put the finial back into her purse and said, "We can't let them go yet."

Peter said, "We don't even know *where* they're going."

"I'd just like to say good-bye."

So they jumped up and headed for the stairs, and their movement snapped everyone into motion. Suddenly, half the people in the place were making for the stairwell.

Peter and Evangeline got to the exit first. Henry had positioned himself in front of the door.

Peter said, "Which way did they go?"

Henry jerked his thumb west toward Broadway.

Evangeline gave Henry a kiss on the cheek, then she and Peter stepped onto Wall Street as Henry raised his .44 and fired it once into the air.

The sound of it, in that space, was like a cannon shot that stopped half the business leaders of New York right . . . where . . . they . . . were.

"Now, folks," said Henry, "seein' as this is the most powerful handgun in the world, you don't want me to go all Clint Eastwood on your ass, so why don't y'all just go back up there and watch the Supreme Court do its thing while we wait for the FBI? There's a lot of folks here who got some explainin' to do, includin' me."

PETER AND EVANGELINE were standing now in the bright sun, looking west on Wall Street.

"I can't see them," said Evangeline.

"But they just left," said Peter. "They shouldn't be more than a block ahead."

"I can't see them."

So she took his hand and they ran.

They ran along a street that Gil Walker and Loretta Rogers would have known by its shape and light if not by the height of its buildings. They ran past the Morgan Bank where Tim Riley had thought his last thoughts and prayed his last prayer. They kept running toward Trinity Church that, like St. Paul's, had survived the steel and concrete storm of 9/11.

And when they got to the corner of Broadway and Wall, they looked north and south, uptown and down, toward the old common and the older Bowling Green.

"I don't see them," said Peter.

"It's like they disappeared," said Evangeline.

And they stood there, at one of the oldest intersections in America.

Then Evangeline said, "Let's go south. I bet they're heading to the Bowling Green."

"I think they'd go to St. Paul's."

"Bowling Green," she insisted.

"All right," said Peter. "You found the bonds. You're on a roll."

So they turned down Broadway and hurried along sidewalks that in the sad September of 2001 had been covered in five inches of concrete dust . . . past buildings with windows blown out in September of 1920 . . . along block after block that had been an impenetrable wall of fire on a terrifying September night in 1776. . . .

And life went on.

In New York, life always went on. . . .

As they passed the Chase Bank, they noticed a video screen, tuned to CNBC. Stocks were up, and a reporter was standing on the steps of the Supreme Court in Washington. "The ruling, in a suit brought by financier Austin Arsenault, says the 1780 bonds are valid. However, the court rejected all compound interest arguments. So, a hundred dollars at five percent, simple interest, over two hundred and thirty years is worth one thousand two hundred and fifty dollars, instead of seven-point-four million."

Peter Fallon laughed out loud.

"A split decision," said Evangeline.

"Everybody wins and nobody wins."

The reporter was saying, "The full text will be found on our Web site . . ."

But Peter and Evangeline were already hurrying south.

They ran past the Wall Street bull and onto the Bowling Green. But there was no sign of Jennifer or Joey, not on the benches, not by the fountain.

Peter and Evangeline were not surprised. They stood for a few moments, watching the fountain send a sparkling jet of water into the air. Then they walked a bit farther south, into the bright sunshine at the entrance to Battery Park.

The Sphere greeted them. It endured. And the harbor flashed blue and silver beyond.

Evangeline said, "They're gone."

And Peter said, "No, they're not. They're"—he waved his hand around—"here. They'll always be here. They've always been here. They were here from—"

"From the very beginning."

"It feels that way."

And Peter and Evangeline looked up into the blue spring sky, as if they might see Joey and Jennifer somewhere up there, rising into the air and mixing their elemental selves with the essence of the city they loved.

Then Evangeline slipped an arm into Peter's. "So, Mr. No-Pete, did we save America from itself?"

"Not even No-Pete and the E Ticket can do that alone."

"Then what about living in New York?"

"Let's talk about that tomorrow."

"Okay. Then what time is it?"

He looked at his watch. "Quarter to one."

"As Henry says, we have a lot of explaining to do, but I'd like to get cleaned up. We could be in my apartment by one thirty."

"One thirty?"

"As in one thirty . . . er."

Peter looked into her eyes. She kissed his cheek.

And they turned away from the waterfront where it had all begun, where the Indians had bartered their island for beads, where the Dutch had built their settlement at the edge of a wilderness, where the British had built their wharves, where Americans had built their businesses, where so many immigrants had come to build their dreams.

And Peter Fallon shouted, "Taxi!"